Sea of

Stars

Books by Amy A. Bartol

The Kricket Series

Under Different Stars: Volume 1
Sea of Stars: Volume 2
Darken the Stars: Volume 3 (coming in 2015)

The Premonition Series

Inescapable: Volume 1
Intuition: Volume 2
Indebted: Volume 3
Incendiary: Volume 4
Iniquity: Volume 5

Sea of

Stars

The Kricket Series
Volume 2

Amy A. Bartol

47N⬤RTH

Published by 47North, Seattle

www.apub.com

Amazon, the Amazon logo, and 47North are trademarks of Amazon.com, Inc., or its affiliates.

ISBN-13: 9781477828236
ISBN-10: 1477828230

Cover design by MaeIDesign

Library of Congress Control Number: 2014953732

Printed in the United States of America

For Shelly Crane: may all the stars align for you.

Contents

Sea of

Stars

CPROLOGUE

WAR

In the dark spaces of every residence of the Alameeda Brotherhood, the ghostly half-light of holographic projectors simultaneously flickers on. A Star of Destiny—official symbol of the Alameeda Brotherhood—appears as a three-dimensional image within the glowing confines of the projectors. The sapphire star is on the verge of going supernova. Turning in circles, its pale pink carbon dust and silver solar flares reach out with scorching color from its surface. As the transmission strengthens, silent, strobing screams of light burst forth from the image of the Star of Destiny until it speaks.

"Brothers," the transmission begins, as a ripple of blue fire vibrates from the star, "we who comprise the strongest, bravest, and the most intelligent men in the history of our world. We stand together as a unified force of destiny. In this, our most monumental moment, we teeter upon the precipice of a new dawn: the rise of the House of Alameeda.

"Just as Black Math, the ancient plague that decimated the population of Ethar, formed the five houses of our planet known to us all as: Alameeda, Wurthem, Peney, Comantre, and Rafe, we are poised to dismantle all who oppose Alameeda's supremacy. Like points of a star, the five clan-houses have always been diametrically opposed. This opposition is a weakness—it denies our right to rule over all inferior creatures; it makes us complicit. The time has come for Alameeda to take our place as the one true star of destiny. The Supreme Alameeda Brotherhood, rightful heirs to the kingdom of Ethar, keepers and safeguarders of the vessels of the one true race, decree that a New World Order will come to pass. It was prophesied by our race of priestesses that we are sworn to protect. The signs they have given to us are clear. The stars of fate have aligned.

"The priestess, born of two worlds and of two houses, has returned to Ethar as prophesied. Kricket Valke, the stolen daughter of our order, is a hostage in the House of Rafe. The Rafe Regent, Manus Grayson, has repeatedly ignored our attempts to negotiate for her safe return. This pretender of power has allowed for the degradation of our priestess by attaching the taint of the Hollowell name to her. His insanity has not ended there. The weakling Regent has had the audacity to think himself worthy of an Alameeda priestess, touting a false engagement to her with malicious intent to demean and deny our claim of ownership of her. He has sought to use her genetically engineered gift of precognition, a trait she inherited through our bloodline, against her creators. For this offense alone, he has earned the penalty of death.

"Last evening, the Rafe Regent's crimes against Alameeda were met with swift and righteous justice. Our attack and infiltration of the Rafe palace in the Isle of Skye has left Manus Grayson critically wounded. We will not stop until he is dead. It is our intent to eradicate him from the face of Ethar, along with his entire house and all of his subjects. Anything short of the House of Rafe's complete and utter annihilation is unacceptable for the grave insult they have dealt to our Supreme Brotherhood. The prophecy will be fulfilled: one House of Ethar will fall.

"The House of Rafe.

"One House will rule.

"The House of Alameeda.

"A warning will be issued to any House that harbors Kricket Valke: 'Return her to us or you will meet the same fate as the House of Rafe. She's our rightful property. We created her bloodline. We own her: body, mind, and soul. She is the intended consort of Kyon Ensin, Supreme Brother and heir to the seat of the Loch of Cerulean. Any failure to meet our demands will seal your agonizing fate.'

"This, Brothers, is our declaration of war."

CHAPTER 1

OUTSIDER

Before me, sunlight warms the wall-length window as it streams into Trey's living quarters. An enormous expanse of blue sky stretches out ahead. I exhale a deep breath, assessing Rafe's floating fortress—this Ship of Skye. Beneath the window, the levitating city hustles. Massive, glossy skyscrapers of silver alloy and glass jut upward from the base of the ship. My gaze travels with them from the two-hundred-and-some-odd floors below me until I tilt my head back and lose the edifices to the ceiling above. Hoards of skiffs, the ultrafast hovercars, bustle around the buildings on amethyst-lit tracks of air. Everyone and everything here moves at a brisk, urban pace—a sharp contrast to the Regent's palace where I used to reside. There, sedate grace is valued over efficiency.

Several dark-winged fighters and slashing silver troop-movers cast dragon silhouettes over the arbors of grass on the open mall outside. Flying between the Ship of Skye's tall buildings and spires, the fire-breathers push upward from the ship's half-sphere base. White vapor trails evaporate like smoky breath in their wake while they patrol the area for any sign of an Alameeda attack. The antimissile guns, mounted strategically within the parapets of the Ship of Skye, track the fighters' progression too, even though they're Rafe ships. The *click*s and *whirl*s from the guns vibrate the windowpane, indicating that no one here is taking anything at face value.

My stomach clenches with fear as I listen to the hum of the aircraft. The sound resembles that of the Alameeda warships that swarmed the palace last night; my hand trembles on the glass. I focus on the clouds beyond the edge of the city to calm myself. They're so thick that if I knew how to swim I might attempt it within their depths.

As Trey paces near me, his image in the glass becomes sharper. I turn and lean my back against the window, crossing my arms over my chest. He moves in front of a white-cushioned, horseshoe-shaped divan. It's built into the sunken, recessed level of his impressive apartment. This area, divided from the main floor by a few black marble steps, is a gathering area for entertaining. Above our heads is a glass balcony that overlooks this common area from his bedroom. It has an amazing view of the wall of glass behind me.

When Trey pauses in his pacing for a moment, the shadows from the violence of yesterday are visible in his eyes—a new world-weary look that I haven't seen from him until now. The blind faith in his mission that was there when I first met him is absent. I've been the catalyst for that change. When he found me in Chicago, he was so certain that he was doing the right thing by remanding me back to Ethar, the planet and culture from which my parents hid me. He was a soldier then, one who just wanted to accomplish his mission and move on to the next thrill. Now he has doubts—I've caused him to worry—I've caused him to change.

Trey's frown deepens as he listens to the communicator pressed to his ear. Whatever Wayra is telling him is not something he wants to hear. The frustration is clear in his tense shoulders as he resumes pacing back and forth. He's been like this ever since my scheduled meeting with Skye Council this morning was abruptly canceled without explanation. Not long after that, Trey had received a message on his communicator. He wouldn't show it to me, but it had him sending Jax and Wayra, my other military bodyguards, away to facilitate a meeting with Head Defense Minister Vallen, Trey's boss. Now Wayra must have some information to report, since he's been briefing Trey for several minutes.

Frustrated or not by Trey's refusal to share his earlier message with me, I can hardly keep my eyes off him. My foray to the window has garnered only a brief respite from my need to track his every movement. The creases between his brows deepen. I want to reach out and smooth the furrow, then trace the lines of the thick, black tribal tattoos that run from his throat, beneath his pressed uniform, to his broad chest and over his flat-muscled abdomen. I want to rest my cheek against his chest—hear the sinfully melodic beat of his heart. Maybe if I did, it'd stop me from worrying about our uncertain future.

"Keep me informed, Wayra," Trey barks, his lips straightening in a grim line. "The moment you know something, contact me." He ends the communication with his thumb to its screen. Staring at nothing at all for a moment, he's lost in thought. Then his violet-colored eyes, an almost universal Rafian trait, connect with mine. My heart stutters to a halt before taking off again at a dangerous beat, leaving me breathless. *He's so handsome it hurts*, I think.

He relaxes a little, his hand plowing through his short, dark hair, making it less militarily precise and more sexy and unkempt. I like it like that; it makes me want to entwine my fingers in it and muss it up some more. His ruggedly attractive face loses its scowl as he studies me in the same manner that I'm studying him. A blush heats my cheeks; I'm suddenly fidgety. I tuck the long strands of my blond hair behind my ear.

"What's going on, Trey?" I ask him in a soft murmur.

"I'm not sure." The edginess in his tone, although subtle, is apparent to me. "I'm attempting to find out." That's not exactly true. He may not be sure, but he has an idea of what's happening, and I'd bet it has something to do with the message he received earlier.

I'd also bet that it's extremely bad, whatever it is, because he's being tight-lipped about it. I witnessed his expression in the moments after viewing the message. Gone was the sultry air with which his eyes had followed me. It has been replaced by a protective, almost possessive mien that has me worried.

I sigh. "Okay, you must have forgotten that I know when someone's lying—it's one of my special, freaky priestess gifts, remember—the one you love to use until it becomes inconvenient for you? You can try to throw me off, but even half-truths ring false with me. So, what do you *think* is happening?" I rephrase my question.

Trey gives a low, sexy growl of frustration as he approaches me with a stealthy gait. I love the way he moves—confident and in control. He stops in front of me. I have to tip my head back so I can see his face. Grasping the lapels of the black uniform jacket he gave me to wear this morning, he straightens my collar and tweaks the line of matte black buttons down my front so that I have an immaculate, military rightness to my look. He's not even really touching me and it's doing crazy things to my insides. No one has ever affected me like he does. "All of this would be so much easier if I could lie to you," he states.

"It would, would it?" I ask, giving him a flirty smile, trying a different tactic with him to cajole the information from him. My finger comes up to trace the buttons of his Cavar uniform. I like him in it. When he was my bodyguard at the palace, he wore plain clothes to fit in. Dressed in a gennet's rank, with silver pins on his collar in the shape of saers—the saber-toothed tiger that are a symbol of Rafe—he looks even more formidable than normal.

"I never want to lie to you—"

"Good, because you can't," I interrupt.

"But," he goes on, "I like frightening you even less, so until I understand exactly what's going on to explain it to you, I'd rather not discuss what little I know at the moment."

He's been treating me like I'm breakable ever since our arrival here last night. I've been trying my best to act normal, but everything from our location to our hard-fought relationship is still so new. I'd spent last night with him—talking mostly, exchanging a few kisses. He had let me cry on his shoulder; he'd wiped away my tears, keeping the memories of the massacre in the palace ballroom yesterday at bay. I'd fallen asleep in his arms.

"Is it the Alameeda? Have they done something else?" I try to be nonchalant, but the shudder that runs through me belies my words. It's beyond my control to stop it. No matter what I claim, I'm still half in shock from last night and more than terrified of them. I stabbed Kyon. Neither he, nor they, will let that go unanswered.

"Shh." Trey's large hand brushes my cheek. He entwines his fingers in my hair. The warmth of his body manages to calm my fears a little, if not my racing heart—that increases by the sheer nearness of him. "I missed you, Kricket. Every second of every rotation that we were apart was torture."

My breath catches, and I have to wait a moment before I can respond. If he's bent on distracting me from my thoughts of the Alameeda, he's done it. "It was the same for me," I admit, laying my hand on his hip. My touch affects him as well. He bites his bottom lip, giving me a devouring look.

Inhaling the scent of my hair, Trey's cheek skims mine. The sensation makes my insides come alive with desire. His soft breath falls on my ear. The deep vibration of his voice sends a wave of pleasure through me again. "I promise that it'll be you and me from this moment forward—whatever happens."

I fall into his embrace as if he's my home. "Things are really bad, aren't they? What are we going to do?"

He leans down and presses his lips to mine. It elicits a soft gasp from me. My lips part, and the ache of desire he creates with his kisses clouds my thoughts. "I know what we're not going to do,

Kricket," his sultry voice assures me. "We're not going to allow anyone to come between us again."

His strong hand on my back travels down me; it glides over my bottom to the back of my thighs. Trey picks me up in his arms, continuing to kiss me as he takes me over to the cushioned divan. As he sits, I sink onto his lap. Shifting in his arms, I straddle his hips; my form-fitting black slacks slide against his thighs as I settle upon them. My hands rest around the nape of his neck. Both of Trey's hands come up to hold my face. He gently pulls away from me to look in my eyes. "I need you to do something, Kricket," he says.

"Anything," I murmur, shivering when his thumb traces my bottom lip. My platinum blond hair spills over his thick forearms, blanketing them.

He keeps his tone deliberately calm as he says, "I want you to try to see the future."

He's never asked me to do that before, my mind whispers. I tense. "I don't know if I can—it just happens—you've seen it—"

He stops my stuttering by leaning forward and kissing me again. Uncertainty and fear fall away, replaced by desire. He ends our kiss to say against my lips, "I know that in the past you've had no control over what you see in the future or when you see it. If it doesn't work, then we'll have to take things as they come. But if you can use your gift of precognition, we might have an advantage and an opportunity to change the future if we need to."

I pull back from him farther so I can read his eyes better. "You're really worried."

He doesn't deny it; he just waits for my answer.

I chew on my bottom lip. "Okay. So—the future? Anything in particular you wanna see?" I smile and tease, "Like—" my eyes glance up at the ceiling as I think "—will I meet a tall, handsome stranger in my future?" My breath curls out of me in an icy plume of smoky air, choking off the rest of my teasing. I'm disoriented, but

I don't leave my body like I have in the past when I go to the future. This is different. My consciousness isn't ripped from me.

With my hands cuffed behind me, I'm restrained to the high-backed seat as I gauge the man approaching me. The grim expression on his handsome face as he draws his arm back squeezes my heart in my chest, causing it to ache. The open-palm slap to my cheek from his rough hand makes my face turn away from him. Blood sprays outward through my parted lips in an array of red. If I hadn't been in a fight before, the sting of it might've shocked me. I never know whether to clench my teeth or loosen my jaw when I see it coming. If I clench my teeth, I usually end up with a few loose ones. If I loosen my jaw, I run the risk of biting down on the soft, fleshy tissue inside and shredding a hole in it. The best thing to do would be to duck, but that would be counterintuitive, since I want him to hit me.

His green eyes lean near mine; his breath is warm on my rapidly swelling skin. "Does a priestess feel pain?" he asks.

Lowering my forehead, I drive it into his nose, hearing it crack as blood spurts out to spatter my cheeks and his. As I reel with dizziness and an aching skull, I try to smile when I murmur, "Yes. Do you?"

⊱•⊰

When I become lucid once more, Trey's smile of encouragement is gone, replaced by a look of deep-seated concern. My hand reaches up to touch my throbbing cheek. I wince. With one hand on my hip, he gently squeezes my side. "Kricket, are you all right? What just happened?"

"I don't know," I answer. Holding my head in my hands, it aches for a second with remembered pain from a dream, and then the pain is gone.

"Did you see something? You didn't lose consciousness, but you feel like ice." He rubs my arms, attempting to make them warm.

Was that the future? I wonder. "How long was I like that?"

"Twenty, maybe thirty seconds. Are you okay?"

"I'm . . . fine." I opt for a truthful answer. I *am* fine right now. If I have another freaky blipisode, I won't be; but for right this second, I'm okay. "I saw something: it was like a different film spliced into the movie of my real life, but with sound and the sensation of getting my head bashed in." I quickly relate to him what I saw.

"Was it an Alameeda soldier—the one hitting you?" he asks, his jaw tensing. He looks as if he's having a hard time remaining calm.

"No—at least, I don't think so," I say. "He didn't look Alameeda—he had green eyes." Trey knows what I mean. Most Alameeda have blue eyes and blond hair—my color hair. I'm half Alameeda, but I didn't inherit their eye color. I have my Rafe father's violet-colored eyes instead.

Trey strokes my pale hair. "Your eyes became almost blue for a few moments, Kricket," he says.

"They did?"

He nods; his thumb brushes my cheek. "The most startling color blue pushed outward from your pupils like a rolling cloud, infusing your irises."

"Maybe I should try again—this time concentrate on the context of what I want to know. This vision just sort of happened—it pushed its way in. I wasn't focused on a direction—a time or place."

Trey lifts his hand to rub his brow for a moment. "Maybe you should rest—"

"We need me to learn how to do this, right?" I ask.

He nods slowly.

I square my shoulders. "Okay then, let's try again," I tell him.

I can tell he wants to know more about the vision I just had. He's disturbed by it. So am I, so much so that I don't feel like repeating it—ever. Trey lets his hand fall abruptly from his forehead. "If you want to try again, let's try something a little different. Try jumping ahead in time just a quarter of a part," he suggests, using his word *part*, which translates to an Etharian "hour." "See if you can get a handle on this new flash-forward technique."

"Okay," I agree, trying not to show my anxiety. I take some deep breaths, attempting to calm my racing heart. "Ready?"

He sits up straighter, his hands going to my waist and holding me steady as he looks into my eyes. "Okay, I've got you," he breathes the words, sounding anxious too.

I stare into his sexy, violet gaze, trying to think in terms of five minutes ahead. It's so abstract to me. I'd much rather stay in the moment—with Trey. I blink. Nothing. After a few minutes, Trey leans forward and kisses me. He captures my bottom lip, tugging on it until I groan with pleasure. "You shouldn't reward me for failing," I whisper against his lips.

"You're incapable of failure," he replies. "You just need practice." He holds up his wrist communicator. "Here." He takes it off, holding it out in front of me. He presses the screen, displaying the time for me. "Focus on this." He changes the time, setting it a few minutes ahead.

I try again to concentrate. I take a cleansing breath, inhaling Trey's clean, masculine scent. I relax a bit. My eyes blur as I watch the timepiece tick away the moments. When I exhale, my breath is visible as cold, smoky plumes.

A trumpeting noise sounds near the entrance to Trey's apartment. The holographic projector near the door lights up with the image of Wayra's face filling the space. First Wayra's nose is huge and then Wayra moves so that only his eye is projected. It spans the space of at least six feet. "May eye remind you," Wayra's voice pipes through the speaker in the wall, "that time waits for no one? Open the door."

As my focus returns to Trey's alert expression in the present, I break out into a smile. Trey smiles back and it causes my heart to race in my chest. "What is it?" Trey asks.

"Wayra is on his way here," I reply. I begin to climb off Trey's lap. He steadies me with an arm beneath my elbow. I don't wait for him to rise, but hurry up the few steps to the main floor. From there I walk to Trey's foyer and stand by the door. Over my shoulder, I tell Trey, "When Wayra arrives, he's going to project an enormous, giant eye on the hologram." Trey nears me, leaning against the wall by my side. He crosses his arms and waits. In a few minutes, a trumpeting noise sounds. Wayra's nose appears larger than life and then his eye comes into focus. Through the intercom, Wayra's voice booms, "May *eye* remind you—"

I push the button on the side of the door, triggering it to open and recess into the ceiling. "—that time waits for no one?" I finish for him.

Positioned with his eye nearly pressed to the black camera lens mounted by the door in the corridor outside, Wayra's violet eyes widen in surprise before they quickly narrow into a scowl. "Don't do that, Kricket!" He shivers as if he finds me creepy. "How did you know what I was going to say?" His broad, uniformed shoulder pushes past me into Trey's apartment. He's almost as big as Trey; they could be brothers in that regard, but Wayra has more of a brutish look, whereas Trey's is refined.

"A lucky guess?" I offer.

Jax follows close behind Wayra with a serious expression on his face. It throws me off for a second, because Jax is usually very easygoing. He combs his dark hair from his eyes with his fingers, highlighting his need for a haircut. He's probably the most lax Cavar when it comes to his hair. He let it grow a little longer when he was at the palace as my military bodyguard. I think it suits him as a medic.

"You've been playing with the future again, haven't you?" Wayra asks. "Good, because we need your help. Something's wrong." He looks past my shoulder to Trey. "We can't get close to Defense Minister Vallen's office—it's surrounded by Brigadets."

My brow wrinkles. "Brigadets?"

Jax pipes in, "They're another branch of armed forces separate from the Cavars. They're not like us. Cavars are like your Marines—Brigadets are like . . ." He trails off, struggling for a word.

"Wackers," Wayra says unhelpfully.

"Military police," Trey provides the answer from behind me, frowning at Wayra for swearing in front of me.

"Yeah, they're like military police," Jax agrees.

"They're knob knockers, Kricket. Stay away from them." As if using his favorite filthy swear words is not enough, Wayra punctuates his words with a finger point in my direction. He glances past me again to Trey. "They're following us. I clocked at least a dozen. What do you wanna do, Sir?"

Walking back into the apartment, I near the window again. From just behind me, Trey asks Wayra, "Are the cycles ready?"

Wayra nods. "Always."

Trey looks in my direction once more, but his attention rests there only briefly before he focuses over my shoulder on the window at my back. Tensing, Trey moves to me, pulling me away from the window and behind his broad back. The sunlight that was streaming in the glass dims, casting a shadow on us. He gives a soft whistle, nodding toward the window. Wayra swears again under his breath and reaches for the pistol-like weapon on his belt that they call a harbinger.

"AFA," Jax's voice is steely.

"What's that?' I ask, hearing stress in his voice.

"Armored Fugitive Apprehender," Jax replies, and then looks at Trey. "What does it want?"

I can't see over Trey's shoulder, so I have to glance around his side to see what has set them off. A dronelike robot hovers in front of the window outside. Its shape resembles an inverted pyramid the size of a soda machine. The surface of the drone is dull, metallic nickel, but the triangle face is black. Within the center of the triangle resides a round lens eye that glows red. As the red iris adjusts, focusing its omnipotent camera lens on us, I'm struck by its likeness to the all-seeing eye on a dollar bill. Then it moves, the two points of the top of the triangle shift downward and twist so that they adjust rapidly to form pointed barrels—not unlike the barrel of a gun . . .

"It's arming!" Jax's voice is anxious. The AFA sends out a strident, deep-moan sound; the noise vibrates the pane in front of us, shattering the window-wall into twinkling, glistening pieces that billow in an explosive cascade of glass. Trey turns and dives at me, bringing me to the ground and covering me with his body to protect me from the sharp, jagged pieces. He takes most of his weight on his side so that I don't get crushed when we land.

As we lie on the floor panting, the entry door to Trey's living quarters slides open, disappearing into the ceiling. A blur of shiny black boots make clipped, tapping noises on the floor's hard surface. Fully armored combat-uniformed soldiers enter the foyer. Blue dots from mini-Gatling-like machine guns freckle my skin when Trey rolls off me.

I'm fairly certain that the men with their guns pointed at us are Brigadets; their uniforms are different from Cavars'. "Kricket Hollowell!" the leader of the unit barks. "Remain still!"

I don't move. I can't: I'm a shattered ceramic garden gnome, rooted to the floor by fear.

"By administrative order nine-four-two-four-six, you are hereby charged into the custody of the head of Civil Defense, Minister Telek, for interrogation."

Trey rises to his knees slowly. Blue spots make connect-the-dot patterns on him as well. "Kricket," he says to me in a calm tone, like he doesn't want to alarm me. *Too late!* "Tell them that you intend to comply."

My voice is calm—numb—as I say, "I intend to comply with the order."

Two soldiers move forward; one grasps me and hauls me up to my knees from the ground. He holds my hands behind me while the other one removes what looks to be an aerosol can from his belt, spraying my hands and wrists with it; it feels like foam coating my fingers. The foam hardens, welding my wrists and hands together in a tight clump. In shock, I glance at Trey. His fists are encased in plastic behind him too.

Looking over his shoulder at the soldier who read the order, Trey asks, "When did Minister Telek become the head of Civil Defense? Where's Minister Vallen?"

In a matter-of-fact voice, the soldier answers, "Minister Vallen is dead. They found him this morning with his larynx torn out. Our report says you visited him last night, Gennet Allairis."

"I did." Trey answers honestly. "We discussed the Declaration of War he intended to sign."

"The Declaration of War was signed this morning by Minister Telek after he was appointed to the post and sworn in. He has some questions for you, Gennet Allairis—for all of you."

Trey becomes tight-lipped. Jax and Wayra hold still as they're foam-shackled like us. One of the soldiers grasps me by my upper arm, lifting me up from my knees to my feet. My knees want to knock together, but I know how stupid it is to show weakness, so I square my shoulders and look straight ahead.

"Aww, look how tough this one be, Leelenaw," the soldier who holds my hands behind me says. "She's a right pixyish look for a shefty Alameeda boosha." I don't know if I'm right in my translation, but I think he said I have a pretty fairy look for being a shifty Alameeda slut.

Before I was brought to Ethar, Jax had surgically implanted a language translator into the area of my brain located behind my ear.

Since then, I've learned that the implant has branched out from the module, creating pathways to the frontal lobe, affecting centers in my brain that control not only language, but speech and sound as well. It deciphers several of the dialects used on Ethar, but it doesn't always get everything right. Just like with any technology, it's only as good as the information loaded into it. Slang, as well as some other Etharian-to-English translations, can sometimes still be confusing and insufficient to me. The way in which things are said—the use of idioms as modes of expression—can throw me off. I'm going to have to have Jax upgrade my language chip to accommodate this kind of slang.

Growls come from Trey, Wayra, and Jax as they eye the soldier like he's meat.

The soldier grins. "Whah-ho! Have yous *all* had her then?" He laughs at his own crudeness.

Wayra scowls at the other soldier who seems to be in charge. "Since when are you letting foreigners into the Brigade?" he demands.

"Since we're at war. Comantre sent us reinforcements," he answers Wayra with a look of resignation. Then he directs his comments to the rude Comantre soldier, "Shut your maw, Raspin. You speak only when I say you speak."

Raspin looks unfazed. "Don't stretch your underbits," he says with a sly, insubordinate smile, "I was just makin' friends." He winks and makes kissy faces at me. I turn away and look straight ahead again, ignoring him.

Leelenaw, the soldier who'd lifted me from the ground, leads me out of Trey's quarters. Several more soldiers in combat gear await us in the corridor. They eye me curiously as we pause and wait for the others to file out. Trey somehow maneuvers into position next to me, not an easy feat with so many wanting to get a look at me. The floating triangle-vending-machine-of-terror follows us into the hall; its stalking, all-seeing pyramid eye focuses its attention on me.

"So that thing's creepy," I murmur to Trey.

"It's a programmed killer. Don't provoke it."

"Okay," I agree, trying to hide my shiver of fear. There are times when acting like a raving lunatic can save your life. In the foster care system, when another kid thinks you're crazy, she's more apt to leave you alone. Even when she's much bigger than you, you know that she knows there's such a thing as "crazy strength." Crazy doesn't hold anything back—doesn't save anything in reserve. It doesn't fight fair. It just goes ballistic . . . and crazy never stops. I've gone crazy before with a broken beer bottle, fending off drunken men. In a situation like this, however, crazy gets you killed—or worse—and there are things worse than death. I glance over my shoulder at Raspin behind me; he scratches his wiry red hair with his two fingers beneath his helmet, giving me a wicked grin, but there's something dishonest about it. It confuses me.

"Look at all the Brigadets they ordered to arrest us," Wayra starts mouthing off to Jax. "Cavars everywhere are laughing at you!" he says to the soldier with a hand on his upper arm. "Why's everyone so afraid of her?" he nods his head in my direction because his hands are a plastic paperweight behind his back. "She's just a little lost Etharian. You should be *protecting* her. She's Rafian. She has proven her loyalty to us."

"They're just doing their jobs, Wayra," I say, trying to calm him down. He's never been in this situation. He's never felt this kind of betrayal.

"Blow their jobs!" he snarls.

Winding through a few curving hallways, the high-end elegance of the sconce lighting on the walls falls away the farther we get from Trey's door. As we progress and turn down several more corridors, the soft lighting is replaced by silver tracks of light in the floor and ceiling.

On the next corridor, we enter a bridge-tunnel of pure glass suspended two hundred stories or more above the base platform of the ship. Stretching between two separate towers, it's illuminated by the sun, giving us an unimpeded view of blue sky. I squint, unable to shield my eyes from the glare as I assess the height of the tower we're about to enter; it's the tallest within the floating city, almost reaching the top of the iridescent defensive shield that covers us the way a dome protects the scene within a snow globe. As we cross the bridge to it, I peer through the transparent floor; beneath us is a breathtaking reservoir of crystal-blue water. The water streams into a deep blue moat around the base of the gleaming silver tower. Beyond it, lush green lawns divide beautifully structured gardens.

As we cross to the tower, glass doors slide open for us to enter through; the lead Brigadet strobes a pattern of light onto the crisscross of blue security beams barring our way. The blue lasers evaporate, allowing us to proceed into the tower. A fem-bot hologram materializes as we move forward, floating along with us. "Greetings and welcome to Premiere Palisade's level 210," her sultry robot voice says, "featuring the offices of some of our most prominent members of Skye Congress and Skye Council. The main concourse of Palisade Station is one level below. The Sonic Rail Line, transport to surrounding skyscapes, can be located on the main concourse, one level down. Overups to destinations within Premiere Palisades are located on the main concourse, one level down. Do you require a guide?"

"Cancel guide," one of the soldiers barks, resulting in the hologram's disappearance from sight.

We continue through the corridor. Military personnel in the Premiere Palisade begin to take note of us. Most of the tall, willowy women we encounter slow their progression as we pass them—sometimes with mouths agape. At first, I think they're looking at just me, startled to see someone who looks Alameeda, but then I notice the adoring stares that Trey is getting when their eyes move from me to him. Blushes and soft whispers behind hands greet me as I glance over my shoulder.

Walking by an elaborate wrought-iron balustrade, we arrive at a gallery that overlooks the round chamber below. It's an ultramodern elevated train station. The tracks intersect the building and run between skyscrapers, linking them together. The arrival and departure area is the size of a high-tech coliseum. All along the walls of the chamber below are elevatorlike doors, which must be the entry points to the overups referred to by the guidebot. The doors project television images featuring some kind of news program that I can't make out from here. Passengers enter the small chambers and disappear behind their doors. My eyes move on to the gleaming silver tile that lines the chamber, noting that the black-tiled pillars and arched niches of its architecture give the space an old-world-meets-new-world look.

I lift my eyes to stare across the gallery from us. A lone figure leans over the railing, his elbows on the balustrade with his hands clasped together. He's between two columns that are carved in the image of saers. What sets this Etharian apart to make me notice him is that he's not Rafian; his dress uniform is that of a Comantre Syndic. His long, golden-brown hair is rolled into dreadlocks and secured in a ponytail. He looks like a surfer—someone you'd see on a beach in Chicago's North Park playing two-man volleyball. The paler skin on his jaw suggests that he had a beard, but shaved it recently. I can't tell what color his eyes are from this distance as they bore into mine, returning my stare, but I'd bet Wayra an entire venish that they aren't violet.

Dreadlock-man watches us move to the palatial staircase that leads to the main concourse below. My skin prickles with goose bumps as I begin my descent on the stairs, feeling an eerie sense of déjà vu. I've read some things regarding quantum physics: how everyone and everything is made up of energy. It's as if I *feel* the energy between this soldier at the gallery railing and me. Taking the first few steps down, the hard foam securing my hands behind me cracks, loosening to allow my fingers to move.

My breathing quickens and my heartbeat thunders even faster than it had in the last few minutes. For a moment, I'm unable to look away from the man at the railing above. When I reach the main concourse of the station, the pull between us is broken. The soldier steps back from the railing so I can no longer see him, disappearing behind a column.

I inhale deeply, as if coming back to myself. Wiggling my fingers, the pressure that made them numb is gone. *Did he do that?* I wonder. I try to track where Dreadlock-man went, but it's impossible to see behind me as my upper arm is tugged forward and I'm hustled across the crowded room.

A wave of citizens parts for us as the soldiers in front usher them to the sides. Some of the onlookers we pass have starstruck expressions. When we reach the center of the room, a life-size holographic projection captures my attention. It's a newsreel playing out events. I almost trip over my own feet when I recognize one of the realistic images as mine. Dressed in the torn, lavender ball gown from the swank last night, I'm made of light, looking pale and fragile as I'm carried from the palace ballroom in Trey's arms. It also shows light images of Wayra and Jax flanking us with their guns up, braced against their shoulders. That clip isn't long, lasting only a few moments before the camera pans to the chaos of artillery fire and mortar blasts. There's a heart-stopping shot of a hovering, ferocious-looking Alameeda E-One crouching over the palace.

Citizens in the station crowd around the hologram news clip, murmuring to one another in agitation over the events they're witnessing. In a few moments, the newsreel changes again and an image of me is back, descending the elegant palace staircase at my debut, smiling a plastic smile to the crowd below before the fighting began. As I look around, I realize that there are more life-size holograms displaying the events of last night.

People near us begin to lose some of the shock our presence seemed to instill. There's confusion as we continue on. Those who were watching the holograms now trail behind us, hoping to get a longer look. Ahead of us, three dronelike orbs the size of basketballs fly around us. One darts in close to me, crowding me like a hungry seagull at the beach. A black camera lens protrudes from the front of the white-metal orb, making *blink-click* noises. The other two have lenses, as well, that survey everything, circling us with the speed of hummingbirds to capture three-dimensional images.

Trey gestures with his head to the drone cameras. "The media are here."

"What do they want?" I ask as I'm jostled from the pushback of the crowd.

"They want to see you," he replies. His lips thin in a grim line.

The Brigadet soldiers are shoving everyone back, but members of the press keep trying to get to me. Flashes of light strobe us as the reporters shout above the aggressive crowd. A beautiful, dark-haired girl with a small star embossed above the arch of her eyebrow yells to me, "Fay Kricket, is it true you knew about the Alameeda attack before the event last night?" The camera drone swoops near to my face, *blink-click*ing as the black lens focuses in. "Whose side are you on, Rafe or Alameeda?" I drop my chin, confused by the frenzy that surrounds me. "Do you know what the Alameeda are planning?" "Is it true you tried to kill the Regent at the swank last night?" "Is that why you're being restrained?"

The Brigadets are funneling me ahead toward a niche in the wall. It contains a larger overup than the others. This lift is also different because whereas the other overups have embedded video screens in their smaller doors that stream the same newsreels we saw in the holograms, these much larger doors are inlayed with iridescent mother-of-pearl. Etched within the double doors are two Art Deco saers. The saber-toothed tigers are on their hind legs, breathing shiny gray, lavender, and blue flames as they face each other in mirrored symmetry.

I'm pulled away from Trey's side by a yank on my arm and herded toward the enormous elevator with the saers on the front of it. Trey, Wayra, and Jax are taken in the opposite direction, toward the smaller overup doors.

"Trey!" I call his name, twisting as I try to see him being led away from me.

Trey fights the soldiers pulling us apart. "I need to stay with her! We have to stay together." He head-butts the soldier holding his arm. Camera drones hover above him, capturing the fight as Trey roundhouse kicks another soldier who tries to grasp his arm. Wayra and Jax fight the soldiers near them too. Wayra lowers his head and uses it rampaging-bull style as he forces it into a soldier's stomach. The crowd around us begins screaming, as soldiers try to push them back by force. The AFA arms again, focusing its lethal gun barrels on Trey.

I wrench my arm away from the soldier holding me. The cracks that have formed in the foam shackles shatter the restraint, allowing my hands to go free. I stumble into the middle of the fight. Pushing past Raspin with an elbow to his face, the Comantre Brigadet holds his bloody mouth. I run to Trey, throwing myself against him. My arms wrap around his neck as I plead near his ear, "Don't fight them! They'll kill you! I'll be okay; I'm stone, remember? Nothing touches me." It's not true. I have a paper heart and he has written notes all over it.

"Kricket," Trey whispers against my neck. I tilt my face so I can see him. He kisses me hard on the lips. It's a desperate kiss—a last kiss.

My arm is seized and I'm forced away from Trey once more. Behind me, I hear them beating on him. I stumble and try to tear myself away from the soldier holding me again, but he forces me into the ornate conveyance in front of us.

Inside, the chamber is much larger and grander than a standard elevator. A low-lit crystal chandelier hangs down from the center of the twenty-foot-high ceiling. High-back cushioned benches line three walls with dove gray velvet upholstery. The large velvet-covered buttons in the benches make diamond patterns in the fabric. The glass above the benches is antiqued and smoky, reflecting our images in blurred impressions.

When the doors slide closed, I feel the overup move laterally before it begins to rise at a stomach-dropping rate. I'm still panting from the struggle. The soldier beside me lets go of my arm, since there's nowhere for me to run in here. Every part of me wants to sink onto one of the soft gray benches, rest my cheek against the cushion, and cry my heart out, but I refuse to give in to it. Instead, I stand among the handful of soldiers, watch the doors in front of me, and wait.

CHAPTER 2
DON'T MESS WITH ME

None of us move when the doors glide open. I stare ahead into the dim room. The sliver of light from the overup's chandelier falls on a round, dark wood table ahead. In the center of the table is an enormous vase, dripping with a vibrant arrangement of znous, the deadly killer-insect-carrying, turbine-boring-worm flowers. Their scent and stunning color make the blood drain away from my face as I stare at them.

A stern, masculine voice calls from somewhere within the room. "Fay Kricket, you may come in."

I push back images of a brutal foster father I once had, thinking, *Don't show fear. They live for it.* I take a tentative step off the overup. No one else accompanies me.

The dark, hardwood floor beneath my feet squeaks from a loose floorboard, the noise echoes in the tomblike atmosphere of the room. The overup doors slide closed behind me, shutting off the sliver of light. As my eyes adjust to the dimness, I realize I've been let off in the center of the room where just this table resides to greet its visitors.

"Take a flower, if you'd like," the man in the room offers, his tone far from warm. I squint toward the right side of the chamber. In the direction from which the voice came I see a wide, beautifully carved mahogany desk. The dark wing-backed chair behind it is turned toward the wall-window, the glass of which has been darkened so that it doesn't let in much light, but does not impede the breathtaking view of the skyline. Nothing of the man is visible above the black upholstery of the chair.

I clear my throat before I say, "I would take a flower, but I have this thing against cranium-boring worms: I don't like them."

He doesn't turn to face me. "I was told that znous are your favorite. I had the worms removed especially for you."

"It'd be a shame to spoil the carefully planned arrangement," I decline, speaking less about the flowers and more about whatever he has in mind for me.

From the left-hand side of the room, a watery-blue light flickers on, drawing my attention to it. My breath catches in my throat. I reach out to the table in front of me to hold it for support, disturbing the flower arrangement and causing several white and fuchsia znou petals to fall to the dark surface.

"Manus!" My whisper is involuntary.

Ahead of me, the entire wall on the left-hand side of the room is a tank, like the kind I'd seen at Shedd Aquarium for the shark exhibit. This one is a bit different, however, in that it doesn't have exotic fish in it, or a sunken lighthouse, or a treasure chest. It only has one occupant: Manus. With a partial mask over his nose and mouth, he's encased in a maze of tubing amid bubbling, gurgling fluid. Readouts light up one side of the glass, pulsing and flashing in waves and colors. My hand sweeps the table; I grasp some of the fallen znou petals in my fist.

I steady myself before I walk to the tank on trembling legs, gently touching the coolness of the glass that separates us with the tips of my fingers. I pull them back as a display lights up.

The male voice is just behind me now. I don't look over my shoulder at him when he says, "They just finished installing him here a few fleats ago," he explains, using his word that means "minutes." "I said it was for his protection, but between you and me, he's more of a souvenir."

"A souvenir?" *He's totally evil*, I think. I'm afraid to turn around and see him.

"We never did get along." He walks to stand next to me, leaning near the glass. He taps on it with his fingernails. I give him a quick glance, just catching his profile. He's old-looking, with streaks of white in his once-black hair. It means he must be ancient, maybe thousands of years old.

A thin, red scar runs from his left eye to his mouth; it puckers his lip on one side, giving him a snarl. I wonder at the reason he never had it removed—or wrapped, as they call it, like most citizens do when they receive wounds that scar. I doubt it's for the same reason Wayra doesn't: I don't think the blushers would be attracted to him, scar or not. However old he is, though, he's still formidable. He's nowhere near grandfatherly, unless the grandfather was ex–Special Forces and addicted to steroids. I doubt very much that I'd last more than a second with him in a fight, not a fair one anyway. He towers over me.

He holds a very stylized handheld cig-a-like smoker. It's silver with a few gold cog-like coins embossed on the long shaft. He puts the black mouthpiece to his lips and sucks in the water vapor from the pipe. He exhales a puff of fragrance not unlike brown sugar. I silently vow to never eat anything that smells like that again.

I turn away from him, facing Manus in the medical stasis tank once more. "What happened to him?" I ask. One shoulder looks as if it had been bitten off by a rather large shark, and there are burns that go to the bone on his legs, abdomen, and face.

"*Haut* Manus"—his stress on Manus's elite title is less than respectful—"was wounded quite severely. I believe he was struck by sonic sayzers—he has contusions—"

"Excuse me, but what are sonic sayzers?"

"It's a weapon strapped to the arm." He moves his liver-spotted wrist between me and the tank and makes gestures indicating the weapon is affixed somehow on one's wrist and aimed Spider-Man style. "It projects sound in bursts at frequencies that can shatter bones and rupture cells." He drops his wrist to his side, drawing another puff from his cig-a-like.

"Where does the sound come from?"

"Preprogrammed frequencies. Some are milder than others. Injuries can be superficial or substantial, based upon the calibration. The Regent suffered injuries that are consistent with a lethal frequency." He doesn't sound unhappy about the unfortunate injuries suffered by his sovereign.

"So they're killer noisemakers." I interpret. "Where did this happen?"

"The Alameeda caught him in the floral gardens of the palace. The sonic sayzers ruptured cells in his upper right torso, right shoulder, neck, and cranial areas. He had to have regenerative skin grafts and cell modifications." He touches the tank and a log of the procedure lights up, projecting images of Manus and his injuries onto the glass so that I can view it. I wince. It's gruesome.

"But he'll live, right?" I ask, irritated that I'm worried about Manus after all he did to me. He's a complication I don't need, but I don't hope for his death.

"Your fiancé will survive," he assures me.

"I'm no longer the Regent's fiancée. That ended last night."

"Oh, I know. You were never going to commit to him. You haven't asked me who I am yet," the man adds in a sinister tone. This is a game to him and he's enjoying it.

"I know who you are. You're Head Defense Minister Telek."

"You surprise me," he says disdainfully, with a cold glare. *He must not like surprises.* "Is that one of your priestess gifts?"

"Hardly. Your soldiers read your order to us when we were arrested. You ordered me into your custody for interrogation. So . . . here I am."

"Yes, here you are," he agrees. "It has been reported that you had some prior knowledge that there would be an Alameeda attack last night."

"I knew they were coming, if that's what you mean."

"That is what I mean. How did you know?"

"I witnessed the attack before it happened," I answer, meeting his unwavering stare. His violet eyes make me want to shiver from the hatred I see in them.

"You . . . witnessed it?" comes his skeptical reply. "In a crystal ball perhaps? Isn't that what human witches use?"

"I'm neither human nor a witch," I reply, trying not to let him rile me. It's what he wants and I won't do what he wants, not for anything.

"No, you're an Alameeda priestess," he agrees.

"I'm a coriness of Rafe," I counter.

He doesn't miss a step. "You didn't answer my question. Do you use a crystal ball?"

"Not quite. It's more of an out-of-body experience." I blush because saying the words out loud makes me sound crazy.

"That must be a departure for you, not using your body to get what you want."

I know what he's implying, but I ignore the innuendo. "I rarely get what I want, Minister Telek," I reply honestly, "within my body or outside of it."

"Speaking of bodies," Minister Telek segues, "do you know what the surgeons plan to do to Haut Manus's?" he asks me.

I stare for a moment at Manus. His eyes are closed. There are several swimmi-bots tending to him. One looks to be a flesh-layering bot, patching skinlike material over a segment of his calf where the burns are not as severe. Another is like a suckerfish-bot, extracting dead, floating, barely attached skin from his shoulder.

"No," I admit warily.

He gestures to one of the two thronelike chairs behind us that face the tank and orders, "Have a seat and I'll show you what a regeneration looks like."

I slip into the soft chair; it makes me feel tiny by comparison, and my toes have to point to touch the floor.

Minister Telek takes the other. We're angled toward each other but still face the tank. A side table separates me from him, yet I feel as if we're still too close.

"On screen," Minister Telek says, "Trey Allairis—cue to Regeneration file."

The tank containing Manus darkens to opaque. It becomes the backdrop to holographic images, like the video walls at the palace.

My breath catches when a hologram projector shows Trey's three-dimensional images in a rapid stream from his infancy to his childhood. Most of the younger images are Trey with his twin brother, Victus. There are several in which both brothers have one arm over each other's shoulder with Trey holding a rather atrocious-looking fish out to the camera.

Next, in rapid succession, and while the hologram spins to show several angles, I view Trey's adolescence to his early days of military training. My heartbeat accelerates; I can't hide the smile that forms on my lips. Some of the tension I'm feeling melts away as I see him grow from child to adult in a matter of moments.

Then the holograms of Trey slow and blink off as the film changes. Booming sounds of cannon fire dropping nearby rumbles my chair from the holographic images that emerge next. Soldiers scramble to strip off blood-soaked clothing in exchange for clean smocks in a makeshift medical unit on the outskirts of a war zone. A few medics pace by the gaping mouth of the entrance to their enclosure with an air of expectation. One of them shouts for everyone to make ready. My empty hand goes to my mouth from shock as my other hand tightens on the znou petals when I recognize Trey in the center of a pair of soldiers being ushered into the medical unit. Tears spring to my eyes, and I fight them back when I see both of his legs are gone below the knees. He's brought to a podlike surgery table. The table resembles half of a tanning bed positioned under an enormous laser mounted on a robotic arm. The laser-mounted tool goes to work, slicing Trey's armor from what remains of his body. Bloody and torn apart, Trey moans as he writhes and trembles in pain from missing limbs and scalded skin. Agony and fear flatten my lips. The crackle and bubble of flesh is audible as surgeons cauterize the hemorrhaging arteries and scrape dead flesh off his sheared stumps. Trey's repeated vomiting as his flesh is sutured to reattach his hand makes me taste bile in my own throat. One of the physicians screams at the anesthesiologist, directing him to put Trey under before the pain kills him.

I look away, unable to watch anymore lest I vomit. *It is a wonder he didn't kill me upon sight when he found me*, I think. *I look just like the monsters who did that to him.*

"Manus won't require the kind of extensive regrowth as this—" Minister Telek pauses. "Is this too much for you?" he asks with a bit of an amused laugh, then orders, "Console on." A different holographic screen the size of a laptop illuminates in the air in front of him. He squints at icons, activating them by his eye movement. The small screen disappears as a compartment opens in the surface of the table between us. A stout but elegant silver urn with matching cups and saucers arises from the surface on a silver salver. "Would you like some kafcan?" he asks. Steam rolls from the spout of the pot. He pours the hot, dark-roast beverage that is very similar to coffee into a delicate cup.

"No, thank you." I make a vow never to take a thing from him. Owing him would be a crime. He keeps the cup of kafcan for himself, setting it on the table near his hand.

"The Alameeda nearly killed Gennet Trey, did you know that?" I nod my head. "I knew. He told me." I swallow hard.

This doesn't sit well with Minister Telek. His hand moves violently to swipe the steaming cup off the table. It shatters on the floor in front of us with a loud clatter. "Trey will do anything for you, won't he!" he accuses with a growl. The abruptness of his rage is not a foreign thing to me. I saw it seething below the surface, and I know better than to answer his question.

When I remain silent, Minister Telek barks an order to his console. "Stream current headline."

The hologram of Trey disappears and is replaced by three-dimensional images of Trey and me from just moments ago in the Sonic Rail Station. I'm throwing my arms around Trey's neck. Trey leans down and kisses me hard on the mouth. My heart strains the wall of my chest. To Minister Telek, this is somehow damning evidence. The love letter Trey wrote on my paper heart is there; Minister Telek can read it.

His rage is barely restrained as he says between clenched teeth, "They're calling you two star-crossed lovers, romanticizing your relationship. It was already viral by the time you arrived at my office." He wants me to be penitent about it.

"That poses a problem for you," I murmur. "You were hoping we'd look like criminals—that's what you were going for by allowing the media to ambush us."

"You're a master manipulator, just like your mother!" he seethes.

"I doubt you knew my mother," I reply. My heart is beating out of control with panic, but I try to appear as if I'm not bothered by what he says or the violence he displays. I don't know where the line is with him, but the kafcan mess on the floor in front of me indicates that I'm close to it. I have to decide if I want to cross over it.

"I knew your father. I couldn't save him from your mother. I will not make the same mistake again," Telek promises.

"What mistake?"

"Pan was the brightest officer in my arsenal. He was like a son to me. He had a brilliant mind—intuitive with defensive strategy. Your mother ruined him."

"How'd she do that?"

"It was after the Terrible War. He discovered her while on patrol near the border of our territory. She planned to escape the Brotherhood by disappearing into the masses on Earth—or so she claimed. Pan helped her seek asylum in Rafe, and then they chose to violate our laws by deserting to Earth together. She manipulated him into protecting her, much like you've done with the Cavar sent to retrieve you, and again with our Regent. We managed to avoid another war with her. That won't be the case with you." He's laying all the blame for my being here upon me.

"I didn't ask to come here," I point out. "You brought me here."

His fury bubbles to the surface again. "*I* did not bring you here! If *I* had ordered the mission, it would've been extermination, not an extraction. The mission to remand you was ordered by Minister Vallen and the Regent."

"To what end?"

"It doesn't matter. One is dead and the other is very near to it."

"You don't know," I goad him to see if he'll give me a better answer. "You don't know why they went looking for me."

"Minister Vallen believed that your mother had the gift of prophecy," he says with disgust. "He was foolish enough to hope that she'd come back and help him see if the aggression we were witnessing on the borders of Peney were the Alameeda mobilizing for war. He didn't understand that the only gift your mother possessed was the one for manipulating men."

"You don't believe my mother could see the future?" I ask.

"No more than I believe that you can," he says honestly. "You're just like her: a charlatan—a spy. You use your femininity to deceive."

He thinks I'm with the Alameeda! I snort with derision and ask, "How did you come to that conclusion?"

"If you're not a spy, then explain how you became Haut Manus's most trusted adviser in such a short time after arriving here from

Earth? Was it your stunning grasp of Etharian politics or just the fact that you are stunning?"

I blanch. I don't want to reveal to him my ability to divine lies. I make up a plausible excuse. "Maybe Manus was hoping ambassadors from Peney and Wurthem would open up to me because of my mixed heritage? Maybe I appear neutral to those in power?" I suggest as I get a sinking feeling in my stomach.

"It's quite interesting to me that when Minister Vallen sent a team to look for you, so too did the Alameeda. Don't you find that an odd coincidence?"

"No. They have priestesses. One of their genetically gifted priestesses could've alerted the Alameeda Brotherhood to Rafe's plan."

"Ahh, psychically, right?" he asks with sarcasm. "You still think I believe that?"

"You should."

He brushes aside my comment. "If you're not with the Alameeda, why did you run from the Rafe team when it made contact with you?"

I look at him as if he's mental. "They scared me. I believed I was human. Running was a natural response to fear."

Minister Telek pushes out his bottom lip and shrugs. "It could be. Or, you could've been running to meet with Kyon Ensin, your Alameeda handler, in order to brief him on having made contact and receive instructions. You are, after all, his intended consort, as decreed by the Alameeda Brotherhood."

"I don't care what the Alameeda Brotherhood decreed. Your grasp of events is wrong. I attempted to kill Kyon just a few parts ago. You have misread the situation, Minister. The only thing that lies between Haut Kyon and me is malice."

"As an agent of the Alameeda, you needed to plan exactly how to infiltrate our ranks. The alleged hostility between you is feigned."

"You're implying that the knife I left embedded in his chest was just a little friendly banter between friends?"

"You had to make it look like you were fighting back. You didn't deliver a death blow, choosing instead not to strike at his heart."

I feel sick, remembering the twinkling sound of empty shell casings tumbling down the staircase. The smell of acrid smoke hanging in the air from the barrels of the Alameeda mini-Gatling-like mechanized weapons; it mingled with the alpha-male scent of Kyon as my knife first nicked his bony chest plate before it slid around it and into him. "If I'm a spy, as you say, why would I try to warn Haut Manus about the attack last night? I told Ustus Hassek, the head of the Regent's police, as well."

"Manus is in a coma and Ustus is conveniently dead," Minister Telek points out. "There are witnesses who saw you kiss Kyon last night."

"*He* kissed *me*! To him, I'm a possession—he thinks he owns me."

"Does he?"

"No." I'm falling fast, faster than I ever expected. "I'm not your enemy! Review the incident of the previous Alameeda attack—"

"I have."

"So you know then. You know I saw that Alameeda attack before it happened—the one to extract Kyon."

"That's not what I saw," Minister Telek replies. Something horrible is growing in me; it's an ache in the back of my throat. "You were privy to the Alameedas' presence—you met with Kyon that evening and you had access to many of Alameeda's allies at the swank you attended that evening. The Alameeda staged the fake extraction attempt in order to manipulate the Regent, Manus, into believing that a feeble Etharian"—he gestures to me with a look meant to discredit—"possesses foresight."

I'm in my own dark ages, I think, *except in reverse—I can't prove that I'm a priestess.* "I'm not the enemy."

"But you are. You killed Minister Vallen." He takes another deep draw on the silver cig-a-like, and the scent of brown sugar envelopes me.

"How could I have done that?" My voice is feeble. "I've only just arrived here. I don't even know what he looks like."

"You had ample time last night to do it. You convinced Gennet Allairis to help you. He's in love with you—anyone can see it by watching your kiss in the station. You convinced him to help you. You promised him sanctuary in Alameeda—a promise I doubt that you intended to keep."

I crush the silky znou petals in my hand. "You're an amazing storyteller, Minister Telek, but that's all it is: a story. You don't even believe it yourself. You know it's a lie."

He looks intrigued that I'm calling him on his complete fabrication of facts. His smile is worrisome to me. Setting down his cig-a-like on the table between us, he says, "Minister Vallen's death I mark as your doing. And you're going to confess to it."

My mouth opens in disbelief for a moment as I prepare to defend myself from such a ruthless accusation, but I close it after a moment. Something occurs to me. "*You* killed Minister Vallen," I murmur in understanding.

His eyes narrow, as if in affront. "You're accusing *me*! No one would believe it! I'm a well-respected officer. I have no motive," he lies, "whereas you will be implicated in the attempted assassination of the Regent as well. I'll show everyone that you can no more predict the future than you can save yourself—or the Cavar you seduced. But it won't come to that, because you're going to confess to the crime. "

"I don't think I'll be confessing to your crime."

"My crime? You have the motive—he was your enemy. You were sent by the Alameeda to kill him."

"Your motive is better, Minister Telek: You killed him for power—a seat on Skye Council—total control over the Declaration

of War you signed this morning. How very Machiavellian of you."
His eyes widen. "Oh, you're surprised I figured out it was you?" I
flick my hand at him. "I can't understand why that would shock
you, since *I* know *I* didn't do it and I'm positive that Trey didn't do
it. That. Leaves. You."

"Had you never returned to Ethar, there would've been no need
to end Minister Vallen's life. I mark his death your doing."

It takes me less than a second to realize he just confessed to killing Minister Vallen. "So you're going to try to pin it on me anyway
by making me look like a spy," I breathe.

"You *are* a spy," he says honestly, believing the worst of me without any proof.

"I'm not, nor am I a murderer."

He ignores me, looking away as he turns on the watery-blue light
of Manus's med-tank again. Then he says, "After you confess to killing Minister Vallen with your accomplice Trey Allairis, I'll make it
a painless death for you both. You can simply go to sleep and never
awake. But if you refuse, I'll have to torture a confession from you
both . . . and you will confess."

My throat aches with my struggle to hold back tears. I open my
clenched fist. What he's saying is true, at least in my case. I will probably confess, even though I didn't do it—with a long enough time
line, I wouldn't be strong enough to endure pain forever. "You don't
know Trey," I say with a tight voice. "He'd never confess to anything
he didn't do, and I'd never condemn him in that way to avoid pain. I
won't be euthanized like some unwanted pet at the pound."

He looks at me again and shrugs as only a powerful man can.
Reaching for the kafcan pot again, he pours out another cup of it for
himself. "Either way you die. A part of me is delighted that you'd
choose pain. Nothing will bring me more pleasure than to see you
die horribly: a fitting end for an Alameeda priestess."

Sea of Stars

My eyes fix his. He gives me a checkmate smile, and then he takes a sip of his kafcan, swallowing it like it's the best he's had in his life. I watch him savor it.

"I changed my mind. I do have something to confess," I murmur.

He's amused. "Ah, so you aren't as tough as you wanted me to believe. The threat of pain already has you agreeing to confess to the murder of the defense minister?"

"Umm . . . no. I'll confess to the *poisoning* of the defense minister."

"That won't work. The defense minister's throat was cut."

"No, it wasn't. He was poisoned, and if he doesn't get an antidote for znou axicote," I reply, opening the lid of the kafcan pot so that he can see the znou petals floating on the surface of it, "he'll be dead by the end of the rotation."

Minister Telek's eyes snap open wide as he rises to his feet, the kafcan cup slipping from his hand to shatter on the floor in front of his Regent-souvenir. He puts his fingers in his mouth, gagging himself so that he vomits. Wiping his wrist over his mouth, it leaves a blood trail on his sleeve. He turns away from me and stumbles toward his desk on the other side of the room.

I rise from the enormous chair and follow him on shaky legs. "I was never interested in botany when I lived in Chicago," I explain conversationally as I trail him. "There was never any need for it. But here, it seems like a useful thing to know, don't you think?"

Minister Telek bumps into the table in the center of the room, knocking the vase of znous off it. The flowers scatter as the vase splinters into a thousand pieces. I step on the flowers as we move across the room. "I found it interesting that most of those who had turbine worms drill into them didn't die from that—they died from the poison the worms ingested after eating the petals of the flower. I only steeped two petals into your kafcan—I had six. They'll want to know that when they come for you. I don't think two will be

39

enough to kill you, but you'll begin to feel the poison eating through your stomach soon. There are several cures available if they act fast: Abersuctonal, Hesterfastok, or Lamb's Bottom—I like the sound of that one, Lamb's Bottom—it just sounds sweet. You should ask for Lamb's Bottom. But they're probably still going to have to repair part of your bowel; it's a very caustic poison. And painful." I fake a cringe. "Ooph, it's supposed to be one of the worst."

He makes it to his desk, leaning on it heavily. "Console on," he moans. "Geteron, I need you!" He collapses into his chair, unbuttoning his collar as he pants and writhes.

"Don't look so shocked," I say, sitting on the corner of his desk as I study him. I hold my hands in my lap so that he can't see how they tremble in fear. "I'm my father's daughter. I, too, have a mind for defensive strategy. But I'm nothing like you. I'm not a coldblooded murderer. This is your only warning, Minister: Don't mess with me. And if you try to hurt Trey, I'll kill you."

The overup's doors open and several uniformed soldiers enter the room with weapons drawn. I don't move as they swarm in around us. A couple of soldiers haul me off the edge of the desk and restrain me. As they do, I murmur, "Think about what I said. You need me to bring the future back to you."

CHAPTER 3
BEYOND THESE WALLS

The Brigadet next to me in the overup has a brand new matte black harbinger in his hand. Judging by the way he's holding the pistol-like weapon on me, he'd feel tough if he got to use it. It's a bit of overkill, though; they've already shackled my hands with spray foam and locked a collar restraint on my neck. It'd take only one press of the remote button to make the collar tighten around my throat and have me on my knees fighting for air.

The overup continues to descend as if it were taking us to the Underworld. The five soldiers surrounding me obscure its soft bench seats. I hate the look in their eyes, so I keep mine on the sparkling crystal in the chandelier as it sways with the motion of the rectangular car.

I scan my mind for what I could've done differently with Minister Telek. I can't find a solution that would've gotten me out of the torture I was sure to face with him in charge. *I should've killed him. He'll murder us for sure now—with or without a confession.* My only consolation is that what I just did to him will buy us some time; he would've extorted a false confession out of me right away. Now, he has a corroded bowel to contend with before he can address my supposed crimes. He'll wait until he can watch my interrogation. I've kicked him in the crotch, metaphorically speaking; he'll want to be around when it's time to return the favor. I have only a small window to figure out my next move.

They should have some sort of elevator music, I think, as the awkward silence in the compartment grows. I clear my throat. "I hope someone remembers to feed Manus while Minister Telek is away. It'd be a shame to find him floating on top of the tank."

The soldiers scowl at me.

"What?" I return with a weary sigh. "That happened to a goldfish I once had. I had to flush him."

"Quiet!" the one with the itchy trigger finger barks at me. His voice is loud in the confined space.

I begin to shiver. I'm the kind of cold where it seems I'll never know warmth again. My chest feels tight and I find it hard to breathe. I look around the compartment—there isn't a way out until the doors open. *Why don't they open?* With growing panic, I pull at my restrained hands; they're immobile, locked in amber like some Stone Age mosquito that drowned in sap. I feel claustrophobic; the walls are closing in. *They're going to kill me*, my mind whispers, and even when I want to deny it, I can't. I swallow hard, trying to contain my freak-out. I hope for a drop in air pressure, for the lift to crash, anything so that this silence ends.

From behind me, I hear a masculine voice ask, "Did you really stab a member of the Brotherhood with a dinner knife?" There's something familiar about the voice, but I can't discern why that is. I begin to turn around, but the voice barks, "Face forward and answer the question."

The hair on my arms prickles. My head hurts, and I feel as if I couldn't turn it if I wanted to. "Yes. He was murdering everyone," I answer.

"He wasn't killing you," he points out.

"No," I agree. "He wasn't killing me."

"Why didn't he kill you?"

"He thinks I'm his."

"Are you?"

"Not if I can help it."

There's silence for a moment. I try to see him in the smoky mirrors, but I can get only an impression of him. He's not Rafian—his hair isn't black. "What are your talents?" he asks.

I moisten my lips. "I can rub my stomach and pat my head at the same time, but you'll have to free my hands if you wanna see."

The soldier holding the harbinger on me looks suspiciously over my shoulder at one of the soldiers behind me. "Who are you? What unit are you with?"

"I'm a Comantre conscript from Westway," he lies. His speech is very lovely, refined in a way that would suggest some sort of upper class. He's not Comantre and I doubt he's ever even been to Westway.

"Then shut your mouth! You're not here to interrogate our prisoner."

The man behind me replies, "Don't interrupt me." He moves closer to my ear, as he asks, "When will they attack next?"

"I don't know," I reply.

The Brigadet in front of me scowls at the poseur Comantre conscript behind me. "What did you say to me?" The Brigadet shifts the barrel of his harbinger. All the other soldiers on the overup do the same, pointing their weapons away from me and in the direction of the soldier behind me.

A heavy sigh comes from the Comantre impostor. "I told you not to interrupt," he replies. The air in the chamber becomes supercharged. The harbinger is torn from the Brigadet soldiers' hand. His eyes widen in surprise as the gunlike weapon floats in the air before him, its barrel pointed at him. All the other soldier's harbingers follow suit, each doing a one-eighty in the air to levitate in front of its soldier. Even as the shock wears off, no one moves at all.

The soldier claiming to be from Westway says to the Brigadets, "If you speak again without my permission, your harbingers will shoot you. Now, stop the overup."

"Halt overup, authorization five-nine-alpha-wastern-urtza," the Brigadet soldier responds with a tight voice.

"Thank you," the one behind me says politely. "Now, Kricket—"

He knows my name

"—tell me when and where the Alameeda will attack again."

"You move things with your mind," I say, slack-jawed.

"Maybe you didn't hear me. Where will the Alameeda strike next?" the man asks with a low snarl.

"Who are you?" I'm breathless.

He lifts my arms behind me in such a way that I think for a second that he intends to break them. I'm forced to bend away from him so that they don't snap. Driven to my knees, I bend forward more with my face going to the floor. I pant in pain, but bite my lips so that I don't cry out.

"I'll ask you again. When's the next attack? Where? How will they come?"

With my cheek to the floor, I punctuate my answer: "I. Don't. Know!"

"Then you're going to have to find out, aren't you? Open your chakras, meditate—get in touch with your spirit animal," he says condescendingly, "whatever it is you need to do to find out—do it!" He lifts my arms again and I grind my teeth.

"What are chakras? I don't do any of those things! I—" I stop speaking when he pulls me up from the floor to my knees again. He kneels down behind me and places one hand on my throat while the other holds a harbinger to my temple. Near my ear he whispers, "Countdown to death commences in three-two-one—"

I breathe the words, "I wish I knew—" As I exhale, my breath curls into the air in a cold, smoky plume from the chill in my lungs.

My eyes roll up to the ceiling. The poseur soldier's hand slides from my neck to my ribs, holding me against him so that I don't slip to the floor.

I'm violently ripped out of my body to hover above all of them, near the sparkling, teardrop crystals of the chandelier. The man beneath me claiming to be a Comantre soldier is the same one from the gallery balustrade at the rail station. He raises his shamrock-colored eyes to my spirit floating above him, as if he can see me. I realize then that he's the one who slapped me in my waking dream—or he will slap me in the future, depending on how you look at it. "Hurry, Kricket," he orders, "before I decide to kill you." His hand shifts back to my throat, gripping it like he'll strangle me.

I hope he can see my spirit finger as I flip him off.

The next moment compares to a solar flare or the heat of a thousand stars as I blast out of the chamber, thrown back up the elevatorlike shaft. The galvanized steel beams that construct the maze of overup channels fall away. I eject from the top of the skyscape and into the sea of clouds. And then . . . the real fun begins. I flash-forward; the trap of ordinary things that one gets used to slips away too, by an explosion of time. The fabric of matter is different here: soothing as it is disturbing, with the sense of being whole and complete but not content—cleverly striving for the suggestion of perfection. Somehow, I know that if I twist, if I move in another infinite direction, the fabric will fold in around me and I'll arrive somewhere else.

Before I realize it, I'm in the stratosphere, climbing higher and higher. The blue sky fades in the absence of air and is replaced by the darkness of space. A gleaming white mass grows larger as I approach it, becoming discernible as a space station. Shaped like a capital I, the station tumbles end over end in its orbit of Inium, the smallest of Ethar's moons. This moon is a favorite of mine; it glows blue and it's so near to Ethar that I imagine it has heard all the wishes I've made on it.

I pass through the side of the space station either because it doesn't exist in this space yet or I don't or both. Thinking about it is likely to fry my brain. Instead, I concentrate on a silver transport trift landing in the open bay of the capital-I station. When the enormous bay doors close with a heavy thump, sealing the area like a tomb, the doors of the elegant falconlike trift open just below the wing. Free-floating steps emerge from the craft to form a convenient walkway to the causeway.

I'm surprised when three females alight from the trift, pausing on the gangway. They're each taller than me by just a few inches, with longer white-blond hair than mine and varying shades of blue eyes, but otherwise, in form and in feature, their likeness to me is undeniable.

A very masculine-looking blond male appears behind them. He's a golden god of a man—heaven-faced, cut from stone, and maybe just as lovable. He leans near to one of them, saying something to her in a low tone before he nuzzles her cheek. She doesn't turn her lips to his or respond to his affection. She's cold and distant. Her demeanor bothers him; he frowns at her, but takes her arm solicitously and leads her ahead, helping her navigate the steps.

She reminds me of a queen bee. Her pale blond hair is piled high on her head with a mass of intricate braids down her back. Her elaborate dress has to weigh a ton. It's not the least bit practical, with a flowing train of rich brocade silk and a corsetlike rib breaker. The neckline plunges in a deep vee, lined with sharp points that could be the stingers of drones she's killed. The dress has to hurt like hell, but she carries it as if it were her skin.

As I watch the pair together, I wonder, Is that her Brotherhood consort? Her cult-master who simultaneously owns and worships her? She seems so very important to him: owned by the drones and unable to fly away without them following her—forever. I can't imagine a worse fate than to be a queen-slave.

The other two priestesses follow closely behind her arm in arm. They each have similar style dresses as the Bee, but only one has an exaggerated collar of stiff, swanlike feathers: the Bird. The other has a high, round orchid-colored collar: the Flower. *Two more handsome, chisel-cut blond males trail them, engaging in sedate conversation like old friends.*

I have no choice but to follow them. I thrust forward, joining their party as they converge in a solemn chamber filled with several embryonic vessels. It's not hard to ascertain that this is a medical room and these steely pods are the equivalent of Manus's shark tank back on Ethar. Uniformed personnel stand far back from them, almost in reverence at their presence.

A small discussion commences about which one he's *in. A stuttering worker shows them to a particular unit. The six figures gather around this unit. The Flower breaks away from her friend, the Bird, and lays her hand on the lid. The coffinlike capsule opens, emitting a pressurized hiss. I ghost-move around the open lid so that I can see who is in it, but a part of me already knows.*

It's Kyon. Unconscious. Naked. Damn my eyes!

The beautiful flowerlike woman with the full, petal-pink lips places her hand on Kyon's broad chest. She covers the angry red stab wound I gave him. His masculine, steam-shovel jaw tenses. Blood raises the color in his cheeks. Readouts on the lid of his pod go ballistic. His eyes open wide, the irises of which shine pure silver. When his mouth falls open, that same silver light emits from deep within him, gray embers from a blast furnace.

When she removes her hand, there is a thin silver scar in place of the angry wound. The Flower glances behind her with a radiant smile to one of the granite-cut men she arrived with, but that stone won't notice her. She loses some of her smile.

The Bee flutters forward, helping Kyon to sit up. He does so awkwardly, which is very uncharacteristic of him. He rubs his blue eyes, trying to clear his head. His blond hair is pulled back from his face and tied so that it doesn't fall into his eyes when he slumps forward. He's weak, I think, *but I don't have a moment of guilt about it.*

"How do you feel?" the Bee asks. Her fingers rest on his shoulder, covering the dark military tattoo that interconnects to form circles there. The tattoo spans his neck, chest, and abdomen, stopping where his hip forms one angle of a dramatic vee.

Kyon ignores her, choosing instead to gaze over her shoulder at the Bee's consort. "Chandrum, was Kricket brought to Alameeda? Is she here?"

Chandrum shakes his head. "She's still with them. The extraction was a failure."

Kyon growls. "What's being done?"

"There is a new plan," Chandrum offers as he watches the Bee wring her hands.

"Tell me," Kyon insists.

"In due course," he says before looking over his shoulder and snapping his fingers. A medical attendant rushes forward with a blanket, forcing the Bee to step back from her post.

The Bird looks in my direction, piercing me with her eyes. She sniffs the air and says, "She listens now. Your Kricket."

"I feel her too," the Bee agrees.

A slow smile spreads over Kyon's lips. "Kricket," he says with a rough voice of someone who has been unconscious for a few days. I startle, not expecting him to say my name, let alone speak to me. "Must I wait for you to catch up to my time?" It's a rare joke, since in my time he's still in the pod, stabbed and unconscious, but here, he's maybe a day or so ahead of me, unconscious as I am in the overup.

The Bird giggles. "You've frightened her, Kyon. You mustn't amuse yourself at her expense or she'll never love you."

"As long as she respects me, I can live with her fear," he replies.

Oh, I'm *so* going to put a knife in the other side of your chest, *I think, feeling stabby.*

"Fie! Now she's angry with you. She indicates that next time the stabbing will be on the other side of your chest," the Bird crows. "Oh, I like her!" She claps her hands like this is all a game.

The Bee's tone is waspish. "Permission to make her go away?"

Ugh, you have to ask for his permission? Gross.

The Bird clasps her hands together with a look of pleasure. "She's a free spirit!"

Kyon looks in my direction. "Catch up, Kricket. I'll be along soon."
With Kyon's approving nod, the Bee's hands lift in my direction.

"Can't wait, freak—" *I'm blown off my feet and out into the blackness of space where I'm falling, falling, falling. I land on my back upon the enormous mahogany desk in Minister Telek's office. Grasping my head and holding it, I realize I'm still somewhere in the future. I search around, trying to decide* when *I am.*

Sliding off the desk, I rifle the room, looking for anything that will indicate a date. A steampunk-looking clock on the shelf nearby makes a metronome sound. Drifting near it to watch the pendulum, I see that it swings faster than it would on Earth. I read the dials that whirl as I interpret the date: it's sixteen parts, Fitzmartin, which is Wednesday, two days ahead in time. In my time it's still Fitzlutzer—Monday.

I move to the round table in the center of the dim room. It's empty, having no flowers to replace the znous. Across from me, Manus's watery habitat is no longer occupied; he's gone but the tank remains. A small tremble causes ripples in the water, disturbing the soft murmur of the tank. Then, another much larger thump shakes the water a bit more. Golden light from the window behind me causes me to turn around. Through it, I track a burning ball of fire hurtling downward into the building next to this one. The impact of the explosion blows out the window, sending cascading glass into the room. Since I'm made of air, the glass passes through me, shining with fiery reflection.

I back away from the terror reining down on the Ship of Skye. I move toward Manus's empty tank again, not knowing what to do. More explosions thump the ship; it begins to list to one side.

In a savage progression, the thumps grow louder: th-thump, thump, thuMP, th-thUMP, THUMP, THUMP—*the wall to my side vaporizes in a fireball that engulfs the room and blows me sideways into the overup shaft.*

I tumble, down, down, down.

I awake in my body with a wide-eyed gasp of air. My lungs burn as I struggle to take another breath. *I feel like I'm waking from the dead.* I'm shivering from cold, and my teeth chatter. I try to lift my hand to my forehead, but they're both still confined behind my back.

Someone shakes me, rattling my already jangled nerves. "What? Stop it," I grouse. I cringe because I'm in the arms of the dreadlocked soldier.

Sitting with me on his lap upon the soft, gray bench, he looks down at me with angry green eyes. "Can you hear me?"

"Yeah, I hear you," I groan. "Now shut up. My head hurts."

"I thought you were dead," he murmurs. I squint at him. He'd be worth a second look if he weren't such a knob knocker. His hair is light brown, but it has streaks of burnished gold in it. His hands are strong and rough. He doesn't get his physique from exercise equipment. If I had to bet, he earns his strength in other ways.

"I'm not dead. Disappointed?" I scowl back at him.

"I'm becoming more so by the moment," he replies with a frown. "Did you see the future?"

"It's more like I went there. And I thought I told you to shut up." I rest my forehead against his chest only because I can't hold my head up on my own. I have a ridiculous headache. I might have stayed away from my body too long; I'm half-dead from it.

His hand slides up and down my arm and it takes me a second to realize he's trying to warm me up a bit. "Tell me what you saw," he orders.

Lifting my forehead off his chest, my eyes meet his green ones. "Kyon Ensin is alive . . . by tomorrow he'll be fine—up and around and plotting our deaths. The Alameeda will attack on Fitzmartin—in two rotations—midday—sixteen parts."

"How will they infiltrate the shields?"

"I don't know—I didn't see that part. The fact is that they do, and then they start blowing the crap out of this place."

"You said you stabbed Kyon!" he says in an accusatory tone.

I take offense to the tone. "Don't yell at me! My head hurts like someone hit it with a golf club! And I *did* stab him. The Flower-looking freak healed him—err . . . will heal him . . . uh, I mean—whatever! The fact is that by tomorrow night, he'll be as good as new."

"The Flower-looking freak? What's a Flower-looking freak?"

"She's a priestess—she had on an orchid dress—never mind!" I say in exasperation. "I don't know who she is. I've never met her! But they completely knew I was there—will be there—ugh! They could sense me listening. This is such a paradox to think about."

"Are you getting this?" the man asks aloud.

"Yeah, we got it, Giffen," comes a voice from a small device on Giffen's uniform.

"You're not Comantre," I state.

"No, I'm not," he agrees.

"Who are you?"

"No one you know."

"Fine," I retort with growing hostility. "I'll leave you to it then. I have to go." I try to move from his lap, but his arms tighten around me.

"You're leaving with me," comes his calm reply.

"Yeah," I say with a fake laugh, "that's not happening."

"I wasn't asking for your permission."

"Good, because I'm not giving it. I have to warn everyone—"

"You're not in charge," he says with a snide twist of his lip.

"I'm not leaving!"

"Has anyone ever told you that you're irritating?"

"No. Everybody likes me," I counter.

The communicator on Giffen's uniform makes a static noise. "Gif, there's a problem," the com-link voice relates in a stressed tone.

"What is it?" Giffen asks.

"They detected our trift."

"Are they moving on you?" he asks.

"Affirmative. We need to move the ship."

"Leave us here. I'll find a way off Skye."

"But, Gif—"

"Go! Now!" Giffen orders.

"Happy landings, Gif," his com-link partner reluctantly says.

"To you, as well," Giffen replies.

"Aww, your ride's leaving. Looks like you're toast," I smirk. "So, let me go and you can save yourself."

"You are very strange. I don't know what bread has to do with this," Giffen says in confusion.

"You're moving things with your mind and I'm strange?" I counter.

"Shh," he hushes me as he sizes up the mess he's in—we're in. It's a colossal debacle. The overup jerks abruptly. Giffen rises to his feet with me in his arms. The elevatorlike car begins to descend once more.

"I think they just noticed us," Giffen mutters. "This is going to sting a little."

My eyes narrow in suspicion. "What's going to sting a little?"

He closes his eyes, and his brow creases. I cringe as a shock charges through me the equivalent of touching an electrified fence. The overup trajectory shifts with a jerk and starts moving sideways, and then slantways.

"Owah! That hurt!" I whine. "What was that?"

"I redirected the overup." He frowns at me, adding, "It didn't hurt that bad."

"Yes it did! Put me down!" I demand.

"You can hardly stand."

"I'm fine." I wiggle in his arms. It's feeble; I'm weak.

With a heavy sigh, he sets me on my feet. I pull away from him.

He reaches for my neck. I shy away from him. "What're you doing?"

"Hold still," he orders, reaching for me again.

I shy away again. "No!" I give him my severest scowl.

"I'm going to take off your collar! Don't move," he says in frustration.

"Oh." I hold still. "Do you know the code?"

"I don't need the code," he grumbles.

I mock him silently, mouthing: *I don't need the code.*

A click of the metal latch sounds; the collar around my neck slips off me to fall to the floor. The sound of the hardened foam cracking is next. I glance over my shoulder at Giffen; he has his eyes focused on my wrists. Pieces of the foam shed off. The increased circulation in my hands causes my numb fingers to sting as I wiggle them, breaking the foam.

I turn to face him. "What are you?" I demand as I rub my wrist with my free hand.

He raises one eyebrow. "What are you?"

I shake my head, glancing up at the ceiling for a second with a humorless laugh, before I look him in his eye again. "I'm not human, I'm not enough Rafe, and I'm too much Alameeda," I reply.

For a moment, he just stares at me, and then he says, "I'm too much Alameeda and not enough Wurthem." The overup lurches again, making me hold the wall for support. We begin to plummet downward once more. Giffen grinds his teeth in frustration. "There's too much going on; I can't control it all. We have to get out." Giffen puts his harbinger back into his shoulder holster. He summons a soldier's harbinger by holding up one hand in the air; it flies to his palm.

"You're a bit of a oddball," I observe.

Giffen frowns. "No more so than you."

He lifts his hands again to the doors in front of us. They slide open, but the compartment keeps dropping. Floor after floor streaks by in a blur. I look at him and say, "I'm not going with you." The overup slows, and then it comes to a stop in front of ten or so Brigadets who appear to be waiting for the lift. They look stunned when they see us. "Not our floor," Giffen growls.

The doors snap shut forcefully before they can react. "You don't know what you're doing!" I accuse him. "You don't even know where we are!"

"Quiet!" he orders, pointing at me belligerently.

I ignore his suggestion. "You're going to get us killed! They see me with you and they'll think, hmm—I don't know—conspiracy! If I didn't appear guilty enough before, you've pushed me over the edge."

"I'll push you over the edge," he says as the overup slows down again. He opens the doors and literally pushes me out of it as he jumps. I land hard on my side, bruising my hip. I roll a little, trying to catch my breath that was forced from my lungs. We're beneath the ship's main platform, within the half-sphere base. Giffen raises his hands to the lift; closing the door, it activates again, and the overup car leaves.

I sit up, glaring at Giffen as he gets to his feet and looks around. The corridor is illuminated with sky-blue track lights in the floor and ceiling. It's utilitarian—unadorned—and by all appearances, utilized only by the drone-bots that carry supplies from storage bays to restock the area up top. I watch the robotic carts move past us with shiny, chrome-plated shells. "Come on," Giffen says, holding out his hand for me to take. "Let's go."

Another resupply-bot passes us carrying stacks of enticing beverages in colorful bottles. *It's a barback-bot*, I think. I remember working at Lumin, the nightclub in Chicago. It's where I first met Kyon. *He's going to destroy this place and everyone in it.*

"We have to warn them," I say as I look at Giffen's outstretched palm in front of me. My eyes travel up him. He's really tall, like most Etharians. He has the form of someone who scales mountains: all muscle without a trace of body fat. "We have to make them listen."

"No," he says, shaking his head, "we don't." Reaching down, he hauls me up with a fistful of my black jacket, popping off a few of the buttons. "We're getting off this ship if I have to throw you over the side."

As I look him in the eyes, I kick him as hard as I can in the knee-cap. His eyes shutter in pain. I wiggle out of his fist, running full out down the corridor.

I don't make it halfway before I'm lifted off my feet, and I crash sideways into the wall. With my back to it and my toes nowhere near the floor, I hang on it like a trophy animal. Giffen hobbles over to face me with a seething look.

"Your gift is more useful than mine," I grunt, trying to pull my arm away from the wall. It won't budge.

"If you want to call it that. I tend to think of it as a curse, since it puts a price on my head," he replies. "But in this instance, I don't mind it so much."

"Was your mother a priestess too?"

"She *is* a priestess."

"She's alive?"

"Last I knew."

"You have the freak gene, like me. I heard that most males don't inherit it."

"They don't, and when they do, they're killed."

"They didn't kill you," I point out.

"You have a gift for the obvious."

"Are you taking me to them?" *I will kill you if you try.*

"To whom?" he asks.

"The Alameeda."

"Why would I? They're my enemy."

"Why do you want me then?" I ask in exasperation.

"You can see the future. That makes you valuable to us." He places his hand on my throat again, but this time he doesn't squeeze it; he merely strokes it softly. "If you want to save yourself, start being useful. Otherwise, you're a danger to us. And we eliminate danger."

"Who are 'we'? I thought that Wurthem is Alameeda's ally." I'm so confused.

"I may be from Wurthem, but that doesn't mean I subscribe to their politics or their shortsightedness! Whom do you think Alameeda will target once they've killed everyone else?" he rails at me.

"Why would they kill their allies?" I ask.

"Citizens of Wurthem aren't part of their master race."

"You're all one race, aren't you?"

"Not to them."

"Why would the Brotherhood want to kill you? I would think that you'd be an asset to them as well. You can move things with your mind—you're telekinetic."

"That makes me stronger than them, and they fear anything stronger than them."

"You're a lost boy," I murmur. "I've seen your type before in foster care. Run off by a father or stepfather or sometimes just an abusive mother's boyfriend. It's in your eyes. I know you."

"You don't know me and I don't know you. But I will kill you if you try to run from me again," he states honestly.

He lets go of my throat. Whatever force he used to hold me up against the wall releases. When my feet touch the ground, he grips my upper arms and yanks me down the hall.

Skittering around the bot approaching us, we have to grip the wall as another flying bot carrying parcels almost brains us. We pass a corridor with signs marking it as the cookery. It's the advanced automated area where most of the food is prepared and then conveyed throughout the ship to the commissaries located in private quarters. Winding through corridor after corridor, we turn the corner, stumbling upon sliding doors leading to a loading bay. Access to the bay is restricted, monitored by a holographic soldier and a few mounted guns on the walls that are operated remotely.

"This way," Giffen says, tugging me toward the checkpoint.

I try to tug my arm away from him. "I can't leave! I have to warn them about the attack!"

"They'll never believe you," he snarls at me, "you just poisoned their defense minister. The best you can expect from them is that they'll kill you quickly if they capture you."

"If I leave then everyone dies!"

"Everyone dies anyway. You saw it."

"I can change that! Let me change that!"

He stops. "You can change it?"

"I've changed it before."

"But you can't stop the attack."

"Maybe you're right, but Rafe can be ready for it when it comes."

He shakes his head. "It's too great a risk. This house will fall."

"What do you mean?"

"Rafe falls. It's prophesied. One house will rise to rule and one will fall. It's foretold."

"I thought the house was never named!" An incredible ache squeezes my heart.

"Rafe's done—Alameeda will begin exterminating them soon. If you want to survive, stop resisting me, because I'm your only chance."

"You're lying! You don't know it'll be *Rafe*!" I shout.

He covers my mouth with his massive hand. "It's obvious it will be them, and I don't care if Rafe falls," he whispers with a severe scowl. "They're not my people! I'm here to make sure the Alameeda don't rise to power, or we're all dead! So you're going to go through those cargo bay doors in front of us. You're going to follow wherever I lead you. We're going to find a transport that's leaving and we're going to get on it. Any deviation from the instructions I've just given you will end with me crushing your skull. Nod your head if you understand me."

I nod my head.

"Let's go," he orders.

He removes his hand from my mouth and moves it to grip my hand, tugging me to the door. With every step we take, my panic grows. If I leave with him, I may survive, but Trey won't. I can't live with that. For the first time in my life, my survival is not as important to me as someone else's.

The holographic soldier that guards the doors doesn't have a chance to detect our presence, because Giffen raises his hand and the projection apparatus smolders, making short-circuiting noises. Next, he shorts out the cameras and the eyes on the mounted guns; they swivel in several directions, but none of them aim at us. He forces the sliding doors to open telepathically, and then he uses a laser eye on one of his uniform buttons to strobe the security wall. The blue beams that guard the bay disappear.

Giffen moves his grip to my upper arm again, pulling me into the cargo bay. It's automated with supply-bots, but at the far end a handful of Brigadets mill around behind the security glass.

We edge toward the monstrous ellipse-shaped Cargo Goers on the launching pad that are waiting to jettison to the surface of the planet. They all resemble the Bean sculpture from Chicago's Millennium Park; each one is a massive, chromelike ellipse, weighing several tons. The skins of the vehicles can alter to blend in with the environment, but right now the one we're heading toward is shiny and new-looking, reflecting everything around it. Supply-bots cruise around the deck, loading them with pallets of medical supplies that need to be transported to the surface of the planet. Giffen pulls me to duck behind a moving bot, skirting between several more so that we avoid detection by the patrolling soldiers near the other end of the hangar. Choosing the Cargo Goer in the center, he drags me over to it. He lifts me up like I weigh nothing and stuffs me into its yawning mouth. Swinging himself up next to me among the crowded pallets and hovering skids, he slumps against a shiny metal crate.

In a matter of a few minutes, the rumbling of the Cargo Goer's doors shake the floor. A look of smug relief crosses Giffen's lips as he stares at me. He breathes out a sigh that makes my heart bleed in fear as he relaxes. I send him a fake smile, and then I bolt to my feet and slide to the right, fitting through the closing doors right before they crush me. I fall hard on the grated floor outside the transport. The doors *thump* close behind me. Getting to my knees, I cringe, looking down at my shredded palms. The engines of the Cargo Goer fire up; the wind from the forced air that propels the craft to hover blows my hair around, whipping me in the face. Scrambling away from the craft, a loud *bang* sounds behind me.

Looking over my shoulder, the chrome doors fling wide open once more. Giffen's eyes hunt for me, and the moment they find me, my feet leave the ground. Caught in his telepathic gaze, I fly backward toward him. A supply-bot, in route to another junction, gets between Giffen and me. The crab-shaped metal bot cuts off his connection, causing it to careen toward him as I drop to the ground again. On my hands and knees, I crawl behind a stack of metal crates. The crates shake and fly off the stack one by one. Taking a deep breath, I get to my feet and run full out toward the sliding doors where I'd entered with Giffen. Before I reach them, a metal crate skidding into my path broadsides me. It knocks me sideways, pushing me into a wall. The jolt bashes my ribs, but it stops short of crushing me entirely.

Winded, I cough and gasp for air. Realizing I'm not dead, I glance toward Giffen. He has jumped down from the Cargo Goer and is making his way toward me. My heartbeat pounds painfully in my chest as I wait for him to crush me like he threatened to earlier.

Shouting abruptly draws my attention from Giffen's furious face. A soldier barks out an order to him, "Cease! Drop to your knees!" Brigadets call from different points around the loading area, swarming in with weapons drawn. Giffen ignores their orders. Instead, he waves his hand, lifting them into the air and throwing them in the opposite direction. A few Brigadets by the door fire on him, but their projectiles get only halfway to Giffen before the shiny metal ammo stops and rains useless onto the floor, making a twinkling sound that sets my teeth on edge.

The next shots that come at him are in the form of electricity from the tricked-out black riflelike frestons. He puts up his hand to ward them off; some of the surging, yellow lightning deflects away from him, but not all of it. Energy slips into him in a singeing stream. He stumbles, clutching his sides for a moment as the sizzling current causes him to stiffen. Gasping for breath, he manages to keep on his feet, but he stumbles as he moves closer to me.

His handsome face is transformed by rage into that of an avenging god. "We would've made it!" he grits between his teeth to me. "You've just killed us."

"You were stupid to come after me!" I retort as I wiggle from between the crate and the wall, holding up my bloody hands so no one shoots me.

"You just pulled off our mutually assured destruction!"

"Nothing about the future is assured!" I counter.

He gets to within a few feet of me when he's hit with another surge of electricity. Bright yellow current infiltrates him, running over his flesh and dropping him to his knees once more.

When he raises his hands in the direction of the soldiers, I interject, "Don't fight them, Giffen!" Rafe soldiers dot me with their blue laser scopes. I kneel, putting my hands to the back of my head.

"I should've killed you," he pants as he struggles to put his hands behind his head.

"I know the feeling," I murmur, as soldiers approach us.

CHAPTER 4
BLEEDING OUR COLORS

Our hands are shackled with cuffs and then sprayed with foam. When the foam hardens, a soldier approaches Giffen with a black pillowcase-like bag in his hand, preparing to toss it over Giffen's head. They want him blind. Giffen's intelligent eyes stare at the soldier for a long moment. The black bag is torn from the soldier's grasp and thrown over the soldier's face. A malicious smile touches Giffen's lips. "Hit him again!" says one of the soldiers. Giffen is struck with another long jolt of electricity that makes him drop to the ground face-first in an unconscious heap.

"Hold still!" The order comes from behind me. I don't move. My face is covered with the same type of blackout fabric, rendering me blind.

Pulled to my feet, I'm stuffed into a hover vehicle, pressed between the broad shoulders of the soldiers assigned to guard me. One of them thrusts something hard against my ribs, making my teeth clench in pain. He says near my ear, "Give me a reason to kill you." I don't make a sound, pretending not to have heard him.

I breathe in shallow breaths as we begin to move. The bag is soft on my face, pulling against my nose and mouth every time I breathe in too deeply. It's hot too and it smells like the mouthwash I used this morning. As we move, I'm grateful for the smoothness of the air propelling this vehicle, because every little breath I take now is a stab of pain to my ribs. I have no sense of where we're going, other than that it feels like we're moving downward at several points in all the twists and turns that we make.

Finally, the transport comes to a stop. I'm ushered out of the vehicle; a large hand seizes my elbow, and I'm pulled almost off my feet. I try not to make a sound. I'm made to walk at a clipped pace until we reach some sort of checkpoint. A male voice says, "This is her, Rutledge?"

"It is," replies the one holding me.

"She's so little! How did she overpower an overup full of Brigadets?" he asks.

"She's a priestess, Coda. She can probably melt you with her hideous face."

"I've seen her face on the holovision. It's not hideous."

"She's a murderess," Rutledge accuses. His grip is painful on my already bruised upper arm.

"You believe the rumor that she killed Minister Vallen?"

"She tried to kill Minister Telek too," Rutledge grits out in anger. "What cell is she in?"

"This way," Coda says, all business now.

I'm yanked forward again, my feet making clicking noises against what sounds like a metal grate floor. We pause here and there for heavy security doors and the distinct sound of laser security walls being disabled.

The temperature in the place drops several degrees, so if they intend to put me on ice, they really mean it. The space begins to feel cavernous—infinite. The metal grate beneath my feet echoes our footsteps. When we pause once more, I'm pushed forward into a space where the sounds around me muffle. The hand on my arm releases me. I startle as a cold trickle of liquid runs over my imprisoned fingers, dissolving the foam shell on them. "Don't move," Rutledge orders. He removes the metal shackles, allowing my arms to go free. I lift one wrist with my hand, rubbing the circulation back into my fingers. When someone behind me pulls the blackout bag from my face, I squint against the glare of light coming from the walls, ceiling, and floor. With a cursory glance around, I note that I'm in a honeycomb-shaped cell—a hexagon. A metal cot platform juts out from the wall, a metal sink is near it, and a metal toilet is hidden in back behind a small partition. When I look over my shoulder, the soldiers who brought me here are retreating.

"Wait!" I yell to them, following them to the front entry of the cell. When I near them, I come up short, running into an invisible barrier that must've activated after they had crossed the threshold of the cell. I drop to the ground, holding my nose that took the brunt of the impact.

One of the soldiers goes to a panel on the wall to the left of my cell and turns on an intercom before he squats down so that his face is level with mine. His clear voice comes through a speaker into my cell. "You're not that smart, are ya?" The voice is Rutledge's. He taps on the glasslike divider; his thick finger doesn't manage to make a sound that I can hear. "It's an invisible bulkhead to keep deviants like you at bay." I stare at the half-moon scar on his chin, wondering for a moment how he got it. He's massive, this soldier. His arms are like the haunches of a bull, thick and beefy. Even with all that, he doesn't look as formidable as Trey and the other Cavars. I think it's because he lacks the tribal tattoo that distinguishes them as elite.

I take my hand away from my nose. "I need to speak with someone in charge! I have information that's vital to Rafe!"

"Oh, we know you do. Don't worry, you're gonna talk," he says with a sinister grin that has goose bumps rising on my flesh. "We'll be back." He laughs at my stunned expression and rises.

Behind Rutledge, two soldiers drag an unconscious Giffen to the dronelike cell next to mine. "You miss your boyfriend?" Rutledge asks. "He looked like he was about to bash your head in when we found you in the supply hangar. Let's make you two cozy, shall we?" He touches the control panel on the left side of my cell. The wall between my cell and Giffen's cell becomes translucent. I watch the soldiers dump him on the floor. One soldier pulls Giffen's blackout hood off, but neither of them takes off his shackles or hand restraints.

"You have to free his hands," I insist.

"We don't have to do anything," Rutledge scowls at me. "This isn't the palace."

"You think?" I retort. "Listen to me. There's going to be an Alameeda attack in less than two rotations—"

The soldiers who hauled Giffen into his cell join this soldier outside my cell. They all begin to laugh. "Does she really think we're going to listen to the traitor who just tried to kill our minister of defense?" one of them asks Rutledge.

"She looks so earnest too," the other one laughs.

I answer them sternly, "You should listen to me or we're all dead!"

One of the soldiers loses his amused expression. He glances around uncertainly and asks, "What if she's not lying?"

"She's an Alameeda spy. She'll say anything to make herself look like one of us."

"But what if she's right?" the one insists.

"I *am* right!" I interject.

"She's here to assassinate our leaders," Rutledge growls, leaning his face near mine and trying to stare me down.

"I haven't killed anyone," I reply. "And you must think I'm completely brilliant if you believe I could plot all of this supposed espionage in my childhood on Earth!" I put my hands on my hips. "I never knew any of you existed or that you'd come looking for me."

"You're a priestess. You know things," Rutledge states vaguely.

I put my hand to my forehead and rub it. "So now you believe I have the ability to know things, but you think I'm making up the most essential thing to our survival: an assault from Alameeda?" The Brigadet's expression loses a little of its bravado. "You don't have to believe me. Go ask the Cavars whom I've lived with for the past few specks! They know me. They can vouch for what I can do."

"Should I ask them now? We could do it together," Rutledge says with a twinkle in his eye. He moves to the right side of my cell, touching another control panel. The wall to my right becomes translucent. I lose my ability to breathe for a moment. Trey stares at me in an assessing way from the other side of the glass-like barrier. He's shirtless, attired in only his uniform trousers. I blanch when I scan his chest; he's already been roughed up. His chest is covered in bruises and abrasions. There are singe marks on his skin. Judging by his reaction at seeing me, he already knew I was in this cell. He must've seen them bring me in.

Trey puts his hand up against the transparent wall as he says my name, but I can't hear his voice. The cells are soundproof.

My knees feel weak. I shake my head in confusion. "Why would you hurt him?" I ask Rutledge. "He'd never betray Rafe. He loves this house."

"It would seem that he needs more motivation to tell us about you," comes the soldier's reply.

I raise my chin. "I'll tell you whatever you want to know. There's no need to involve him."

"Oh, I know you will," he agrees, "but we won't be questioning you now."

"Defense Minister Telek wants to be present for it," I state.

His smile evaporates. "How did you know?" he asks. His eyes narrow in suspicion.

"I'm psychic," I say with derision.

His eyes darken in anger. "Minister Telek can't be here now. He's having part of his intestines removed. Did you know that as well?

They're imaging his replacement parts now. They won't be ready for a few rotations."

"We can't wait a few rotations! We have to speak now!"

"He has holes in his esophagus now," the soldier says drily.

"Minister Telek killed Defense Minister Vallen so that he could assume his post on Skye Council. Please let me speak to the council," I beg.

Rutledge appears unimpressed with my story. He shakes his head. "You only get to talk to us. We're aware of your priestess ability to influence your adversaries."

"My ability to do what?" I ask after I close my gaping mouth.

"We have proof of your trait," he counters.

"Oh! You've proof?" I scoff with rising eyebrows. "What's your proof?"

He walks across the metal grate catwalk to the adjacent rows of stacked honeycomb-like cells that go up as far as I can see. Hundreds of catwalks like the one that he's standing on service the levels above. He touches a control panel on the wall, illuminating several of the cells in front of me. Inside one, Wayra stands watching my encounter with these soldiers. He, like Trey, has been interrogated, as the bruises and scrapes on his face and bare chest attest. Next to Wayra's cell is Jax's cell. Above him in individual cells are all my Cavar bodyguards from the palace: Drex, Hollis, Gibon, Dylan, and Fenton. Their cells are all clumped together.

I put both my hands flat against the invisible barrier in front of me, smearing it with my blood. "Let them go! They're not your enemies."

"They all refuse to answer any questions about you. Don't you find that strange? Their loyalty is to you and not to Rafe."

"They're more than loyal to Rafe! They're decent men. They believe that I saved Cavars when I reported an attack by the Alameeda!

They were assigned to protect me, and that's what they're doing—protecting me is part of their duty."

This takes him aback for a second. "We're the authority here."

I make a derisive sound. "They're Cavars. They don't see Brigadets as authority—just as you'd scoff at their authority. They were answering to Minister Vallen until he was murdered. They're intelligent men. They understand motives, and no one had a better motive to kill Defense Minister Vallen than Minister Telek."

"You're accusing Defense Minister Telek of murdering Minister Vallen?"

"I know he killed him. He told me he did it. He wants me to take the blame for it."

"So you admit that you poisoned him!"

"Oh, for sure. Wouldn't you? He murdered your defense minister! He wants to kill me to cover it up. Why do you think I poisoned him?" I ask.

"I think you poisoned him because you're a spy and you were under orders to kill him."

"Under orders from whom?" I ask with a cold stare.

"The Brotherhood."

I frown. "I wouldn't walk across the street if they ordered me to," I reply honestly. "Listen to me: I could've killed Minister Telek, but I didn't. That's not important now. What's important is what you plan to do to intercept the Alameeda invasion coming on Fitzmartin." My tone becomes harsher as I speak.

He looks uncertain. "This is your influence, isn't it? I'm not falling for your skills."

"What do you think I'm doing to you? I'm just being reasonable. If you believe nothing else other than there's an imminent attack planned, then we're good. Everything else we can sort out later. At least check into it. Go over whatever protocols you use to defend this place and see if there are any holes. They come in with an air strike—big bombs. The shields will be ineffective because they'll already be inside," I ramble. He turns the intercom off so that we can no longer hear each other while he discusses something with his fellow soldiers. I pound on the barrier between us, yelling, "It starts at sixteen parts on Fitzmartin—sixteen *parts*! Do you understand?"

They turn their backs on me and walk away. I panic, beating on the wall between us. "They're coming on Fitzmartin! They'll kill us all! Please listen to me!"

Losing sight of them, I turn to look at Trey. He's watching me, taking in everything about me. I look down at myself; I'm a complete mess. My hands are abraded from my fight with Giffen. The black jacket Trey gave me this morning is torn and missing several buttons.

Quickly, I go to the wall that separates us. I wring my hands as I say, "We have to get out of here! The Alameeda are going to be here soon."

Trey mouths the words: *Slow down. I can't understand you.*

I cringe and put my hands to my head. "I don't know what time it is!" I say to myself, as fear overwhelms me. I try to take a deep breath to calm down before I lose it. I touch the wall between us, using the blood on my fingers. I smear a picture of the Ship of Skye among the clouds. Then I add flying ships dropping bombs on it. Next to it, I write in backward letters: NITRAMZTIF NO STRAP 61.

Trey's hand touches my drawing of the Ship of Skye. He moves his hand to mine as I lean against the wall. I know he can't hear me, but I say, "It'll happen in about 48 parts from now! They get inside the shields! They bomb everything! It's like the Hindenburg—ahh, you wouldn't know what that is!" I scold myself as I thrust my hands in my hair, pulling it back from my face. "It's like the whole place is on fire!"

His expression is grim. He nods in understanding. Turning away from me, he goes to his sink, to the soap dispenser. He takes the soap to the entrance of his cell, to the invisible barrier.

He uses the soap to write on the barrier: STRAP 84 NI TLU-ASSA LAIREA ADEEMALA.

Wayra leaves his post at the entrance to his cell for a moment. When he returns, he writes in soap on his wall: BAW-DA-BAW. Jax and the rest of the Cavars do the same.

I sit down on the metal cot and rest my cheek against the cool transparency of the wall.

"I have to think," I murmur as I look around at the cell. It's a nightmare in terms of escape. If I were to somehow break through a wall, I'd only find myself in the next cell. The only way out is through the front wall, and my nose still hurts from running into it. I glance at Giffen in the cell next to mine. He hasn't moved yet. I wonder if he's dead, but I see his chest rise and fall, and I know he still lives. I'm not sure whether that's a good thing, or a bad thing. On one hand, he might be able to free himself once he wakes up, but on the other hand, a free Giffen may not be healthy for me. He might decide to kill me once he figures out I'm here too. Either way, the odds are looking like I'm going to die in here.

I close my eyes for a moment, fighting despair. *What good is seeing the future if you can't get out of its way?*

When I open my eyes again, I meet Trey's as he slouches next to me on his side of the wall. His eyes ask me questions. The first is: *What happened to you?* I shrug, and then cringe; my bruised ribs ache, making me not want to breathe. He motions for me to take off my jacket. He rises from the floor, waiting for me to do the same. Getting to my feet, I face him again. I gingerly peel off my black jacket and lay it upon the slab. I almost don't want to look as I grasp the hem of my white top, inching it up my left side. My shirt is stiff, because it has ribbing sewn into it that pushes everything up and in, a fact that probably helped protect my ribs to a certain extent but now causes me to pause and wince, holding my breath for a second with my elbow pointed up. Finally exposing my ribs, I glance at them; they're the color of midnight.

Trey's reaction is pragmatic, except when his hands ball into fists. He gestures that I should wet my jacket with cold water to use it as a compress. Following his advice, I dampen the jacket and take it with me to the cot against our adjoining wall. Lying down on the metal slablike cot, I face him. He sits right next to me again against the floor, since his cot is located on his far wall.

With a lift of his chin in the direction of the hand clutching my side, his eyes ask, *How did that happen to your ribs?*

I point over my shoulder to Giffen stretched out on the floor in the next cell.

He nods his head in Giffen's direction with a raise of his eyebrow.

I shake my head and say, "He's like me." I point to myself. "He has gifts." I point to my hair and say, "He's part Alameeda."

Trey's eyes open wider in surprise. He lifts both hands, palms up. *What gifts?*

I sigh, trying to think of a way to describe telekinesis without using words. I take the balled-up compress in my hand and rest it on my mattress, between us. I stare at it, pointing from my eyes to the compress and back again. Without looking away from the compress, I lift it up by sliding the flat of my hand underneath it, pretending I'm really levitating it with my mind.

When I look over at Trey, he mouths the word in English: *telekinesis*. I nod vehemently before I wince again in pain. Then I say aloud, "I think he'll try to kill me when he wakes up. He's gonna have to get in line, though. Minister Telek would like that honor, unless Kyon gets to me first."

I can tell right away that Trey didn't understand the last bit I said about Telek and Kyon. He knows English well enough, but still, reading my lips is not easy. He shakes his head and studies my mouth, waiting for me to restate what I just said. Instead, I point to the picture I just drew on the wall and say, "Kyon."

Trey gets to his feet and starts pacing back and forth in front of me. He makes a stabbing gesture to his chest, and then points at the drawing.

I sit up on my cot. "I know! I did stab him," I reply with the same sort of frustration, "but he's still coming. In a few hours he'll be healed by a priestess—they're like a menagerie of misfit toys at his beck and call—and they have a space station! Did you know they have a space station? Please tell me you guys have a space station too!"

It's clear that Trey didn't catch what I said, but he seems to accept the fact that Kyon will be responsible for the attack.

Trey points up to the ceiling, mouthing the words, *What happened?*

"Oh, you want to know how my interview went with Minister Telek?" I tap my chin with my finger. "Hmm, how do I put this? Not good." I look away from him for a second before I look back and say sheepishly, "I poisoned him."

Trey gives me the did-I-hear-that-right expression and mouths the words, *You poisoned him?*

I nod my head.

He looks confused as he asks silently, *How?*

I point to my brain. "Remember when we were running—" I use my two fingers to show running "—through the Forest of O?"

Trey nods.

"Remember when I—" I point to myself, and then pantomime picking a flower "—picked a znou and put it behind my ear?"

Trey nods again.

"Well." I pantomime pulling the flower from behind my ear and plucking petals from it. "He had znous in his office, so I took the petals." I pantomime picking up a kafcan pot and pouring some kafcan into a cup. I pretend to take a sip from the cup before dropping the petals into the cup and holding the imaginary cup out to Trey. "I poisoned his kafcan with those flowers." Understanding crosses his face, but he doesn't seem upset with the fact that I just tried to kill a minister of his house. He looks impressed by it.

Telek killed Minister Vallen? Trey asks me by mouthing the words, but I know he's just affirming what he's known since the pyramid-shaped Automated Fugitive Apprehender came crashing through his window this morning.

I nod. "He's going to say that we did it." I gesture to him, and then to myself.

Telek's not dead? Trey mouths.

I shake my head no. "This is so bad, Trey," I whisper, looking around my cell, my eyes filling up with tears. I choke them back. The last thing he needs is for me to cry. "I didn't kill him. I know I should've, but I—"

A hiss sounds from above my head. Startled, I look up, noticing small holes forming in the ceiling. The first few drops of cold water that land on me feel good. I hold up my hand as the water rains down harder, wetting everything in the room. I get to my feet again, standing in the center of my cell. I glance at Trey who has a grim expression from his dry cell.

Water runs in streams over my face and drips from my chin. It soaks my white shirt, turning it translucent. I pull on my wet, black jacket. Soon my black pants are soaked as well. My body temperature drops, causing me to shiver violently. From my perch on my cot, I watch water collect on the floor. The grate in the center of the cell must be plugged. It doesn't take me long to figure out what's happening. It's psychological warfare. They're not going to interrogate me right away, but that doesn't mean they can't start the torture.

At first, I'm just cold, but after a few hours, the drops of water are needles piercing me. I crawl under my bunk to get some relief, but soon the water is too cold to sit in. Trembling, I rise up from under the cot, glancing at Trey. His face is rigid with anger. He uses his fingers, pointing to his eyes in a look-at-me gesture. He starts doing jumping jacks. I follow his lead, although I can only raise my right arm above my head. Every movement is painful to my ribs, but it's better than freezing to death. In no time, I'm warm enough to stop shivering.

I give Trey a small smile to reassure him that I'm okay. Abruptly, the water turns to mist, losing some of its ferocity. I sigh in relief as my smile broadens, but only for a moment. The small holes in the ceiling disappear as they widen to become several large holes. A moment later, cold water pours from them, turning into a deluge. The standing water that was at my ankles lifts to my knees. Moving to the cot attached to the wall, I stand upon it, but within minutes the level rises to its edge then spills over it, lapping at my feet.

I glance at Trey's handsome face. He can't hide the fear in his violet eyes. "They don't know I can't swim, do they?"

He shakes his head no. He turns and runs to the front of his cell, pounding on it with his fist. I can tell he's shouting, but there's not even a whisper of it in my cell; I hear nothing above the roar of water. Wayra and Jax start beating their fists against the fronts of their translucent barriers. They can see what's happening to me. They know what it means.

As the frigid water rises and swallows my legs, I try to find something buoyant enough to hold me above the water. There's nothing that floats in this cell—not even me. The fabric of my clothing isn't the right type to hold air in, so I can't make a flotation device. Panting in shallow breaths, my heart is demanding more oxygen as adrenaline circulates through my system. I grasp my side with my hand, trying to control the pain as I attempt to breathe deeper. When the water is to my chin, I tilt my head up and look at the ceiling. Water still runs in unchecked, making choppy waves on the surface. Whimpers of fear escape from my lips; I remember what it feels like to almost drown. I'm not looking forward to repeating it. My palms reach out and flatten against the wall that connects my cell to Trey's. I try to climb it, forcing my knees up against it, but my hands keep sliding down it.

I take a deep breath and hold it; the water closes around my mouth, and then my nose. With my eyes wide, I straighten my neck; my head submerges beneath the water. A mass of blond hair waves in my face. Trey's blurry image presses near me, so close and yet a world away. I see him move away from the wall to his sink. He kicks it, smashing his booted foot on top of it until it breaks away from the wall. Water spouts up as he grasps the metal basin in his hands and rips it out of its housing. With a shovel-like piece of it in his hands, Trey runs at the wall between us, slamming the metal basin into it. Cracks form and spider along the surface. He winds back and strikes it again. The noise is a soft clang in the water. Liquid streams out from the cracks he makes, but its not enough to allow the level to go down so that I can breathe. I try to hold my breath as he winds back and hits it once more, but I choke in water. Reflexively, I cough, gasping, taking liquid into my lungs. It burns with an unnatural fire. In my confusion, I see Brigadets scrambling en masse outside our cells. They have their weapons drawn on Trey's side, but on my side they're rushing to the control panel. My lungs ache and my head feels like it will explode at any moment, but I can't feel my extremities; my fingers are numb and cold.

I wish I could get away.

I slip out of my body and become a spectator to the events swirling around me. I stand behind the soldiers on the catwalk. The sweat on Trey's brow slides over the curved lines of the tribal tattoo on his neck. Thick veins stand out on his strong arms as he continues to pound the barrier with relentless strokes. With one more swing, Trey shatters the dense wall that lies between him and my limp body. My figure spills into his cell in a tidal wave. Trey catches me in his arms, wiping the mass of blond hair back from my face. He pinches my nose and breathes into my mouth. Soldiers open both of our cells. The water rushes out of the opening and falls through the metal grated floor outside.

Trey lays me on the floor. My face is pale and my eyes are closed. He begins chest compressions on me, but a few soldiers grab him, hauling him back from my supine form. As Trey struggles against them, savagely fighting them off in an attempt to get back to me, he renders a few of them unconscious.

One soldier doesn't join the fray; instead, he kneels down beside my unconscious body. With quick fingers, he pulls something from a shiny silver case. It squirms and slithers, wrapping itself around his hand like a live, albino snake. It's not an animal; it's a twisting, writhing snake-bot. The body is smooth and alabaster with pink lights within it that glow with an eerie fire. The Brigadet holds the gruesome sidewinder near my mouth. The snake-bot opens its wide mouth, clamping onto my face and ratcheting my mouth open. From inside the skin of the snake-bot, a smaller, slimy, internal snake-bot slides out into my mouth and down my esophagus. In the next moment, water is pumping out of the other end of the snake-bot like a primed hose.

Standing outside of my body, I'm a horrified observer of the scene. I know it's me, but it doesn't feel like it's happening to me. I feel nothing. I feel numb. Next to me, a feminine voice says, "How do you like my gift?"

I turn my head; the lovely, fragile image of the Bee stares back at me. I recognize her as the priestess who blasted me out of the space station earlier today. Attired in the same waspish dress as before, she's now made of light and air—a perfectly formed nightmare.

"How did you find me?" I ask her.

She doesn't answer my question but says, "I was told you can't swim." She watches as the medic inside the cell works to revive me. That battle doesn't seem to be going well. Nothing he does is bringing me back to consciousness.

"You did this," I accuse her. "You filled my cell with water."

She gives me a maleficent smile.

The soldier extracts the snake-bot from my esophagus, looking grim. My lips and my skin have a bluish tint that bodes ill for me. When Trey notices the medic sit back on his heels and shake his head, he loses his mind. He becomes a raging bull, tackling the soldier next to him. Trey wrestles the tricked-out freston from the startled hand of the soldier. Turning the weapon on my limp form upon the floor, Trey fires a yellow lightning electro-pulse straight at my heart. The electricity flows through me, and then through the water as well, shocking everyone in the room. My spirit self is ripped from the air and stuffed back into my body with the force of a cyclone.

Wide-eyed, I gasp as my back arches in agony and I writhe in pain. My heavy, granitelike lungs don't feel as if they can process air. Above me, the Bee comes into focus over the shoulder of the soldier who's patting my cheek.

With a look of disdain, the Bee says, "You'll live." She sighs in frustration before her sapphire-blue eyes narrow in contempt. "If Kyon brings you back here, I will kill you," she promises. "Run, little Kricket. Run far away."

"Who are you?" I whisper through cracked lips, but I never hear her reply. She evaporates into the ceiling and is gone. The chaos of Trey's cell becomes loud and disorienting. Soldiers who have roused from being shocked are trying to subdue Trey, who's pointing his freston at the head of one of the soldiers he's taken hostage. The soldier next to me has recovered somewhat from his shock as well. He pulls the trigger on a gunlike syringe he has inserted into my arm. As the drug he gave me careens through my arteries, I slip into darkness.

CHAPTER 5
THE DISHERY

I suck in my bottom lip as I awake to aching muscles and a stiff neck. A dull pain in my upper arm makes me lift my chin off my chest. A smirking soldier draws a gunlike syringe away from my skin. Trying to move, I find my hands are restrained above my head. I breathe faster through dry, cracked lips, and there's a saliva trail running over one side of my cheek. I squint, disoriented, my eyes unfocused; I'm aware enough to realize that there's a metal post against my back.

I push up onto my feet, which relieves some of the pressure on my arm sockets, but I'd give anything right now to be able to put my arms down. Looking up, I find my hands are shackled and latched to a metal peg on the post. The post goes up for as far as I can see through a hole in the ceiling of the room. I'm terrified. I pull as hard as I can against the restraint, hoping it'll loosen or break. It does neither.

The soldier who revived me walks away. He crosses out of the circle of light in the center of the room, moving into the shadows toward a door on the far wall. As he leaves the room, I think for a moment that I'm alone, until I hear a male voice say, "Your name is Kricket?" It echoes in the open space.

I squint, trying to locate the voice. It's in the darkest part of the room. I taste blood on my lip. My voice is hoarse and raspy when I answer, "Yes."

"Do you know who I am?" he asks.

"No," I answer. "But I'll be your best friend if you let me go." He laughs, but I'm not kidding. "How long have I been out?"

"You mean unconscious?"

"How long?" I repeat with growing panic.

He sounds amused as he says, "I was told that you're psychic. You're not omnipotent, then?" He moves away from the far wall, closer to the circle of light I'm in. He's slight in stature in comparison to all the Rafian men I've encountered. He's only a few inches taller than me. To them, he's probably a curiosity—being short. He stays on the fringes for a moment, walking around me in a circle. I wait to see what he'll do next.

When he faces me again, I say, "If I were a better psychic, Geteron, I wouldn't be here."

"I thought you didn't know me," he says in a surprised tone.

"It took me a second to recognize your voice. You're the one Minister Telek called for after I'd poisoned him. You were the first one in his office."

"You admit you poisoned him?" he asks with some degree of astonishment.

"Telek murdered Minister Vallen and threatened to use me as a scapegoat. I call what I did self-preservation. Are you in charge in his absence?"

"I'm his second in command. I'm in charge until he recovers."

I raise my chin. "Congratulations on your promotion."

"Apparently, I have you to thank for that."

"You're welcome. Now let me down."

"I don't think so. I have a few more questions for you."

"I have one for you too. How long have I been unconscious?" My mouth is dry, as if I hadn't almost drowned recently.

"Why is it important?"

"There's going to be an Alameeda attack at sixteen parts on Fitzmartin. It's an aerial assault. You need to prepare for it."

"I've heard the rumors you started regarding this attack from a few sources." He checks his watch. If what you told my soldiers is true, then we only need to wait a couple more parts to see if you're correct."

"It's Fitzmartin?" I ask in a panic. I try to pull my hands down, but the chains holding them merely rattle and clang.

"It is a little earlier than midday. We found you less formidable unconscious."

"There will be an attack soon!" I warn. "You can't afford to refuse to act on what I'm telling you. It'd mean the destruction of this entire floating fortress—your military headquarters."

He gives me a skeptical look. "There has never been an attack like the one you describe in the history of this ship."

"This ship will *be* history. Please save us."

"Why should I trust you?"

"Because you can't afford not to!"

"Give me something to build my trust."

"What do you want?" I ask in desperation.

"Tell me where they are."

"Where who are?" I ask.

"Your companions."

"Trey?" I ask in confusion. "He was in the cell with me—did he escape?"

"He did, and so did the other one."

"What other one—Jax? Wayra?" I ask.

"Your accomplice: the Comantre Syndic who tried to rescue you."

"He's not my accomplice and he wasn't trying to rescue me! He was attempting to kidnap me, and when he failed, he tried to kill me."

"Who is he?" he asks.

"I don't know," I reply, "but he's not Comantre. He's something else entirely."

"He picked up my men and threw them without touching them."

"I know. I saw that. He has gifts."

"Is he Alameeda?" he asks.

I shake my head. "I don't think so. Did you lose him?"

"He escaped from his cell when you created a diversion for him."

I scoff. "It wasn't my plan to almost drown in my cell. The diversion was created by someone else."

"It wasn't our plan either. Something went wrong. Your cell was set to rain—nothing more."

"Someone changed the setting to tsunami."

"So it wasn't you trying to distract the guards?" he asks.

"I don't have any abilities like that, and if I did, I would've picked a different way to distract them," I retort. "I can't swim." I want to ask him about Trey, but I can't. I don't want to give him any information that may lead them to Trey. If he's hiding on this ship, I need to find him. "What about the other Cavars? Did they escape as well?"

He mulls over what I said, approaching me with caution. "No. We still have them—your bodyguards from the palace. They're still tucked away safely in their cells. When we locate the other two, they may not be so fortunate."

"What do you want to know? I'll tell you anything—just don't hurt Trey. He's only trying to protect me, nothing more. He loves this house. He's loyal to Rafe."

Geteron steps into the ring of light I'm in. "How do the Alameeda get past our defensive shields?" he asks.

I exhale a deep breath, because he wants information on something I don't know. I'll have to bluff him. Before I can answer, though, a loud, squeaky hinge sounds from behind Geteron. From the open doorway, Kyon strolls into the room. His arrogant mouth twists into a smug smile. "It's not very difficult to infiltrate your defenses. You deny the supernatural. You find her gifts illogical, even when the proof of her abilities stares you in the face."

Geteron is confused for a moment. I'm not. I beg him, "Let me go! Please! He's going to kill us!"

Kyon ignores me; his focus remains on Geteron. "How many times did she tell you I was coming?" he asks Geteron as he moves closer to us. "A handful? More?"

"Who are you?" Geteron asks with a wary tone. "Who let you in here?"

"No one let me in here. I killed all your guards. You didn't answer my question. How many times did she warn you that I was coming?"

"You're Alameeda!" Geteron sneers in an outraged tone.

"I was worried she'd convince you of our arrival scheduled for a few parts from now. I decided to change our plan—make it earlier. I thought if we arrived silently, I'd have a chance of locating her before we decimate you. I believed she'd at least attempt to warn you of my new plan. She doesn't trust me at all; it's a failing of hers. So I have to assume you either didn't believe her or you harmed her in some way, making her unable or unwilling to help you. Which one is it?"

"Please let me go," I whisper to Geteron, eyeing Kyon as he shark-smiles at Geteron.

Geteron reaches for his harbinger, but he's not quick enough. Kyon throws a star-shaped blade; it lights up, glowing with blue fire. It makes a whirling sound as it whips forward, striking Geteron in the middle of the forehead. Once implanted, it does the scariest thing I've ever seen, it latches onto his skin and drills into his head, boring completely through until it comes out the other side. The shiny stars continue to spin, boomeranging back around. Kyon lifts his wrist in the air as the killing star comes back to him, docking itself on the metal wristband. Geteron teeters on his feet for a moment before he buckles and falls backward to the floor. Brains shoot out of the hole in his forehead upon the impact.

Kyon walks to him, kicking his foot with the toe of his boot. Then, his eyes lift to mine. My stomach clenches in fear as he assesses me with a cold stare. "For someone who can see the future, you don't do it so well."

I laugh humorlessly, belying my terror. "It sometimes sneaks up on me," I say as I raise my chin.

"You shouldn't allow it to do that," he admonishes.

"It's a moot point now."

"Why's that?"

"You said you'd kill me when you found me."

"And I always keep my word with you, don't I?" he asks.

"No. Not always. You seem to flake a little when I outsmart you."

"You *are* resourceful," he replies in an offhanded way. "But you appear to be less so now." He walks around the post, knocking on it behind me. It makes a hollow sound. "Forget how to blend in?"

"Ugh! Just do it already and get it over with," I snarl. I feel like I'm half dead anyway. I'm sick with fear—that part ending doesn't seem like such a bad thing. But as soon as the words are out, I regret them.

"Do what? Kill you? Do you want me to?"

"It seems like the lesser evil at the moment."

He nears me, his massive form has never made me feel as small as I do right now. He extracts a long, sharp dagger from a shoulder holster beneath his arm. With the hilt in his hand, he lays the flat of the blade just under my ear; the metal feels cool against my fever-ish skin. The fingers of his other hand weave in my hair, pulling it back, forcing my eyes up to meet his steely blue ones. The flat side of the knife shifts in his hand, moving to the back of my neck. He twists his wrist; the sharp edge rests firmly against my nape. With one broad stroke of it, he can probably cut off my head.

"Any last words?" he asks me.

I remain silent, because screw him.

"You're so defiant," he says, but there's an admiration in his tone that he can't quite hide. His hand tightens on my hair. "Aren't you going to close your eyes?"

I glare at him.

A smile grows on his lips. "You're stronger than them all." With one brutal stroke he cuts off my hair. I bite down on my already swollen bottom lip as my hair is ripped from me. Bringing his massive hand in front of my eyes to show me, we watch my hair turn black and shrivel to dust. Kyon opens his fingers, letting the ashlike residue fall from his grasp. Reaching out, he threads his fingers in my silky blond tresses, which are growing back to their former length before his eyes.

"Do you know why it does that?" he asks me. "Why your hair regrows so quickly?"

"No, do you?" I quirk my eyebrow at him in question.

"It's part of your genetic engineering. Do you know what happens when I cut your hair?" He lets my newly regrown hair spill over his fingertips, and I'm reminded of a miser and his gold.

"It renders me unable to sell it at Gurlz Need Weaves?"

Kyon's blue eyes dance with suppressed humor. "Is that a drawback?"

"Where I come from, a little extra money would've been handy."

"You'll never have to worry about money again."

"I guess that's one good thing about dying."

"Do you know what hair is?" he asks me.

I sigh, tired of his game already. "A collection of dead cells," I reply.

"To be more accurate, it's made up of long chains of amino acids joined together by peptide bonds forming polypeptide bonds. When I cut your hair, it forces your body to regenerate cells more rapidly. It rejuvenates you, making you—"

"—freakish?" I ask, attempting to find the word for which he's searching.

"Immortal . . . or very near to it. You won't physically grow much older than you are now, if you continue cutting your hair on a regular basis."

"That won't make me immortal, because you can still kill me with your knife."

He trails the sharp edge of steel over my cheek, heading for my mouth. "I find pleasure in your ability to reason. I'm growing tired of inane blonds."

"That sounds like a cultural hazard for you as an Alameeda. Most of you are pretty stupid."

He lets my insult roll off him, as if he agrees with me. "Priest-esses can be very naïve, and most of them are spoiled to the core."

"So you deserve each other. How nice for you."

His blade rests against my lips. He lifts it and holds it away from me so I can see my mouth reflected in its silver gleam. "Look at this . . . your bottom lip is not so broken anymore . . ."

I suck in my lip, running my tongue over the surface of it. The cracks that were there have healed a bit—the marks aren't gone, but they're no longer scabby.

A shiver tears through me. "It's ridiculous that you know more about my body than I do."

His knife skims lightly over my chin, down the front of my neck, over my chest, pausing above my frantically beating heart. "I should know everything about your body. It belongs to me."

"Yuck!" I make a face, "I think I just threw up a little in my mouth."

He stiffens. "You're so melodramatic."

"So your plan isn't to kill me? You plan to keep me," I say, already knowing I'm right. Part of me is relieved that he doesn't want to cut out my heart right away, but another part of me is desperate because he still believes he owns me, and I can't have that.

"We're going to destroy this ship. I came here to save you."

"I have another way you can save me: go away and don't kill any-one. It's a simple plan, one you can grasp."

He shrugs. "Eh, my way's better," he says with a smug smile. "It's the prophecy, Kricket. A house will fall. We're making sure that it's not our house."

"You're the *only* aggressors here," I counter. "Rafe isn't looking for a fight."

"Oh no? Why have they been after the Tectonic Peninsula? It's a staging point to mount an attack against Alameeda."

"Probably because you moved your troops to the borders of Peney first. Don't try to spin this. You guys were there when I arrived in Rafe."

From the pocket of his uniform, Kyon pulls out a silver disk. He touches it to the manacles on my wrists; it sticks to them like a magnet. Lights flash as it makes a high-pitched sound until one cuff clicks open on my wrist. "I wouldn't dream of spinning anything with you. You're a Diviner of Truth." I don't try to correct him with the fact that I can discern only lies, not necessarily the truth. He plucks the disk off the cuff, transferring it to the other one as he remarks, "You cannot deny that Rafe went looking for you at the same time as we did. That wasn't an accident. They have an agenda, Kricket." When my other restraint clicks open, I'm unable to hold myself up. Kyon catches me in his arms before I fall down. With a deep scowl, he murmurs, "You're weak."

"I'm fine," I say, as my cheek rests against his neck. I'm really not fine, though. I feel like I may pass out at any second. Black dots swim in my vision.

Trying to focus on something concrete, I stare at Kyon's tribal tattoos on his throat. They're military—a distinction for those who serve, but Kyon's are more than that because they're unlike the ones I saw on Forester or Lecto, his former bodyguards. He has special markings, about which I know nothing. Whereas Trey's markings are black swirls and flowing lines, Kyon's are more like black, connected crop circles.

"How long were you unconscious?" he asks, holding me to him.

I lift my head from him trying to gain some distance, "Long enough."

"You never even had a chance to see me change our plan, did you?" he asks.

"You wouldn't be here if I did."

He scoffs at my bravado. "I think you overestimate your skills for diplomacy. You're Alameeda; no one here can see past that."

"All of you Etharians are racists. You guys pretend to be more progressive than humans, but it's really just a front. You hate each other for the most ridiculous reasons: different eye color, hair color, and skin tone. Seriously, I know a stylist in the 'hood who can make you a brunet in less than an hour."

"That's an oversimplification of the situation."

"Is it? Okay, let's lay it on the line: your lifestyle choices scare the hell outta me. You can't own people. It's wrong!"

"We take care of our priestesses. We make you our consorts."

"That's bullshit if there's no choice, and you know it!"

"Every civilization on both of our worlds has slavery."

"Not legally. Not anymore."

"But it exists, legal or otherwise, correct?"

I ignore his point. "But it's wrong. Might does not make right," I retort.

"Become mightier than me and we'll discuss it."

He lifts me onto my feet, putting his enormous hand on the back of my neck. He bends like he's about to scoop me up off my feet, but I stop him. "I can walk," I say testily, trying to shrug off his possessive paw gripping me. His hand tightens, causing me to wince.

"You're still weak. Do I need to cut your hair again?" he asks.

"No," I mumble. Under my breath I add, "You total freak."

Kyon walks me past Geteron's corpse. I want to kick Geteron because if he'd listened to me in the beginning, he'd probably still be alive. When we reach the doorway of the interrogation room, Kyon slips his hand around my waist, pulling me to his side. He raps on the door. It swings open to show a handful of heavily armed Alameeda soldiers. Amid them is a slight, waifish form of an Alameeda priestess. Her look is Goth-like, with thick, black eyeliner, making her blue eyes resemble hot-spring pools ringed with volcanic sand. Her hair is long, platinum, and wavy, pulled back in a ponytail. Attired in a dark Alameeda military uniform, she looks delicate despite the sharp lines it creates on her.

In my confusion, my mouth gapes as Rafe soldiers walk through the corridor near us. No one raises an eyebrow or sounds an alarm. It's as if we don't exist to them. I scream to a pair of soldiers who get close to us, "Hey! Over here! Help me!" I wave my arm, but I can't get anyone's attention; they just walk on by as if nothing is out of the norm. I want to cry, but I clamp down on my emotions as my respiration doubles.

Kyon's hand shifts to my nape again. "They can't hear you," he warns.

"Why?" I retort.

Goth-girl's eyebrows raise in surprise. Maybe she can't believe the tone I've taken with him, or my hostility, or the fact that I'm resisting him at all, I don't know, but it startles her. She murmurs, "You've become a shadow to them, and like all shadows, you're dark and silent."

"Is that your schtick? Making us shadows?" I ask scathingly.

"Schtick?" she echoes in confusion. "What is schtick?" She looks to Kyon for guidance.

"Ignore her, Phlix," he advises. "She's a savage."

I can hardly believe what I just heard. I let loose on him, "*I'm* the savage? Me? I'm not the one bent on eradicating whole houses of Etharians. That's you, freaks!" I point to all of them.

Kyon ignores me, "Lead us out of here, Phlix," he orders Goth-girl.

"What did she mean about us eradicating whole houses of Etharians?" Phlix asks in a weak, whispery voice.

Kyon doesn't bother to answer her question, but barks, "Phlix!"

His tone startles her; she must be unaccustomed to him yelling at her, especially in a tense situation like this one. She turns and leads us away from the interrogation room, past laughing Rafe Brigadets gathered around another animated soldier who is telling the story of how Trey shot me with the freston, restarting my heart.

All around me, life continues as if we don't exist. Whenever someone comes across our path, we skirt them, maneuvering against walls. It doesn't sit well with the brawny Alameeda soldiers that Kyon has amassed, though. Their disdain for their enemies is apparent in the way they hold out their guns to the heads of the oblivious who pass us by.

As we walk, I size up my genetic rival, frightened by her power. But when she glances back at me, I don't get the sense that she sees me as her enemy, much less her rival. Phlix is simply curious about the savage priestess Kyon has uncovered.

While we weave our way up and out of the underbelly of the floating city, the unsuspecting citizens surrounding me make my stomach ache. They have no idea that their world is about to end. Entering the deck level of the ship, I shield my eyes from the streaming sunshine that illuminates through the geometric windows.

We pass through great domed lobbies with gleaming floors and lush atriums; they make the City Insurance Building where I once worked in Chicago look like a hovel. To my right is a beautifully appointed cafeteria-style dining station where officers and their staff are eating at round tables. Delicate urns of kafcan arise from the center of tables on gleaming trays. Embedded in the tables are menus whose selections are delivered by floating tray-bots. The aroma of the food is enough to make my stomach growl. It's been too long since I've had something to eat.

Feeling faint, I sway against Kyon. My hand goes to Kyon's back in an attempt to keep myself on my feet. Kyon pauses for a moment. Holding me to his side with his arm around my waist, he lets me rest my cheek against his chest. He strokes my hair. "My little savage isn't infallible after all? Shall I carry you?" he asks.

My hand brushes up against something cold and steely holstered on his thigh. I snatch the weapon off him, holding his harbinger in my hand. I press the Gatling-like barrels up under his chin. "Welcome to the future," I murmur. My hand trembles from the weight of the weapon. "You're on time delay, Kyon. You do only what I want you to do." I bluff, as if this is all part of my plan.

I back away from him, keeping his harbinger that I have no idea how to fire pointed at him. His entourage trains their weapons on me. Kyon waves them off as he barks, "I kill anyone who harms her!" He brings his eyes back to me and says, "Kricket, no one wants you here. You need to come home now. I'll take care of you."

"I'm not a part of your cult! You don't own me," I growl. Stumbling back from them, ice-cold air permeates the space. I push through it, stirring black smoky swirls around me. The smoke rises in plumes and evaporates into the air as I burst from within Phlix's shadow world bubble.

I bump into the table behind me, scattering the contents of a half-eaten meal unto the floor. The soldiers at the table jerk to their feet, startled by my sudden appearance among them out of thin air. I shiver in dread, no longer able to see Kyon and his entourage in their circle of secrecy. I push past the table, colliding with a chair and almost falling over it. A Brigadet reaches for me; I turn the harbinger on him. He raises his hands to me in surrender. I randomly swing Kyon's weapon around, pointing it in the most unprofessional way at anyone who comes near me as I continue to retreat.

"The Alameeda are here!" My tone is desperate with unshed tears. "They're going to kill all of you if you don't stop them! You have to do something!" I look at their faces frantically. "Do something! Please!"

A Rafe soldier near me draws his weapon, but he doesn't point it in my direction. Instead, he asks, "Where are they?"

I take a gasping breath, choking back my urge to cry at his apparent acceptance of what I'm saying. "They're right there!" I stab my finger in Kyon's direction, repeating, "They're right there."

He lifts his harbinger and fires at the spot I indicate. Nothing happens.

"Do it again! I swear they're there!" I insist.

He fires again, and then pauses. It's silent for several seconds. Watching the spot in the center of the lobby, I search for any movement. Then, I jump in horror as the ear-piercing, sickening sound of ammunition rounds are pumped into the crowd of Brigadets and civilians standing in the commissary. The scent of weapon fire and blood vapor fills the room along with the screaming voices of Brigadets returning fire on thin air. Suddenly, one of the hulking Alameeda soldiers from Kyon's hunting party falls out of the invisible circle, writhing in pain from a wound to his abdomen. He clutches his middle, trying to stave off the flow of blood wetting the ground. He reaches out in the direction of the empty space in front of him, motioning for them to pull him back into their cloak of invisibility.

Someone near me screams, "Alameeda!"

Kyon comes crashing out of the hidden circle, black smoke swirling in a disturbed burst around him. He murders three soldiers with precision shots before they even know he's there, but he never stops moving in my direction. Behind him, some of his men come into view, killing Brigadets as they trail him, protecting his flank. Kyon bashes heavy tables out of his path. I'm frozen in fear for a few moments, and then I turn, desperately searching for a way to escape. I plow forward, squirming between the soldiers who are now wholly engaged in the firefight with their enemies. I glance over my shoulder. Kyon is only steps behind me, killing everyone in his path. Because I'm watching him, I miss the hovering service-bot bussing a table of dirty dishes in front of me. Plates shatter onto the floor when I crash into it. The robot holds its ground by forcing me sideways. I smash into the dirty-dish receptacle embedded in the wall, almost falling into its conveyor chute.

With Kyon bearing down on me, he points an accusing finger as he promises, "You will learn to obey me!"

I turn away from him, frantically squeezing myself headfirst into the small dish chute in the wall. It's a conveyor system used to transport dirty dishes to a place called the dishery. My shoulders barely fit within the chrome-lined space; it's so tight that I have to round my back so the sensors along the walls and ceiling won't abrade me. As I enter, thousands of tiny little round air holes beneath me propel me forward into the darkness of the sloping tunnel. It feels as if I'm floating on a magic carpet of air as I glide along, my hair lifting and pushing and slapping me in the face.

From behind me, Kyon's stern voice calls out my name in frustration. Reaching his long arm in, he grasps the toe of my boot, but I kick back as hard as I can and it slips from his fingers, allowing me to slide away. "Kricket!" Kyon howls my name again, eliciting terror in my frantic heart.

Though I continue moving away from him, I'm too shaken to feel any relief. It takes me a second to realize that choking sobs are racking my body while I move at a steady pace for a bit in the near absence of light. Twisting and turning, I'm gently rolled along the dish corridor, a passenger in the aftermath of a monstrous tea party. Up ahead, light flickers and before long I'm unceremoniously shifted onto an adjoining air-powered conveyor where I'm whisked off at a much faster pace. This corridor leads to an open factorylike area. With a gasping sigh, I'm able to sit up and move my arms as the conveyor of air flows into another enormous one. A menagerie of stained dining settings and sticky utensils surround me that range from chintz to futuristic elegance. I spy the matte-black harbinger that I'd stolen from Kyon among the rabble of dinnerware. Reaching for it, I take the heavy weapon in my hand and stuff it under my shirt against the waistband of my pants. Looking over the side of the conveyor, a Penrose-stairs-like maze of conveyor lines come and go in a seemingly infinite paradox of wine-resin stemware and kitsch plates. I shiver at the size of this facility and desperately search around for a way out.

Ahead of me, robotic arms line both sides of my conveyor. Nimble metal claws select drinking glasses, tumblers, mugs, and flutes from the chaos of floating china, sorting them into racks that get transferred to a different conveyor line. Unable to find a way off this river of air sweeping me forward, I throw my arms around my head and duck as I come abreast of the surgically extracting arms. A scanner passes over me, but nothing else happens. The robots continue to select only the drinking glasses from the mess and leave me be.

I breathe a sigh of relief, but it's short-lived, because rows of bristly rollers line the conveyor ahead of me. Thrusting back and forth and side to side, the bristles roll over the plates and cutlery, scraping away excess food. The food is pushed off to troughs on the sides of the conveyors and shuttled away onto different conveyors.

As I near the brushes, I scrunch up my face, covering my head with my arms once more. The first brush pushes me flat into a lieback position. The bristles bounce over me, scrubbing my skin with delicate, crumb-encrusted fingers. When I pass by them all, I sit up again on the cloud of air, exhaling a deep breath.

I'm propelled into the next section with significantly more force than the previous ones. Pushing forward, I travel under an arching tunnel of metal jets that shower me. Hot water drips from my chin, as I'm thoroughly soaked. A sharp hiss draws my attention to my right side. Steam rolls from a glass tunnel on an adjacent air-conveyor line. A roiling cloud of steam blasts from it, the temperature of which is enough to sizzle butter. Endless streams of crated glasses trundle into the car-wash-like tunnel, which soaps, lathers, rinses, and sanitizes them. The current temperature reading on the side of the mechanism is equal to a whopping 180 degrees. I shudder, grateful that I didn't fall onto the skin-melting conveyor with the glassware. But the conveyor I'm on rounds a turn, and I'm met with the same type of hellfire dishwasher ahead of me.

Wild-eyed, I flail my arms, trying to halt my progression forward. I knock dishes over the sides of the conveyor, watching them commit to gravity and fall several stories before they catch a different conveyor and are whisked away in another direction. A sharp hiss of scalding steam emits from the passage ahead of me, turning the air white into a billowing cloud of heat. Desperately, I rock back and forth on the cushion of air beneath me in an attempt to gain enough momentum to pitch myself over the side.

Almost to the tunnel, I whimper as the first flood of steam touches me, turning my skin rosy. I lift my arms to shield my face from the burn. *Thump*, a muffled noise rumbles and rolls out, becoming louder and louder until the whole dishery ripples in a wave of shaking chaos. The conveyor tilts to the side, catapulting me off it before I reach the dish inferno. I hurtle through the air, arching upward in a flying heap before being caught in another slipstream. The forced air jerks me sideways before dumping me off the end of the belt of air. I fall with the other scraps of meat into a gigantic composting silo.

The walls of the compost silo are steely and high. I take a few deep breaths, stunned that I'm still alive. As I lie atop the mound of squishy leftovers, I cringe in horror. More uneaten food pours out of a giant, overturned bucket swinging from a hook above me. I roll to the side, narrowly avoiding being buried. Floundering amid the carnage of discarded cuisine, I crawl to the side of the compost vat. I try to gain some footing, but I keep sinking into the sludge beneath me.

When I spy metal ladder rungs on the opposite side of the vat, I flail toward them. The bottom of the vat makes a choking gasp; it rattles and come to life with a groan. The food beneath me moves in a circular motion, swirling as if it's being flushed down a drain. In merry-go-round fashion, I'm dragged around the rim of the garbage silo. Coming to the ladder, I palm a rung, but it slips out of my hand as my feet lodge on the muck. I growl in frustration, gritting my teeth. I'm swept away from the ladder. A hole forms in the center of the vat; compost feeds into sharp, churning blades, shredding everything into crumbs with the viciousness of a wood chipper.

I blanch, scrambling with renewed vigor to dislodge my feet from the muck miring them. Pulling on my calf, I can't get it unstuck and I miss the ladder rung as it passes. Hurriedly, I unfasten the straps on my boots. An avalanche of rubbish careens into the middle of the centrifuge, rolling down to get sucked into the belly of the shredder.

My lip curls in determination. I reach down, finding a jam-smeared piece of bread; I smash it between my hands, rubbing my palms with the sticky residue. I crouch in preparation as I go around again. When I near the ladder rung once more, I grasp the metal in my hand, getting a good grip. Pulling myself up, I loop my arm through the rung, catching the bar in the bend of my elbow. I lock my wrist with my hand and draw it to my chest. Stretching to full extension, I'm torn out of my boots while I cleave to the rung. I close my eyes for a moment, panting hard and holding back tears. When I open my eyes, I look down and see my boots tumble into the jaws of the composter.

As I clamber up the ladder, I miss my footing several times in my haste and nearly fall back in. I pull myself over the lip of the trough and I lie gasping on a grated catwalk. *Thump, thump, thump.* Bombs! I'm nearly shaken off the walkway, but I manage to hang on by wrapping my arm around the railing. The lights flicker in bolts of yellow. Dishes crash down in pelting shards from the interrupted airflow on the conveyors; luckily, I'm shielded from most of it by the catwalk above this one.

Sirens shriek in warning. When the trembling abates, I rise, my knees shaking. I clutch the railing and take my first limping steps. Pipes burst above my head, raining warm water on me, bleeding the splashes of muck from my hair and clothes. I stumble along the causeway, where a pearly light catches my attention and illuminates a hatchlike door.

I lift the latch of the door, ease it open, and find myself in an empty room. The loud siren continues in here, echoing off the tiled walls while a light on the ceiling strobes the room in ominous flashes.

I scream when metal showerheads drop from the ceiling and a clear glass tube rises from the ground, trapping me just over the threshold. I gasp, staring up at the spouts, and my hands press and push against the solid walls surrounding me. A fem-bot voice activates, "Contamination detected. Please remain still for decontamination."

The showerheads rain down foamy soap and warm water on my head while an arch of mini-jets hits me from all sides. I cringe, scrunching my eyes closed. Loose strands of food and slime flow away into the drains at my feet. After a couple of minutes, the showerheads turn off and retract. The clear tube disappears back into the floor, freeing me.

Holding my breath, I wait to be apprehended again, but it's clear after several moments that I'm entirely alone here. The place is deserted, and through an observation window, I note that the control room is empty. I move forward tentatively to a steel bench in front of the clear-fronted, lighted lockers lining the walls. I try the latch on a few, but they're all locked. To my left, there's a shower room— a lavare. I raise my shaky hand to my wet hair; a shower is a moot point now. Instead, I hunt around for something to wear that will hide my hair.

In a bin near the door, I find discarded cherry-red, industrial overcoats. They must use them to wear over their clothing when they go out to inspect the dishery. I rummage through the bin, drawing one out. It's enormous. I toss it back in and hunt for another that's a little smaller. When I locate one, I try it on. It reaches all the way to my ankles. I pull up the attached splash-guard hood, shrouding my hair. I pull the harbinger from the waistband of my pants, and tuck it into the outer pocket of the trenchlike coat. I tiptoe over to a door on the adjacent wall, leaving a trail of wet toe prints on the floor behind me.

The door slides up automatically as I approach. I hesitate as people run by, too preoccupied to even glance my way. I watch them for a few minutes, but it's clear that they're abandoning their posts at the dishery as fast as possible. Cautiously, I enter the sterile, white corridor. Merging into the chaos around me, I leave the dishery behind.

CHAPTER 6
HANG ME UP TO DRY

A fem-bot voice, piping through the audio system, calmly states, "All active-duty personnel are ordered to report to assigned combat stations. Code Amber. Enemy infiltration is detected. All noncombat personnel are ordered to seek shelter in your designated areas—follow protocol Alpha Indie." The voice pauses for only a few moments before it restates its message. "All active-duty personnel . . ."

I run down the bright white corridor with no thought of direction, guided purely by fear and adrenaline. When I come to the end of it, I search the wall and ceiling for some kind of marker that will help me find the detention area. *Nothing! There's nothing!*

The tap of booted feet hurrying to their assigned positions in the battle echo the flight of my rapidly beating heart. In the next corridor, everyone I come across is outfitted in combat gear. The light that runs down the center of the wide passage is flashing from white to amber here. There are several hallways, but I continue straight ahead.

When I turn onto a new passage, a holographic male figure materializes in my path. I stumble to a halt at his country-club smile, recognizing his handsome visage as being one of a Rafian actor with a role on *Violet Shadows*, a soap opera program that women seem to follow religiously here.

"Welcome to the Beezway, the express superhighway to get you to where you need to be by the most efficient means possible. Shall I call for your transport?" he asks me.

My mouth opens, and then shuts as I think of a response to that question. Finally I murmur tentatively, "Yes?"

The actor's image gives me a toothy grin. "Excellent! Please scan your wrist communicator into the kiosk to call your vehicle to our current location." His holographic hand gestures to the lighted, cylindrical docking station near a wall of glass ahead of us. I begin to realize that he's a glorified valet-slash-doorman.

I hold up my bare wrist to him. "I don't have my wrist communicator available—I misplaced it."

With a genuine look of concern on his lighted face, my attractive companion replies, "I'm sorry to hear that. Shall I call for a general mode of transportation for you?"

"Uhh . . . sure," I say with my bottom lip rolling out.

"Please state your destination."

I falter for a moment. *Where do I want to go? Where would Trey go?* I wonder. He's looking for me—I know it. When the Alameeda attack starts, though, he'll go to the detention center to try to free our friends. "I want to go to the detention center . . . where prisoners are held?" I ask him, keeping my face averted beneath my red hood as a group of soldiers run past us.

"Please wait one moment while I input your destination," he says apologetically.

As I wait, I walk a few steps away to the wall of glass that separates us from outside of the ship. Beneath the window, a concrete tunnel shelters a lavender channel of light. The channel is a superhighway, ferrying all sorts of hover vehicles along its wide berth in two directions. The highway acts as a link between buildings and around the perimeter of the ship.

I turn away from the window, observing the lobby of this hovercar station. I realize this part of the ship is quickly becoming a ghost town. Several other holographic images of soap opera actors are calling forth hover vehicles for Skye personnel, evacuating them from this area.

I startle as I glance to my side and find the hologram has joined me at the window. "I'm sorry," the actor-hologram says, "all general transportation has been suspended due to Code Amber. Would you like me to contact a security detail to assist you?"

"No!" I state, holding up both my hands. "That won't be necessary. I will locate another means of transport." Dropping my hands, I back away from his smiling visage.

"Okay." He gives me a sultry look. "Don't forget to check in with *Violet Shadows*, airing tonight at nineteen parts."

"Will do," I say, before turning and moving toward the outside doors.

I keep my face down while the last few technicians from the dishery move to their hover vehicles and merge onto the highway. I wave my hand in front of a panel and open the doors to the Beezway. I walk through and stand at the railing. Several fast-moving hovercars zip past, creating a slipstream that nearly blows the hood of my overcoat back from my head.

There's nothing left for me to do but to climb over the railing and onto the glowing lavender roadway. I press to the side abruptly as a bullet-shaped hover vehicle fires down the tunneling passage; it's carrying troops dressed in Cavar uniforms. After taking a deep breath, I turn and follow in the direction they're going. More shiny silver hovercars with Cavars inside go by. The hopelessness of locating Trey crushes me, squeezing my heart.

In desperation, I sprint down the center of the express track. A hover vehicle rounds the bend in front of me; this one is black and built for speed. I stop and put my hands up, waving at it frantically.

The driver cuts the air jets; the vehicle loses buoyancy, hitting the ground. As the car bounces, it sends out sparks, screeching as it grinds across the lane. Stopping right in front of me, the driver's eyes widen in surprise, and then narrow in anger. The door of the vehicle opens, sliding in an arc over the ceiling.

He flicks his hands at me. "Are you demented?" he asks as he approaches me. "I almost flattened you!" He's at least a foot and a half taller than me and he's all brawn with short, military-style hair. His Cavar uniform is that of an officer. The tribal tattoos on his neck are a comforting sight. "Who are you? What are you doing in the middle of the Beezway?"

Blood is roaring in my veins. He comes and stands right in front of me. From my pocket, I pull out the harbinger. As I point the weapon at him, I'm surprised that my hand isn't trembling. "Take me to the detention area," I order him. "Now!"

He glances at the harbinger in my hand for a second, and then he meets my gaze. Before I can react, his hand closes over my heavy weapon, pulling it out of my grasp. His other enormous hand wraps around my neck. He twists me around so that my back slams hard against the front of his black hovercar. Holding the harbinger he confiscated from me to my forehead, he says through clenched teeth, "Give me a reason not to kill you."

I wheeze and cough, all the air inside me knocked out. "Baw-da-baw," I manage to say as he squeezes my throat so hard that tears come to my eyes. Immediately, his grip on my throat eases. I cough more and gasp for air.

Thump. I turn my head as an Alameeda missile hits the Ship of Skye in the distance, sending out a rolling wave of fireworks. The shock of the blast causes the tunnel in front of us to shudder and then collapse. Rock dust spews outward, shadowing the destruction. It cuts off the flow of traffic, making it impossible to move in the direction the hovercars were traveling. Had the hovercar I stopped kept going, everyone inside would be dead now, crushed beneath the weight of the tunnel ceiling. A fast-moving vehicle behind us isn't able to stop in time. It crashes into the caved-in debris and explodes into an inferno. More hovercars follow it into death.

"It's the Alameeda," I say, when the soldier with his hand to my neck looks down at me, "they're attacking."

With a grim expression, the Cavar tightens his grip once more. "Really? I hadn't noticed the triple nitronium fritzwinter sonicdrites hitting the ship! " he growls. "Who are you?"

"It doesn't matter. Cavars are trapped in the detention center—Trey Allairis, Jax Roule, Wayra Waters—they're locked in cells, guarded by Brigadets. If we don't get them out, they're dead."

He lets go of my neck and sweeps the cowl of the red overcoat off my head. My wet hair falls in waves onto the hovercar's shiny black veneer. "You're the Alameeda priestess—Kricket Hollowell—the one Wayra has been guarding," he states.

"You know Wayra?"

"The wacker owes me money!" he says.

"It's going to be tough to collect; the Brigadets have him incarcerated in the detention area. He's likely to die in there with the Alameeda attacking."

"You're Alameeda," he says with renewed hostility, pressing the barrel of the harbinger harder against my forehead. I wince.

"Yes. You got me. You should take me back to the detention center where I belong," I suggest.

"Maybe I should just kill you as a traitor," he counters with a malicious sneer on his lips.

"Kesek Alez," a voice behind him says, addressing his superior as the rank of major, "she may not be a traitor. Look at this!"

"Report, Cyphon," Kesek Alez growls. He pulls me off the hood, twisting me around so that my back is to him. One of his hands holds my neck while the other presses the harbinger to my temple.

In front of me, two armed combat-uniformed Cavars have their weapons drawn on me. The other two Cavars on the transport I stopped have exited the vehicle and are now trying to stop the traffic from plowing into the death trap ahead of them.

The one who spoke holsters his weapon, saying, "HQ is running this on a loop." The one I take to be Cyphon holds his arm out in front of us. From the watchlike band on his wrist, a mini-hologram projects a surveillance camera view of me appearing out of thin air in the commissary. The image of me then points to the middle of the room—the Brigadet I was near soon fires on the spot, and then moments later, the Alameeda soldier falls out of the circle.

The soldier with the wrist hologram looks at his commanding officer. "It looks like she was trying to help the Brigadets."

Kesek Alez turns me loose. I step a few feet from him and pivot to face him. He frowns at his subordinate. "I don't give a fat shickle, Cyphon, if she was trying to help the Brigadets. Right now she's impeding us."

I interrupt them. "I just saved your lives from that." I point to the debris in the road. "I need transport to the detention area. Gennet Trey Allairis is being detained by Brigadets," I lie. "They claim to be the authority here. Defense Minister Vallen would never have allowed that. He would've appointed Cavars to be in charge of Rafe's defenses." Honestly, I have no idea what Defense Minister Vallen would or wouldn't have done in this situation.

"They're calling Gennet Trey a traitor too," Kesek Alez says with an arrogant sneer. "And he has escaped from the detention center. There are bulletins alerting us to the fact that he's armed and extremely dangerous."

"Sir," Cyphon interjects, "I served under Gennet Allairis when he was Kesek. I'll never believe anyone who tells me he's a traitor."

I latch on to Cyphon's bit of support. "If you don't give them the benefit of the doubt, all the detained Cavars in those cells will die if this ship goes down. Let them fight for their lives against the Alameeda. You can figure out their guilt or innocence after we survive."

"If they're traitors and I let them out, they can destroy this ship!" Kesek Alez shoves his finger in my face.

"Take me there—talk to Wayra—you know he's not a traitor—if you know him at all, then you know that."

Kesek Alez thinks for a moment, seeming to be swayed for a moment by my argument. Touching a spot on the collar of his combat armor, he activates a communicator. He speaks into it, "Command: we've intercepted a fugitive in the area of Griffin Flow and Hurst Haven."

"Identify fugitive," a fem-bot voice pipes in from the console within the vehicle near us as well as the earpiece that Kesek Alez has.

"Kricket Hollowell," he states.

There is hardly any pause at all before he gets a response. "Remain where you are—sending fugitive transport to secure prisoner," the feminine voice coos through the speaker.

"You knob knocker! You can't give me to them! Why won't you help us? You're a Cavar!" I scream at Kesek Alez in frustration.

He gestures toward the hovercar they vacated with a nod of his head. "Put her in the back until they get here," he orders Cyphon.

Cyphon grasps me firmly by the elbow, pulling me toward the hovercar. "C'mon," he says, not without sympathy, "it'll be okay."

"You don't know that!" I sneer at him. "I wish you'd help me!"

He presses his hand to the back of my head, making sure I don't bump it as he directs me into the backseat of the vehicle. Once inside, he makes me scoot over so that he can sit next to me while we wait for the fugitive transport to arrive.

Kesek Alez turns his eyes on his men. "After we get rid of her, we'll find an alternate route to station . . ."

Whatever else Kesek Alez says doesn't register with me. I have the worst feeling: as if I'm entering an ice storm. I exhale a breath; it curls up in front of me like wintry air. *The future,* I think, wanting to stave off any notion of it while at the same time ready to embrace it if it helps me out of this. I lean back against the seat, staring straight ahead of me at nothing at all—until a different movie of my life begins to play out . . .

The Cavars are pacing back and forth outside the hovercar, anxious for the fugitive transport to arrive. One of them checks and rechecks his gun. He glances at Cyphon in the backseat next to me, "You got an extra D-Cell? Mine's nearly gone." He indicates his gun, pointing the barrel away from us.

Cyphon speaks to him through the open window. "You're supposed to keep your D-Cell charged, Ancil."

With a sullen expression, Ancil replies, "Yeah, I know! I guess I didn't expect to get ambushed by the Alameeda today." He looks past Cyphon to me, glowering as if I'm responsible for the attack. When his eyes shift back to Cyphon, he asks, "You gonna help me out or not?"

Cyphon sighs heavily. He rummages around in a soldier's gear pack at his feet. Locating a rectangular pronged case made of metal, he hands it out the window to the other soldier, who loads it into his gun. The gun makes a humming sound, like it's powering up.

Ancil begins to walk away, but Cyphon stops him. With a good-natured smile, Cyphon says, "Hey! Gimme the other one so I can charge it, ya jackwagon."

Ancil turns back around, handing him the other D-Cell. "I didn't think you'd notice."

"I notice everything," he retorts with hubris.

Behind us, I hear a noise that makes the hair on my arms stand on end. I turn my head and, looking through the back window, I watch as an E-One approaches us on the empty side over the divided guideway. The wasplike heli-vehicle flies next to the line of hover vehicles behind us. The forced-air engines raise dust in its wake. The mean, predatory form makes my insides churn.

Unimpeded by the lack of traffic on the opposite side of the Beezway, the pilot of the E-One has no problem coming abreast of us. The craft lands with a decisive thunk *on the guideway. The doors of the black beast open in a graceful sweep as floating steps descend from the interior of the craft.*

With his back to me, Kesek Alez walks toward the E-One to greet them. He waves his arms over his head nonaggressively, signaling to the fugitive apprehension squadron. A lone figure steps out onto the stairs of the E-One, attired in black combat armor. He raises a long-barreled weapon. Pressing a button, several silver darts fly from the gun in rapid-fire succession.

The first dart embeds in Kesek Alez's neck. When he pulls it out and looks at it, he drops it in horror. His body immediately swells up like puff pastry. He expands to three times his normal size before he explodes into a red vapor cloud while his blood and entrails paint the tunnel red.

The other Cavars who are hit by the darts suffer a similar fate. Ancil tries to fire his weapon, but his bloated fingers no longer have dexterity, and then it's too late; he becomes a Jackson Pollock all over the side of our hovercar.

Kyon exits the craft, walking down the steps at an unhurried pace with several other Alameeda soldiers. While Kyon moves toward our hovercar, the Alameeda soldiers fan out to protect him, firing their weapons at anyone who looks their way.

With a strangled cry, Cyphon bursts out of the seat next to me, hitching up his gun as he goes. Kyon lifts his arms and fires one shot, hitting Cyphon in the forehead, exploding his brains out the back of his head.

I don't move; I just remain where I am. When Kyon reaches the car, he bends down, extending his hand to me. "Take my hand before I throttle you," he says. His blue eyes are as threatening as his words . . .

I blink several times. My breath curls out in icy waves from my mouth. *I didn't leave my body . . . I just saw—*

"You got an extra D-Cell? Mine's nearly gone." It's Ancil; he's at the window.

I blink again, tongue-tied.

"You're supposed to keep your D-Cell charged, Ancil," Cyphon replies.

With a sullen expression, Ancil replies, "Yeah, I know! I guess I didn't expect to get ambushed by the Alameeda today." He looks past Cyphon to me, glowering as if I'm responsible for the attack. When his eyes shift back to Cyphon, he asks, "You gonna help me out or not?"

Cyphon sighs heavily. He rummages around in a soldier's gear pack at his feet. Locating a rectangular pronged case made of metal, he hands it out the window to the other soldier, who loads it into his gun. The gun makes a sound like its powering up.

Ancil begins to walk away, I reach out and grasp Cyphon's wrist. "They're coming!" My heart is in my throat; fear is a violent thing in my chest, tearing from inside me, desperately trying to get out. I have to gulp to hold down the bile that threatens to spew from my mouth. After a few deep breaths, I turn to Cyphon and say, "Get ready to go. It's not your command; it's the Alameeda. They intercepted your kesek's transmission. They're coming here and they'll kill them—" I nod out the window at Kesek Alez and the other Cavars he's with "—and then you. They'll force me to go with them—we have to change that!"

Cyphon stares at me with a blank expression. "What are you talking about?" he asks.

With my chin I point to his unit. "We're about to be attacked. They die, but you can live. Things are about to get insane," I reply with an anxious plea in my voice. "I'm sorry."

Cyphon lifts his eyes to his commanding officer, half in confusion and half in denial. The E-One lands across from us. Kesek Alez moves forward to greet them. A lone Alameeda soldier steps out onto the stairs of the E-One, attired in black combat armor. He raises a long-barreled weapon. Pressing a button, he shoots Kesek Alez and several other soldiers with darts. The mayhem that follows mirrors my glimpse of the future.

Cyphon makes a move to leave the hovercar. I jump on him, locking arms with him. "You can't help them!" I scream. "They're dead! You have to save us!"

"How did you know?"

"We have to go!" I yell instead. "Drive!" I urge as we both lie across the backseat of the vehicle where I've pulled us down.

Lifting my head up, I peek through the window just in time to see Kyon alight from the interior of the E-One. Turning to Cyphon, I say in a desperate voice, "If you get out, they'll kill you and take me! You don't have any options but to drive."

Cyphon's jaw clenches as he scans my face. I nod once, letting him know he has only one choice now. He doesn't listen to me, though. He yanks his arm from my hands, opening the door to the hovercar. He throws himself out of the vehicle, lifting his riflelike weapon and firing at the Alameeda scattered around the Beezway. In seconds, he's cut down, falling into the roadway, turning it crimson with his blood.

I sit frozen in the backseat of the vehicle, unable to move. Shouts and the deafening report of automatic weapon fire coming from the Alameeda soldiers echo from outside the hovercar. My head doesn't duck. I don't cringe in fear. I know they're not shooting at me; they're massacring everyone in the tunnel.

There's a pause in the noise. I turn my head and glance out the door. Kyon is still by the E-One, his handsome blue eyes are on me, watching my reaction to what's happening. He looks proud of me—proud of the fact that I'm not screaming, or covering my ears, or crying for them to stop. I'm not doing any of those things because I know that they won't help. No one here will help. No one here will stop him. He's probably also proud that I don't look at all surprised by what's happening—I knew it would happen—I saw it happen. He knows I saw it.

Kyon takes a step in my direction, but then he stiffens. The door to my right opens and I startle, expecting to see a blond-haired goon looming over me. Instead, the exquisite face that greets my eyes melts my icy heart in an instant. I feel myself go limp against the seat. "Trey!" His name tumbles from my lips. "How did you find me?"

Trey ducks into the backseat; his long arm reaches past me to close the door, blocking Kyon from me. I inhale Trey's sultry scent and it's like a drug running through my veins, creating a poignant ache inside me. The door locks as Trey takes me in his arms for a bone-crushing hug. I endure it, unable to breathe. His deep voice is hushed as he says, "I've been monitoring communications. They've been airing footage of the Alameeda shootout in the commissary. It showed you slipping into the dishery chute. I escaped and have been hiding out—trying to find where you were being held since they took you from my cell. When I saw the footage, I figured you had to be around the dishery somewhere, so I started this way, hoping I'd find you."

Lifting me up, he shoves me over the barrier that divides the hovercar; I fall into the front seat. He climbs over the barrier between us to the front seat next to mine. He doesn't look at me, concentrating on the vehicle instead, and then he adds, "I overheard the transmission the Cavars issued, reporting that you'd been detained."

He presses a few buttons. Seat belts twist up and secure both of us to the vehicle. I look around the compartment. There's no steering wheel on either side; it's just a dashboard of lights with readouts on the windscreen.

"Engine on—engage manual transmission," Trey orders. The hovercar immediately hums to life and lifts off the ground. The panel on his side of the vehicle opens up, emitting a joystick controller from the interior of the dashboard. Atop the joystick is a round, floating ball. As Trey grips the joystick, his thumb rubs over the top of the roller ball; the vehicle swings in a ninety-degree turn, facing the heli-vehicle and Kyon. "Secure compartment," he orders the cabin of the vehicle. All the open doors slide closed and lock.

Kyon has gathered his Alameeda soldiers to him. He holds up his hand, signaling to the pilot behind him to hold his position. Slowly, Kyon raises his weapon at arm's length, aiming it at Trey. He pulls the trigger, firing a round at Trey's side of the hovercar. Projectiles pelt the hood and the windscreen of the military-grade vehicle, leaving dents, but they fail to penetrate the interior.

I grimace. "Why aren't they firing on us with the E-One?" I ask as he revs the engine and we stare down the missiles and other scary weapons mounted on the outside of the lethal E-One.

"Kyon doesn't want to risk killing you. He needs you alive," Trey replies.

I know he's right. Trey squeezes the trigger on the front of the joystick; our hovering vehicle charges forward, accelerating so quickly that I'm plastered to the seat back. Kyon scrambles to get out of our way, as do the other soldiers with him, leaving just the E-One in front of us as we race straight ahead. I cringe, holding my breath. We rumble over the road divider. Right before we hit the E-One, it lifts up from the ground, allowing us to pass beneath it.

Trey moves his thumb, spinning us onto the open lanes of the wide tunnel. "Project rear trajectory," he barks. An area of the windscreen darkens to show a watermark image of the area behind our hovercar—a rearview image. Pressing the accelerator, we move faster than I have ever traveled in any type of vehicle on Ethar. I lose my stomach when he spins up onto the wall as we bank into a turn. Light ahead of us shocks me because it also means we've run out of road.

I give a cry of alarm, "No road!" drawing up my legs and bracing one hand against the ceiling and the other against the window, preparing to plunge off the edge.

"It's a guide—we don't need a road," Trey explains while concentrating on driving. I sag in relief for a second when I realize we're not going to plunge to our deaths. He glances at me. "This is a troupedo; it drives on air, Kitten. The Beezway makes it faster, it propels at the same time, allowing a vehicle to go twice as fast as normal, but it's not necessary as a road."

Around us in the sky, fighter aircraft of all types are engaging in fierce dogfights. Brilliant sprays of colorful light erupt as the Rafe Dragon ships spew fire into the air, looking for chinks in the Alameeda's swarm of attackers. The Alameeda have supersonic aircraft, each with a pointed-shaped fuselage in front of a huge, round turbinelike forced-air engine in the back. These ships are able to outrun the Rafe ships with both speed and agility. The Rafe ships, however, have more precise weaponry. By locking onto targets, they're able to predict where the Alameeda will be.

"How did you escape?" I ask, before a startled scream rips from me as we're rammed from behind by the pursuing E-One.

Trey veers to the left, using the agility of the troupedo to counteract the immense speed of the E-One, keeping it off us. His jaw clenches tight as he whips us around the bend of a cylindrical building. When he puts some space between the E-One and us, he gives me a sidelong look. "I have the Comantre Syndic in the cell next to yours to thank for my escape."

"Giffen?" I ask in a high-pitched voice. I'm holding on to the seat with both hands, and I still feel like I'm about to hit the windscreen in front of me.

He nods, watching the watermark image of the E-One on the windscreen. He points us directly at the fiery blaze billowing up from the base of the Ship of Skye, the result of one of their mega-ton bombs. Choking smoke pours around us as we fly through the destroyed and smoldering buildings. The E-One is on top of us again, ramming us from behind, making my teeth rattle. Trey slips between two buildings just before one topples into the other. The E-One has to veer up to avoid being crushed.

Trey's jaw loosens its rigid line. "Giffen broke through to your cell when he awoke, pulling me through the shattered wall."

"With his telekinesis?" I ask.

He nods in answer. "He demanded to know where you were."

"What did you tell him?" I ask.

"Nothing."

"What did he do when you refused to talk?" I look him over; he's full of scrapes and bruises. He's wearing a Brigadet's uniform shirt. I don't want to know where he got it.

"I'm not sure. But when I regained consciousness, he was gone and there was a trail of dead Brigadets leading out of the deten-tion center. I tried to free the other Cavars, but I was almost appre-hended—I had to escape instead. I'll have to go back for them."

We're rammed once more by the E-One behind us. The entire vehicle shakes, and it takes a Herculean effort by Trey with both his hands on the joystick to steady the troupedo once more.

"They're going to kill us," I whisper in fear.

Trey shakes his head. "They can blow us out of the sky whenever they want to, Kricket, but they won't. Kyon's obsessed with you. He can't give you up."

"That doesn't make me feel better."

From behind us, an electro-pulse slams into our hovercar. All the readouts on the windscreen disappear along with the lights and everything else that was propelling the vehicle forward. We begin to free-fall because the vehicle is no longer operational.

"What just happened?" I whimper at Trey as the hovercar goes into a dive. I brace my hand against the door and ceiling, fear suffocating me.

"They just killed our power!" He scowls, pressing buttons and trying to get the engine to turn back on. The Ship of Skye's landscape grows bigger and bigger with every second we plummet. I realize I'm in a coffin looking out as we sink toward the deck.

The back window of our hovercar explodes. Glass falls around me to the windscreen. Hooks lodge in the backseat, cutting the upholstery and embedding deep in the frame. Our descent is halted; we spin in a dizzying swing, dangling from the bottom of the E-One by grappling cables. As the hovercar pendulums, our image reflects in the glass of one of the buildings. If it were not for the harnesses holding me to the seat back, I'd be kissing the windshield as we face the ground below us.

We twist on the lines like caught fish. Trey looks around the cabin of the vehicle. "What do you want to risk to get away?" he asks.

I swallow past the bile corrupting my throat. "Everything," I reply. "I'll risk everything to stay with you."

"I was hoping you were going to say that," he breathes. He unhooks his seat belt. Holding the seat back, he leans over and kisses me. My heart contracts painfully in my chest. He grasps my hair, and rests his forehead to mine for just a moment. I want to wrap my arms around him, but he pulls away from me. Reaching behind his seat, he opens a console in the back. He extracts a canister from it the size and shape of a fire extinguisher and hands it to me. When he reaches back again, he retrieves another one from the console behind my seat. "Use that to break your window!" he orders me. I turn the canister around, butting it against the glass until the window shatters. He does the same with his. "Brace your snuffout between the arrowing and the bender," he says.

"What?" I ask, giving him a beseeching look. "I don't know what any of that is!"

"Here! Do this!" He demonstrates, lodging his canister between two car parts that look like a gill of a fish on the outside of the hovercar where I'd normally find an auxiliary mirror. "Make sure the nozzle is pointed out!" The urgency in his tone prompts me to turn my canister around as fast as I can.

The hooks holding our hovercar suspended above the ground retract, pulling us upward. The belly of the E-One opens, ready to swallow us up. Trey glances back through the rear window. "They're pulling us in. We have to go now! When I tell you to, open the nozzle of the snuffout." He indicates the control jet on the spout of the fire-extinguisher-like thing lodged on the side of the car. "Light the gas with this!" He digs in his pocket, coming out with something that looks like a lighter. He reaches back behind his seat again, finding someone's gear. Rummaging around in the bag, he locates another lighterlike tool.

As he straightens in his seat, the lines suspending us in the air continue to retract, drawing us closer to the E-One. A bead of sweat rolls from Trey's hairline and over the sharp angles of his cheek and jaw. He narrows his eyes in concentration. "On the count of two," he says, his hand moves to the canister by its nozzle.

"Wait!" I gasp. "How do you light this?"

Trey moves his thumb away from the grip on his lighter, revealing a small groove in the side. "Press here," he says.

I nod. "Got it," I exhale, lighting mine for a moment before I let it extinguish. His hand moves to the canister outside his window once more. He waits for me to do the same with the one on my side of the hovercar. "On the count of two," he says again, and I nod. "One . . ." The hovercar lurches upward closer to our enemy as we swing lazily in midair. "Two!" Trey shouts. I open the control jet; noxious gas spews out of the canisters in a steady stream. Lighting the gas, it erupts into flames that blast us sideways. He grabs my head and pulls me to him, covering me in the center of the hovercar.

Our hovercar rockets laterally; its roof crashes into the side of a building. The glass of the skyscape's window rains around us. The hovercar lands on top of its roof, suspending us upside down in our seats. As the fireballs on either side of the hovercar continue to burn, it spins us around as if we're on a flaming teacup ride in a traveling carnival.

The canisters finally run out of gas and the hovercar comes to a reluctant halt. Dizzily, I grasp the belts holding me in place upside down. From somewhere outside the vehicle, a fem-bot voice announces, "All active-duty personnel are ordered to report to assigned combat stations. Code Amber. Enemy infiltration is detected. All noncombat personnel are ordered to seek shelter in your designated areas—follow protocol Code Amber."

CHAPTER 7
OVER THE EDGE

Trey is already out of his seat, reaching over to hit the release button on my seat belts. He catches me before I fall against the roof, and then he releases me to rest on it. Crawling out the side window, he pulls me with him just as the hovercar lurches backward, scraping across the shattered glass on the floor. The tension of the lines attached to the hovercar slacken for a moment, causing the car to pause. It sits idly, rocking back and forth before the lines attached to it lift upward once more, forcing them taut. Abruptly, the hovercar makes a horrific screeching sound; the metal rooftop drags over the floor as sparks fly everywhere. The vehicle lifts up, careening backward through the smashed window by the twisted lines from the E-One. It dangles outside for a moment before it floats upward and out of our line of sight.

Trey hurriedly lifts me to my feet. His fierce hug causes my ribs to ache, but I don't care. I never want him to let go. He kisses my temple, murmuring, "They're going to realize you aren't in the vehicle soon and come looking for us. We need to make a decision, Kricket." He loosens his arms around me. His hand moves to my chin, tipping it up so our eyes meet. His wary look speaks volumes. "We're both wanted for treason. If we plan to survive, we'll need to leave the Ship of Skye."

"If we do that, what happens to Jax and Wayra?" I ask.

He shakes his head. "They die," he answers in no uncertain terms. "They'll never let them out of their cells. If this ship goes down, they go with it. If it doesn't, they'll be executed for treason."

"I won't leave without them! I won't let them die unable to defend themselves!"

It's in his eyes: Trey can't leave them here, either. "I agree. It's up to us to get them out." He bends down and kisses me. I'm overwhelmed by the potency of his nearness. My knees weaken.

He must feel it because he lifts me up in his arms, allowing my head to rest on his shoulder. Carrying me over the shattered glass and debris that litter the floor, he moves in the direction of a bank of overups that lie open not far away. The fem-bot warning continues to sound, "All active-duty personnel . . ."

Behind us, wind stirs the glass on the floor, causing me to glance over Trey's shoulder. In the gap in the window, the outline of the E-One throws a long shadow upon us. I stiffen in Trey's arms, causing him to pause and look behind him as well.

The static snap of high-intensity electricity sizzles the air near the E-One. Trey turns away from the heli-vehicle and dives with me in his arms. We land behind a concrete pillar; Trey flattens us against it. The crackle of a lightning strike branches out from the E-One with bright, webbed fingers; it glows golden, raising the hair on my neck as it misses our entwined bodies by mere inches. Closing my eyes, my hair whips up around me while the fem-bot voice short-circuits.

After the shock dissipates, Trey's mouth brushes my ear as he asks, "Can you run?" I nod. He puts me on my feet. "When I tell you to, run toward the overups." I nod again. Trey peeks around the pillar for a moment, his strong hand gripping my forearm. "Now, Kricket! Go, go!" He urges me to move toward a grouping of elevator-like doors ahead of us. Behind us, more windows crash in, shattering as Alameeda troops rappel in with jet packs attached to their backs.

We near an overup and Trey practically throws me into it. I hit the back of the lift, holding out my hands against the jarring force. It knocks me to my knees. I shift to fall on my hip in a heap, staring back at the overup doors, willing them to close. Through the small opening, I recognize Kyon. Attired in full black combat armor and a dark helmet, his visor hides his blue eyes. I know it's him though by the shape of his strong jaw—the cut of his elegant cheekbones. When he turns his head toward me, fear makes my legs weak.

"Kricket!" Kyon yells, coming right at us. One of Kyon's fellow soldiers accompanies him. They fly forward; smoky trails of white vapor expel behind their jet packs, forming waving kite tails of exhaust. Kyon has his weapon trained on me; he can kill me anytime he likes. Instead, he shifts the barrel of it at the soldier flying in front of him who also has a weapon trained upon me.

A blue laser dots my chest. My hands come up as I flinch. "Don't!" I yell at the soldier, his finger squeezing the trigger of his weapon.

Kyon fires first. A blue laser blast hits the Alameeda soldier in the arm; it shatters his armor, taking a huge chunk out of his bicep. He spirals forward, cutting Kyon off, propelled by his jet pack. His blood paints the cage of the overup as he crashes into the compartment with us. The doors roll closed right before Kyon can enter.

The overup drops. Trey growls and grasps the Alameeda soldier's laser weapon, turning it on him. Trey fires before his enemy can lift his other weapon from the holster on his hip. The impact of the blast to his chest sends the soldier crashing into the wall of the overup. With his breastplate and skin melted away, his heart lies open to me before he falls forward facedown onto the floor.

My arms are dead weights; I stare at his unmoving corpse. Panting and staggering to the panel on the wall, Trey swipes holographic buttons. The overup goes sideways, and then slantways before it falls again in a rapid descent.

"We need to get his Riker Pak off," Trey says, indicating the corpse on the floor. I stoop down with him. He lifts a panel to a compartment; inside, several buttons blink and glow. He presses a button on the jet pack, and the harness unlatches and retracts off the dead Alameeda soldier. The pack weighs a ton; we both have to lift it together. Helping him position the heavy pack near his back, he reaches around, pressing a button. Automatically, a harness winds out of the jet pack and secures itself to Trey's back. He flips a switch in the pack, and it emits a low hum, propelling itself upward so that he no longer has to hold it up.

"Check and see if he has a pinpointer." Trey gestures over his shoulder with his thumb.

"I don't know what that is," I say in an apologetic tone.

"A pinpointer is a homing beacon. The Alameeda can use it to track us. Here, tell me if you see anything blinking."

The jet pack has two fuselagelike projections that make up its oblong shape. Two separate video screens with digital readouts flank the sides of the propulsion system. Everywhere lights blink and flash with different colors and shapes.

All of my fingers spread wide as I jerk my hands. "The whole thing is blinking!" I respond.

"It's okay; I found it." His deep, rumbling voice answers as he turns around to face me, yanking a glowing yellow disk from one of the harness straps. He drops it on the floor, crushing it beneath his black-booted foot.

The overup shakes as something lands on the ceiling of it. Both our heads snap upward. A red-glowing outline mars the ceiling, turning it aflame. Melting metal drips down to dot the floor, causing me to press to the side of the lift. Kyon's voice sounds through the ceiling, "Allairis, leave her in this transport now and I'll let you live."

"I need the navigation system," Trey says calmly, his eyes on the ceiling as he points his weapon in the same direction. "Can you get it for me, Kitten?" He gestures to the helmet on the dead guy's head. Grimacing, I reach down and pull the black shell off our enemy's blond hair. Examining the helmet, I notice blue-font readouts on the interior of the visor.

Trey plucks the helmet from my hands, squashing it onto his head; it automatically takes the shape of his cranium, negating the need for a chinstrap. He moves to the wall panel once more, waving his fingers over several holographic buttons. The overup comes to an immediate stop. The doors roll open to a parking garage of sorts. Row upon row of hoverbikes, like the ones that Trey used to extract me from the palace, are stored here.

Kyon's roar from above has my eyes on the ceiling once more. He's having a hard time cutting through the thick metal. His frustration is clear as he shouts, "Kricket! If you make me chase you again, I *will* kill him!"

The blood drains from my face. My eyes look to Trey.

"Please come here," Trey asks, holding his hand out to me.

I take it and he tugs me to him. Turning me around to face away from him, a blue glowing belt of the jet pack wraps around my waist and shoulders, securing me in front of him.

In my ear, Trey murmurs, "According to my guidance systems, the detention center is fifty stories below us in the arc of the ship. Are you ready?" He powers up the jet pack on his back. My feet leave the ground as we hover for a moment in the air. "Do you still want to do this?"

"Yes," I state without a hint of doubt.

His whispering voice is soft upon the shell of my ear, "If this doesn't work out for us, Kricket, know that I've loved you from the moment I held you in my arms on Ethar, and every moment in between. I will love you even after my final breath."

Warmth travels through my veins until I realize he's making sure to say good-bye to me. My heart recoils with a savage ache. Lifting my hand, I cup Trey's cheek, feeling the light stubble on it. As I turn my lips to his ear, I murmur, "Know that if this doesn't work out, your job is to stay alive until I can bend time and manipulate the future to bring you back to me."

My fingers feel his smile as he murmurs, "And just when I thought I couldn't love you more . . ." Taking my fingers from his cheek, he kisses them before wrapping his arm around my waist.

We rocket from between the doors of the lift, entering into an open area several stories high. There are tiers of every type of hover vehicle here, waiting to be claimed. Trey takes a winding tunnel supported by concrete columns; my hair flies behind me and I lose my stomach. Every sound is muted except the beat of my heart. Terrified that we'll crash into something—that we won't make it—I soon forget my nervousness about jet-pack travel when the greater threat, in the form of another bomb, hits the Ship of Skye. Around me, the walls tremble; pieces of the ceiling crumble away, covering my hair with a fine powder as the hovercars shift.

From behind us, a laser shot obliterates a support column in front of us. Rock dust spews out at us, choking our air. Avoiding a falling pillar shattered by the pursuing Alameeda, we swipe the wall flanking us. We ricochet. Twisting, Trey maneuvers us so that the jet pack skims the ground. As we fly upside down on our backs, Kyon is able to fly above us. He dives down, trying to release the belt of my harness. I kick up at him to make it harder for him to get me, but my bare feet don't make much of an impression on him.

Trey waits until the last possible moment to make a sharp turn, leaving Kyon raging in the wrong direction. We branch off into a different corridor. The severe angle of our turn causes us to bounce against the wall. Ricocheting, he fights to keeps us from crashing into the adjacent wall. We flip around once more so that I'm again beneath him. When we pass the next rows of columns in the tunnel, Trey aims his stolen Alameeda weapon, shooting at the stone supports. The ceiling above us begins to collapse, bringing down debris and mortar, blocking the path behind us—cutting off the Alameeda Strikers following us. We take several more turns in an attempt to lose Kyon and the Alameeda soldiers for good, angling toward an enormous pillar in the parking garage that's wreathed by guardrails.

"Clutch yourself," Trey growls in my ear.

While I try to figure out what he means by that, I look for something to hang on to, but there's nothing but air between my fingers. We swoop over the guardrail so fast it seems inevitable that we'll hit the vertical support column rapidly approaching. I put up my hands to shield my face, even though I know it'll do no good.

At the last possible second, a warning signal on the jet pack beeps loudly: *dee dee dee, dee dee dee.* It activates some sort of preservation protocol in the engine, cutting the power to the forward thruster. The jet-pack engine flips the thruster from forward to reverse. We slow up. Trey kills the power completely and we drop, abruptly changing direction. Falling headfirst through the open-air gap between where the floor ends and the support column begins, I do, indeed, clutch myself; my arms crisscross in front of me, circling my waist. The power to the pack is reengaged, and we plummet toward the belly of the ship at a breakneck pace.

We plunge several stories, and the light dims the farther down we fly. When we reach a junction illuminated by white fluorescent lights, we turn like gulls in the wind, soaring through a long tunnel. We travel until our shadows settle on large chamber doors ahead of us; thick and steel, they scream all of the reasons to stay away.

Touching down on a platform in front of the dull-hued doors, the jet-pack engine ceases firing. The whine of sirens is muffled here, several stories below the surface of the ship. The flashing of amber lights is all too apparent, though, turning our pale faces from ghostly to sickly in intermittent intervals. A fem-bot voice advises, "All non-essential Detention Center personnel are ordered to Code Amber stations at the surface of Skye. Defensive protocol: Vector Six. All nonessential Detention Center personnel—"

Trey releases me from the harness; it disappears into the jet pack along with his restraint. He shrugs off the jet pack, and it clatters to the deck with a loud noise. "Most of the Detention Center personnel are being ordered to battle stations," he whispers as he clutches my upper arms to steady me. "They'll be operating with a skeleton crew."

"That's good for us," I murmur.

A wary scowl crosses his lips. "You're my prisoner. Do you think you can sell it?" He subtly nods his head in the direction of the imposing doors, and then he shakes me roughly. It's not painful, only disorienting, as I lose my feet and stumble while he holds me up.

When he pulls me almost nose to nose to him with his hand balled in the front of my jacket, I glare at him in mock anger and murmur, "We don't even need a pencil to draw them in, honey."

"I love you," he says under his breath.

He yanks me into the pools of spotlights in front of the edifice. The light becomes brighter, causing me to shield my eyes. The portal in front of us becomes translucent, revealing a checkpoint with mounted guns and an admissions area manned by only two worried-looking Brigadets. "State your business," a voice pipes through the communicator located above the trigger of the doors. A heavily armed Brigadet approaches the barrier between us. Trey lets go of the front of my jacket. He straightens his Brigadet uniform shirt.

"Let us in. I've located your escaped prisoner." He gestures to me, swiping my hair farther away from the already fallen cowl of my red cloak. Pale strands of it spill forward to drape my shoulders, exposing my Alameeda heritage to them. "I'm being pursued by Alameeda Strikers." He points his thumb over his shoulder at the empty tunnel behind us. "They're attempting to recover their spy. I've been charged to remand her back to your custody," he lies, trying to hide the strain in his voice from them.

"Where'd you find her?" the soldier says as he scrambles forward.

"The Beezway. The Alameeda destroyed the west end of the transfer tunnel. We just made it out," Trey answers honestly.

The sentinel activates a hatch door beneath my feet, causing me to fall into a chute when the ground gives way beneath me. My arms are flung above my head. Air propels me rapidly through a cylindrical tube, forcing me under the barrier. I emerge on the other side of the doors, but I'm trapped within a clear gerbil-style cage. My gasping, frantic breath fogs the transparency of the walls as I press my hands against the box restraining me.

Trey is left standing on the platform outside the door. His eyes search for me immediately. "Let me in!" he insists with a troubled frown from his lone position outside the gate. "I'm dead if you leave me out here!"

"I've been ordered not to admit unauthorized personnel. Most of our detail has been relocated by the Amber Code," the Brigadet explains unapologetically. "We're operating on lockdown here."

From behind Trey, a firework of blue light explodes. His shoulders round while his hands come up to protect his head. Laser fire ricochets off the once-steel-looking screen that separates Trey from the sanctuary of the detention area. At the other end of the tunnel behind Trey, Kyon and several other Alameeda Strikers with Riker jet packs come into view; they show no fear of the defensive guns that automatically return fire upon them. Blue bubble-shields that look to be made of light form around the Alameeda Strikers, deflecting the lethal Brigadet laser light from penetrating their targets, acting as a force field against it.

Trey turns and fires on them too. Finding his efforts useless, he backs away from the onslaught of Alameeda. Pounding his hand against the barrier, he screams at the guards, "Open the gate!"

Confusion shows on the Brigadet's face, but he acquiesces, moving to the console on the wall again. The floor beneath Trey opens, sucking him into it before the hole evaporates once more. Next to me in a separate, transparent cage, Trey jets upward, filling the space like sausage meat. "Let me out," Trey urges them. "You need my help to defend against them."

The Brigadet moves to release Trey from his hollow pillar prison. The moment the tube surrounding him retracts into the floor, Trey raises the weapon in his hand and fires a shot at the Brigadet. Electricity pulses in yellow light over the guard's body, driving him to his knees before he falls forward on his face. Trey immediately lifts his gun to the other two soldiers; before they can react, he pumps them full of energy that makes them fall to the floor, twitching like fish out of water—tased but not dead.

Running to the panel near my restraining tube, Trey deactivates it. The cage retracts into the floor, allowing me to leave its claustrophobic atmosphere. Breathing deeply, I jump down from the platform that separates me from Trey. I look toward the barrier, and Kyon is there, watching me. He lifts the mirrored visor on his navigation helmet, showing me his piercing blue eyes. I shiver at their intensity.

"Stop," I whisper. "Please."

No, Kyon mouths back before he gnashes his teeth. His eyes search the barrier for a way inside.

Trey doesn't notice our exchange. He clutches my shoulder, forcing me to turn away from Kyon and follow him out of the open door on the opposite side of the admission area.

We emerge onto a grate-floored catwalk, our footsteps echoing in the cylindrical hivelike arena surrounding us. All of the aisles join together in star formations. Amid each star, there are hundreds of mirror-reflected shiny orbs; they're moored above an abyss of prison levels that go on for miles beneath us. Thousands upon thousands of stacked hexagon cells form a grim honeypot.

Jax, Wayra, and my other Cavar bodyguards are in those cells, but which ones? I wonder, as we make our way over the grated bridge toward a large metallic orb. Emerging from a sliding door in the mirrored orb chamber, a soldier lifts his weapon to defend his position. Trey is a better shot; he drops the soldier with a stunning burst of electricity.

Jumping over the incapacitated soldier, Trey enters the chamber of the orb through its open door. Another Brigadet rises from his seat at a holographic panel of controls in order to ward off Trey's attack, but he's dropped to the floor in short order by a blow from Trey's fist.

Once we're inside the orb, the controls and holographic screens indicate that the orb is a craft of some kind. Trey drags the unconscious soldier out of the control room and onto the catwalk. When he returns, he goes directly to the holographic console and gazes intently at the screen of readouts in front of him. Within moments he says, "I found them."

"How'd you do that?" I ask in awe and disbelief.

"I'm a Cavar," he replies with hubris. "They're on level four ipsacore in section twenty-two."

"How do we get to them?"

Trey scans the hologram, sliding moveable icons around a grid-like screen. The door of the control orb closes. The catwalks that attach to the orb retract, unmooring it. The orb falls from its position at the top of the hive. Descending several stories, the orb slows and fits itself through a narrow, silver tunnel of light to the left. Like a silver ball in a pinball machine, we glide along to another sector. Shooting out into a separate stack of cells, I notice the mark of section 22. The orb floats to the middle of the sector and hovers there. Grated catwalks expand from bridgelike walkways that line the fronts of the cells. When the star pattern of bridges moves to connect to the orb, Trey slides the door to the orb open.

"Which ones are they in?" I ask.

His hands rapidly conduct an orchestra of information on the holographic screen, pulling out its secrets from within the control module. Wayra's face flashes up on the screen, and then Jax's. I feel tears sting my eyes.

"That's them," I exhale.

"They're all clustered in the same area—south." He points behind us. "You need a slipshield to help me unlock the cells. Here." Trey finesses more holographic buttons. A small panel in the control console opens and emits a clear sticker that resembles the symbol on a USB port. He takes the small patch and peels it from the backing like one would an electrode. He grabs my hand, turning it palm up before sticking the tattoolike symbol to the skin over my wrist. I examine it: it's created from a gel-like substance with wires embedded in it. "That slipshield will unlock the cell door when you scan it. The system will consider you a guard."

The silver orb transport pod slows until it hovers in the open-aired space beyond the grated catwalks. After Trey manipulates more icons on the holographic screen, a docking catwalk slides out to our transport, attaching itself to the lip beneath the door. Trey rises from the control seat and takes my hand. He leads me to the door and opens it. He scans the area outside for Brigadets, but there seems to be no one about at the moment. He tugs gently on my hand, and we exit the pod through the open door. Trey takes the catwalk that leads to the southern grated walkway. I follow him, running with my face turned toward a row of empty cells as I scan them one by one, looking for my friends.

Trey comes to a halt in front of a cell. I peer into it and find Jax sitting on his cot looking forlorn. When he sees us, he jolts to his feet. He shouts something, but we can't hear him at all through the barrier. As a bewildered smile forms on Jax's haggard face, Trey immediately moves to the console near his cell, working the slipshield to free him.

I move around Trey to the cell next to Jax's and find Wayra. He's doing push-ups in the middle of the floor. His powerful back is covered in bruises and burn marks. I wince as my stomach twists. The assault against him is clear—they think he's a traitor, because he insisted upon protecting me.

Going to the panel on the side of the cell, I square my shoulders. He'd hate any show of sympathy or remorse, so I activate the intercom and ask, "Are you done with your set? Can we go now?"

Wayra pauses in midpush; his face lifts to see me at the mouth of his cell. One eye is swollen and he has bruising around his jaw. He gets to his feet, wiping at sweat rolling down his face with his forearm as he walks unhurriedly to the clear barrier between us. "Poison, Kricket?" He shakes his head like he disapproves. "You're not a very good assassin. This is the second time you've failed to kill the target. It's becoming a pattern with you. We're going to have to work on it."

The Brigadets must have told him what I did—maybe while they were interrogating him? I shrug as I swipe my wrist beneath the console's scanner. The barrier between us disappears, freeing him. "The poison was more of a warning."

"In that case, it was a strong message," he remarks with approval.

"I really meant it," I admit as I crane my neck back so that I can see his face as he steps in front of me.

He picks me up and hugs me to him. I expect him to crush me because he's so big, but he surprises me by treating me like I'm fragile. "I thought they drowned you," he says.

I rest my cheek against his shoulder. "I think they almost did. I need to learn how to swim soon."

"We'll make it a priority," he replies, setting me back on my feet.

Trey hasn't paused in his mission to free the other Cavars. In short order, Hollis, Drex, Dylan, Gibon, and Fenton emerge from their cells. They're all disheveled messes, each having endured some form of abuse.

Jax grasps my chin gently, turning my face so that he can scan it. His frown makes me wary. "What?" I ask.

"You've been beaten." It's not a question. "Are you in pain?"

I've been beaten? I gently pull my chin from his grasp. "No," I answer. "I was when I woke up, but I'm not now. Why do you—why do you think I was beaten?"

"Kricket, you're bruised and battered," Jax replies with the kind of gentleness that I've never found in anyone else.

The urgency in Wayra's voice, as he walks to Trey, distracts me from Jax. "There's a guard pod at the end of this catwalk," Wayra says, pointing his chin in that direction. "They have emergency evacuation protocols. If we can get in, we can infiltrate the system and open all of these cells. If we let everyone out, we'll have a better chance of getting out of here—safety in numbers." He looks around, his eyes rising to the hundreds of stacked cells surrounding us.

"Will they shoot us if they find us escaping?"

"On sight," Wayra replies.

Trey hands Wayra one of the guns he'd confiscated from the Alameeda Striker on the overup. "Take this. They'll have a stockpile of weapons there. We'll need them to gain our release. Is everyone up for the mission?" Trey asks each of them.

In unison, they each respond, "Sir."

Trey nods toward me. "Kricket and I will remain here with the transport and map an escape route out," he says, indicating the silver orb that brought us here. He hands Jax his other gun. Jax takes it, running his hand over the Alameeda weapon and checking its load. "Signal me with that if you need an extraction. Otherwise, meet back here upon completion."

"Baw-da-baw," Wayra says with a roguish smile.

The unit of Cavars goes in the direction Wayra indicated earlier. Trey walks to my side. Gently he takes my arm, leading me over the catwalk back to the shiny silver transport pod. He stops near the opening of the transport and hands me into it. I lean against the entranceway next to him, nervously looking around for Brigadets.

There aren't any. This section is desolate. They isolated us from the general population for a reason. Now, with the Brigadets all on the surface fighting the Alameeda, the place is a tomb.

Chewing my bottom lip, I jump when Trey leans near me, murmuring, "They told me you died." I hesitate, glancing at him. He has a hollow look. He anxiously rakes me with his eyes, as if he doesn't believe it's really me.

"When?" I ask. I have a desert in my mouth; I try to swallow past the lump of sand in my throat.

"When they took you from my cell. They taunted me with it—they told me you drowned."

"Did you believe them?" I ask.

He grimaces. "No. Yes. No. I went back and forth. I don't know which was worse." My eyes widen as he adds, "I knew what could happen to you if you survived." Now his look is sorrowful.

"Nothing happened," I reply, but I know what I just said is untrue. I can't remember the last couple of days. I woke up and it was Fitzmartin—Wednesday. I've lost time. A deep ache forms in the pit of my stomach.

"Something did happen, Kricket," he replies. "It started soon after you were taken from your cell."

"What started?"

"After I escaped, I looked for you. I hacked the Ship of Skye main systems. The location and surveillance of your interrogation was encrypted with a security code I couldn't decipher without some of my more advanced programs. I didn't have access to the tools I needed to find you—they were stored in my wrist communicator." He holds up his wrist to show me his watchlike device. "I had to get it back, but it was in my apartment. I'd dropped it when they came to arrest us." I remember him taking off his wrist communicator so he could use it to help me focus on trying to project into the future. "I couldn't infiltrate the system to look for you until I retrieved it.

It took me several parts—my apartment was being guarded—they were looking for me. When I did get it back, and I was able to scan the system for you, I found their recording of the interrogation sessions with you in the ship's database—"

I shake my head. "I . . . I don't remember anything—I only became conscious a few hours ago—I mean *parts* ago."

His expression turns angry. "I don't know if I saw all of it—if there were more sessions—but I saw enough. I heard your screams—they tortured you, Kricket."

I shake my head in denial. "I would remember—"

"Turn around. Let me see your back," he orders, his lips flattening in a grim line.

"My back?" I ask numbly.

"Yes. Show me your back. Lift your shirt."

Slowly, I turn around in the doorway of the silver transport. I stare over the metal guard railing ahead of me. It'd be a long fall to the bottom of the detention area should I slip over it. I let the red trench coat slide off my shoulder. Pulling back the collar of my shirt, I hear Trey's intake of breath. I glance over my shoulder at my exposed skin and see a thick bruise that's turning from black to yellow. It looks like it was really bad at one time, but it's healing now. Abruptly, I pull my collar back up and cover my shirt with the red trench coat once more.

I shake my head slowly, trying to clear the fog from it. "I don't know how that happened. I've been trying to escape—the dishery—" I turn back around to face him.

"They used hallucinogens mostly—drugs—when they questioned you, so that's probably why you don't remember it," he interrupts. "When you didn't answer a question, you were struck."

I blanch and ask, "What did I say?"

"You spoke about Earth—mostly—and me," he replies solemnly.

"Oh," I murmur, unable to come up with a suitable reply.

"At one point, I thought they killed you," Trey confesses in a rough voice.

I shake my head again, trying to think. "No. Not yet." I don't meet his eyes because I might cry if I do. Instead, I laugh; it doesn't contain a hint of humor, though. "Despite their best efforts, I've managed to outlive my expiration date. If it's any consolation, most of them are getting pounded by the Alameeda now."

"It isn't, but if it's any consolation to you, the one who beat you is dead."

"He's dead? How?" My voice shakes. I can't help it.

"I couldn't find where you had been taken after the interrogation, but I located Rutledge's apartment."

"Rutledge—the Brigadet guard who brought me to my cell?"

Trey nods. His voice hardens as he says, "He was on the recordings of your interrogation. He was easy to find. He wept when he told me he didn't know where Geteron had taken you after he'd interrogated you. Rutledge didn't live long after that."

My body turns toward Trey's, instantly straightening from its stooped posture in total awareness of him. Without hesitation, Trey takes me in his arms; one of his hands extends to the nape of my neck while the other snakes around my waist. He weaves his fingers in my hair, pulling me to him possessively. His nose brushes the column of my throat to my ear as he breathes me in. The gentle, masculine scent of him envelops me. My own breath catches; every nerve ending within me reacts to him at once. Warmth curls through me all the way to my toes. I'm suddenly weak, and my knees bend. I lean into his rigid chest, melting against him.

Something in my own chest tightens as my respiration becomes fluttery. My fingers dig into his strong biceps, looking for support. It's there; his arm tightens around my waist, holding me up now. "Trey," I say breathlessly. He must notice, but he continues to nuzzle my neck as if he's unaware of the exquisite havoc he's creating inside of me. His mouth shifts to my temple, kissing it tenderly. "I'm sorry," I murmur. Trey pauses. He scans my face, trying to read it. "If it weren't for me, this would never have happened to you. It's because of me—I was never welcome here," I manage to say.

Trey tenses. In the same soothing tone that he used before, however, he murmurs, "*We* were never welcome here—"

"It's because of what I am. There's too much history for some of them—people like Telek. To him, I'll only ever be Alameeda—his enemy."

"Then I'm their enemy," he growls. "I'll kill anyone who tries to hurt you again." It's a simple statement of fact, but one that soothes some of the ache in me. With his hand on my back, Trey holds me to him. I wrap my arms around the nape of his neck. Leaning down, he kisses me. His voice is raw as he confesses against my lips, "I thought I'd never see you again." He uses both his hands to cup my face. When he looks in my eyes again, his thumb traces my bottom lip. His other hand draws a path over my cheek, then skims down my body as he bends and kisses me again.

Color infuses my skin while his tongue strokes mine. The breathless feeling I had is gone, replaced by my increased respiration and a building sense of need within me for more. He raises his head so that his lips are just above mine. "Do you know what I thought about after they took you away?"

"No."

"I thought about all the opportunities I allowed to pass without showing you what you mean to me. I'm not going to make that mistake anymore."

"You're not?" I rest my forehead to his lips.

He murmurs against my skin. "No, I'm not." He moves; his nose skims down against mine in an intimate caress. "I can't ever feel that way again."

"What way?"

"The way I felt when I thought you were gone forever," he answers harshly. "I'll do whatever I have to do so that never happens again." He kisses me. When he stops, I feel needy, burning for their return.

As I reach my hand to brush Trey's hair back from his brow, an arm wraps around me from behind. It rips me away from Trey, squeezing the air from my lungs. I'm seized by another arm around my waist and pulled from the doorway of the silver transport orb. A jet-pack-clad Alameeda Striker clutches me to his chest as we rocket upward. The soldier holds me above Trey's head for a moment, hovering in midair, before he flies with me over the catwalk and metal railing into the open-air abyss.

Dangling me in the middle of a coliseum of detention cells, my feet stop kicking him as I look down. Panic seizes me. *If he drops me, I'm dead; the fall goes on for several hundred stories!* I whimper.

Another Alameeda Striker joins us. I can't see the soldier's eyes, concealed as they are behind the mirrored navigation visor of his helmet, but his wide, pearly-white grin speaks volumes. "You found her!"

"It'll mean a commendation for sure—for both of us!" the one holding me says near my ear.

Distracted as the soldiers are by me, neither one of them is paying any attention to Trey. As I lift my chin and look toward the catwalk, Trey lunges forward, leaping into the air. He plants one of his feet on the bottom rung of the metal railing and steps up, his other foot touching the top rail. Pushing off, he jumps toward the idling Alameeda soldier near to us. Sensing Trey's movement, the soldier in front of me tries to raise his weapon at the last moment, but he doesn't have time. The back of Trey's knee wraps around the Striker's throat, snapping his neck, while pulling him down into a horizontal position. Trey tears the navigation helmet from off the dead soldier's head, placing it on his own. The limp Striker turns over on his back. Trey lands with both feet on the Striker's supine chest. He widens his stance on his enemy, riding the jet-pack-clad corpse like a skateboard.

Then Trey grabs the Alameeda gun and brings it up to his shoulder. He aims near my head, firing a blue laser strike over my shoulder. I feel a jolt as the soldier behind me is struck in the face. His head snaps back and his arms loosen around me. I slip from his arms, falling toward the bottom of the ship as he flies upward.

In the next instant, I'm caught by Trey. He clutches me to his chest with his arm beneath my legs. The jet pack beneath the dead soldier at his feet makes a turn, and we surf back to the railing of the catwalk, navigated by the helmet on Trey's head. Once we're there, Trey lifts me over the railing, placing me on the grated metal pathway. After he lets me go, he pulls himself over the railing as well to join me.

Peeling the helmet from his head, he tosses it over the side. Striding to me, his large, rough hand grasps mine once more, before he gazes down into my stunned eyes. "Are you okay?" he asks urgently.

I nod my head, unsure of my ability to speak. All at once, the walls of the cells surrounding us evaporate. Trey looks around, "They did it, Kricket. It's time to go." He pulls me back in the direction of the silver transport orb.

Coming around the arch of the catwalk, we run into a battle between more jet-pack-clad Strikers and a recently liberated contingent of Rafe's most wanted, whom the Cavars have freed from another section of the detention center. The Alameeda birds with blue, fiery OMS tails rise above our catwalk, diving and firing upon the hive dwellers, scattering them. Swarms of freed prisoners rush about, mingling with the Cavars that were once my bodyguards.

I spot Jax fending off an inauspicious Alameeda birdman. Trey drops my hand. With the gun he took from the soldier he killed, he takes aim and shoots the Alameeda Striker harassing Jax. He doesn't stop shooting but picks off several more Alameeda; their jet packs go berserk, flying off in every direction as their navigation is skewed.

"Stay behind me," Trey orders. He moves along the catwalk, killing enemy soldiers with exacting accuracy; he never misses. I keep my hand on his strong back; his muscles bunch and strain beneath my palm.

Without warning, Kyon drops down behind me, forcing me out of his way. I fall against the metal railing, my ribs aching as I hurt that tender spot once again. Trey glances at us over his shoulder, but before he can react, Kyon lifts him up off his feet and throws him over the side of the catwalk. I scream as Trey falls from sight. My knees buckle and I kneel before Kyon on the catwalk in stunned agony with my hand clutched to my side.

"My little savage," Kyon murmurs, raising his mirrored visor so that I see the wicked gleam in his eyes, "have I finally brought you to heel?"

CHAPTER 8
BENEATH THE CLOUDS

Kyon lifts me from my knees, pulling me to him. I look up; the dark tattoo circles on his neck wink at me, watching me like a many-eyed beast within. I can't answer him; I'm incapable of speech. His eyes darken at my expression. I must be very pale; my heart hardly beats. He clutches me tighter. "If you'd learn to obey me, you wouldn't have to witness this. I'd have protected you from it." I don't respond—nothing works in me at the moment. After a few seconds, Kyon picks up on my unhinged state. He frowns and growls, "You shouldn't be here at all. I'll see you home."

Home? Who's home? What home? I think, but it's all a jumble in my mind. My worst thoughts were just realized. *Trey's gone—over the edge—I never saw it coming.*

Kyon doesn't release me. He drops his visor over his eyes before he bends and leans toward me. He activates the harness of his jet pack, and belts snake out of it like sidewinders, wrapping around me and securing me to him. As he straightens, my feet leave the ground. I can't see anything; I'm pinned to him, facing his chest. His scent is everywhere—it wouldn't be an unpleasant smell, except I associate it with him, so now it's like I'm smelling raw fear. It makes my stomach ache. *Trey's dead.*

I turn my face, attempting to breathe in deep gulps of air to the side of us, but instead, I retch. I heave again, but nothing comes up; there's nothing in me to expel. I try to hold back my choking gags, but I can't. Kyon notices that I'm ill. He reaches down and extracts a sharp dagger from the outer sheath on his black boot. Quickly using it, he slices off my hair below the base of my skull. Instantly, my hair regrows and my queasiness lessens. He strokes the blond waves of my hair gently, murmuring, "Better?"

I stop trembling and my nausea ebbs a little, but I shake my head with a grim expression, denying that anything can ever be better again. He says nothing more but replaces his dagger in his boot before straightening. He signals to a few Strikers near him. They snap to his command, coming nearer to us. Kyon's eyes are fixed upward.

I turn my face to the side again, needing to breathe. From underneath Kyon's arm, I spy an Alameeda Striker rise from the level below our catwalk. His head lolls forward, arterial blood pumping down from his slit throat. I recognize Trey, latched onto the Striker; he's piggybacking the dead Alameeda soldier. A navigation helmet covers Trey's head; the mirrored visor denies me a glimpse of his beautiful eyes. With one hand, he aims the confiscated Alameeda gun at Kyon and pulls the trigger.

A blue bubble-shield activates as the laser strikes near Kyon's head; the bubble-shield repels the shot, causing it to bounce off. Kyon turns so that I have to move my head again to see Trey. With a gesture, Kyon orders his escorts to move on Trey.

In the very next instant, my hair slicks back from my face as Kyon and I launch straight up from the catwalk. Passing thousands of empty cells on our way to the surface of the ship, they become a blur as I struggle to focus. Casting my eyes downward, Trey and the Strikers become smaller and smaller until we pass through a connecting tunnel, leaving them behind.

❦

I must have lost consciousness, because the next thing I know I'm being jostled from the jet pack harness and caught up in Kyon's arms. He holds me to the black Kevlar-like armor that covers his chest. He calls out, "Curer! I need a curer!"

He lays me down on a cool floor. The sound of running feet and the buzz of voices sway around me. Kyon takes off the jet pack from his back; he bends again to pick me up in his arms. Someone leans near my face, shining light into my eye. "She has violet eyes," a male voice murmurs above me. I try focusing on him, but I just see flares of light.

Kyon ignores his observation. "Where's the med-station? She's ill."

"This way—I'm a curer," he says. We move at a clipped pace, my head lolling against Kyon's broad chest. I open my eyes, trying to regain my wits; I can't keep them open. Shapes and colors move around me until I feel myself being lowered onto a soft cushion. My cheek lies close to the edge; I'm on some kind of hover cot in a partitioned area. Next to me, a bandaged Alameeda soldier lies unconscious and still on his floating bullet-shaped bed.

"Who is she?" the male voice asks.

"She's why we're here. Find out what's wrong with her and fix it."

"Yes, Brother Kyon," the male responds with a military tone, knowing exactly who Kyon is. I feel a dull pain stick my arm. The blond male hovering over me says, "I've injected her with nanobots. They'll circulate in her bloodstream. I should know what ails her momentarily."

"I've cut her hair twice in the span of less than a few parts. Nothing should be ailing her," Kyon says, and he sounds worried. *About me?*

"Is she the rogue priestess? The one we've come to rescue?"

"She is. She's also my intended consort," Kyon says between his teeth. "If she dies, I will make sure you follow not far behind her."

All business now, the curer responds with a clinical tone, "We can't assume her physiology is exactly like that of other priestesses. She deviates from the norm with her impure Rafian DNA. She needs to be studied."

"Your only concern should be in keeping her alive. As I said before, your life depends upon it."

There's a pause while the curer scrutinizes a handheld gadget as it makes sporadic blips and beeps in his hands. He exhales a breath. "She's dehydrated. Cutting her hair wouldn't solve that. Her electrolytes are depleted and she's anemic—when was the last time she has eaten?"

"I don't know," Kyon says sullenly.

The curer clucks his tongue in a shaming way. "As her intended consort, it's your job to know. She has an abnormal amount of adrenaline in her bloodstream. Has she suffered a shock of some kind?"

Kyon grabs him by the throat. In a sinister voice, he says, "Rehydrate her and give her a nutrition supplement."

"Right away," the curer rasps. When Kyon releases him, the Alameeda medic gets up from his knees next to me and hurries away.

Kyon sits beside me on the floating cot; the fingers of his hand brush mine once, but he doesn't move to entwine them. His touch is feather-light, almost wistful. "We'll be home soon. It's peaceful there—on the Loch of Cerulean. You'll be safe. I'll train you to obey me so this never happens again."

I bite my tongue. He moves his hand away from mine when the curer returns.

"This is a rehyde-pack," the curer explains, holding up a chrome cylinder the size of his palm. It's time-release." He holds the cylinder against my skin. From the bottom of the tube, a small, needlelike tail elongates before it digs into my skin, finding my vein. "She should be fine as soon as this runs its course."

"How long?" Kyon questions him.

He shrugs. "Less than a part."

I struggle to bring their faces into focus. My cheek moves on the cushion, finding a cool spot. I try to see where we are. It takes me a second to recognize the saber-toothed open mouth of the saer-shaped carved columns above me that line the gallery. I'm in the rail station of the Premiere Palisade Building. My eyes search for the staircase that leads up to the gallery. When I locate the stairs, I realize where they go: to the skywalk over the reservoir—to Trey's building—to his apartment.

I begin to feel more lucid as I process that the whole place is crawling with Alameeda soldiers. They're using this area as a base of operations. Troops cluster around officers who are using the station's holograms to study the aerial combat maneuvers taking place outside in the airspace above our position. My eyes move on to just beyond them, falling upon a pile of bloody bodies pushed into a heap in the corner—not one of which has blond hair. Panic hits me and with it comes the urge to vomit again.

My head rises from the cot; I turn away from the dead, finding Kyon's blue eyes watching me. I let mine slip out of focus. Feigning the panic of delirium, I whimper, "Don't lose the white rabbit! We have to follow him!" I allow my head to rest upon the cushion again.

"Eh?" the curer says beside me, his fascination with me piqued. "What's a rabbit?" he asks Kyon, who glowers at him in response.

Coldness seeps beneath my skin. I begin to shiver uncontrollably, but I'm okay with it because it makes me sound more credibly incoherent. "You killed Kenny," I groan with my lips chattering, "you bastard . . ."

Kyon scowls at the curer, who immediately says, "The shivering is normal. It's standard with rehydration—it lowers her body temperature. Her delirium should end quickly." The medic pats my arm. Kyon glares at his hand on me, and it is quickly removed. The medic uses his hand instead to wipe his sweaty brow, apparently taking Kyon's earlier threat to heart.

Kyon strokes my arm, trying to get my attention. "Kricket?"

I groan again, "The eagle has landed . . ."

"Brother Kyon," a clipped, military voice says from somewhere behind me. "We've located the Regent. We're attempting to move him now. He's in medical stasis, but there's a problem with the regulator."

"Have someone else see to it," Kyon responds with a wave of his hand in a dismissive gesture, returning his concerned eyes to me. "I'm attending to my priestess."

"Brother Excelsior wants to consult with you on this matter," the soldier replies in an insistent tone.

The name makes a noticeable difference upon Kyon: he stiffens and exhales a frustrated breath. "Very well," he acquiesces. "I'll be there momentarily."

The soldier's retreating footsteps tap on the marble floor. Kyon glowers at the medic beside him. "You have to stay with her. Do not let her out of your sight. Am I clear?" he asks.

The good doctor swallows his anxiety and replies, "I understand."

"Give her a sedative; I don't want her to panic if she becomes lucid."

The medic immediately reaches into his pocket and extracts a needlelike gun from it. He holds it up to the light and calibrates the needle with the dial-like gauge on its side. He draws the needle toward me when Kyon grabs his wrist. "That's too much. You'll render her completely unconscious. She's small. She needs half of what you have there."

The doctor dials back on the tranquilizer. He holds up the gauge on the readout for Kyon to approve. Kyon nods his head. "Good."

Leaning forward, the curer holds the sharp instrument to my neck and pulls the trigger. A pain jolts me and I have to stifle the torrent of swear words I want to rain down upon his head. Instead, I murmur, "Did you try the znous? They taste lovely."

Kyon reaches out and gently rubs my cheek with the back of his fingers. He has an unguarded look, one I've never seen from him before as he murmurs, "And you are very lovely in your madness."

Unfocusing my eyes, I give him a lunatic grin as I mirror his action: rubbing the back of my fingers over his cheek. "You should start a blog."

His enormous hand covers mine, warming my cold fingers as he closes his eyes for just a moment. I lie still while attempting not to show my surprise at his reaction. A moment later he gently pulls my hand from his cheek and lets go of it. He gets to his feet, saying gruffly to the medic, "Monitor her. I won't be long."

The medic watches Kyon's retreating back as he moves across the station. A youngish-looking Striker meets Kyon at the other end of the long room and leads him to the gilded saer doors of the overup; they're the same ones I'd taken to Defense Minister Telek's office. When Kyon's large frame disappears behind the sliding doors, the doctor turns his attention back to me. That's when I reach up and shoot him with the same tranquilizer gun I'd pulled from his pocket.

Holding him by the collar with one hand, I use all my weight to pull him nearer to me again. He exclaims loudly, "What are you doing?" His hand goes to his neck as he growls at me.

My thumb dials the dosage higher as I say between my teeth, "Not enough?" I press the needle of the gun beneath his chin and pull the trigger again. His tongue swells up in his mouth and he slobbers unintelligible words while his eyelids droop down over his eyes. He falls face-first next to me onto the cot. "Good night," I whisper as I look around to see if we're being observed.

No alarm is raised, so I peel off my red overcoat and toss it over the medic's face. I'd like to trade him for his uniform jacket, but he's too freaking big to move, and it would look odd on me, attracting the kind of attention I want to avoid. Upping the dosage on the tranquilizer gun, I check the pathway to the stairs. It's not very far away, but I have to make it to the top if I have any hope of getting out of here. Taking a deep breath, I stand. I sway on my feet, light-headed.

Hiding the tranquilizer gun in my waistband, I stumble away from the cot occupied by the curer. Reaching the edge of the partition, I pause, waiting for the soldiers near the stairs to finish their conversations so I can go. I clutch the column next to me, letting my cheek rest against it as a bout of dizziness hits me. Pressure on my elbow alerts me to the fact that someone's at my side.

"Do you need help?" It's a tall, blond-haired soldier; his gun is strapped to him in a shoulder harness, its long barrel is pointed away from me. He seems young, but they all do, so I have no way of gauging his age. I must have an apprehensive look because he says, "I'm Keenan. Brother Kyon sent me to sit with you. I'm here to protect you."

"Oh," I murmur, looking down, "I was just looking for the umm . . . you know," I whisper shyly, "the Commodus." As a point of fact, it's not a lie; I'm so scared I'm about to pee my pants.

He doesn't laugh at me. Instead, he looks around, gauging the state of things. "You want something . . . private," he states, not like a question.

"Preferably," I agree.

"Can you climb stairs?" he asks.

My heart leaps in my chest. *Is he serious?* "Urr, yeah. I think so."

"There's a Commodus in the gallery above. Would that work, Elle Kricket?" his eyes soften in concern. "I'll help you up there."

"Lead the way," I return with a small smile.

I lean on his arm as he guides me to the stairs, needing his support more than I care to admit. Once there, we climb them together. He pauses several times to let me rest. I play the part of an invalid, because I sort of am one, but I cringe every time he stops, covertly looking over my shoulder to see if anyone has discovered the medic

I've left in a drug-induced stupor on my cot. I'm also terrified that Kyon will return at any moment. He's much harder to lie to than everyone else, because he knows what I'm capable of.

When we reach the top of the stairs, I'm ushered to a doorway nearby. "I'll wait for you here," he says, allowing me access to the Commodus. As I shuffle in, I search for another way out. The facility is elegant, but there's only the one point of entry, which is currently being guarded by an enormous, armed giant. I exhale an irritated breath. "Really?" I mutter sarcastically to myself. Since I'm here, I quickly use the facility.

Afterward, while showering my hands with the warm steam spray at the beautiful shell-shaped niche in the wall, I study the ceiling for vents that I can fit into. Nothing. My knees feel weak. I sit down on the floor, and then lie down—the tile is cool, it chills my skin through my dirty shirt. Staring up at the ceiling, I wonder for the millionth time, *How did I get here?*

After a short time, Keenan's voice sounds through the open doorway. "Elle Kricket, do you need some assistance?" I don't reply; I just stare at the ceiling—it's beveled with clouds projected onto it— it's a little like being outside on a summer day—blue sky.

Keenan's bootsteps echo off the elegant walls. "Elle Kricket?" he asks hesitantly, when he sees me lying on the floor. I don't make eye contact, continuing to stare at the ceiling.

Keenan squats down next to me, touching his hand to my shoulder. "Do you need me to call you a curer?" he asks, nervously looking into my eyes.

I whisper real low, "I need . . ."

He leans his ear close to my lips, trying to hear me better. I move my arm up, pressing the tranquilizer gun against the side of his neck. The gun makes a sharp hissing sound as I pull the trigger. His shocked eyes meet mine as I load him full of sedative. My arm falls away, resting again on the floor with a thud.

His pupils dilate within seconds. "Why?" he asks as he slips to rest with his elbows on the floor. He reaches for his weapon, but his eyelids droop. His cheek crashes onto the tile next to my ear. When his eyes close, I exhale a deep breath.

Gazing up at the ceiling once more, I point to a passing cloud on the screen—it looks like it has a long neck. "Giraffe," I say softly to my unconscious companion.

I ease myself up off the floor. My joints creak like I'm a thousand years old. Every muscle I own is stiff to the point of cramping. I glance at the gauge on the tranquilizer gun: it's empty. I let it drop to the floor. Next I strip off the rehyde-pack from my arm, letting the discarded cylindrical tube bounce with a clatter onto the hard surface.

I pull Keenan's weapon from his shoulder and place the strap across my chest, before examining the gun. It's not as heavy as it looks. It has readouts on the side. Notchlike finger grooves indicate where the gun is supposed to be held. It's long like a rifle, and unfortunately, my arms aren't nearly long enough to hold it the way it should be held. I let the gun swing around me so that it rests against my back.

Turning toward Keenan, I pat him down, searching him for something I can use. I tug an earpiece from his ear. I hold it up near my own ear and listen—I think I hear Kyon's voice coming through it, but it's faint. I rub the earpiece on my pant leg before I place it in my ear.

"Keenan, report. Give me your location," Kyon's voice growls. A pause and then, "Report—do you have Kricket with you?"

I touch the side of the earpiece to press it farther into my ear; a small microphone snakes out, stopping near my mouth. I breathe a shallow breath.

"Kricket," Kyon says my name like a warning. "Where are you?"

"How'd you know it was me?" I whisper. I forget about searching Keenan and hurriedly tiptoe to the doorway of the Commodus.

"Call it the electricity between us both," he replies in a softer tone, like the one he'd used with me earlier when he'd called me lovely. "I know the light sound of your breath—it falls heavy on me."

I peek around the door frame. There are soldiers at the top of the gallery steps, looking in all directions, presumably for me. I'll have to go soon; they'll find me in here if I wait.

"Why do you want to hold on to me? Find someone else—just let me go." I slip out the door and hug the illuminated wall, quietly backing away from where the soldiers are. I glance over my shoulder to make sure I go down the hallway that will take me to the skywalk between the buildings.

"I don't want another for my consort; I only want you. I'll be your first lover—"

"No you won't, because even if you are, I'll *never* love you," I retort.

"There'll be no martyrs here, Kricket. I'll tear your heart off your sleeve and bury it deep in my chest. Your savage heart will beat for me. Run if you think you can—I'll hunt you down."

My tongue is heavy in my mouth. "I'll have my finger on the trigger when you get here."

"You best have more than that—have a bullet with my name on it. It'll make no difference. I won't allow you to deny me anything— your mind, your heart, your body—"

My limbs are weighted down by fear. I have to get him out of my head. I pull the earpiece from my ear, throwing it away just as Kyon reaches the top of the staircase. His eyes are on me immediately, like he senses me. He gives me a dirty smile, one that makes me feel as if he's seeing me naked.

As he pauses to assess the fact that I haven't drawn my weapon on him, like I'd promised to, I can't help noticing the same of him. He doesn't pull out his gun; he doesn't need it. He's bigger than all the other soldiers near him—physically perfect—and a hell of a lot stronger than me. I can see the intimidation on the faces of the other Strikers. It's not his rank that does it either; it's the fact that he exudes raw power. I'd bet most people in his life do exactly what he tells them to do when he tells them to do it. I'm probably the only one who doesn't.

Kyon's cold blue eyes warm the longer he looks at me. He scares me like no one ever has. I know he's capable of anything. *He was very gentle with me when he thought I was sick . . . Would I have loved you if you'd managed to keep me in the beginning?* my eyes ask him. He tilts his head to the side, like he hears me.

His look devours me, and I'm fairly certain now that he truly *is* picturing me naked. My breathing becomes shallow, and I turn and run from him on shaky legs. In my panic, I'm unable to think of a reason why no one is guarding this entrance to the building. The feminine guide-bot hologram materializes once more as I approach the exit leading to the skywalk. "Thank you for visiting the Premiere Palisades—" I blow past her, glancing over my shoulder.

Kyon is not far behind, catching up fast. The door slides open for me. Passing the threshold, I realize now why there are no guards to the skywalk: it's been destroyed. There's a huge gap between the buildings now. Unable to turn back, I run down the glass tunnel to its jagged edge, finding shattered pieces of debris where the skywalk has been torn away. I run over it, cutting my feet on sharp pieces.

Nearing the edge, I realize the gap is entirely too wide for me to jump to the other side. I gaze down over the edge. The fall is around two hundred stories—not survivable, even with the reservoir at the bottom of it—even if I could swim.

I glance back over my shoulder. Kyon slows, and then comes to a stop. He holds up his hand to the soldiers following him. They stand down, not coming any nearer to me. "Kricket," Kyon says gently, like he had before when I was sick, "come here."

It's an order, however softly it was spoken. I glance over the edge once more; it nearly gives me vertigo. I press a shaky hand to my forehead, rubbing it. My head feels like it's going to burst. Kyon takes a cautious step toward me. He murmurs, "Remember the last time you jumped?" he asks me. "This isn't the same thing. You were only two stories up in your Chicago tenement—you broke your ribs and your clavicle. You wouldn't survive this fall."

My eyes widen in shock. *He knows about my past—the night I jumped from my foster father's apartment after he'd nearly killed me. But he's wrong about one thing.* "My ribs were already broken before I jumped," I murmur.

He growls at this information, his face darkening more. "He hurt you badly," Kyon says. He takes another step toward me, and I inch to the precipice of the skywalk.

"You've hurt me too," I say honestly.

"I didn't understand you before," Kyon admits. "I'm beginning to now." He pauses again, and then he says in a gentle tone, "Do you know what I've thought about since I awoke from medical stasis?"

"Killing everybody?"

He smiles at my accusation and shakes his head. "No, not everybody. I thought about what you said to me—how you think I'm like your foster father, Dan. Do you remember telling me about him?"

I nod. "Yes."

"I've made a point, since our misunderstanding at the palace, to read every file that we've collected on you. I had largely ignored your past on Earth until now, thinking it wouldn't be very important to me because I'm your future. But it is important, Kricket, where you come from, is it not?"

I just stare at him, not understanding where he's going with this. "I'd rather you know nothing about me. In fact, forgetting about me would be the best thing you could do."

"I'm going to find him," Kyon says softly.

My eyebrows rise in surprise. "Find who?" I ask, my mouth going dry.

"Dan O'Callaghan." As he says my foster father's name, he takes another step toward me. "He doesn't get to live after what he's done to you."

"You've done worse," I reply.

"Have I?" He advances toward me again, his movements stealthy.

"You know you have." The backs of my heels cross the edge of the skywalk. Kyon stops abruptly once more, my threat implicit.

"I've never been in a position to betray your trust, or your love, like he has."

"I don't want you to hurt him," I state forcefully, so that he gets the point. "I mean it. I don't want anything other than to never see either one of you again."

"I don't believe you."

"It's true."

"Don't think of the consequences; there are none for us. He brought this upon himself, whatever I choose to do to him. He brought you up in the dark. I thought you couldn't feel pain, but you do . . . you just hide it well. You need strength, someone you cannot manipulate with your intelligence, someone who gives you boundaries. It's the only way you'll ever feel safe."

"What?" I pale.

"I want you . . . your beautiful face, your taste, your mouth full of lies, your sad, violet eyes—I hate them, but I want them."

"Kricket," Trey's voice says from behind me.

I whip around, seeing Trey coming toward me on the other side of the skywalk. He's not alone: Jax, Wayra, and several other Cavars who were incarcerated are with him. Immediately, the Strikers behind Kyon open fire on the Cavars. The Cavars drop to the glass floor of the tunnel. I step between them to the middle of the skywalk, blocking a clear shot to Trey.

With a wolfish scowl, Kyon barks an order to his men. "Cease fire!" When his eyes return to me, he has a concerned expression on his face. He extends his hand to me. "Kricket," he says gently, "come here."

I glance over my shoulder at Trey again. He must have come from his apartment—he has on one of his black combat shirts, it molds to his muscles like a second skin. Gone is the jet pack that he clung to the last time I saw him. He's on foot now and has his weapon drawn up to his shoulder, but he hasn't fired any shots. He's assessing our situation. He holds his hand up to the Cavars behind him, silently ordering them not to fire.

"How'd you find me?" I ask Trey, raising my voice to be heard over the chaos swirling around us. Aircraft blast through the air overhead; dogfights between Rafe and Alameeda pilots tear up the sky. Ammunition fire rains showers of orange and red, turning the twilight to day for brilliant moments. Our skywalk trembles as bombs hit the deck of the ship.

Trey holds up his watch on his wrist; it blinks with a blue light. "We're tracking the slipshield on your wrist."

I lift my wrist, studying the clear sticker that resembles the symbol on a USB port that I'd used to open Trey's cell door. The small patch is blinking with a blue light. I look back at him and see anguish in his eyes. He doesn't have a jet pack to reach me. I'm stuck on my side, a world away from him.

Kyon calls to Trey, "Tell her to come away from the edge. She's too close—she's going to fall." Kyon is no longer wearing his jet pack either; none of the Strikers with him are. It's a fact that makes Kyon's jaw clench tighter the farther I lean over the gap.

Trey's jaw tenses too, as he steps to his edge of the skywalk. He judges the distance between us. Lowering his gun, Trey touches his wristband again; the flashing blue light stops throwing its pale light on his face. When his eyes meet mine, I see fear in them. "Do you trust me?" he asks.

Amy A. Bartol

I nod my head, whispering, "Yes."

"Then jump!" he says. I flinch, my heart pounding in my chest like he struck me. *Do it!* Trey implores.

Kyon moves behind me; he lunges in my direction, making a grab for my arm. I twist back around to face Trey; he's watching me, his every muscle tensing, his eyes begging me to move. I take a deep breath before jumping from the edge of the skywalk and lurching into the air toward him. To my surprise, Trey jumps from his side at the same time, meeting me in the air between the broken pieces of skywalk. His arms go around me, hugging me to him while we fall toward the reservoir of crystal-blue water far below.

CHAPTER 9
SKYE BELLS RINGING

As Trey and I plummet away from the skywalk, my hair streams back from my face. Panicking, I'm unable to breathe in more than shallow breaths. The wind is so loud and it tears at our clothes as they ripple in the descent. Trey lets go of my waist, moving away from me so that we're no longer clutching each other, but only clasped together by his hand in mine. I'm facedown, spread out like a starfish, watching the water growing larger by the second.

My view is obscured for a moment as an unmanned hovercycle careens beneath us. Recognition dawns on me; it's Trey's hoverbike—the same one that brought us here from the palace a few nights ago. *Was it only a few nights ago?* I think in confusion. The hovercycle positions itself directly under Trey as the hatch opens, allowing him to fall into its open cabin. His legs straddle the seat while he pulls me by my hand so that I fall onto the vehicle behind him. He brings my hand to his waist; I seize it and wrap my other arm around him, gripping him tightly. My cheek presses against his back as I hug him with what strength I have left.

The hatch closes around us; the sound of the wind is immediately cut off. It's very quiet, with only the hum of the hovercycle. Trey takes control of the bike; it veers to the right, banking and coming around the other way. Through the sound system of the vehicle,

Wayra's voice echoes as he emits a loud whoop. "Baw-da-baw! I want to do that again!"

His elation is matched by that of Jax's voice, as he asks, "Did you see the look on those knob knockers' faces when we all jumped from the skywalk?" Jax's hovercycle comes abreast of ours, hugging our side in a defensive position. I shift my face to look in the other direction and see Wayra's hovercycle as well. A small group of hoverbikes joins us, weaving around buildings. The darkening denim-blue sky is unzipped by choking columns of black smoke. I recognize Hollis. Drex has Fenton on his hovercycle with him. Seeing the destruction of the ship, however, causes their laughter to die down quickly. "We have to evacuate," Trey's voice rumbles through his back, tickling my cheek.

"Do we follow protocol seven one nine—evacuate to ground—regroup—hook up with a ground base?" Wayra asks.

Trey's voice rumbles again, "We're hunted—by both sides. We act like civvies for now until we can make our case with whoever is left to take command. For now, our mission is to protect the priestess against all enemies. Anyone who can't do that needs to tell me now."

They have to pretend to be civilians—lose their identities as Cavars?

The com is silent; no one speaks up. "Right," Trey says. "Diamond formation. Make ready. They won't let us leave without a fight. Kyon has probably diverted every available ship to search for us."

At first, I think he's wrong; none of the big ships pay attention to us as we slink away, heading to the edge of the Ship of Skye. The shields are down, so there's nothing barring our way from leaving. Darkness is falling fast as we emerge over the lip of the main deck. My heart nearly stops at the fleet of warships beneath us. Trey hugs the contour of the ship, blending in with the dark, hieroglyphic-shaped metal.

In the next few moments, everything gets turned up way too loud outside. I can't slow anything down. We're weaving through the crowd of ships that converges on our small group, firing unbelievably scary weapons upon us. Explosions on the lower deck of the Ship of Skye force Trey to make sharp turns to avoid falling metal and debris.

We dive into a cloud; I can't see anything but white, and then dark sky as we emerge. I'm in a bird machine and the only objective is to get low. I clutch Trey's back; his muscles bunch beneath my cheek. The side of his face lights up in orange and red when a ship near us explodes. He swerves to avoid the explosion. Something hits and then bounces off the lid of our hovercycle. It takes me a moment to realize it was a person. I cringe, tasting fear. Trey's neck stretches as he tries to keep an enemy ship in his sights so they don't outmaneuver us. My mind keeps up a steady mantra of *go, go, go, go, go* . . .

A gleaming silver ship near us fires off a round of shots that light up the sky with blue fire as it passes right in front of us. I don't think the shots were intended to hit us; they were a warning to surrender. Trey's back becomes damp with sweat, and he growls when we avoid colliding with another ship as it tries to absorb us into its tractor beam.

Boom, boom, boom, boom, in rapid-fire succession. The vibrations tear into my chest, and my already fluttering heart beats twice as hard from the shock waves. The sky lights up as lightning strikes turn it to the color and texture of marmalade. A loud groan of metal shifting whines above us.

Above us, a dark shadow looms. The entire Ship of Skye leans over us, careening sideways. As I look up, it topples over, changing direction as it charges toward the ground and into our path just beneath it. Trey stands the hoverbike on its head. We point straight down to avoid being crushed by the tons of ship hurtling toward us. As we bank, g-forces exert too much pressure upon my body. I can't breathe or think as my world turns to black. The only thing I hear is the sound of ringing in my ears—a bell clanging—a Skye-blue bell.

❦❧

My head aches. Night sky greets me as I open my eyes; two moons preside king and queen over the stars. I hear the beautiful, rasping whisper of Trey's voice, the rumble of it in his chest trembles my cheek. He strides with me in his arms. "Almost there, Kricket," he says.

I get a lump in my throat. I ache; it's a broken paradise to be in pain, but still to be in Trey's arms. He's running through the dark to keep me from the cage of Alameeda control. He moves us between concrete buildings that creep into the sky—majestic stems whose flowers are too tall to see. We enter a building into a dim corridor where the elegant sconce lights make rainbow halos until my eyes adjust to them.

From behind us, other booted feet click in the corridor. It must be the other Cavars. My eyes focus on Trey's chin, which has a determined set to it. I know I should try to walk, to say something to lighten the moment for him, but nothing about me seems to be working like it should. I'm so tired.

We emerge into a grand lobby, security at which should be tight, judging by its opulence, but we walk through all the checkpoints unchallenged.

"You own this building or something?" Gibon asks, as Trey's face is scanned at an unmanned checkpoint and cleared immediately.

"No. I designed its security system. I own the ones on the other side of the park. We can't go there; they may check them. This one is owned by a family friend."

"Is he here?" Wayra asks, his voice echoing off the ceilings. No one is about.

"Not if she can follow directions—everyone here and in my buildings were advised to evacuate to estates outside the city after the palace was attacked," he responds.

He continues to the back of the skyscraper, to rooms on the ground floor.

"*She* must be cut from amethyst to be able to afford ground-floor suites," Fenton says in awe; his eyes are wide as he assesses the posh, modern style surrounding us. It's clear he's not being sarcastic; all of them but Trey seem to be impressed that we're bypassing the bank of elevators to remain on the main floor.

He leads the way to a suite of rooms that encompasses almost the entire side of the building. Once at the grand doors, Trey pauses for a moment for a facial scan to pass over him. It catches my face as well. A loud warning alarm echoes, scaring me half to death.

Trey's brows pull together before he growls, "Cease warning. Access code: tonic triad."

The tall doors sweep upward, recessing so that we can enter. He knows the floor plan, crossing through the immaculate foyer. Illumination switches on; we enter a formal entertaining area. Three enormous chandeliers fall out of the ceiling to settle above us as they glow with shimmering golden light that makes everything look that much more elegant. In the center of one wall, there's a cascading water feature; liquid flows over beautiful tiles with a tranquil, satisfying sound. On either side of it are full glass walls that show a large expanse of formal gardens. Low topiaries define beautiful pathways that light up with well-placed ground sconces.

Trey growls again. "Light protocol for occupy only. Dim to half measure. Set privacy at five. All security up—alert status five—silent alarms active."

Immediately, the garden lighting outside dies, so too does most of the lighting in the dwelling. The room we're in remains lit, but dims to a much lower setting than before. With the lights off outside, the horizon glows red in the distance. Ripples and shocks tremble the ground, just as it had when the bombs where hitting the ship.

But now, it's not bombs but pieces of the Ship of Skye pelting the ground.

The walls of glass fill with a thickening fog between the panes, darkening them quickly to become opaque. I'm hypnotized by the smoky swirls that make them look as if they're breathing. It's somehow better and worse that I can't see the destruction going on outside. A part of me wants to deny it, while another part of me wants to watch it so that I'll know the exact moment I need to move.

Trey turns and I catch a glimpse of Wayra, Jax, Drex, Hollis, and Gibon. *Where are Dylan and Fenton?* I wonder as I take roll call in my mind, assessing my Cavars. I feel my heart flutter, like I'm missing vital pieces of me. They're all looking at me with worried expressions.

"Wayra and Drex, mine the place—find whatever provisions we need," Trey orders them. "Hollis, you head back toward the lobby—wait for Fenton. It shouldn't take him long to destroy the beacons on the hovercycles."

"Is Dylan with Fenton?" I ask. My voice doesn't sound like mine. It's tight, a couple of octaves higher than normal.

"Kricket," Trey says, relief in his tone.

"Where's Dylan?" I ask again. I can hear panic in my voice, my breaths coming in shallow pants.

Trey doesn't answer me. He nods at Jax, a clear indication that he's to follow us. He walks swiftly to an adjoining room and crosses the large sitting room before leaving it and entering a palatial bedroom. Definitely feminine in design and decor, it has white and lavender tones. Large, velvety-soft chairs with high backs face an opaque, smoke-filled window wall that must also hide the expensive-to-maintain garden outside.

As he walks by the chairs, it's clear he intends to put me on the bed.

"Chair." I motion to them. I don't want to lie down. I want to find out where Dylan is. Trey frowns and ignores me. He takes me to the bed and places me gingerly upon it. Jax is next to him; pulling a medical pack from his back, he rummages through it.

He pulls out the "grandma goggles" from his pack that I know to be an ostioscope—a medical device that performs full-body scans.

Weakly, I fight Jax, trying to look him in the eyes instead. I croak softly, "Dylan?"

Jax's jaw tenses. "They got him, Kricket. He's dead," he says with a shrug I know he doesn't feel. In shock, I don't fight him when he puts the ostioscope on my eyes. Green lights flash and readouts flicker on the lens, but I couldn't read them even if I wanted to, because my eyes blur with tears. A single tear slips out, sliding down my cheek. I try to hold the rest back. *I don't cry in front of people. It's weak. It doesn't happen. It can't happen.*

Jax says to Trey, "She has bruises everywhere. Some look several days old—not new, but she didn't have them days ago. Some of the stages of healing I'm seeing are off somehow . . . they're not reading right. Three of her ribs had hairline fractures—here and here." He touches my ribs lightly. "But now they're recalcified—growing stronger than before, I'd say. Did someone give her a rapid bone regenerator recently? If they did, I can't find a trace of it in her system—and yet . . . she's healing at a rate I'm not used to seeing. Still, this has to hurt, Kricket." He touches my ribs lightly before touching sore patches on my back. "Have you been suffering with these contusions for long? How did you get them all?" he asks with a surly disgust that's not aimed at me.

He pulls the glasses from my eyes, but I avoid looking into his. "I haven't been suffering," I murmur numbly. "I was drugged most of the time since they pulled me from my cell—I don't remember much from the last couple of days." I rub my wrists where I'd been shackled. Thick, yellowish armband bruises tattoo my swollen skin. "I only woke up today—midday." I meet his eyes. "Did they . . ." My throat squeezes tight. "Did anyone . . ." I inhale a deep breath.

With a concerned expression, Jax waits patiently for me to ask my question. Finally I ask, "Was I raped?"

He looks startled. For all his experience, he's shockingly naïve. He jerks his head to the side, studying the readouts on the glasses again. I look over his shoulder at a point on the wall. I can't look at Trey; it's impossible. I don't want to know what he's thinking.

Jax begins to shake his head. "No, Kricket," he says in a gentle tone. "You must have suffered a beating—your back is—there's bruising there, but there are no internal injuries evident aside from your ribs. No internal trauma associated with rape. And everything is normal—just like when we did this before."

I nod my head expressionlessly, acknowledging his words. It takes a second for relief to flood me and with it, the unbearable need to weep. I hold it back.

"Are you thirsty?" Jax asks me, pulling a canteen from his pack. He offers it to me. I nod silently, taking the canteen and putting it to my lips. Swallowing big gulps helps to ease the rawness of my throat.

"Here," Jax says, taking the canteen from me and shoving a protein bar into my hand.

My stomach rebels against the thought of putting it in my mouth. "I can't eat—"

Ignoring my protest, Jax nudges my arm up, urging me to eat it. "It's not the same kind as the ones we ate in the Forest of O. Those were especially made to ward off parasites—this one is just nutritious. You need to eat it—your stomach is completely empty—you're *literally* starving. Do you want to be the weakest link on our team?"

He knows me too well. I sniff the protein bar tentatively. It smells like peanut butter. I take a bite and find it tastes good. I chew it slowly, worried that my stomach will reject it.

Jax glances at Trey; they both visibly relax a little. Jax's eyes return to me again. "Lean back against the pillows, Kricket," Jax says while unrolling a canvas medical pack full of vials that are each secured by an elastic band. I try to move to follow his request, but I'm achy. I wince.

Trey moves beside me onto the bed, gently pulling me back with his arm around my shoulders. He leaves his arm there, bracing me against himself. Jax lifts up my ankle, examining the bottom of my foot. He selects an aerosol-like can from among the vials. Pointing it at my foot, he sprays it generously over the area. It instantly numbs the bottom of my foot. He presses on that area with his finger. "Do you feel this?" Jax asks, while probing the cuts I suffered while running over broken glass.

"I feel pressure, but I wouldn't call it pain," I reply. I feel far away, like none of this is real.

"Good. Keep eating," he grunts. He uses a tweezerslike implement to extract a piece of glass embedded there. Blood drips off my heel, teardrops of red on the lavender-colored blanket. Jax's brow furls as he concentrates on his task. Finally, he drops a jagged, bloody shard of glass onto the coverlet, unconcerned that it will probably stain the beautiful silk. He probes for more glass, but finding none, he rests the tweezers on the bed next to the glass.

Wrapping a cloth around my foot, Jax applies pressure to it. Selecting a silver tube from his pack, he unwraps my foot and smears ointment inside and around the lacerated area. Taking out a clean bandage, he diligently covers my wound before letting my foot return to the bed. He quickly lifts my other foot off the bed and performs the same action. When he rests my other foot against the cover once more, they're both wrapped in bandages.

All my thoughts are far away when Jax looks up at me again. "I'm sorry that hurt you. Here," he says softly, extending a clean bandage for me to take.

I look at it in confusion. My breath hitches as I say, "You didn't hurt me." I realize then that I'm crying. Tears are running over my cheeks, dripping off my jaw.

Trey takes the bandage from him and wipes my face with it. He rises from the bed to gather the blanket he was sitting on, pulling it over me. He returns to my side, snuggling up next to me and spooning me with his large frame while I cry big, racking sobs that I can't control. Jax packs up his gear; he turns to leave but pauses instead.

Coming back to the bed, Jax squats down so that we're eye level. "You saved our lives, Kricket. We would've died in our cells if you hadn't gotten us help. Thank you. Get some rest. I'll check on you again soon. " He kisses my hair tenderly. I sniffle in response.

When Jax is gone, I hear Trey say behind me, "The Alameeda won today. They pulled us out of the sky, but that won't defeat Rafe, just as it won't defeat us. We're together again. What were two is now one." His warmth seeps into me and I find it hard to keep my eyes from closing.

∂๑⁓๑

Soft male voices flow around me, moving me toward the surface. My heavy eyelids open reluctantly. I recognize Jax and Wayra seated in the plush, high-backed chairs that they've turned and pulled nearer to the bed. Trey is sitting next to me on the mattress, facing them. Between the three, they have a 3-D map of the city blocks. Trey is pointing to a highlighted section that seems to be beneath the streets. Trying to focus on what they're saying gives me a headache. My eyes lift to the window wall beyond them; it's still opaque—I can't see anything outside. *How long have I been asleep?*

I lift my head, but my neck is really stiff, so I don't attempt to turn it. Groaning, I lie back onto the pillow. They all look up from what they're doing to stare at me. Trey's hand touches my hip. "How do you feel?" He strokes me lightly.

"Tired," I murmur. I don't recognize my voice as being mine. I sound ancient.

Wayra and Jax both get to their feet. Wayra lifts the Alameeda gun; I recognize it as the one I stole from Keenan after I tranquilized him. He comes to my side, bending down to look in my eyes. "You hungry?" he asks me with a concerned expression. "I found some venish—I'll share it with you."

I frown, my eyes closing involuntarily as I say, "You're gonna share your venish with me? I must be dying."

A surprised laugh comes from Jax at my comment. "Don't scare her like that, you knob knocker." His voice is soothing as he adds, "You'll be okay, Kricket. You just need to rest."

I want to say something else, but I'm so tired that I just listen to their soft voices as they go back to discussing our position in relation to our enemy.

CHAPTER 10
EAST OF EDEN

It's dark in the room when I wake. Rolling over, I find Trey asleep next to me in one of the plush chairs that he pulled up close to the bed. He has his hand near the barrel of a Kaiser Gat that is leaning against the side of the chair. He looks exhausted, like he hasn't slept in a while. Not wanting to wake him, I slide over the mattress slowly and move toward the opposite side of the large bed. My joints are stiff when I get to my feet. I pause, realizing that the bandages that wrapped them are gone now. I don't know when they were removed, but as I take a few steps, I can tell that the wounds I had are nearly healed. Jax and his horabus plant ointment are miracle workers.

When I near a large bureau on my way back to bed from the Commodus, I pause. Movement from within a gilded frame catches my eye. A video is playing within the frame, which is arranged in a place of prominence among a few others in the middle of the beautiful wood surface. I recognize two of the figures in it immediately as being those of Trey and Victus, Trey's twin. They're on either side of a very beautiful young woman. Each brother has his arm wrapped around her shoulder. There's no sound as Trey mouths the word *One*, the girl next to him mouths the word *Two*, and just after her, Victus mouths the word *Three*. Trey and Victus turn and kiss the girl on the cheek at the same time. Laugh lines form around her eyes as she closes them, giggling, exposing a very attractive set of dimples.

Then, Trey and Victus both lift their lips from her at the same time, running away from the frame as she opens her eyes with a stunning grin. The picture resets again and it replays the same scene over and over as I stare at it.

I glance back to the chair. Trey still sleeps, hardly making any noise at all. Numbly, I change direction, walking to the lavare attached to the bedroom. I close the door to it when I'm over the threshold. Leaning against the door frame, I notice that the entire wall ahead of me is mirrored, the reflection interrupted only by a glass vanity countertop.

My image stares back at me, but I hardly recognize her. She's so pale and haunted—something wild and savage, but not unbeautiful—no—she may be even more so because of the lack of civility to be found there. But she looks nothing like the girl in the frame. They don't even seem like they belong on the same planet.

I go to the mirror, wondering what it is that Trey can possibly see in me if that girl in the picture is actually Charisma, his ex-fiancée. Deep down, I know that she is. *She looks like the sweetest thing ever to walk Ethar, and I broke them up.* That thought doesn't make me feel good.

I gather my hair back from my face, trying to comb it with my fingers. It does no good, so I give up and touch the countertop with my hand instead. With my finger on the glass surface, I draw a square. The movement activates a recessed compartment in the vanity. A medicine cabinet rises from the surface of the glass. I'm not at all disappointed by the treasure trove of feminine products lining the glass ledges. I do, however, have a Goldilocks moment when I think about the fact that this all belongs to someone else.

I try not to dwell on it as I choose a vial that contains something akin to mouthwash. Tipping the pink liquid to my lips, I swish some of it around in my mouth. As I touch my hand against the glass countertop again, I use my three fingers to draw squiggly lines over the surface, the symbol for water. The countertop opens up, revealing a small sink. I spit out the mouthwash and watch it swirl down the drain.

Next, I select an aerosol can from the many colorful scents and bottles aligned in the compartment. Lifting my arms, I spray the aerosol on my armpits one at a time. The small hairs melt away instantly, leaving my skin smooth to the touch. I pull up each pant leg and apply the spray liberally to my legs. It leaves them hairless and shiny, like they're coated in a moisturizing aloe.

After straightening my pant legs, I replace the aerosol can on the shelf. I realize that it'll take more than dry shampoo to tame my hair, so I clean the countertop, putting everything back into the compartment. Drawing a square in the reverse direction allows the compartment to be absorbed once more by the countertop.

Avoiding the posh porcelain spa tub, with its complex buttons and controls, I turn on the water in the luxurious shower. Steam rolls up, clouding the shower doors. Fans click on, whisking the hot air away so that the rest of the room doesn't get overly steamy.

In front of the mirror once again, I attempt to peel off my dingy shirt that was once white, but now has several different smudges of brown, dull red, and gray. I grasp the hem to pull it over my head, making my ribs ache just enough so that I wince and pause. Weakly, I drop my arms, breathing heavily.

The water to the shower turns off. Behind me, Trey moves away from the glass partition. He's looking at the floor, at the sticky, ointment footprints I've left on the pristine white tile. Without a word he walks to the gigantic spa tub and activates it. It's not like a normal one, taking several minutes to fill from a spout. No, not at all like that. Water comes up from the floor of the tub, filling it to capacity in a matter of moments. Steam curls up invitingly. From his pocket, he produces a small vial. He unstops it and pours the liquid into the water.

I must look confused, because he says, "Jax gave me this. It's for your skin—to help heal any of the cuts you may still have. He also gave me this." He holds up another vial. "It's for pain."

"I don't need that one," I murmur, nodding my head toward the additional vial. I need to stay lucid; dropping my guard now is ludicrous. We're hidden in plain sight here. We can't count on this position to harbor any real shelter—not for much longer, anyway.

"You're in pain. You can hardly lift your arm up," Trey observes.

"It's not that bad—really—I'm just a little stiff is all."

"How am I to know that when you minimize everything that happens to you?"

"I don't do that—"

"You do," he counters in a quiet way. He believes it. He must be upset about what I asked Jax when we arrived—about whether or not I'd been raped. I look away from the mirror for a moment. Right now, I don't want to talk about the interrogation or anything that has gone on in the last few days. I want to pretend like none of this is happening—like we're not at war. The thought of Kyon is enough to make my stomach ache. He's probably out there hunting for me, and there's nothing I can do about it except hide from him.

I try to reel in my thoughts and change the subject. "How long have I been asleep?" I look at my wringing hands.

"Almost two rotations."

I glance back to the mirror to see his expression. It hasn't changed from his look of concern. "Should we have moved from here by now?" I ask with an uneasy grimace.

"We couldn't—"

"Because of me?" I ask worriedly.

He shakes his head. "No. The enemy has occupied the city just east of here and they have positions north and south. There's resistance fighting just outside the city limits—Rafe troops are mobilizing there."

"Oh," I say. I should want to know more, but I don't. I'm afraid to know more.

Trey waits for me to ask questions. When I don't, he grows more concerned. His voice is softly soothing as he says, "We're safe for now, and that's not likely to change soon. We'll know before it does, and then we'll leave."

"You promise?" I fiddle with the countertop, closing the sink with a wave of my fingers on the glass.

"I promise," he vows.

"Do you have a plan just in case?"

"Yes," he says, nodding.

"Is it a good plan?"

"The best of plans."

"Is it better than crossing fields at night occupied by saers with only a recurve?"

"Much better than that plan," he says with a reluctant smile. "And we have much better food this time."

I exhale a breath I didn't know I was holding. "Okay then."

"Why didn't you wake me when you got up? I could've helped you," Trey asks.

I wave my hand dismissively. "You looked exhausted. Have you slept more than a few parts since we've been here?"

"I've gotten rest here and there." He shrugs as if it's no big deal.

In the mirror, he grows larger as he moves nearer until he towers over me. He stops just a breadth away, but I feel him as if we're touching. His closeness is a physical thing, pulling me to him. Warmth radiates from him, enveloping me. I lean back against his broad chest. He bends his neck so the new growth from his beard tickles my throat, sending a shiver crashing through me. My cheeks flush, adding color to them as he reaches for the hem of my shirt.

"Your ribs are still healing—let me help you with this." He begins to lift the fabric up when I cover his hands with mine. It's so intimate, letting him undress me, I don't know if I can handle it. I struggle to meet his eyes in the mirror.

When I do, he says, "It's just me, Kricket. Lift your arms." The earnestness of his request wars with my senses. Before I met him, I never let anyone help me do anything.

Slowly, I obey, raising my arms up. He ratchets the hem of my dingy shirt. I wince again, sucking in my breath when the stiff lining in it scraps against my bruised flesh. Trey's large hand covers my fragile ribs, holding them firmly beneath my bared breast. The pressure is just enough to relieve the ache from them as he pulls my shirt over my head with his other hand. His thumb brushes the lower edge of my breast when I drop my arms. His forearm covers my nipples while he pulls me against him once more. I close my eyes as my skin reacts to his against my bare flesh. When I open them, he's watching me in the mirror, his eyes dark and unreadable.

He sweeps my hair off my neck, directing it over one shoulder. I watch him in the mirror as he leans down and brushes his lips over my back. He kisses my bruises, like he'd take them from me if he could.

"It's okay, they don't hurt—"

He pauses but doesn't look at me when he says harshly, "It's not okay. I will never be okay with this."

Trey turns me around to face him. His hand reaches up to entwine in my hair; it tilts my face up to his. He kisses me softly, afraid that he'll hurt me. When I kiss him back, my tongue stroking his, the need within him becomes increasingly apparent. His kisses become bolder, unrestrained, as if he'll extract some kind of retribution for the time that was stolen from us.

His touch fills me with yearning; I ache to wrap myself around him—to hang on tight. My heart flutters with desire and fear at the all-consuming feel of it. *You can't need him this much,* my paper heart warns me. *If it doesn't last, and it can't last—you know that—how will you survive the loss of him?*

I ignore those feverish thoughts. My bare skin presses to him, rubbing against the soft fabric of his shirt. This isn't simple infatuation that I can just ignore, hold my breath, and hope to have pass. It's something that I can no longer protect myself against. *If something happens to him now, it happens to me as well.* The thought scares me to death. *I've always been better off alone—always.* That thought comes with a squeezing of my heart that is hard to ignore. *I don't want to be alone anymore, not when I can be with him.*

My arms come up to wrap around the back of his neck. Trey reaches down, lifting me off the floor, his arm under the backs of my knees. The thick bones of his forearm and the muscles of his bicep press me gently against his chest; I feel the power he controls beneath his skin. My fingers play over his strong shoulders, the breadth of which seems to go on forever. His assault on my lips continues; they're more cathartic than if I were to slink into the corner alone to cry. Trey's hand moves from the nape of my neck to stroke a path over my back. He turns away from the mirror, taking me to the sunken tub.

My pink-painted toes lower to the soft white carpet when he sets me on my feet again. The spell is broken for a moment while our lips part; I want to stay in his arms to keep any fear from creeping back in. His hands slip down my sides, and with them a shiver washes an intense wave over me, making me aware of nothing but him.

His fingers glide beneath the waistband of my black pants, sliding them off as his fingers move over me. I make a soft noise, somewhere between a gasp and a moan. At the sound, Trey's eyes darken. His hand cups my bottom, squeezing me and pressing me against him. Something within the core of me clenches exquisitely tight. My hand clutches his chest, gathering the material of his shirt to steady me.

I move my legs to step out of my pants, letting them pool under my feet. When I do, I'm aware of my nakedness. Biting my lip, I meet Trey's gaze. He looks me over; his stare makes me feel bold and shy at the same time. Reaching for the hem of his shirt, I pull it up to expose his abdomen. He accommodates me by yanking the material off over his head, dropping it by my clothes. My fingertips float over the deep vee of muscles that leads to the waistband of his pants. His hand covers mine as he takes one and brings it to his lips, kissing it.

"Kricket." He breathes my name like he's blowing on tinder to start a fire. Lifting me up in his arms again, he eases me into the spa tub. With his hand under my arm, he steadies me. I submerge in water that reaches to my shoulders. There's a bench lining the perimeter of the bath, I stand next to it with the heat of the water turning my skin from pale to a soft pink.

Leaning my head back, I soak my hair, dampening it. Trey strips off his trousers and enters the spa behind me. He sits on the bench and draws my back to his chest, so I'm on his lap. I gaze up at the high ceiling, my head resting against his neck. The scent of him makes the blood run faster in my veins.

Trey touches a few buttons on the panel beside us; a compartment lined with glass bottles emerges from a recessed portion of the tile. The bottles look like potions from some long-ago apothecary in different shapes and colors. He selects one of the stout, red bottles, unstopping it and pouring a small portion of it into the palm of his hand. After rubbing his palms together, he gently touches them to my hair, lathering it and working cinnamon-scented soap into each strand. When he's finished, I twist so that I face him. I rinse my hair by leaning my head back into the water once more.

Straightening, I gaze at him. Trey's eyes wander over what he can see of me. *I'm the dark secret that he can't keep hidden—his crossed fingers—his hold-my-breath-to-keep-from-feeling. But I make him feel everything.*

He reaches his hand out; his thumb traces my lower lip. I take it in my mouth, sucking on the pad of his thumb gently. He in turn sucks in a harsh breath. Finding my waist, he pulls me to him. Settling me on his thighs, I straddle his lap. His hands explore my curves, running down my sides, skimming the outline of my breasts.

Releasing his thumb from my mouth, I lean near him, reaching to take a honey-colored bottle from the ledge near his head. My breasts press against his chest with my cheek brushing the stiff hair on his face. He turns his mouth to kiss my neck. My eyelids flutter closed briefly, and I release a soft "Ahh." I thread my fingers in his hair to hold him to me. His lips are heaven, making me want him more.

Opening my eyes, I take the bottle from the shelf. I unstop it, inhaling its scent—sandalwood. I pour some of its syrupy body wash into my hand. Unhurriedly, I run my soapy hands over his hard shoulders and chest. I trace the path of his tribal tattoo as it winds over his ribs and downward. His eyes stalk me, taking in my every movement as he rests his shoulders against the side of the spa. Reaching out, Trey cups my breast, his rough hand sliding gently over it. The love letter he's writing on my paper heart stutter-stops, and then riots within my chest with scribbling beats.

He leans forward and captures me in his arms; the water sloshes over the side of the spa. His lips press to my breast. Something within me stretches taut: it winds and coils until it elicits a soft cry from my lips. My head falls forward while I wrap myself around him, a vine of soft skin and golden hair clinging to him.

"Do you know what you mean to me, Kricket?" Trey asks in a raspy voice, looking up into my face. "You're my every thought. If you don't feel the same, you should stop this now—I won't touch you again. But if you decide that you want this—us—once I have you, I won't be able to give you up—you'll have my soul."

His words make no sense to me: I could no more stop what's happening between us than I could stop the wind from blustering in Chicago. *You already have my soul*, I think. *It must be written all over my face as it is written all over my heart.* "It scares me, how much I want you, Trey," I admit against Trey's lips.

My words soothe him. "No matter what happens, Kricket, I'll fight for you. Until death do us part . . . and then forever after that. I love you," he says honestly. "Say you'll be my consort."

"Yes," I breathe out the word. "I promise I will. I love you. Now . . . finish what you started. Show me what it feels like to be yours."

⚜

Stealing oxygen while being tethered to the sky, that's what it feels like to be loved by Trey. His mouth strokes me while I pull his hair, my lips cooing with bribes not to stop—never to stop. My pale skin turns the pink of a desert flower. I drown in fire. My paper heart is a folded, flaming phoenix. He shifts me against him, claiming my soul in exchange for his own . . .

Trey emerges from the tub, leaving me to languish a bit longer while he retrieves a towel. He wraps it around his hips before selecting another one for me. He brings it back to the tub, extending his hand for me to take. I step out of the water onto the white carpet. Trey unfolds the towel, wrapping it around the back of me but leaving the front open. With the ends of the towel, he pulls me against him once more, capturing my lips with his own for a deep kiss that makes my knees weak. My hands rest against his chiseled abdomen, before slipping around him and hugging him tight. I never want to move; I want to stay like this forever.

⚜

The silky sheet leaves my calf and thigh exposed. As I lie on my stomach, my head turns against a sumptuous pillow. I'm half asleep, having only just finished another round of lovemaking with Trey in the enormous bed. Every available inch of which has been covered by one of us at least twice. The sheet inches downward, slipping over my skin like water over a river rock. Firm lips press a soft kiss to one rounded cheek of my posterior. My lips curl in a satisfied smile as Trey straightens and rests his back against the propped pillows near the headboard. He pulls me to him so that my head rests on his chest. He toys with my hair, smoothing it and wrapping strands of it around his fingers.

"Sleepy," I say as though dead.

"Am I keeping you awake? I just wanted to hold you."

"You should sleep," I murmur.

Trey grunts like I said something ludicrous. "You have no idea how long I've been dreaming of this moment, do you? I don't plan to miss any of it to sleep."

"You've been dreaming about this?" My eyebrow arches.

"When I said you're my every thought, I meant it."

"When did you first begin dreaming about it?" I ask, warming to the subject.

"After I first saw you. My daydreams of you were nightmares," he says.

"Do tell," I say, all in for this conversation.

"I didn't intend to smack you on your bottom—when you were pretending to be unconscious in the limousine on Earth," he admits.

"Oh, no?" I asked him, suddenly not as tired as I was a second ago, feeling him caress my bottom now.

"I'd been next to you for hours with your perfume filling my nose, your hair tangling around your body—and then there were the sounds you made right before you became conscious—"

"The sounds I made?" My cheeks flood with color, trying to think of what sounds I could possibly make while I was unconscious.

"Breathy sounds—just like the ones you made a second ago when I was—"

"Got it." I blush.

He peeks down at my face. "Are you blushing?"

"No!" I lie.

"You *are* blushing." Bending down, he lifts my chin up so that he can give my lips a quick kiss. When I rest my head back against his chest, he continues, "And then, when you sat up and you called me a chester, I thought for sure that you could read my mind, or that everything I was thinking was written all over my face."

"I had no idea you felt any attraction to me whatsoever," I retort. "In fact, I thought you thought I was trash."

He sobers immediately. "How could you think that? I thought you were the most remarkable person I'd ever met—surviving like you had, all by yourself—and you managed to escape us on the train. That never happens. We don't lose prisoners."

"Really?" I lift my face to see if he's being serious.

"Yes, really." He leans down and kisses me again, sucking on my bottom lip with a sensual growl that makes me feel it everywhere. "You mean you couldn't tell that I was infatuated with you by the fact that I was holding your hand at every opportunity?"

"I thought you were making sure that I stayed with you."

"I didn't know what I was doing; my hand just kept seeking yours out on its own. Then you took my hand when we saw the Alameeda ships—" He sucks in his breath like his heart is being squeezed. "You were afraid the ships would see us. Do you remember?"

"Yes." I'm fascinated by what he's saying. I trace my fingertips over his abdominal muscles and watch as they tense.

Trey's voice deepens. "You were wrapped in a blanket, but you held it to yourself so that your back was almost entirely bare. Your hair fell in waves down to here." His hand moves now to caress the curving flesh below my back. "You were arguing with me about the direction we should take to avoid the Alameeda."

"I wasn't arguing. That was me *suggesting* we go the other way so no one would get caught and tortured."

"You were inserting yourself into my heart was what you were doing. I never had dreams about anyone like the ones I've had about you. You are all I ever think about."

"I am?"

"You and your stone heart."

"It's a paper heart now, like I told you before, and your name is written all over it."

"I want it to be burned there permanently."

"You brought me to the end of the Earth—then you made me jump off it with you. I can safely say that you stole me and my heart."

"If it's any consolation, you own mine," he admits. "You should hear it beat when you're near. My heart has a special rhythm for you." He pulls me on top of him so that my hips straddle him. My hair runs over my shoulders and pools on his chest. His hand goes to my nape, pulling me down to meet the lust on his tongue.

"Show me this rhythm," I murmur against his mouth. When he demonstrates the rhythm with his body, I cry out his name as my heart beats as one with his.

CHAPTER 11
STOLEN MOMENTS

"What was that?" I ask, startling awake by the ground trembling.

"It was nothing," Trey murmurs next to me. His voice is deeper; he must've fallen asleep too. It's no wonder; he hasn't slept much since we've been here.

"There's something going on outside, Trey!" I hiss with alarm. "The ground is shaking."

I rise from the bed, wrapping the sheet around me, taking it with me. I pass the high-backed chairs in front of the massive window wall. The smoky glass swirls around inside the panes, obscuring my view of the courtyard outside.

"How do you make this transparent?" I ask Trey over my shoulder.

"You don't want to see outside right now, Kricket," he says softly from the bed.

"Why not?" My alarm turns to deep-seated fear instantly. He doesn't meet my eyes.

"It'll scare you. I don't want you to worry. I'll take care of you. We're going to remain safe. There's a plan in place to move from this position. We just have to wait a few more parts until it is feasible to do so."

"Is there a way to unsmoke the window so I can see what's going on?"

"Yes," Trey says reluctantly, sounding irritated that he isn't able to lie to me, "but I don't want you to see what's out there."

A part of me trusts him to know that I shouldn't see it, but another part of me, the survivalist—the chameleon—has to know what's happening—has to take it in—has to learn from it so that I can somehow avoid a similar fate in the future.

"Please let me see what's going on."

Trey climbs off the bed, his naked form a distraction from fear. He moves to the lavare, retrieving his clothes. When he returns, he has on black military-issue pants. He shrugs into a black shirt he normally wears under his combat gear. As he passes the closet, he ducks into it for a moment, coming out with a long, black robe. He brings it to me, holding it open.

"Won't the person who owns that robe mind if I wear it?" I ask casually, but there is nothing casual about my question. It makes my stomach tighten.

"It's Charisma's and she wouldn't mind—but it won't matter anyway. She's not coming back here," he says grimly.

I wonder at his response while he holds the robe open for me. I turn away from him and allow him to ease the robe around my shoulders as I step out of the sheet. It's more like a gown than a robe. I fasten the thongs that hold it closed before tying the ribbonlike belt that wraps around my waist several times. When I'm done, I suspect that I look like a blond-haired geisha in it. The black silky fabric trails on the ground; the waist is stiff with an internal corset. The bell sleeves fall over my hands; only my fingertips are visible. Turning to the window, I weave a fishtail braid into my long hair, tying the end of it in a knot while I wait patiently for him to defog the glass. I worry my lip between my teeth, afraid of what I'll see.

Trey watches me for several moments, aware that I'm unrelenting in my need to see outside. He sighs heavily. "When I transition the window, Kricket, you'll be able to view what's out there, but nothing will be able to see in. Is that clear? You'll remain obscured from the outside."

His words cause me some panic. I nod, feeling my hands tremble. *Why did I allow myself to believe that we were okay here?* I wonder. *Am I naïve or am I stupid?*

Trey takes a deep breath before giving a voice command, "Quadrant four casement. No fenestration. Transparency one way only: interior to exterior."

The roiling smoke between the glass panes dissipates, showing the courtyard beyond. It's dark outside; the stars are the only things I recognize. Rubble covers the once pristine grounds, bathing the topiaries in gray with a thick coating of rock dust. Fires rage in some of the buildings surrounding this one. Others that aren't on fire light up sporadically with blue flashing lights. It looks like blue lightning strikes behind the glass of the tall buildings. I wonder about it until I realize that Alameeda laser fire glows blue.

"They're death squads—they execute civilians," Trey says behind me, following my line of sight.

"Wait. Civilians?" I ask, feeling like I might vomit.

"Alameeda don't take prisoners. It depletes their resources to keep them alive—so they don't do it. But that's not the only reason why they don't. They hate our blood—our genes. They want to eradicate us."

War is raging—they're killing more people. I take an involuntary step back from the window as a dark shadow blots out the stars; it's a drone ship flying nearby. No bigger than a hovercycle, the Stealth-like drone flies through the wide, grassy streets that are now killing fields. Bone-white lights shine from the drone into the crawl spaces, alleys, and niches of the vacant street. Searching slowly, the evil unmanned bot passes over garbage and debris stirred up by its forced air; the rubbish skips past it in the wind like dead autumn leaves.

Amy A. Bartol

Trey's mouth is close to my ear, causing goose bumps to form on my arms when he says, "We did a controlled detonation of the top floors of this building when they were bombing the area, so that they won't be tempted to land here."

"When did you do that?" I ask. "I never heard an explosion."

"Just after we arrived. You were hurt—Jax made sure you slept through it. I gave the order. Hollis executed the plan; he's quite precise with explosives. The architecture was designed with a reinforced core. The debris slid to the sides of the building, allowing the core of the structure to remain intact.

"How did you know it would do that?"

"I designed Charisma's building with defense in mind—the way I designed all my buildings. This one has layers of sensor jammers installed in its infrastructure. It won't show heat signatures if it's scanned from without—the drones will detect no signs of life. It's soundproofed to a hundred and eighty xerts—that's nearly the same in decibels—you'd lose hearing if anything were louder than that. The glass panes are equipped with hologram imaging. We've been projecting a desolate interior—broken windowpanes, looted and burned-out lobby, and uninhabited rooms. Right now, it looks like a shell from the outside. We only need to maintain this façade for a few more parts, until the Alameeda extract their death drones and attempt to take over the city. When they mobilize, so do we."

"How?" I ask, trying to be an active participant in my own survival.

"We have a few options available to us. We'll choose the best course when the time comes."

"When were you going to tell me all this?"

"When it was time to go."

"Why?"

"You didn't ask me your thousand questions—when we were in the lavare. You were different—fragile. Nothing I said then about this would've been to your advantage. I didn't want you to be afraid."

"*Fear* is a good thing, especially in a situation like this." Just as I say that, a drone enters the rubble-infested courtyard of the building. Sharp, white lights pass over the fountain feature in the center of the yard. The machine creeps stealthily over the terrain; it pauses on a topiary in the shape of a spix, scanning it with a grid of blue lights before it moves on, coming closer to where we're standing behind the glass. My heart beats so hard that it hurts.

"Wayra," Trey says in a low voice, speaking into the com-link on his wrist communicator.

"We see it," Wayra's voice responds immediately. "Do you want this one too?"

"I want them all," Trey responds with a hushed, hunterlike quality, "but we let this one go home. It's too close to our position. We don't want them tracking its last-known position and then coming here to investigate."

"It's hard to let it go," Wayra murmurs from wherever he is.

"We don't have to let it go unscathed," Trey replies.

"You got something special for this one?" Wayra asks.

"I do. I'm sending it to you now." He presses buttons on his watchlike communicator.

"What's this program called?" Wayra asks.

Trey replies, "I think we should call this one *whahappened*."

Wayra gives a low laugh, "Is it as good as your *someone-elsie* virus? I truly enjoyed hacking the last drone's navigation and taking over. It felt so right flying it down the throat of that death squad."

"I thought you'd like that. This one is a little different; we don't get to navigate the drone, but when it gets called back to its deployment ship, they'll wonder *whahappened* when it explodes upon docking."

The drone moves closer, searching everywhere for living creatures. Suddenly, it flashes its light right at me and holds it there. I gasp.

Trey hugs me from behind. "I promise you that it can't see you."

I want to turn and run; this thing is so freaking scary. It has two guns with multiple barrels on either side of its bat-shaped wings. One yellow-lighted camera eye swivels around while stark-white lights bleach everything it touches. The light shines directly at me, but the beam doesn't penetrate the room.

"The program I have in place will compensate for new data from the drone. It'll incorporate the drone's searchlights into the holographic image, while still projecting a desolate interior by adding the light elements."

I hold my breath. When the white light swings away from me, I let out a sigh and sag against Trey. His arm across my chest tightens. "It's just running its protocols. It's not intelligent, not like you," he murmurs against my hair. The drone moves back through the courtyard.

Trey holds up his wrist and speaks into his communicator. "Did you get the job done, Wayra?" he asks.

"Yeah, it's done. *Whahappened* is now a part of its nomenclature. When junior returns home to the mother ship, he'll be a harassenger instead of a passenger, and then BOOM!"

The drone slips out of the courtyard; it joins up with another hovering creeper. Their ghostly lights paint the street as they move on. My breath returns to normal until the other drone halts abruptly, flipping a uey. Its lights bear down on something moving in the darkness. The blood in my veins turns to frost.

"It's homing on something," Trey murmurs into his communicator. "Wayra, do you have eyes on it, the second drone?"

"Negative," Wayra replies between his clenched teeth.

"I've got eyes on 'em," says Gibon, joining the conversation. "The ratwacker's got someone." From where I am, I witness a dark-haired couple crawl out from beneath an overturned hovercraft. My insides coil.

Bathed in a light, the couple clings to one another while the drone hovers threateningly above them. The drone with Trey's virus follows it, circling them menacingly. I cringe and pull away from Trey, going to the glass. My breath fogs it as I watch the drone project a holographic image in front of them. *It's me!* I recognize my face, larger than life.

"What's it saying? Can anyone hear it?" Trey asks urgently.

"It wants to know if they've seen Kricket. It says it will let them live if they give it information regarding her whereabouts," Gibon says in a whisper. When the woman shakes her head, the drone reacts violently, turning a flamethrower on her. She instantly catches fire, and the intense heat melts her skin off her. The male beside her catches fire too. He lets go of her, draws a harbinger, and begins to fire on the drone. The companion drone executes him by pumping more than fifty consecutive rounds of bullets into his body in under twenty seconds, reducing him to nothing more than a pile of flaming flesh. The drones take another sweep of the area before they move on up the street once more and disappear from my line of sight.

I rest my forehead on the glass, staring out at nothing in particular. Trey says, "Revoke transparency. Continue camouflage protocol five." The window wall becomes opaque once more as smoke swirls between the glass panes, obscuring the outside world.

I lift my forehead from the glass, looking behind me to Trey. "I need a weapon," I say softly.

"You're safer without one," Trey replies. "The Alameeda don't want to kill you."

"Are you joking?" I ask him incredulously, turning around to face him. I lean against the smoky glass for support.

"No. They want to own you. They won't kill you unless you force them to."

"Maybe I want to decide my own fate should the need arise."

My response does not go over well with him. He grows angry. "You're looking for an OTBD?" he asks in a very predatory way, watching me as if he can see inside my soul. Maybe he can; we traded souls not too long ago.

"Define *OTBD*."

"Out The Back Door. Death by suicide."

"That's about right. I'm not looking to get caught again."

"You're a survivor, that's what you do." Trey's eyes burrow into mine. "I'm counting on you for that," he says in a biting, clipped tone. His eyes look me over as if he's seeing my battle wounds even though they're covered.

"Weapon," I insist, holding out my hand to him.

"No. Not for that. Never for that," he retorts.

"You want to see me with them again?" I ask with my hands on my hips.

"No. I'm not looking to let you go."

"You might not have a choice."

"Why do you say that? Have you seen something I should know about?" he asks, like I'm hiding something from him.

I point my thumb over my shoulder to the window at my back. "Yeah," I scoff, "I just saw two people get killed over me."

"That's war, Kricket. People die."

"They do," I agree. "Badly. But some live. Maybe I don't want to be one of them. Anyway, how am I supposed to defend myself without a weapon?"

"You weren't speaking of defense just now, you were looking for a way out, and I promise you that I'll never give you one. I gave you the opportunity to leave; you didn't take it. Now I can't let you go."

"Why not? You're okay with them torturing me?"

"You made me love you!" he says harshly. "You're not allowed to give up, do you understand? No surrender to death. Whatever happens, you have to survive it."

"But what if things get really, really bad?" I ask.

"Then you fight, like you always do, and we'll pick up the pieces of us later."

"We will?" I ask.

"Yes," he says without a hint of doubt.

I exhale a deep breath. "Okay."

"If you want to learn to defend yourself, then I'm definitely the person to help you do that. Everything is a weapon," he says. As he nears me, he takes his shirt off. I don't have a thought in my head for a second. He pushes the chairs out of our way so that we have room to move around. When he stops in front of me, he looks down at my face. "The problem you have is with your height. You're short."

"I'm not short. You're all freakishly tall," I retort.

He smiles and I lose the fight I had immediately. "If you were taller," he amends, "I would advise you to go for the throat or the face. They're both vulnerable, you can grab the larynx—" he mimes grabbing the front part of his throat "—or strike the cartilage here." He demonstrates a fake chop to his own Adam's apple. "This will gain you some time to get away, but not much."

I listen closely as he explains all the most vulnerable points on the body. He shows me how to exploit them in the most efficient ways, although it's difficult to concentrate, because his body is ridiculous in its perfection. He really needs to put his shirt back on if he wants my full attention. When he demonstrates several ways I can take him down, my focus becomes razor-sharp. He lets me stalk him, as we practice different moves to incapacitate my enemies.

After rehearsing a takedown move at least a hundred times, I finally manage to get Trey flat on his back. Breathing heavily, I pounce on his chest triumphantly. Straddling him, I ask, "Did you just let me beat you?"

He hesitates. "No," he lies.

"Ugh! Little white lies are beneath you, Trey. I need more practice."

"You're doing fine. I've been fighting for a long time. I don't know what kind of practice you can do now that will make up for that."

"I need an equalizer."

I see the reluctant agreement in Trey's eyes. "Yes. You do. But it has to be one that your enemy can't easily take from you and then use against you." His words remind me of the incident in the Beezway with Kesek Alez, when he took the harbinger away from me like he was taking a toy from a child. "I have an idea," he says.

He sits up and lifts me up as he gets to his feet. Playfully, he tosses me on the bed before he moves toward a display console built into the far wall.

There's a menagerie of crystal figurines on the shelves. Some of the cut-glass images are of animals and some are Etharian forms—dancers and musicians. Trey touches a drawer and it slides open. He extracts a long, black lacquer box. Tucking it under his arm, he closes the drawer. Then he selects a few of the crystal figurines from the shelves and brings them back with him to the bed.

Sitting cross-legged on the middle of the bed, I scoot over to make a little more room for him to join me. He does. Sitting cross-legged too, he sets the black lacquer box in front of me.

"What's this?" I ask him, looking at the box curiously.

"What you're looking for."

I try to lift the lid, but it won't open.

"Oh, sorry. I forgot that it's security locked." Trey places his hand on the lid of the box. A blue light scans it. A decisive *click* sounds as the catch of the lid unlatches.

"How come you can open it?"

"I gave this to Charisma," he says, like it's no big deal.

Instantly, I'm irrationally jealous. "Really," I respond by snapping the lid closed again. "Maybe I shouldn't be looking at it then."

Trey frowns. "I think you're looking at this the wrong way. I gave these to Charisma as from one *friend* to another. She wouldn't mind if you use them. She'd want you to be safe."

"Why do I get the feeling that you know very little about how women think?" I ask him.

"I know Charisma very well. You, on the other hand, are often a mystery to me."

I don't know whether to be offended, jealous, or flattered by that statement. As it turns out, I'm a little bit of all three.

He places his hand on the lid again, letting the security program scan it. "You need this, so whether or not either of you likes the fact that you're borrowing it doesn't really matter that much to me."

When the lid unlatches once more, Trey opens it without preamble. Inside, the box is lined with lavender-colored satin. Resting in the center of the bed of satin are two silver cuffs. The jewelry is Gothic in design; each resembles the framework that holds panes of stained glass in a lavish church window, but without the colored glass itself.

I raise my eyebrow at Trey. "If these are some kind of freaky, sexy restraints—"

Trey's shoulder nudges against mine as he chuckles softly, like I'm joking. "No," he replies, before grinning and showing all his perfect teeth. "Sweet furroo, I love you. But, no, these are weapons, though I like where your mind is going—"

I have no idea what *sweet furroo* means, but a part of me wants desperately to hear him say it again with the same sexy groan. Instead, I nudge my shoulder against his arm to stop him from whatever he's about to say. "Just show me what you have here."

Lifting one of the cuffs from the box, I see it's clearly made to fit a feminine forearm. I depress a small groove in the side of the cuff, and it opens with the spring of a hinge.

"This is a sonic sayzer, Kricket," Trey says. He lifts my wrist with his other hand and pushes back the silky material of my robe.

Delicately, he clasps the cool metal device to my forearm. It's heavier than I expected, weighing at least a pound. "It can kill things—"

"—with sound," we say together.

Trey looks up at my face. "That's right. How did you know that?"

"Defense Minister Telek explained it to me when he was showing me Manus's wounds. He had Manus in a tank in his office."

"Telek's one sick Etharian," Trey replies grimly. Looking back to my wrist, he adjusts the cuff so that it's properly balanced before he closes it over my skin.

"Well, the poison I gave him probably didn't help with that either," I reply.

A small, reluctant smile forms on his lips. "You're so intelligent. You probably don't even need this weapon. You just need time to assess a situation to find the best solution."

"I'd feel better if I had something like this, though. So, how does it work?"

Trey flips my hand over so that it's palm up. He touches the metal column of the device, stroking the metal plate over my wrist. A lavender-colored beam of light shines on my open palm. The light projects a keypad on my hand. Trey begins entering codes to the prompts. After he enters the first series of numbers, letters, and symbols, the metal on my wrist warms and becomes malleable, shrinking to fit me like a snug sleeve. The metal takes on the feel of stiff fabric as it moves to just below my elbow. The cuff grows over the top of my hand, threading through the gap between my index finger and my middle finger, my middle finger and my ring finger, and again between my ring finger and my pinky.

I turn my hand over several times, examining the fit and structure of the weapon I'm wearing, or is wearing me, depending upon how you look at it. "They're going to love me at the Robotic Renaissance festival this year," I say softly, admiring the arching metal design. It's engraved with scrollwork that resembles Trey's tattoo.

Trey doesn't laugh; he only looks confused. "Any festivals you were planning to attend have probably been canceled, Kricket."

I nod, not wanting to explain. "You're probably right. How does this work?" I ask instead.

Trey rises from the bed and moves back to the display cabinet where he retrieved the sonic sayzer. He opens a different drawer and extracts a small, black conelike apparatus. He takes it and moves back toward the window wall at the far end of the room. Setting the conelike apparatus on the floor, he squats down and touches a few buttons. Light pours up from the machine on the floor, projecting holographic stars over the room in that area. "Dim lights," Trey orders, and the room darkens, allowing us to see the galaxy of stars more clearly.

From his pocket, he extracts a few of the crystal figurines and tosses them into the cone-shaped sea of stars. Instantly, the figurines float in the air as if they've entered zero gravity. It does something else to each one. The figurine shaped like a spix animates and rears up on its hind legs, pawing the sky like a wild mustang. The saer opens its saber-toothed mouth, stalking the other figurines and swiping its paws at them, but it never quite seems to actually touch any. The elegant couple in formal attire dance together. I recognize the moves as the dance that Tofer taught me to do for my debut swank with the Regent. Those memories scare me, so I clear my throat and ask, "What are these things called?"

"Targets," he replies with an evil grin.

"You mean we're going to shoot them?" I ask.

"Oh, we're going to destroy these targets," he breathes like he's been waiting for this day all of his life.

I roll my eyes. "What are they *really* called?"

Trey searches his mind. "Sacred Moments? Special Moments? Crystal Moments—Crystal Clear Moments!" he says, excited that he remembers their name. "They were really popular about seventy-five floans ago, before the war—the Terrible War—the war before this one," he amends.

"Really? You don't seem to be a fan of them."

"I'm not. They annoy me. That's why we're going to use them for target practice."

"You can't do that, Trey!" I say, "They're not yours!"

"They're not going to make it through this war, one way or the other, Kricket. We might as well learn something from them before they're destroyed," he replies. "Charisma didn't like most of them anyway. She only kept them because they were gifts from family. This one"—he points to the elegant couple—"was supposed to be us at her coming-out swank. She hated it. She thought it looked nothing like either of us."

While he goes back to the display cabinet for more figurines to murder, I walk closer to the dancing crystal couple. They're perfectly matched as they spin in synchronization through the stars; the female holds her billowing crystal dress while the male's capable arm at her back holds her frame close against his powerful chest. The crystal male figure bears a strong resemblance to Trey, although he's much stronger and more muscly looking at present. The male bears more of a resemblance to Victus than Trey. *I still hate it for what it represents—Trey and Charisma forever entwined in each other's arms.*

When Trey returns, he tosses a mastodon into the mix. It raises its noble, crystal snout in a defiant posture. "A mastoff to represent her first trip to the Forest of O," Trey says. He tosses an expensive-looking trift into the air; it catches in the zero gravity pool. "Gets her license." The Stealth-like trift flies around the galaxy in twisting, fantastic maneuvers, avoiding the other crystals by centimeters. "Graduates from Robard's Academy for Blushers," he tosses a pointed-toed ballerina-looking dancer into the mix.

"The school wasn't really called Robard's Academy for Blushers, was it?" I ask him with a smile.

He shakes his head, grinning again. "It was Robard's Academy for Accomplished Young Fays, which really is just code for 'pampered blushers.'"

I watch the ballerina-like figurine circle the rest in a hypnotic spinning motion. *I like her.* I relate to her solo dance—I used to always dance alone, just for me. "What was the spix for?" I ask, as she passes by it.

Trey squints at the spix, watching it rear up again and paw the air. "Best in Show. Charisma trains spixes—breeds them for competition. She also rides them in tournaments. That's why I bought her these sonic sayzers; she uses them to shoot targets while riding her competition spix through a course. The competition itself is called Biequine. She's quite skilled at it too—a perfect shot."

My eyes return to the spix. *I like that one too.* It reminds me of Trey—the Knight. He dumps several more crystal statuettes into the Milky Way pool. When he turns to gather a few more, I rescue the crystal spix from the sea of stars. Quietly, I palm it, feeling an instant connection to it. I then slip the spix into the pocket of my black robe.

Trey moves to the bed, extracting the other cuff from the box. He quickly calibrates it, adjusting it to fit his much larger arm. Then he joins me in front of the menagerie of Stolen Moments, or whatever they're called.

"We need to move back." He pulls me back to the far wall. From the side of my wrist, he touches an empty windowlike arch in the metal. It opens a compartment that contains a small earpiece. He extracts it and pushes it into my ear. A mouthpiece slides out from the earpiece and positions itself in front of my mouth. "It's not armed yet," he says, "but when it is, make sure that your sayzer isn't pointed at anything important—like me."

I nod solemnly. "I understand. How does it arm?" I ask.

"We'll have to enter a sequence of finger movements that will arm it. It will be personal so that only you can use the weapon. I've overridden Charisma's settings with the master code I used to set it. I've got this on a practice setting. It will only shoot short-frequency bursts. They'd sting if they hit skin, but it would be more like a small pellet—not lethal."

"Okay." We come up with a combination of finger movements that Trey says will become a muscle memory response the more I practice with the weapon.

He walks me through the basics of how to use it, but when I raise my wrist Spider-Man style and say the words that are supposed to fire the weapon, the rotten thing does nothing but vibrate.

"Seriously?" I ask after Trey strikes two more crystal figurines without even trying by using the word *fire*. But when I say it, nothing happens!

Trey examines the weapon, checking and rechecking it. "It's working. Maybe you just need to try different tones of voice."

Trey uses his sonic sayzer, hitting a couple more crystal figurines with the words "knob knocker." He's so good at it—he never misses.

"You're enjoying this, aren't you?"

"You mean destroying these statuettes?" he asks.

"Yes," I say, nodding.

"Yes."

"Why?"

"I can't explain it."

"Try."

"Ever since I was old enough to know who I was, I knew that the future everyone wanted for me wasn't what I wanted for myself. I wasn't encouraged to make a career in the Cavars; I was only supposed to serve for a few fleats—do my service, and then leave it behind to go into the family business."

"The family business?" I ask.

"Allairis Engineering," he replies. "My family designs buildings, estates, ecostructures, as well as other things. My father particularly looks to me for security infrastructure. And at every step along the way, Charisma and I have been present for every single milestone in each other's lives, not by choice, but because it was expected. I would've been there for her by choice. She's my best friend, but there's no spark there—no worry that if I don't see her in the next few parts I might lose my mind. Do you know what I'm saying?" he asks me.

"No passion?" I ask.

"No passion," he agrees. That should make me feel better, but it doesn't. It makes me feel worse. Passion is fleeting. Friendship is forever.

"*Fire*," I say with my wrist up, aiming at the dancing couple. When nothing happens, I growl at my shiny sleeve, talking to it, "This is so frustrating! Why won't you work, you stupid piece of—"

Strong arms encircle my waist from behind, causing me to jump. Trey pulls my back against his chest. His mouth nuzzles my neck, instantly taking away my frustration by shifting it to intense desire. "Relax," he says near my ear. "You don't have to be perfect at everything."

"You don't know me at all, do you?" I ask. "You don't understand. I really need to destroy the dancing couple."

"Annoying, aren't they, Kitten?" His rumbling laugh is heaven against my throat.

"The worst, honey." I whisper the last word because his kiss against my sensitive skin makes me breathless. Then, *BOOM*, my arm retracts violently as my gloved wrist fires a sonic boom into the floor. The foundation shakes from the blast while the lights in the room flicker.

"Ho-ly Fffmmm—" Trey covers my mouth with his hand and cuts me off.

"Shh," he whispers in my ear. Jax and Wayra come bursting into the bedroom.

"What the shickles, Trey?" Jax asks angrily when he sees us together, each with a sonic sayzer on our arms and locked in an intimate embrace. "Is this some kinky—"

Trey interrupts him. "It's not what it looks like. I was showing her how to use a sonic sayzer and it went off unexpectedly."

"You should lower the setting," Wayra advises while inspecting the deep crater in the floor.

"It's set to practice mode," Trey growls. He doesn't move his hand from my mouth until he pulls the earpiece and microphone from me, inspecting the device for any outward flaws.

"It's not supposed to do that in the practice setting," Wayra replies unhelpfully.

"Thanks, Wayra," Trey growls.

"With all mercies," Wayra replies with the polite Etharian you're-welcome response.

"What word did this," Jax asks, joining Wayra at the hole in the floor.

"She said a phrase. I'm not sure which word it responded to."

"What was the phrase?"

"'The worst, honey,'" Trey answers.

"The word *fire* did nothing," I add.

Jax looks at me with a shrug. "Well, it wouldn't."

"Huh?" I ask.

"You're not speaking Etharian. You're speaking Earthling."

"I'm speaking English," I correct him.

"Which is Earthling," he says defensively, like I should never have corrected him for it. "We just hear everything in Etharian because we have translator implants with an English upgrade. But you're not speaking my language, sister."

"You're right!" I grin at Jax, who grins at me in return. "Mystery solved."

"We can't risk shooting it off in here again," Trey says. He replaces the earpiece back into the compartment of my sayzer sleeve. "Enter the secondary code, Kricket." I move my fingers awkwardly, like I'm playing keys on an invisible piano. The sonic sayzer shrinks from its expanded sleeve back to a shorter cuff. "We'll try it again when we're in our new location."

"Where is our new location? When are we going? " I ask, worried about leaving as much as I am about staying.

Trey glances at Wayra, who is rubbing his chin and staring into the hole in the floor like he's trying to figure out where it ends. "How are the preparations coming for our departure?"

"We're solid," Wayra says absently. "We're just finishing up our prep to welcome the knob knocker's troops to our fair city. We're waiting for our patrol to return. After that, we can leave any time. The tunnel is fully operational—we're evacuating civvies as fast as we can move them."

Trey nods. He turns to me and says, "I need to see to some things. Do you want to change"—he indicates Charisma's closet—"and meet me in the other room for dinner?"

"Yes. I'll come find you when I'm ready," I reply.

Trey, Jax, and Wayra leave while I hunt for clothes in an impressively large closet. Walking past aisles of printed fabric pressed between glass panels, I marvel at the selection—it rivals my own at the palace. Soft, flowing patterns create dreamy shapes and cloud-like waves as coats, blouses, skirts, and trousers billow, suspended in midair by constant streams of perfectly positioned forced-air vents between the glass panels. I select a pair of form-fitting pants by touching the surface of a panel. The glass opens and the article slips into my waiting hand from its hanger of air. The pants are too long for me, but since the tight black fabric clings to my calves, they gather, creating a surprisingly stylish look.

I have the same problem with the tops; all of them are too long for me. I select a sleeveless black blouse that's cut in a deep vee in the front. It's made for someone with less curves than me, so it pushes what I have up and exposes more skin than I'd like, but I can't worry about that now. I locate a wide, black belt, cinching it to ride low on my hips. I move on to footwear. The shoes prove more difficult. Most of the ones I try on are too big for me. I settle for some black boots that aren't too big once I stuff a small, silk handkerchief in each toe.

Rising from a soft-cushioned bench after buckling them, I move to leave the closet, but I spy a row of masculine clothes in the corner of the room. On impulse I follow the line of clothing, noticing everything from casual attire to formal wear. I look to see if there are any Cavar uniforms, but there aren't. *Are these Trey's clothes? Did he and Charisma live together at some point?* I wonder.

Deciding that it's none of my business, I find a soft leather jacket that's about my size and deposit the crystal spix I rescued into its pocket. Putting on the jacket, I walk out to the reception area. It's been turned into a virtual command center. Holograms of several different battlefields follow Alameeda death squads rampaging on the city streets. Explosions throw bodies onto the red-and-copper-colored dirt.

I jump when Trey touches my elbow. He lays a soft kiss on my cheek when he sees that I can't find any words for what I'm seeing.

He speaks instead: "The fighting is taking place on the opposite side of the city. We'd have trouble getting there from here. We're undermining the Alameeda resupply, wreaking havoc on their ability to fight effectively."

"How are you doing that?" I ask, but swiftly turn my attention to the wall near us when the twinkle of cascading water ceases.

In lieu of a fireplace, a stunning waterfall is the focal point of the space. The green-tiled water feature positioned between the two smoke-filled window walls has stopped working abruptly. From somewhere beneath the wall, a series of knocks sound. Drex moves to the wall, knocking back on it. Another series of knocks sounds from the other side. Drex smiles. He touches several of the green, jade, and white glass tiles on the wall.

There is a change of air pressure in the room as the wall recedes to show descending steps. Fenton emerges from the dark depths of the staircase tugging on the ends of the silky threads of a sky blue parachute. He's covered in grit and has smears of gray greasepaint on his face. His snow-white teeth shine against his matte gray lips as he grins. "Success! The satellite uplink worked! Trey's program hacked their drones, loaded them by supply-bot with sanctum amps, and flew 'em into their formations." He produces a perfect red apple from his pack and takes a huge bite of it, noshing, and wiping his mouth with his sleeve. "Anyone hungry?" Behind Fenton, Hollis drags part of the parachute covered with food into the room. Fenton smiles and adds, "We brought down a chow ship along with several others."

Hollis scowls at Fenton. "Help me bring it in, ya jackwagon!" The Cavars all converge on it, bringing the prepackaged food into the room, tossing various items around as each calls out his selection from the treasure trove.

"Did you bring back the satellite uplink?" Trey asks Fenton.

"Yeah, we got it. It was close, though. Gibon is bringing it up now. They targeted the building and reduced it to rubble after we jumped off the roof. The glide suits worked well." He extends his arms, showing us the chameleon-fabric squirrel-like jumpsuit he's wearing. "I'd like to get my hands on a Riker Pak, though," he admits, referring to the jet packs the Alameeda use.

"They'd be helpful," Trey agrees, "but your glide suit doesn't leave a heat signature that they can trace. They're blind when we don't use technology."

"But they go *boom* when we do," Wayra interjects with another smug smile. He moves forward and bumps his shoulder against Trey's in some kind of sign of camaraderie.

Gibon comes up from the depths of the tunnel beneath the water wall carrying a small dishlike apparatus with him. He has greasepaint on his face as well. He selects a fancy bottle from among the plethora of others in the parachute. Walking to the elegant kitchen, he goes to the commissary unit and collects two elegant glasses. He depresses a notch on the side of the bottle, and a spout emerges from its neck. He pours the brown liquid into the two short glasses. Meeting my eyes, he extends a glass out to me, knowing I'm watching him. I leave Trey's side, going to him in the kitchen. I take the drink he offers me. Lifting it up to him in silent salute, he mimics my movement. "To Dylan," he says, raising his glass to our fallen friend.

"To Dylan," I agree with a sad smile. We each put the glass to our lips and drink together. It's definitely alcohol and it definitely makes me cough a little.

Gibon drains his glass in one swallow. He sets it on the stone countertop. "I should've had his back," he says like a confession.

Looking down into my glass, I swirl its contents with a twist of my wrist. The cuff of the sonic sayzer peeks out from beneath my sleeve. "It was chaos, Gibon. We barely got out alive," I reply. I take another small sip of my drink.

"I messed up." He pours himself another glass of the brown liquid. "It's not like that was my first day on the job and I overslept or something. He got smoked and I did nothing. They blew him out of the sky." He tucks the alcohol away with one swallow.

"The Alameeda picked the world up and dropped it on us, Gibon. You protected us." I nod at the Cavars hustling around in the Great Room.

"You've got it wrong. You saved them," he says with a frown, "and me. There is no Ship of Skye now; it's gone, and we'd be gone with it if not for you."

I don't know how to respond to that, so I change the subject by saying, "You're kind of amazing at driving a hovercycle. Do you think you can teach me how sometime?"

His violet-colored eyes soften. "I'll teach you how to fly anything you want."

"I think that's my job," Trey says as he enters the kitchen and stands next to me.

"Is it?" I ask him with a raise of an eyebrow. "I didn't want to overload you with too many tasks. You already have to teach me how to swim and climb enormous trees. I was just trying to lighten your load."

He puts his arm around my waist, drawing me to his side possessively. Smiling in a predatory way, he murmurs, "You're my intended consort. It's my pleasure."

I silently finish his sentence: *And no one else's.*

"Well, you'll have your work cut out for you then, won't you, because I've never driven anything before. I never had a bike, or a scooter, or a car," I reply. Gibon chokes on his liquor, coughing as he looks from me to Trey incredulously.

Trey shrugs and says, "She's from Chicago."

Gibon wipes his arm on his sleeve. "So I've heard. I just never— you've never even driven a flipcart?" he asks, as if it would be a crime not to have done so.

"I don't even know what that is," I reply honestly, taking a larger sip of my drink and paying for it with a wheeze.

Jax approaches our little party. He hands ration packs to Trey. "Here, you might want to take a couple of these. We're packing up the rest. Are you hungry, Kricket?" he asks me.

The alcohol is making me feel light-headed. It's not unpleasant; in fact, it's kind of nice. I look toward the bottle. "I think I want some more of that."

"Negative," Trey says right away, taking my empty glass from me. "You've recently been dehydrated and malnourished. You need food. Come with me."

Trey leads me to a formal dining area. I sit in a chair that he holds out for me. He brings us both a plate and sits right beside me. Breaking open the ration packs, he unloads the fare onto both plates. As we begin to eat together quietly, Drex approaches us. He stops in front of me, laying down a package of cocoa-covered wafers tied with a ruby-colored ribbon in front of my plate. He also lays down a large, shiny metal object that looks suspiciously like brass knuckles. With a respectful nod to Trey, Drex moves away from the table. I stop chewing in confusion.

Hollis approaches the table next. He smiles at me as he sets a bottle of fazaria, Manus's favorite after-dinner drink, in front of me. Along with the bottle, he leaves a wicked-looking clawlike implement that appears to be made to disembowel something. Gibon follows with several pieces of fresh fruit and a simple-looking short jade club. Fenton continues the line with an assortment of candies that he leaves amid the other gifts, as well as a small weapon that would fit in the palm of my hand. I think the proper name for it on Earth is a katar, but I have no idea what they call it here.

When Wayra sets a freeze-wrapped petite venish in front of me, I have trouble keeping my mouth from falling open. He also rests a small knife on the table. "I'll teach you how to use it later." I nod to him in acknowledgment. He moves aside and lets Jax through. Jax gives me their version of chocolate, called hohoban; it's in the shape of flower petals. He also leaves me two sharp metal implements that resemble deadly chopsticks.

With both my eyebrows raised in surprise, I murmur, "These are for me, I assume."

Grinning, they all nod and talk at once in what I gather are affirmative answers.

When they quiet, I murmur, "Thank you, guys, but I didn't get you anything." I look at Trey, who's trying really hard not to laugh.

The Cavars, however, laugh at me like I'm an adorable idiot. Drex pipes up, "We're not the ones who just agreed to commit to our gennet, so it wouldn't be proper to give us a gift in return."

Hollis explains, "The treats are to honor your announcement to commit to a lifetime of submitting to his will. We know what that's like. You have our deepest condolences!" They all roar at that, like it's the funniest thing imaginable.

"The weapons are a tribute because you saved our lives," Jax explains.

Trey takes my left hand in his, turning it over so that my palm faces down. He encircles my wrist with an intricately scrolled silver armband. The armband immediately shrinks in size from what was clearly a male fit to a feminine size. After he touches the crest in the middle of the thick bracelet, a wicked-looking, sharp-pointed silver star emerges from within the bracelet; it's magnetized to its cradle of metal, waiting to be touched and used. "Before I was able to locate you on the skywalk, I had to retrieve my spare wrist communicator from my room. I managed to get that as well while I was there. It belonged to my father; he gave it to me when I went to war the last time. Now I give it to you as payment for my life." Trey takes the star from the top of the bracelet. "It's a starcross." He holds it up for me to see. I recognize it. Kyon has something similar to it that he used to kill Geteron in the interrogation room on the Ship of Skye. The star is like a boomerang; it returns to the bracelet after it's thrown.

"I can't take this," I say, afraid of such a gift as this. It's a family heirloom and I don't even know if his family will accept me. "You can't give me this."

"I already gave it to you. You can't give it back," he counters, setting the starcross back on top of the bracelet. He touches the middle of the star-shaped metal; it slides back inside its home within the bracelet, concealed by the crest once more.

My fingertips pass over the etched crest on top of the bracelet reverently; it's the Allairis crest. I've seen it on a ring that Victus wears. "But you saved me on the skywalk and at the palace. You've saved my life more times than I've saved yours." I try to take the bracelet off so I can hand it back to him.

He won't help me remove it. Instead, his hand covers mine on the silver bracelet. "It's my *job* to protect you—not only as a Cavar, but as your intended consort."

That's stupid machismo thinking. "And I'm not supposed to protect you in return?" I ask.

He blinks. "Well . . . no."

"I'll never understand you people," I murmur in frustration.

"Yes, you do," he replies, taking my hand in his. "You live by a code. So do we."

"You know my code?" I ask him.

"I'm getting to know it."

"Really?"

"From an early age, you've learned never to trust anyone but yourself. You let almost no one help you, but the ones you do allow into your life have special significance to you: you love them, even when sometimes you wish that you didn't. Because when you love someone, Kricket, it means you're completely loyal to that person, you'll sacrifice anything for him—even your life. How am I doing so far?"

I shrug, noncommittal. "So you fancy yourself a code hacker?"

"On occasion," he replies.

"I used to have a simpler code."

"Let me guess: I'm an island."

"Something like that. It wasn't working out for me as well as I would've liked."

"If it's any consolation, I'm shipwrecked on your island. To use your words: deal with it."

We're interrupted then by music streaming in from the amazing sound system within the walls. Drex approaches me by the side of my chair. "I pulled the watch shift with Hollis. We'd like our dance now."

Drex pulls me into an area next to the dining room. Thanks to my private tutor, Tofer, I'm well acquainted with all of their popular formal dances, as well as some of the informal ones. Drex chooses an informal dance called the Hop Step, which is literally a really fast hop-step-clap kind of dance. I'm quickly passed around from dance partner to dance partner, until my cheeks are rosy and I'm out of breath.

The tempo of the music slows and I find myself in Trey's arms. The Cavars have all suspiciously cleared out and left us alone in the elegant room. I don't think that what we're doing now can be called dancing by the standards of either Ethar or Earth. Trey's hand strokes my hair as I rest my head on his solid chest; we sway to the rhythm as the music plays.

◦𝔰▽𝔰◦

It's late when Trey gets into bed. Stretching out beneath the blankets, he pulls me against him, burying his nose in my hair. His skin is cold, like he's been outside and he smells of night air. I turn toward him and smile sleepily. "Hi," I whisper.

"I love that word," he says. "It used to make me look up for something high, did you know that?"

I giggle and shake my head. "I didn't," I admit.

"Now I know that it's your way of greeting people, but you say it differently to me," he says, smiling.

"I do?"

"Yes. You say it breathlessly to me," he explains.

"Well that's because I haven't really been saying 'hi' to you; I've been saying: 'I love you.'"

He kisses the hollow between the valley of my neck and shoulder. I gasp softly, my hand reaching out and gripping his bicep, feeling the smooth skin over powerful muscle. My hand moves to his back and strokes him over the woven tapestry of muscles that make up the intricate texture that's Trey.

"I'm slowly learning all the subtle nuances of you, Kricket. I want to discover your every thought . . ." his kisses travel down me, over my clavicle " . . . your every look . . ." he kisses the pink tip of one breast, and I inhale deeply " . . . every curve . . ." he moves farther to kiss my stomach " . . . and every other freckle."

I giggle as much at his comment as at the feel of his bristly skin against my sensitive flesh. Grasping his face, I make him look at my eyes. "Why every *other* freckle?" I ask him. "Why not all of them?"

"Well, I didn't want to sound obsessed, and also some freckles aren't as good-natured as others." As I laugh harder, Trey rises on his elbow, smiling down at me. "That's the sound that I want to live in for the rest of my life."

I rise on my elbow to meet his lips with mine. He sits up and pulls me onto his lap so that we're face-to-face. He makes love to me then, eye to eye and skin to skin. I watch his every expression and he watches mine.

Just after I call out Trey's name in a breathless haze of pleasure, I hear a feminine voice speak from across the bedroom. "You've been hard to locate." I stiffen in Trey's arms. Looking over my shoulder, I find the Bee priestess seated in one of the tall wing-backed chairs that are facing the bed. Her legs are draped over the arm of it with her back against the other arm.

"How did you get in here?" I demand, as outrage and fear war inside me. Outrage wins.

"Who are you talking to?" Trey asks, startled by my abrupt change in demeanor.

I wave my hand at the blond girl in the chair. "An Alameeda priestess," I growl my response. Slipping from his lap, I pull the sheet up to my chest as I face the Bee.

"Where is she?" Trey asks, reaching for his pants on the floor near the bed.

"In the chair." I nod my head toward where she's slouching. "Can't you see her?"

"No," he growls in response.

She looks at her fingernails. "Well, technically, I'm not really here. I'm just projecting myself here. Normally, no one can see me. You are the first person who's been able to detect my presence."

"Who are you? What do you want?" I ask.

"My name is Nezra and I want you to die," she answers honestly.

"Well, Nezra, I don't think I'll accommodate you. I sort of enjoy breathing," I reply.

Trey whispers in my ear, "Keep her talking while I alert the others for a random change in plan." I nod.

Nezra watches Trey slip on his shirt and gather the clothes I had on earlier, bringing them to me. He leans down and kisses me, before moving quickly to the door. When he's gone, Nezra says, "So the big Rafian soldier is your lover. Felicitations, little sister; I didn't think you'd have it in you to defy the Brotherhood in this way. You surprise me."

"Trey's my intended consort."

She laughs mockingly. "You're either really brave or really stupid. Kyon will kill him in front of you when he gets here. You know that, don't you?"

"I'll kill him if he tries," I counter savagely.

She straightens in the chair at once, anger showing on her beautiful face. "I'll kill you if you harm him. You don't deserve Kyon."

"Ugh, gross! Do you like him?" I pretend to vomit in my mouth a little before I slip the black sleeveless blouse over my head once more, pulling it down over me.

"He was supposed to be *my* consort, but our mother ruined it all."

"*Our* mother? You mean you're my sister?" I ask. I'm unable to think for a second.

"Half sister," she amends with disgust. "I'm not blood-tainted like you. I'm full-blooded Alameeda."

"We have the same mother?" I repeat, stunned.

"That's about all we have in common."

"Did she raise you? How old were you when she—"

"—faked her own death?"

I stare at her in shock.

"She faked her own death so that she could leave me. Does that sound familiar?" Nezra asks.

I feel like I can't breathe. "What?" is all I can muster at the moment.

"You don't really think she's dead, do you?"

"Yes, I do."

"She's far too brilliant to die from Crue. Maybe she just wanted to get away from you."

I want to kill her. "How come Kyon never mentioned you to me?" I ask incredulously.

"He doesn't like talking about me," she says.

"Why not?"

"Because it's too painful a subject for him," she lies.

I snort and decide that she's pathological. "Uh-huh. You're a lurker, aren't you?" I pull on my pants and then get up from the bed to put on the belt.

She gasps audibly. "I'm a priestess! It's an honor to be in my presence!"

I roll my eyes. "Who are you people? You're so conceited! You must bore him to death. No wonder he said he's tired of inane blonds. I can only assume he means you."

"I am *highly* intelligent," she growls, pointing her sharp fingernail at me. "If you must know, my suit was awarded to his cousin, Chandrum, instead of to him!" She's breathing hard, as if what I said offends her.

"So they forced you to commit to Chandrum instead of Kyon?" I ask with an aloof air, putting on one boot and buckling it.

"Yes," she nods.

"Why'd you let that happen? Why didn't you fight for him?"

She makes a derogatory sound. "No one fights the Brotherhood. That's a ridiculous statement."

I pull on the second black boot. "Well, why'd they choose Chandrum for you and not Kyon?"

She ignores my question. "Why haven't you left the city yet?" she asks. "You're hiding like cowards here. Kyon will be here soon. It's like you're waiting for him."

"I'm not waiting for him. The Cavars have been infecting your drones so you freaks can't use them to kill civilians. Why has it taken you so long to find me?" I bait her.

"You've been blocking me. Ever since I tried to kill you in your cell, you've been reluctant to let me near you. I guess I've caught you at a weak moment," she smiles, nodding toward the bed.

"There was nothing weak about that moment. Did you tell Kyon I'm here?" I ask.

"Oh, he knows. If you're too stupid to use your gifts to find out what he's planning and stay ahead of him, then you deserve to have him find you and kill your lover."

"As soon as I do figure it out, you'd best run, Nezra. I could maybe excuse you for trying to kill me in my cell—I'd chalk it up to sibling rivalry—but now you're starting to piss me off." I walk past her, gather up the floating crystals in my arms, and take them to the black lacquer case that contains both of the sonic sayzer cuffs as well as all the weapons I was given at dinner. I put them in the box as well.

Taking a deep breath, I try to think more clearly. I take out one of the silver cuffs. Slipping it on my arm, I move my fingers, making the weapon elongate into a sleeve. I walk past Nezra again, returning to the zero-gravity apparatus. Shutting it off, I gather it from the floor. It, too, goes into the weapons' box, next to the crystals and the other cuff.

Nerza's blond bee's nest that she calls hair bobbles as she asks, "Why is he obsessed with you? What have you done to him to make him this way?"

I slip on Charisma's black jacket. "Who? Kyon?" I ask with a raise of my eyebrow. "Well, that's simple, Nezra. I ran away from him and swore to him that I'd never do anything he says. You should try it sometime. It's called 'I hate you, leave me alone.' It gets all the psychos foaming at the mouth for more. Add a little 'I'll never love you,' and *bam*! Instant crazy."

"You belong to him. He can do whatever he wants to you. You'll find out."

I point my finger at her. "That's where you're wrong. He can't do whatever he wants to me, because I'm not going to let him."

I go to the closet to get a messenger bag I'd seen there earlier. I stuff clothes into it as fast as I can. Back in the bedroom, I gather up the black box, sliding it into the bag. Slipping the bag over my shoulder, I look at Nezra standing by the chair.

"Why are you still here?" I ask. I'm halfway to the door.

"Falla wants me to ask you a question."

I pause. "Who's Falla?"

"She's the priestess who likes you—although she cannot explain to me why she does with any clarity." I wrinkle my brow at her in confusion, trying to remember which one was Falla—the Bird or the Flower? "The one who sensed your presence when we were tending to Kyon."

The Bird, I think, remembering her as being the one who helped Nezra force me out of their future. The Flower was the other one who healed Kyon with the freaky silver light.

"I'm not interested in answering her questions," I reply, almost to the door.

"She just wants to know if you love the other one too."

I stop where I am and look over my shoulder at her. "The other one? What other one?" I ask.

Her smile, I decide, is sinister as she says, "The one from Wurthem: Vance Giffen."

I flip her off as I leave the room.

CHAPTER 12
KEEP THEE TO ME

There's a shickle load of them outside," Wayra says to me, as I join him and Trey in the Great Room. Trey takes my hand, bringing me closer so that he can wrap his arm around my waist and pull me to his side.

"Everything's ready," Jax says as he joins us.

"Then it's time to go," Trey states. They all look at ease, like having the Alameeda outside is a normal, everyday thing.

"We're going out there?" I ask, fear making my knees weak.

Trey whispers in my ear, "Did you lose the other priestess or is she still about?"

I search the interior of the room, but nothing out of the ordinary catches my eye. "I think she's gone. I left her back in our room. She hasn't followed me—I don't know if she can."

From somewhere outside, Kyon's voice booms bullhorn-loud. "Kricket, do not make me come in to get you. I will kill everyone inside if you do."

"Uhh," I exhale, as if he hit me in the stomach. I cover my face with my hands, rubbing it involuntarily. *They're gonna break down the doors.* "I have to go to him."

Trey's arm squeezes me tighter. "I don't think so. You're not going to him, Kricket. Today you're a magician's assistant and I'm going to make you disappear."

I drop my hands from my face. "What do you mean?"

Trey leads me to the wall of falling water. He touches the jade and ivory tiles; it turns off the water and opens the descending steps. Handing me night-vision glasses, he says, "Now you see us."

He leads me down the steps into a tunnel lined with a conduit of wires and pipes.

"Now you don't," I breathe.

"This is how we've been getting people out of the city. We've been patrolling the streets, saving the ones we can by funneling them through these passageways. I never filed any of the schematics for my tunnels to any of the Isle of Skye zoning authorities. They don't exist in any databases. They're sort of illegal."

"Trey, you're a doomsday planner."

"Guilty," Trey agrees. He leads us to his waiting hovercycle. "Unlace compartment," he murmurs. The lid of the hovercycle opens for us. Trey mounts the seat, pulling me down behind him. He waits for me to wrap my arms around his waist. "Ready?" he asks as he starts the engine. I lean against him, my cheek resting upon his broad back. I nod so he can feel my answer. The compartment lid closes around us. The other Cavars are mounted on their hovercycles, moving ahead of us through the tunnel.

Our hoverbike rockets forward, away from Charisma's sanctuary. I silently make a note to thank her for her generous hospitality, even though she had nothing to do with it. A few minutes later, the ground trembles as a *boom* shakes the walls around us. The tunnel behind us collapses, spewing out a volcano of rock dust. Wayra's laughter comes through the hovercycle's com-link; it sounds a little bit like a goat being strangled. When he catches his breath, he says, "What a bunch of knob knockers."

"Do you think we got Kyon?" Jax asks from his hoverbike beside us.

"I wish I knew," I murmur. My breath becomes an icy coil before my eyes. The world around me melts away.

Seabirds fly overhead; their cries are mocking laughter on the ocean breeze. Kyon's eyes, the bluest of blue, stare down at me. He reaches for the nape of my neck, tying a red flower around my throat. It's a black-ribboned choker adorned with the rarest bud. His elegant black dress uniform seems out of place in the fading light of the setting sun upon the water. With sand between my toes, I stare at the lapping waves on the beach. Gold and silver shine in the tide along the shoreline, a seaside with all the stars of the heavens captured within it. The thin veil covering my eyes parts, his eyes lean to me, bringing with them havoc within my bones. I stifle my instinct to recoil. "With this flower," Kyon says, smiling down upon me, "I keep thee to me . . . always. Welcome home, Kricket."

"Kricket . . . Kricket," Trey rubs my arms that have gone slack around his waist. "Answer me. Are you okay?"

I lift my head from his back. We're still moving stealthily through the underground tunnels on his hovercycle. I'm disoriented, but I manage to say, "I'm fine." I hear the thickness in my own voice that makes my statement sound like a lie.

"Did you faint? Were you unconscious?" he asks, trying to discern the problem.

"No. I don't think so. I wasn't unconscious."

"You had a vision, didn't you?" Trey asks, continuing to rub life back into my dead hands.

"I don't know."

"You went limp against me—your skin is like ice—you were unresponsive." He lists the facts.

I worry my bottom lip between my teeth. We're both quiet for a second with only the sound of the hovercycle's hum as we weave through the tunnels. "Something happened."

"Did you see the future?"

"I don't know. Whatever it was, it just turned on, playing like a scene from a movie with me starring in it."

"Was it similar to what happened to you in my apartment before the Brigadets arrested us?"

"Yes," I admit.

"What was it about, Kricket?"

"What I saw when we were in your apartment together hasn't happened, so maybe this one won't either." I tell him quickly, attempting to minimize the impact of what I saw.

"Please explain what you mean by that."

"I mean that I know who the man is from my first vision. It's Giffen, but when I met him, the incident I saw didn't resemble what actually happened. So maybe this one won't either."

"Okay. Back up. You think Giffen is the man who struck you in your vision?"

"I know he is," I reply with certainty.

"But he didn't hit you when you met?"

"Well, he hit me, but not with his hand. He hit me with a metal crate that he moved with his mind. Oh, and he twisted my arm when we were in the overup. And he pushed me out of a moving overup. And he hung me on the wall when I tried to get away from him, but he never hit me in the face."

The muscles of Trey's abdomen and back stiffen. After I tell him everything I know about Giffen, he says, "Tell me about the vision you just had."

I feel myself growing pale as I stammer, "I think . . . I . . . I think Kyon and I—Kyon was in it."

"Do you think he lived through the explosion back there?"

"I know he did."

"How do you know?" Trey asks.

"I'd feel it if he died."

"Why do you say that?" he asks.

"Because our lives are so tightly wound together that I'd know," I reply, trying to explain the unexplainable.

Trey doesn't argue with what I just said. He accepts it. "What was Kyon doing in your vision?" he asks.

"He . . . he tied a ribbon around my throat—it had an exotic-looking flower on it—I'd never seen a more beautiful bud—"

"It's a copperclaw," Trey says in a low tone. "The Brotherhood uses it in their ceremonies when a Brother commits to his priestess. It's symbolic of the binding."

I'm having trouble at the moment being inside my skin. I want to escape from it—let my skeleton spill out of me. I need to tell Trey everything. It feels like a confession when I whisper, "Then he said, 'With this flower, I keep thee to me—'"

"'—always,'" Trey finishes for me. His tone is grim.

"Yeah," I whisper. Neither one of us says anything. The silence makes me feel smaller and smaller. After a while, I straighten, finding my spine. "We don't know if it'll happen. Like I said, Giffen didn't slap me when we met. He forced me to meet the future, but he never slapped me to get me to do it." I sound desperate. When Trey still says nothing, I blurt out, "I'll change it—I've done it before—I can do it again—I can change it."

Trey lifts my hand to his lips, kissing the back of it tenderly. I feel it tremble against his mouth. "You're not alone, Kricket. I'll help you change it. We'll do it together. Now, tell me everything that's happened to you from the time that I was separated from you until this moment."

❧❦❧

When Trey's tunnel ends, we move into the drainage line leading out of the city that they had shut down a couple of rotations ago. Not long after, Trey cuts the engine to the hovercycle and lifts the lid to the compartment when we arrive at the end of the pipe. There's a service tunnel with connecting drains that leads outside. The sun is still up, streaming light into the grate that covers the hole to the outside world, the opening of which is hidden in a drainage ditch. Beyond it, a large pasture spreads out for as far as the eye can see.

All of the Cavars dismount from their hoverbikes, stretching their arms and legs after being slouched in the same position for so long. "We're going to rest here until the sun goes down, Kricket," Trey explains.

I scan the cement tunnel that leads to the drainage cover. It's only wide enough to fit one of us at a time. The hovercycles won't squeeze through it. Turning to Trey, I ask, "Are we leaving the hovercycles?"

Trey nods his head. "We can't take them, Kricket. They have a heat signature that's easily detected."

"We're mammals. We all have a heat signature," I point out.

"What's a man-imal?" Wayra asks, wrinkling his nose. "I'm no man-imal."

Jax looks puzzled. "Sounds like she called us half man, half animal in her Earthling."

"It's English," I say with a grin.

"That's what I said," Jax replies, deadpan. "Earthling."

"Kricket." Wayra insists upon my attention, like he's trying to teach me something, "We're not human or animal. Jax—" he points at him menacingly "—weren't you supposed to teach her about anatomy? This is getting ridiculous."

Trey ignores Wayra, saying, "We have something to combat their sensors, Kricket. You don't have to worry." He comes to me and leads me to a quiet place to rest while we wait until dark.

Nestling against Trey's side, I fall into an exhausted sleep. I awake with my head resting on Trey's thigh. He's stroking my hair, watching the other Cavars move around the tunnel. As I sit up, I hear a soft nicker outside. Curious, I rise to my feet, walking stiffly over to the mouth of the smaller tunnel. I duck my head, crouching as I walk nearer to the grate covering the opening. Outside in the field, hundreds of spixes roam the meadow grazing on the lush, thick grass that is the type of green one sees in pictures of Ireland, but that don't exist in Chicago.

"Have you named any of them yet?" Trey teases as he crouches down behind me.

"That one"—I point to a huge beast of a spix—"I'm calling Flea. And that one"—I point to the white spix with brown socks—"will henceforth be known as Compost. And that little one over there—"

"The plump one?" he asks.

"No, the really little one next to Scoundrel; the one with the short horns."

"I see it—the docile one," he whispers in my ear. His nearness is causing my insides to do backflips.

"That one is Raging Bull."

Trey chuckles. "I love you." He presses his lips to my cheek. "And to prove it . . ." He pulls out the gifts that I was given at our engagement announcement.

"You brought the venish!" I say with delight. We sit down opposite each other with our backs to the circular walls as Trey unwraps the meat pie and hands it to me. I take a bite, finding it delicious. Breaking off a piece, I hold it up to Trey's lips for him to eat. He looks at me for a moment, surprised by the offering, but then he leans forward. Opening his mouth, he allows me to feed him.

"Yum. Venish," I coo, chewing greedily. "Wayra's the best when it comes to food." I break off another piece, feeding it to Trey as he watches me hungrily.

The next time I feed him, my fingertip slips into his mouth along with the morsel. He sucks it softly. Immediately, my insides riot as my abdomen clenches tightly. I stop chewing and swallow. Setting aside the nearly empty tin, I lean forward; Trey meets me half-way. The next thing I know, I'm straddling his thighs with my arms wrapped around him. His hands are running over my back, while his tongue strokes and teases mine.

"Ahem." A clearing of a throat at the other end of the narrow tunnel makes us break apart abruptly. Glancing in that direction, I see Drex and Hollis with their backs to us. Drex says over his shoulder, "We need to get in there and cut the grate off or we'll fall behind schedule, Gennet."

"Of course," Trey says absently, while running a hand through his mussed-up hair to try to straighten it. "We'll move."

With as much dignity as we can muster, we put our little feast back in Trey's pack and move out of the way of the soldiers. After they enter the smaller tunnel and begin cutting the iron tie bars away, Trey leans near my ear. "We might have a problem. I can't seem to keep my hands off of you."

"That's a problem?" I ask, biting my lip and trying not to laugh.

"That question shouldn't make me as happy as it does," he replies.

"Shouldn't it?" I tease him.

"Stop distracting me," he admonishes with a sensual smile and a quick kiss. "I have to help unload the supplies from the hovercycles. Stay here and try not to get into any trouble."

"Leave the venish." I smile, bouncing a little bit as I suck in my bottom lip so that I won't grin like a total fool. He hands me the small pack with yet another kiss. I watch him move away.

I shouldn't be happy; I know that. The entire world is one big series of scary events, but right now, at this moment, I'm having a hard time focusing on all that. I just want to live in this moment—in these seconds—with Trey. I know it's wrong. I know when it ends there will be no soft landing.

In no time at all, all the gear is unloaded from the hovercycles. Dusk is quickly turning to darkness when Trey joins me. "Wayra and I are going to gather the transport. It shouldn't take long."

I lose any hint of a smile I had. "What? You're leaving?"

"I'll be back in less than a part."

"Where are you going?" I ask.

He leads me to the mouth of the smaller tunnel once more. "You see the roof of that building over there?" he asks.

I nod, fear turning my stomach. "Yeah. It looks like a barn of some kind."

"Wayra, Fenton, and I are going there to gather spixes. I know the owner. I've worked with him for many floans—he's a family friend. We'll bring the spixes back here, load up the gear, and we'll be on our way."

"Ohh . . . no. No, no." I shake my head. "That's not a good plan." I clutch his forearm. "We need a trift—or a skiff. Spixes are unpredictable. You can't just put fuel in them to make them go."

Trey smiles like I made a joke, but I'm completely serious. "Kricket, no technology means the Alameeda can't find us easily. That's why we were so successful at avoiding them in the Forest of O. We didn't use anything they could track. It will be nearly impossible to hide from them as it is. They can employ aircraft and satellites at will here."

Everything he is saying is true. "Okay," I agree, "that makes sense. I'll help—I'll go with you."

"Wayra, give me a fleat," Trey says to the waiting Cavars. Leading me away from the opening, he takes me to a quiet place by the hovercycles. Raising his eyebrow in a questioning look, he asks, "I need you to stay here while I do this. Is that going to be a problem?"

"Um, yeah."

"Why?"

"Because we always stay together."

"There are going to be instances where it will be better to have you remain in a safe place while I scout ahead. Are we going to have an argument every time something like this comes up?"

I point my finger at him. "Don't make me sound like a crazy, clingy girlfriend," I retort. "This isn't the same thing."

"Kricket, just listen to me. Stay here. I'll be fine. I'll be back in less than a part."

He turns and walks toward where Wayra and Fenton are waiting for him. I panic. *Don't go!* I think, wringing my hands. "I wish I knew if it was safe," I whisper.

My breath turns to ice as my body turns to fire. I try hard, but I can't stay on my feet. It's almost like the floor rises to hit me in the cheek; blood spits out of my mouth and from above my body. I watch Trey run back to me and pick me up in his arms.

❧

When I return to my body, I'm dead cold. Gasping for air, my head aches and my cheek throbs. Tasting blood in my mouth, I'm fairly certain that I'll never be warm again.

"Kricket." Trey shakes me lightly, trying to get my attention.

"Yeah, I'm fine," I lie. I feel like I almost died. "It's okay to go get the spixes now. You were right, it was safe—it is safe—whatever." I hold my head, because even a hangover would be better than this.

"Do you mean to tell me that you just forced yourself into the future to make sure that it was safe to go to that barn just over there?"

"Yeah—and I know you're mad now, but—"

"I'm not mad. I'm furious. Why would you hurt yourself like that when I already knew that this task was a minimal risk?"

"Well, now we know to a greater degree of certainty that it's safe."

He looks so angry that if there were nails to be chewed, he could do it. He lifts my head off the pillow of his thigh and rests me on the ground with my head upon a balled-up shirt. He places a blanket over me before he straightens. "Jax," he growls.

"Sir," Jax says by his side.

"Make sure she's okay," he orders.

"Yes, sir," Jax says.

Trey doesn't look at me as he moves away toward the exit again. I call out to him, "I'm sorry too."

He whips around, looking like he has never been this angry in his entire life, not even when I put a znou near my ear in the Forest of O. "I didn't apologize!" he barks in frustration.

"I know," I say weakly, "but you're going to get to the barn and you're going to feel really bad about being a total knob knocker to me right now, and then you're going to apologize to the future me that you know is there watching you. Err . . . or is she the past me now?"

He turns around abruptly, striding out of the tunnel and into the night.

Jax crouches down next to me. He checks my pulse the old-fashioned way: by holding my wrist. "That was a bit unnecessary," he observes.

"This time," I say in a way that lets him know I'm not above doing it again if any of them pushes me.

"Was it worth it, though? You stayed away way too long, Kricket. I thought you were going to stop breathing—so did Trey. If you gave it a few more fleats, you might not have been able to return to your body, even if you wanted to. It was that bad."

"I had to make sure he wasn't walking into anything," I reply stubbornly.

"This is a gift for sure, Kricket," Jax says quietly, examining my cheek. "But if you abuse it, it could become a curse—or your end."

I drop my eyes from his.

"You may have a concussion, and this is going to bruise," Jax says, rubbing his thumb gently over my swollen cheek.

"No it won't," I mutter. "Cut my hair."

"Excuse me?" Jax asks, like he didn't hear me right.

"Do you have some scissors?" I ask him.

"You want to cut your hair? Now?" He looks as if he thinks I've lost my mind.

When I nod, he gets up from the floor and goes to his medical pack. He comes back with a pair of very sharp scissors. I sit up, but I almost have to lie back down again from dizziness. It takes me a second to focus enough so that I can take the scissors from Jax's grasp.

He's gravely concerned about what I'm about to do. "Trey might get angry with me for letting you cut your hair. He seems to really like it the way it is. Are you sure you want to do this?"

"It'll grow back."

His anxiety grows as I put the blades to the back of my head and gather a large handful of my hair. "Sure it'll grow back," he argues, seeing how short I intend to cut it. "But wouldn't it be better to wait until you can have a professional do it—you may not be happy with the results when you—"

I snip off a large section of my hair; Jax winces. As I pull my shorn locks away, they turn black and curl up into dust. New hair springs from my scalp, extending down my back to fall to about the same length as before. Jax's mouth hangs open.

"I'm sort of a freak," I explain with a grimace, but I can't regret showing him because I immediately feel better. The dizziness is receding. He takes the scissors from my hand, using them to cut off another section of my hair. When it regrows, he cuts more off with the same result.

After a few minutes of cutting, Jax grasps my chin in his hands, turning my face so that he can get a better look at the bruise on my cheek—or should I say, the lack of a bruise on my face. It healed much faster than the ones I had before, probably because there's only one this time and no broken ribs. "This is—this is—you are—"

"—monstrous," I fill in the blank for him.

His grasp on my chin grows tighter. "No!" He sounds almost angry. "You are without a doubt the most amazing Etharian I've ever laid eyes upon."

"Thanks, Jax." I try to smile.

"You're a genetic enigma."

"That I am," I agree. He lets go of my face, allowing me to stand with his hand beneath my elbow for support, but I don't need it. I feel fine, just really thirsty. "Do you have some water, Jax?"

"I do. I'll get it for you." When he returns, he hands me the water canteen. We talk about the first time I had my hair cut on Earth, how my foster mother nearly lost her mind over it.

"Does Trey know?" Jax asks.

I shrug. We lean against the cement tunnel wall together, out of the way from where the other Cavars are waiting by the exit. "Well, I told him on the way here about everything that happened to me after we were separated from each other. But, I don't think he actually *knows*. It's a little hard to explain it to someone. Seeing it happen kind of brings it all home, though, doesn't it?" I ask him.

"It does," he agrees. "Do you know how it—" Jax is distracted by the nickering of spixes outside. It means that Trey, Wayra, and Fenton have returned from the barn. Jax pushes away from the wall. "I need to go pack my gear onto my spix. We can talk about this later. It's a long journey and we have to get going soon."

I nod my head. "Okay," I say. "I'll be along in a minute. I'm just going to braid my hair."

"Don't be long. You're already on the naughty list," he jokes.

"There's a naughty list? And I'm on it?" I ask as if scandalized.

"You own that list," he says with a smirk.

As he walks away, I mutter, "Oh, Jax, that I do."

Swiftly plaiting my hair, I warily watch Trey when he enters the tunnel from outside. He doesn't see me right away, searching instead the place where he'd left me on the floor. As I finish my braid, I knot the end of it.

I move to where I'd left my bag earlier. Trey meets me near it. "You were right," he says, reaching out to pull me into his arms for a hug. "I do feel really bad about being a total knob knocker."

"I know. You said that in your other apology."

"I've been so worried about you."

I rest my upturned chin against his chest, looking up at his face. "I know you have. You told me that while you were saddling the spixes—you saw me hit my head and you saw me almost stop breathing. Over nothing, as it turns out."

He takes a closer look at me, his hand stilling on my cheek where it had been swollen only a few minutes ago. Confusion clouds his eyes. "You hit your head—there was blood—"

"Remember when I mentioned that cutting my hair causes my body to regenerate cells at a faster rate than normal?"

He nods his head. "I remember."

"I had Jax cut my hair."

Trey's fingers stroke my cheek for a few moments. Then, he leans down and brushes his lips to where I was hurt. "Is there anything you can't do?" he asks me softly.

"I can't swim," I remind him. He kisses me again. "I'm glad you're not mad at me anymore. I'm sorry—I wasn't trying to be a lurker. It's just that I'm not used to needing someone. I don't know how to handle it."

"You weren't being a lurker. Our circumstances here are extreme. I want you to need me. I don't ever want you to stop needing me." He kisses me; my insides warm as if I'm drinking sunshine.

"Gennet, we're loaded," Wayra says from the exit to the pasture.

Trey and I both become aware of where we are once more. He takes my hand and leads me outside. I take off my night-vision glasses and follow him blindly, gazing at the stars. They're far away again, not like they were when I was on the Ship of Skye. The king and queen moons are holding court among them.

I put my glasses back on while Trey helps me mount a spix. He joins me on its back, sitting behind me. I raise my eyebrows to him. "Is your riding with me a commentary on my equestrian abilities?" I ask him.

"Maybe, but secretly I'm always looking for any excuse to have you this close to me." It's not a lie, which causes me to grin like an idiot. "What shall we name this spix?"

"Honey Badger," I reply.

"Why?" I can tell that he doesn't know what that is. Maybe they don't exist here.

"Because the honey badger is fearless."

Wayra hands Trey a blanket made from the camouflage fabric that I was used to seeing them wear when they were in the Forest of O. Trey unfolds it, wrapping it around himself and covering me with it. I'm grateful for the heat it's giving me. The weather has become decidedly colder than what I'm used to here. The shield that once covered the area is now down, allowing the natural climate to assert itself upon us.

"This will block our heat signature. If Alameeda ships do a fly-over, they'll just see a group of riderless spixes."

"Where are we going?" I ask.

Trey leans near my ear, being deliberately quiet. I think he's worried that one or more of the supernatural priestesses are somehow listening. "There are spix stables and training lodges several rotations, journey from here. It's rural and close to the border of the Forest of Omnicron. That's where we're headed."

"Is it in the Valley of Thistle?" I ask. I've been curious about where Trey grew up since I made up our fake commitment ceremony to fool the Comantre soldiers.

"No. It's south of there. We can't go to Thistle. Kyon will have patrols there searching for you."

"Your family!" I say in a startled tone. The spix becomes restless, throwing its head back a couple of times and scaring me more with its wicked-sharp horns.

Trey makes hushing noises, settling the spix. "They're already gone from Thistle. If all goes well, they'll meet us at the lodges."

"You mean your parents will be there?" This information doesn't help me get a handle on my panic.

"They will. They're looking forward to meeting you."

"I'll bet," I mutter sarcastically.

As the spixes move forward, Trey murmurs, "You'll like them, Kricket. They're good people."

"I'm sure they are. You're their son."

"You say that like it's a bad thing." Trey's cheek brushes against mine, causing my insides to quiver.

"Good people want good things for their family."

"And that worries you, why? You're a good thing, Kricket."

I scoff. "Uh-huh. I'm super good, Trey," I say sarcastically. "Hopefully Charisma will be there too, so they can see what a bullet they dodged by you choosing to commit to me instead of the girl next door whom they've loved forever."

Trey is quiet behind me. I glance back at him. "What?" I ask, reading the worry on his face.

"Charisma should be there too," Trey admits with a cringe.

I face forward once more. "Well, there's still a chance we won't make it there, right? A lot can happen."

"Since when are you afraid of anyone or anything?" he asks, nuzzling my neck.

"Since I found something I don't want to lose."

"There is no chance of you losing me."

"You must not have heard about me. I'm trouble."

"Oh, I know it. I've often said 'There goes Trouble' when you leave the room. Wayra," Trey calls ahead, "what's Kricket's security codename?" He keeps his voice low so it won't carry far.

Wayra glances at us over his shoulder. With a grin, he replies, "That'd be Trouble, sir."

Trey squeezes me tighter. "See? Trouble." He smiles. "You're the navigator for my next thrill . . . and every thrill after that."

CHAPTER 13
WORLD TURNS TO STONE

O nly the wind whispers as we move along dry riverbeds and over lush fields that go on for miles in every direction. As we come to a small knoll, I chance a glance back at the Isle of Skye behind us. The horizon is on fire. Smoke rises into the air as if the city is the chimney stack of Ethar. Soft thumps sound in the distance. Whatever is happening back there is horrific. I look to the faces of the Cavars with me. None of them looks back.

Not too long after we leave, an Alameeda ship approaches us. Hearing the rotorless engine makes me dig my nails into my thighs. My legs tense on the spix's flanks, causing it to dance sideways. Trey has to work hard to control it with the reins. "Relax, Kricket," Trey whispers in my ear, "they can't see us."

I think he forgot for a second that I know when he's lying. As soon as he notices my stark-white face, he amends, "They *can* see us, but they won't. They're using infrared. The blanket hides us from them because they can't see our heat signature; they can only see the heat of what looks like riderless spixes. Since they're not looking for spixes, they're looking for other modes of transport. We're invisible to them. Trust me."

I relax my legs enough to make the spix less anxious. The other Cavars have let their reins go slack on their spixes, allowing them to wander haphazardly, giving them a staggered, unpurposeful gait.

When the ship doesn't notice us and slips away over the horizon, I sag back against Trey.

But, a few minutes later, humming vibrates the ground. Trey whistles softly, waving his hand toward a small copse of trees. We just make it to them when twenty or more low-flying E-Ones move in formation over the horizon line. They're spread out at the same velocity so that they're aligned for miles. What's most disturbing is that they're so low they resemble crop dusters working the fields.

I stare up at the canopy of leaves above my head, grateful that the trees haven't shed them yet. For some reason, I find myself holding my breath. It's silly, I know that, but I do it nonetheless. I don't look at the E-Ones as they grow ever closer; it's as if they'll know that I'm here if I do. With the camouflage blanket draped over our heads, Trey pulls it tighter to me so that our eyes hardly show.

The black sinkhole in my stomach eases a bit as the rotorless heli-vehicles move away, but the goose bumps covering my body don't recede. Even when the E-Ones disappear over the far hill, no one and nothing moves for several minutes, least of all, my goose bumps.

Trey begins to guide the spix out from the safety of the trees. I put out my hand, covering his on the reins. "Wait!" I plead. Wiggling out from under the blanket, I try to gulp in deep breaths of air, but it's no good, I'm going to be sick. Swinging my leg over the side of our spix, I jump down from its back. Falling to my knees, I get up and stagger a few steps to the trunk of a tree where I lean my hand against it and vomit again and again.

We're never going to make it, I think, retching violently. *Kyon is going to find us and he's going to kill Trey and make me watch.* I'm not panicking now. This isn't panic; this is different. This is me finally grasping the reality of what's happening. When you have nothing to lose, failing doesn't come with the same kind of consequences. Now I have Trey. Failure in this means his death. I can't fail.

I think it's the soldier in Trey who knows better than to crowd me. He allows me a little space. Dismounting from Honey Badger, he doesn't rush over to hold my hair back for me. I prefer that. His attention is unwanted at this moment.

When there's nothing left in my stomach, I finally stop retching. I straighten up, wiping my eyes on my sleeve. I glance over my shoulder; Trey is facing away from me with his back leaning against the trunk of a nearby tree. Jax is next to me, handing me a canteen of water. I take it, pouring some in my mouth. I swish it around, and then spit it out. I hand it back to Jax, and he gives me a mintlike leaf that they use to refortify enamel. I take it and put it in my mouth.

Wayra has been leaning against the trunk of the tree adjacent to mine. He pushes off it, saying, "Finally. I was starting to think you were some kind of heartless android."

"Huh?" I ask.

"You finally did something normal," Wayra replies.

I laugh humorlessly. "Puking my guts out is normal?"

He nods stoically. "It is. Some soldiers do it before their first battle. But the courageous ones don't."

"Are you calling me a coward?" I ask him in confusion.

He frowns. "Is this your first fight?"

I shake my head. "No."

Wayra agrees, "No, it's not. It's only the soldiers with courage that puke later on—the ones who've been through something brutal, like being captured and tortured. They know what it means to be recaptured. It's not the same as not knowing, is it?"

I shake my head no again.

"No, it's not. But they go on anyway. They find a way to thwart the enemy. I puked my guts out before a battle; I had just returned to active duty after being shredded by a sanctum amp. I knew what it meant to be wounded. I wasn't looking to repeat it."

"What did you do to get over the fear?"

"I lived through it," he says. "I got good at what I do. I made sure that I was the best at my job. You're a time-traveling polar vortex, Kricket. You can make the future the shape of heartache for those knob knockers if you want to. Do you want to?"

I nod.

He scowls. "Was that a yes?" he barks out militantly.

"Yes!"

"Well, all right then! Puke and rally!" He raises his index finger and moves it in a circle in the air. "Let's go kill something." He turns and strides away, back to his spix. Jax follows him, shaking his head. The Cavars remount their spixes once more. Trey waits for me to join him.

"How hard was it not to hover right then?" I ask him, as he leads me back to our spix.

"You have no idea," he replies. He lifts me up onto our spix before climbing on it to sit behind me. After the blanket covers me once more, Trey pulls me against his chest. He kisses my temple. "This is going to be a long night, but it will end. I'll keep you safe."

He believes that.

The night is filled with near misses and hard riding. After many long hours, I forget to be scared, because my body aches too much to worry about something that *might* happen. Being on a spix like this is its own special torture. I find myself praying for dawn just so we can stop. A few hours before the sun rises, we come to a wooded area. Entering between the trees, the Cavars find a decent tree-shrouded clearing in which to halt the spixes.

Trey climbs off first and then reaches up to help me dismount. When he sets me on the ground, he continues to hold my arm under my elbow, because I'm a little wobbly. I walk around for a little bit, stretching my legs. Everyone but me begins digging a hole in the ground with mechanized shovels that do a lot of the work for the soldiers. In no time at all, the place resembles a mass burial site. As I walk up next to Hollis, who is shoulder-deep in a hole, I ask, "What are you guys, vampires?" I watch him line his grave with a waterproof foam spray before lying down in it to check its level of comfort.

"What's a vampire?" Hollis says, staring up at me from his supine position in the hole.

"You don't know what a vampire is?"

"No. Is it as handsome as I am?" he asks.

I frown to keep from laughing. "Er . . . not exactly. A vampire is an undead creature who feeds on human blood for survival. It sleeps in a coffin and you can only kill one by putting a wooden stake through its heart."

Hollis looks disturbed. "That is terrifying, Kricket. I am never visiting Earth."

My eyes widen as I hold up my hands and say, "No! It's mythical—"

He pulls a small piece of twine that's looped in his camouflage blanket: the pile of blanket at the foot of his trench slides over the top of the grave. The fabric is on a chameleon setting that takes on the color and texture of its surroundings so that the hole and Hollis are completely hidden from sight beneath it. "Good night, vampire assassin," I hear him call from within the dirt.

Jax nudges my shoulder. "Kricket," he says. When he has my attention, he hands me one of the personal toiletry totes, like the kind I remember from when we traveled here from Earth. "You may want to use this now. We'll be staying down most of the daylight hours."

"Thanks." Jax moves away as I rummage through it, seeing things in it that we didn't have before, like hair remover spray and scented oils. I smile, because I know he must have packed these with me in mind. I slink off to find a private place. Hiding behind a large tree, I use the soapy sponge in the pack to clean up as best as I can, and then I use just about everything else in the tote as well.

When I return, the spixes are wandering around free, munching on grass. All the supplies have been buried in trenches. Most of the Cavars are in their holes. Trey is waiting for me by a rather large trench. As I approach him, he jumps down into it, holding up his arms to help me in. After he lowers me in, I realize that I'll need a leg up in order to get out of it because it's deeper than the other trenches. The waterproof foam lining the walls and floor has hardened, giving the trench iridescent shell-like walls. Trey has spread out mats on the floor over the foam, so it's actually comfortable inside our grave. After I lie down, Trey takes off his shirt and lies beside me, pulling the twine so that our camouflage blanket covers the mouth of the hole.

I quickly snuggle up next to Trey. With my head on his chest, I say softly, "This is quite a burrow you're dug for us. It's twice as big as Hollis's hole."

Trey smiles. "There's two of us and we'll have to stay in it for hours, so making it bigger made sense to me. But really, I was just working off some demons."

"Demons?" I ask as I raise an eyebrow at him. My night-vision glasses slip to the edge of my nose when I do. I use my finger to push them back up.

"I had you practically on my lap the whole way here," Trey says ruefully.

"Is that a bad thing?"

"It's a different kind of torture, Kitten."

"Well, we're entombed here with nothing much to do except . . ." I trace the ridges between his ab muscles.

"Don't tease me. I'm about to go off as it is."

I sit up and slip off my jacket, tossing it into the corner. I straddle his hips, saying, "I'm not teasing. You've been rubbing up against me for hours. I'm about as frustrated as you are."

He sits up abruptly, pulling me against his chest while his lips cover mine, searing them with kisses. Strong hands slide up my sides, pulling the cloudy fabric of my black blouse with them. Our lips part as he pushes it off over my head. It joins my jacket in the corner.

From there, it becomes a race to see who can disrobe the other faster. Trey is definitely the winner because I'm completely bare when he pulls me back to him, while his dark slacks are still around his ankles and his boots are both on.

As I sink down on him, I say his name without meaning to. He quickly covers my lips with his to smother my cries. We're both too far gone to be gentle. My nails dig into his back while he roughly presses me against him, lifting my hips over and over until my head falls back and I lose myself to ecstasy. He follows not far behind me, burying his face between my hair and throat, panting harshly in my ear. I relax in his arms, resting my head on his shoulder while we remain locked together in a tight embrace.

Trey strokes my back. "We need to find someone soon who can perform a commitment ceremony."

"I don't need a commitment ceremony to be with you," I murmur against his skin, placing small kisses along the breadth of his wide shoulder.

"I need it." He lifts my hair and unbraids it so that it falls over my shoulders.

"Why? I know how you feel about me."

"Because I need everyone to know that you're mine."

I giggle. "That's a little cavemanish, don't you think?" I ask him teasingly.

The next thing I know, I'm on my back. With the palms of my hands flat against his chest, his warm skin rubs against me while I gasp at the exquisite feel of him. "Most of all, Kricket," he says passionately in my ear, "I need *you* to know that you're mine."

His hands on me are possessive and demanding. "Say you're mine, Kricket." His fingers twine in my hair.

Intense pleasure washes over me. "I'm yours," I whisper, biting my lip to keep from screaming it.

"Whose?" he growls again.

"Yours, Trey, I'm yours." I say breathlessly, as we completely lose our minds and our bodies to each other. For the next few hours, we prove over and over that we belong to one another.

❧

When I awake in our little love nest, I stretch beneath the blanket. "It will be dark soon," Trey says from behind me. His hand moves on my side, stroking my skin possessively. I can't help feeling disappointed that we'll have to leave here soon. It's been an oasis in a sea of scary. I sit up; Trey's hand falls away when I crawl for my bag in the corner. On my knees, I sift through it until I find the personal tote that Jax gave me yesterday. Finding a comb within it, I sit on the mat and attempt to untangle the snarls from my hair. After a few minutes, I realize that it's a hopeless mess.

"Here, let me try," Trey says, holding out his hand for the comb.

Moving nearer to him, I place the comb in his hand and then turn around. Gently, he lifts my hair and begins combing it from the bottom up, carefully working out the snarls without pulling too hard on it.

"How did you learn to do that?" I ask him suspiciously.

"We own spixes. They sometimes wander into briar patches and get burrs entangled in their manes."

"You took care of the spixes."

"Every day for most of my childhood. I could train a spix from wild to tame faster than anyone we knew—even Charisma."

"Really?" I murmur, trying to envision his life as a teenager. It was completely different from mine. "And Victus? Could he train spixes as well?"

Trey snorts. "He could, but he wasn't very interested in them. He's more of a thinker than a doer. He would come with me and talk to me for hours while I took care of things. He's a philosopher—a dreamer. He dreams things up and I make them."

"You sound like the perfect team—in some ways—opposites. I believe you're a thinker too, though. If you weren't such an extremely good planner, we'd be dead inside the city now. And your skills as a hacker are ridic, you know? Reprogramming drones can't be as easy as you made it look."

He pauses in combing out my hair. I glance at him over my shoulder; he leans forward and kisses me hard on the mouth.

"You make me happy," he says in a low tone.

I have to blink a couple of times and look away. "Well, Trey, I think you're the first person who has ever said that to me."

"That's impossible," he says honestly.

"It's the truth." Not wanting to explore my past, I instead nose into his. "And what is Charisma? A thinker or a doer?" I ask.

"She's a doer."

"And me?"

"You are the rare person who is good at everything."

"I can't swim."

"Yet."

In no time at all, Trey manages to unknot my hair. I weave it in a fishtail plait.

"Are you hungry?" Trey asks.

"As a matter of fact, I was just about to talk to you regarding your penchant for starving me." I smile at him, wrapping the blanket around me. "It's really getting out of hand."

"There are still some treats left from our commitment announcement." Trey reaches for his gear, finding the sack full of goodies. He places them between us; the blanket he has wrapped around him is riding low on his hips. He also adds a few items that I'd rather ignore: namely, the kind of protein bar that I was forced to eat in the Forest of Omnicron.

"Umm . . . blak," I say, holding up the meal from hell.

"Jax thought it'd be a good idea if we had these—just in case it becomes necessary to leave Rafe."

"Do you think that could happen?"

He doesn't want to answer me, but he does anyway. "Yes."

"Why?"

"Because at the moment, we're outlaws."

"We're Bonnie and Clyde?"

"We're who?"

"Never mind."

I eat a few of the treats. Trey nudges the protein bar toward me. I ignore him. He sighs. "You know you have to eat it."

I give him a puzzled look. "Do I know that?" I look upward, searching my mind. "Hmm . . . no, I don't think that I do know that." I tap my chin with my index finger, and then shake my head. "Nope. That's not something I know."

He grins and leans forward, reaching out and grabbing me. He starts to tickle me mercilessly. "Trey!" I giggle before laughing hysterically. When he doesn't let up, I have to gasp in deep breaths between peals of laughter. "Trey!" I laugh. "Trey!" I say as sternly as I can. "You . . . have . . . to . . . *stop*!"

"Do I?" he asks while he continues to tickle me before looking upward, searching his mind. "Do I really have to stop tickling you?" His evil grin is turned on me when he looks down again. "Nope. That's not something I have to do."

"Okay!" I acquiesce.

He smiles, leans forward, and kisses my temple. "Thank you."

I wipe tears from my eyes, before I narrow them at him. "You shouldn't do that! I have to pee as it is." I take the gross protein bar from him and lie down, looking up at the blanket covering the trench.

Trey's expression is immediately contrite. "I can take you up. It'll be all right."

"No. I can wait," I assure him.

I take a bite of the protein bar and just about gag. *Ugh, cat poop,* I think.

As I chew, Trey studies me. He frowns, resting with his forearm on the ground propping him up. "You said some things," he says cryptically, in a very un-Trey-like way.

I finish chewing and swallow. "I say lots of things. Anything in particular you're referring to?" I smile at him.

"Who's Astrid?" he asks.

"What? How do you—" I feel the blood drain from my cheeks.

Trey hurriedly explains, "It's something you kept saying over and over—when you were being interrogated. You kept asking, "Where's Astrid? Where did Astrid go? I have to find Astrid."

My chest is in agony. I sit up and pull on my blouse over my head and see him frown at me, as if I'm taking away his toys. "You don't have to get dressed, yet," he says.

"I have to—to—I have to—"

Hurriedly, I dress beneath the blanket, pulling on the black legging pants from yesterday. I get to my feet and go to a shell-coated wall. Jumping up, I try to grasp the lip of the trench so that I can pull myself out and escape.

"Who's Astrid, Kricket?" Trey probes, disturbed by my behavior.

I turn around and face him, covering his mouth with my hand. "Shh—don't ever say that name to me again," I hiss with a sick kind of desperation.

He pulls my hand from his lips. "Why?" he counters, not letting it go.

I turn away from him, jumping up again so I can get away. "Help me get out—please," I beg him, still facing the wall, unable to look at him.

Without saying another word, he pulls the cord attached to the camouflage blanket. It slides away, revealing the faint twilight. Trey hoists himself out of the trench, but he doesn't pull me out right away. Instead, he moves away quietly to scout the area. I pace the trench, walking in circles on the mats.

"It's clear," Trey says, reaching his hand down to me. He grasps my wrist, pulling me out of the hole. Refusing to look him in the eyes, I snatch my hand away from his, moving away to the trees where I'd been the night before.

After I take care of my most basic needs, I don't return to the camp right away. Instead, I walk alone along the division between the high grass and the tree line, holding out my hand so that the tall grass slips over my palm. *Why am I still looking for Astrid, after all this time? Maybe it means nothing, just a reaction to a terrifying situation.* But the loss is there. I have that ache in my chest again for something that doesn't exist. *I keep holding on to nothing as tightly as I can . . .*

"Tell me who Astrid is," Trey says behind me, causing me to jump halfway out of my skin.

"Don't sneak up on me!" I hiss.

"You don't walk away from the camp in the middle of all this mess!" he hisses back. "You were fine, and then I said that name and you completely changed."

"It's nothing." I try to feign a casual shrug.

"It's not nothing. Not the way you said it when you were drugged. It's like a piece of you had gone missing and you needed to find it. You were begging your tormentors. It was gut-wrenching!"

"I was on drugs—people on drugs say weird things. I once knew this guy, everyone called him Tweeker Tony—" I murmur.

"Don't redirect me. I'm starting to know your tactics very well. Explain who she is because I want to understand why she's so important to you."

"Astrid is not important to me. It's no one! One caseworker described Astrid as my imaginary friend—and don't give me that look, Trey," I say, straightening.

"What look?" he asks in surprise.

"I'm not some broken thing you need to fix. Just because I wasn't raised in the Valley of Thistle with a perfect family doesn't make me broken."

"What does it make you then?"

"Resilient."

"You can act like this is nothing. You can walk around with a mind full of secrets, but if you want to let me in, I'll be here for you." He takes my hand and starts to walk in the direction that we came from, saying, "It's not safe for you out here alone. You need to come back to camp—"

I squeeze his hand tightly and blurt out. "I don't know who or what Astrid is." Trey stops, but he doesn't turn around. "Maybe it's someone I used to play with, or a neighbor, or a stuffed animal—maybe a babysitter. All I remember is that I would cry every night for Astrid." Laughing humorlessly, I add, "I can't even picture Astrid in my mind. Isn't that crazy? To need something you can't even remember?"

Trey turns back to look at me and waits for me to continue.

"Remember I told you when there's little left to lose, the consequences for one's actions don't carry the same weight, painful or otherwise?"

"I remember," Trey says.

"I learned that early—just after I was placed—that's what they used to call it when they'd find you a home: *placed*. I hardly remember anything about being placed the first time. I remember the apartment was small—cramped—tidy but poor. It had this awful smell, though—mildew, urine, and pine cleaner. I'll remember that smell for the rest of my life."

Trey nods, but says nothing.

"Some people who take in foster children are borderline saints—selfless and dedicated. These people they placed me with made fun of those people—they were career caregivers. I call their type 'the hangers-on.' They keep hanging on to poverty with both hands, receiving money from a broken system by taking in kids they don't want."

"They didn't want you?" he asks.

"They hated kids. They wanted a paycheck. They wanted me to shut up and do what I was told. And as you know, that's not something I'm good at."

Trey's jaw clenches, but otherwise he doesn't react to what I said.

"I remember asking them, 'What about Astrid? We have to find Astrid.'"

"No one would listen to me, so I ran away to look for Astrid where I used to live—I think I was five, maybe? I don't think I was gone long—some concerned older woman on the bus followed me and then took me to the police station. The police brought me back."

"What happened then?" Trey asks when it looks as if I won't continue.

The palm of my hand feels sweaty in Trey's; I'd pull it away from his, but he's holding my hand so tightly that I don't think I'd be successful. Instead, I exhale a deep breath. "It's the first time I remember ever being hit. It's not smart to make a hanger-on look bad like that with the police. That's like threatening his livelihood. It's dangerous. But it didn't matter what they did to me; for whatever reason, I couldn't let it rest. The next time the police brought me back, my foster father hit me so hard that my foster mother had to take me to the clinic. I don't know what her name was, but she probably saved my life. I don't remember much for a while after that—a couple of years are just gone. I can't tell you what Astrid was or why it was so important to me. I just know that sometimes I still wake up calling that name."

I think Trey is afraid to react to what I said. He's not sure if he should show me how he's feeling. He's angry about what happened to me and sympathetic, but he knows how I feel about sympathy, so he's trying not to show it. He's even a little remorseful for insisting that I tell him something that is obviously painful for me—all of that is there on his face. What he does, though, takes me by surprise. He gathers me to him and kisses me fiercely. What starts off as an angry kiss between the two of us, turns into the all-out desire to possess each other completely.

"I don't know why they wouldn't want you, Kricket. Or why they would do those things they did to you. All I know is that *I* want you—so much more than I ever wanted anything in my life."

My desire for him is insane. He's not sentimental—neither of us is—and yet he says things to me that strike at the core of my being and speak to the fighter in me. He makes me crave him in the most vulnerable way. I can't lose him—ever.

Reaching up, I twine my arms around the nape of his neck. I jump up, wrapping my legs around his waist. His hands cup my bottom, pressing me to him. He leans me against a nearby tree. We fumble with each other's clothes, trying hastily to free ourselves of everything that lies between us. With the bark of the tree at my back, Trey makes love to me again, and it takes us a lot longer than expected to return to camp.

When we do get back, the gear has already been loaded up. Trey helps me mount our spix. Seated behind me, his arms around my hips and his masculine scent are a constant reminder that I'm not alone in the dark.

Our night begins as we gallop across vibrant fields adorned with grazing animals that sort of look like a cross between sheep and pug dogs; they have the white, woolly bodies of sheep, but their faces are googly-eyed and without long snouts. I find them cute and creepy at the same time. When I ask Trey what they are, he calls them skoolies.

The barrage of aircraft overhead is nearly constant now, but it's not all enemy ships like last night. Dogfights break out as the Rafe Air Brigade engages the Alameeda. Their battles light up the sky with colorful laser fire and smoking, orange-flamed explosions. It's easy to spot the E-Ones that are looking for us. They're low-flying and have adopted the same formation as the first night. Each time they come near us, I have to close my eyes. I get the sense that if I were to open them, they'd know where I am. It's silly, but I can't stop.

The next day is spent in the shelter of a dilapidated barn. We're grouped together under the falling-down rafters, which affords no privacy for any of us. I'm so exhausted from the hard ride, however, that when I fall asleep next to Trey in the shadow of the loft, I sleep all the way until sundown.

We spend our time the next night hurrying from one copse of trees to another until the landscape turns hilly. The change in the terrain to dense trees climbing in a gradual slope signals a change in our pace. It becomes a steady clip, neither pausing nor running, but with the underlying urgent need to be somewhere else. We move through paths in between gray stones where water trickles down over the rocks in petite waterfalls. In the distance, mountains rise with smoky peaks covered in green and white trees.

We find a small cave and make our camp. Throughout the day, the Cavars take turns patrolling the area, looking for signs that we're being followed. Nothing turns up. Even the aircraft are less frequent now, not that I can stay awake long to listen for them. As soon as I eat a meal, I find my eyes drooping, and the next thing I know I'm being roused from sleep and hustled to an already saddled spix as darkness falls.

Progressing uphill throughout the night, the grade continues to get steeper. Wearily, I lean back against Trey to keep my seat. "Sorry," I murmur at my weakness.

"I like the feel of you against me," he says in my ear, causing me to smile. I turn my face and kiss his neck. He leans his head down so that our lips can meet. When they do, I reach up, laying my hand on his cheek. Our kisses turn heated. My legs squeeze Honey Badger's sides, causing him to trot ahead next to Wayra.

When Trey notices, he has to rein in our spix, breaking our kiss.

We both look over at Wayra, who is smirking at us. He nods his head in greeting to Trey. "Sir."

Trey nods back. "Wayra."

"Did you need something, sir?" Wayra asks with amusement in his tone.

"No. I have everything I need," he replies. "Carry on." Trey pulls us back behind Wayra once more.

"Do you have everything you need?" I ask him.

Trey smiles and kisses the top of my head. "Yes. Everything I need is right here."

Every now and then we pass through rocky tunnels that cut through the hills. They're shockingly unkempt by the standards of most Rafe construction. Water seeps down stone walls by green crawling vines. Loose rock makes the ride treacherous.

"These tunnels are rarely used anymore," Trey explains, echoing my thoughts. "Once air travel became the preferred mode of transport, there was little need to maintain them. The local population of a few spix ranchers and trainers use them to work the spixes."

As we exit a tunnel, the sun is rising over the valley. We have a clear view of a winding path to a valley below. Low fieldstone walls hem in paddocks and connect several barns and outbuildings. In the corner of the clearing, a large estate spreads out among an orchard of fruit trees and serenely planned-out gardens. I take off my night-vision glasses, staring in wonder at the incredible vista.

"Whose place is this?" I ask Trey.

"Technically it's mine, but I own it through a charitable foundation that's not overtly attached to my name. It serves as a camp for developmentally challenged youths. The campers are all gone now. When I knew war was imminent, after my conversation in the lodge with Kyon, I had the place closed and the children sent home."

"Why do you keep it a secret?"

"Because I sometimes like to hide away from the world here. If I were to attach my family name to it, then every wealthy Rafian with too much time on his hands would want to come and use it for a hunting lodge because of its proximity to the restricted area. That's not what it's for, and I don't have time for it."

Trey directs Honey Badger with more urgency now. There are a few moments when I fear I'm about to be bounced off the spix. Trey doesn't seem at all concerned by the precarious fall over the edge of the cliff should the spix misstep. His confidence speeds us through the descent.

When we reach the valley floor, I'm overwhelmed with relief. I sag against him in complete fatigue. But as we trot down the tree-lined dirt lane, I have to admire the beauty of the place. It's a secluded valley, hidden by mountains and cut off from the constant buzz of technology that I've grown accustomed to seeing in Rafe.

After traversing a rustic-covered wooden bridge, two riders approach us at an easy gait on the other side. I recognize Trey's brother, Victus, immediately. They're identical, with the same dark hair and violet eyes, except Victus is not as broad-shouldered as his brother, and he lacks thick, military tattoos on his throat, chest, and abdomen. Next to Victus is a willowy Etharian woman dressed like him in an outfit made explicitly for riding. Her mount is a dappled gray spix with a white mane knotted in intricate braids, just like Victus's.

"Trey, who is that with Victus?" I ask, even though I already know the answer. I've seen her face in the video picture in her room.

"That," he says with a soft sigh, "would be Charisma."

CHAPTER 14
CANDYLAND BOOGEYMAN

Charisma is an incredible rider; her back is ramrod-straight, and the way in which she sits her spix makes me believe that she may well have been born upon its back. I try to keep my emotions reined in when Trey halts our spix in front of the pair.

To the Cavars behind us, Trey says, "You can go up to the main house over there. They'll provide food and show you to where you can get some rest. We'll go over your assignments after you sleep." The Cavars move around us, continuing on to the large estate.

Trey's hand slips from my waist to my thigh. He squeezes it in an intimate caress before he dismounts from our spix. Victus and Charisma dismount as well. Walking the short distance to them, Trey extends his arms and they both walk into them, group hugging like only a family in my dreams would do. I immediately feel like a lurker. My posture becomes even more stooped and all I want to do is slide to the ground and lie there for hours; I'm so tired. I can't let them see how alone I feel in this moment, so I try really hard to adopt a blank expression.

"Pasdon and Mamon are here?" Trey asks them while they continue to hug. Victus pulls away from Trey first, leaving Charisma to shift in Trey's arms for a solo hug.

"They're at the main house," Victus affirms. "Mamon will be relieved to see you—you know how she worries."

"She makes a career of it at times," Trey replies, while his hand rubs the girl's back tenderly.

"She has every right to worry," Charisma says, wiping a tear from her eye as she pulls away from Trey's side. "You don't make it easy on her with your lifestyle choices." The statement is a fact without the malice of an accusation.

"I know. You're right. I have this thing for danger, though, Charisma." Trey smiles at her.

The next tear that slips down her cheek is wiped away by Trey. "Shickles," she says in a very cute and completely sweet way, "I promised myself that I wasn't going to cry."

Trey hugs her again and she cries more on his chest. I feel sick. Not because it's a disgusting display of emotion, but because it's not. It's love. Victus moves away from them, joining me. He reaches a hand up and rests it on my hip. "Kricket," he says in an affectionate way. "You look like you might need some help getting down from your spix."

"I think I can manage—"

He doesn't let me finish, but reaches his other hand up to my waist, plucking me off the spix as if I weigh nothing. He hugs me to him like a brother would. "We were worried about you too, Kricket," he says in my ear and my heart squeezes tight, but I refuse to cry. *I'm not weak—I need to figure out how to be stone again before this paper heart of mine is the death of me.*

I rest my head on Victus's shoulder, because fighting tears is exhausting and I'm already so tired. Trey is by our side an instant later. "Hey, you want to stop touching her, grabby hands?" he asks Victus in a good-natured way.

"No. I don't." Victus continues to hug me with a teasing smile for his brother. "This is my soon-to-be sister and look at her. She looks like she can hardly stand on her own at the moment."

All humor is erased from Trey's face when he gets a better look at me. "Give her to me," he orders, reaching out and pulling me away from Victus as he hands me over. "She never says anything!" Trey complains to his brother. "She never whines or shows vulnerability. It's so frustrating."

"She's right here and she can walk," I say, wiggling to try to make him put me down.

"See what I mean?" he asks Victus, reluctantly setting me on my feet with an exasperated sigh.

"Ahem." Charisma clears her throat near us.

Victus grins. "You still want to do this?" he asks.

She rolls her eyes at him and nods vehemently.

"Okay," Victus sighs. "Charisma still thinks she can't greet you, Kricket, until she's been formally introduced. I told her it's unnecessary, given the circumstances, but she doesn't want to offend you. So." He makes a grand sweeping gesture toward me as I stand by Trey's side. "Fay Kricket Hollowell, coriness of Rafe and priestess of Alameeda. Soon-to-be Dreykaress Kricket Allairis, it is my honor to present *my* intended consort, your soon-to-be sister, née Minness Charisma Aleesia Sandersault. Soon-to-be Hautess Charisma Allairis of the Valley of Thistle, ancestral lineage House of Rafe, Isle of Skye, et cetera, et cetera, et cetera . . ." He trails off in a bored tone.

Charisma sinks into a deep curtsy before us. When she rises, I have no words to say to her. They've all run away from me when Victus introduced her as his intended consort. I glance at Trey to gauge his reaction. He's grinning from ear to ear.

"My new sister, huh?" He glances at Victus with a quirk of his eyebrows. "Well, it didn't take you very long once I called off our engagement, did it? I saw your clothes in her closet, you knob knocker," he says playfully.

"So you're not upset?" Charisma asks as she exhales a deep breath she's been holding. The relief on her face is exponential.

"The only thing that I'm upset about is that you both made me be the bad guy again," Trey replies honestly. "As if it's my job with you two or something. Why do you think I volunteered for that mission to Earth? I wanted you two to admit that you love each other. I was sick of being in the middle of it, stuck in between you both."

They both look shocked. "You planned for us to betray you?" Charisma asks, looking ashamed. "And you put yourself in extreme danger to do it?"

"No," Trey says softly, "I planned for you to be in each other's company without me around so that you could realize just how perfect you are for one another. You complement each other. Charisma, you like to take care of others. It frustrates you that I won't let you do that with me. But Victus loves all of your attention. You can baby him until next Fitzover and he will be the most contented Etharian to ever walk Thistle. The danger of the mission I agreed to was just a thrill."

"I don't enjoy being babied," Victus lies with a grin.

Trey snorts, "You're a fuss bucket, Vic."

"I love her," Victus says quietly, looking his brother in the eyes with all the banter gone from his expression.

"I know you do. I'm happy for you," Trey returns with a genuine grin.

"Victus and I must look like awful people to you, Kricket," Charisma says to me in a melancholy tone.

I turn my gaze upon her; my emotions over what I'm hearing are a jumbled mess. I don't know what to think or feel. I say the first thing that comes to mind. "It just feels bad right now because your secret's out. But it can't be as bad as it was before, can it? It's not like having your love be an unspeakable thing that you carry around— something you can only daydream about—about the places you'd go with him if you could—the things you'd do—the person you'd be with him. You no longer have to hide behind pretend smiles whenever he's near, hoping no one else will guess what he means to you—hoping he won't guess, either, because he's meant to be with someone else. You must have wondered if you'd ever have a real smile again, and it must have been torture when your paths remained aligned straight ahead, never allowed to intersect, just continuing with the same common symmetry pulling you to him but keeping you apart at the same time."

"How did you know all of that about me?" she asks, stunned. "Is that one of your priestess gifts? Reading people?"

"No," I laugh humorlessly. "I've just drowned in the dark before too."

Charisma links arms with me, tugging on mine gently. "I'll take you up to the house. You need to rest," she says. Trey takes my other hand and follows with Honey Badger's reins in his other hand. Victus trails us leading the two dappled gray mounts.

Charisma takes me up the fragrant garden path where tiny violet flower heads litter the walkway of gray cobblestone and green moss. Nearing a water feature, I want to dive into the elegant fountain that creates a centerpiece to the courtyard. I would rather face Trey's parents soaking wet than in the state I'm in: dust-covered and spix-scented.

Ahead of us, ledgestone steps lead to a long, wide, wraparound porch. The entryway is ledgestone as well, with copper doors. Copper bolts create a beveled framework around them. On either side of the ledgestone are transparent walls like the ones in Charisma's building, allowing the outdoors into the living area of the building. There are multiple rooflines of a gray material I've never seen before. It appears similar to slate, but as I near it, the tiles shift, as the scales of a living dragon do, to seek the most advantageous angles for which to catch the sunlight.

Before I reach the first step, the copper doors open up and a couple walks onto the wide porch hand in hand. I stop where I am. I know immediately that these are Trey and Victus's parents, because the resemblance of father and sons is uncanny. In fact, they could all be brothers, if this were Earth and they weren't all ridiculously old. Trey drops the spixes' reins.

Trey tugs me forward while Charisma drops my arm and hangs back with Victus. I can usually read a room fairly well, but his parents are hard to know. His mom is surprisingly petite by Etharian standards, only an inch or two taller than me. Her hair is very lovely and long, flowing down her back in silky dark brown waves. She could easily be his sister, which is a little disconcerting when you think that parents *should be* older-looking. Her violet eyes are the shape of Trey's. I watch as they fill with tears; she fights to keep them from spilling over.

Trey's dad is a puzzle; I can't tell if he's livid or just extremely upset. Either way, it's too much emotion for me to handle right now. We stop in front of them; Trey gives his father a formal nod of greeting. It's not returned. Instead, his father grabs him by the shoulders and hugs him fiercely. Trey's mom caves in as well, hugging them both and crying softly until they make room for her in their hugfest. I stand there awkwardly with my hand in Trey's until I feel Trey and Trey's dad reach over and pull me into the hug-a-thon as well. It's still very awkward, but it's also sort of sweet, so I manage to tolerate it until Trey's dad lets us go.

"I'm glad you both made the trip here," Trey says to fill the void of silence while his parents try to pull themselves together. He waits several moments for them to dab at their eyes with handkerchief-like swatches.

Trey's dad clears his throat. "Thank you for the timely invitation."

"Let me introduce you. Kricket, this is my mamon, Vessey Allairis," he says while gesturing toward his mother. I sink into a deep curtsy, even though technically I don't have to, because I'm a priestess and in that circle curtsying to her is considered beneath me.

That's one reason why I do it. The other reason is that I want her to know up front that I respect her as the mother of the person I love.

"Greetings, Hautess Allairis," I say formally.

She's still recovering from her sob, but she manages to choke out the word "Greetings."

Trey smiles encouragingly at me. "Kricket, this is my pasdon. Do you know what that word means?"

"Is it like 'dad'?"

"It is. His name is Vanderline Allairis," Trey adds.

"Greetings, Vanderline." I try not to stare at him as I sink into a deep curtsy, sweeping my hand across my chest to rest on my shoulder in an appropriate greeting. I know I'm supposed to avert my eyes in a nod, but I can't. He looks too much like Trey and Victus.

As I rise, I'm relieved that my knee-jerk response hasn't offended him. With a nod, his deep voice is similar to Trey's as he replies, "Greetings, Fay Kricket."

Trey's mamon is still unable to speak, but she has a smile on her face nonetheless. I raise a shaky hand to my forehead, trying to block the glare of the sun as it continues to rise. It takes me a second to realize that I'm so sensitive to it because I haven't been in the sunlight for several rotations; I've seen it only here and there since the war began.

I think Trey's dad notices that I'm a tired wreck, because he steps aside so that we can enter the house, saying, "Don't allow us to keep you out here all morning." Vanderline ushers us both toward the door. "You both clearly need to rest."

I stop before crossing the threshold. "I can't stay here, Trey," I say in a near whisper. I grab onto the sleeve of his shirt to get his attention. "Your entire family is dead if I stay here. They can't be near me. If Kyon finds me here, he'll show them no mercy." I'm trembling like an El platform with an approaching train. I try not to show it.

"Kricket." Trey strokes my pale cheek, talking to me in a calming voice. "I have a plan. We won't stay long."

"What's the plan?" I look at his parents' concerned faces and I know that if I'm responsible for their deaths, Trey will never survive it. They're his family. They've *always* been his family. He can probably live without me, but he'll never be able to live without them. "You need to take me somewhere so that if they find me, I'll be alone and they won't kill anyone else."

They're better off without me and I'm better off when the only person I'm responsible for, or to, is me. Could I survive on Ethar alone? I may know enough now to get by for a little while, but ultimately, Kyon will find me. I have no doubt about that. He has all the resources, and given a long enough time line, he won't fail. I will be forced to deal with him.

I feel like a cornered animal; I want to claw my way out. Trey cups both my cheeks with his hands and forces me to look at him. "There is no safe place in Rafe anymore, Kricket, not for any of us. It won't matter if we're with you or not. The Alameeda are killing everyone. It's just like it was during the Terrible War. Extermination. All of us—myself included. We actually have a better chance of survival if we stay with you, because after you get some rest, you're going to begin to hone your ability to see and affect the future. You're going to make time bend to your will, and I'm going to do everything I can to help you stay ahead of them until such a time as we can fight them."

He looks away from me to the faces of his parents. "This isn't the way I wanted to tell you all of this. It's worse than we first thought. The Alameeda are primed to annihilate us all in this round. No mercy. We have to prepare to move into the restricted area. We can stay here only until we can make ready. The word has gone out. Rafe troops are converging to secret bases in the annexed area. We will try to join them there, in the Forest of Omnicron."

There's shocked silence from everyone present. Trey is in control of the situation, our leader. "We'll talk more after Kricket and I have had a chance to recuperate. In the interim, everyone should get as much rest as possible. The rotations ahead are sure to be trying ones."

Trey lifts me in his arms and brings me into the house. It's all a blur to me. I close my eyes and rest my cheek on his shoulder. I get the sense that it's a very large place by the fact that it takes Trey a while and many, many winding staircases to get us to the top of the house. When we do come to a room, I open my eyes. We cross beyond the enormous double doors that look as though they were designed to keep everyone at bay.

The view in front of me steals my breath. The room itself is masculine in its design and decor. Copper spyglasses of different shapes and sizes sit upon tripods of dark wood by the window wall. Some are angled at the mountain range in the distance and some are pointed to the sky. Low tables with metal contraptions that look like sextants and compasses have homes near the expensive-looking interactive globes and map tables. The room could be the office and bedroom of a nineteenth-century steampunk explorer. The strangeness of finding a room like this on Ethar is just another layer of mystery to add to Trey's already extensive list.

An almost regal bed is off to the right side, centered on that wall so as not to block the vista straight ahead. The panorama that greets my eyes as I stare outside is that of a majestic mountain range that rivals the ones I saw when I first came to Ethar in the Forest of O. Wilderness stretches out, surrounding the white-capped peaks. A wide terrace balcony runs the full length of the bedroom and is accessed through the glass doors in the glass wall.

Trey doesn't take me to the terrace; he turns instead and takes me to the softest bed I've ever lain upon in my entire life. It's four-poster mahogany-stained wood and is carved with stunning detail. A cloud of mosquito netting covers the bed. Beneath the veil of netting lie fat pillows and luxurious white sheets and blankets.

I scoot over; my head meets the exquisite white pillow as if it were falling through a cloud. Trey sits beside me on the bed and begins to unbuckle my boots, pulling off one and then the other. I close my eyes, turning on my side and half hugging, half snuggling a couple of pillows to me. When Trey begins to strip off my clothes, my eyes spring open. "Your parents are just downstairs," I whisper-hiss.

"Is that a problem?" he asks with a small smile developing upon his lips.

"Won't they freak out a little?"

"No. They never freak out. They wouldn't know how to freak out. Anyway, you'll be my consort soon."

"They never freak out?"

"What you just witnessed downstairs is the most emotion, other than worry, that I've ever seen from them. They're usually very stable."

I narrow my eyes at him, but he's telling the truth. "They won't mind us being together here even though I'm not your consort yet?"

He pulls my filthy shirt off over my head. My black leggings, which are also in a disgusting state, follow closely behind it. "The only reason you're not my consort yet is because we haven't had the opportunity to make it official."

When I don't have a shred of clothing left on me, Trey stands up and strips off his clothes as well. He slides into the bed next to me, making me scoot over to make room for him. He spoons me, his head sharing one of my pillows as he tucks me close to him.

"Ugh," I groan. "I smell like a spix."

Trey's nose sniffs my hair. "I smell the same as you do." He kisses the back of my head.

"Are you sure your parents are going to be all right with this?" I know how stiff some Etharians are about any hint of impropriety.

I'd heard enough gossip bantered around at the palace when I was one of its captive residents.

His voice is sleepy already. "I'm over a hundred floans old and this is my house. They'll have to endure it. They're not unreasonable people, Kricket. They won't allow societal rules to supersede wisdom."

I giggle despite everything. "You probably have a hundred rooms in this place and probably half as many beds. Your argument will have to be better than that when you talk to them."

"I can't bear the thought of you being anywhere other than right next to me. That's my argument. Everyone will just have to accept it, including you."

I smile drowsily. "I like that argument. It's a sound angle."

"It's sound because it's true," he murmurs.

Neither of us says anything else as sleep overtakes us.

⁂

When I wake, it's to find Trey missing. The sunlight has disappeared from the sky outside, replaced by a multitude of stars. A small lamp on the table in the sitting area casts a soft glow over the elegant occupant in the chair. Charisma is studying an atlas, poring over it as if it were a treasure map. Pulling the sheet up with me as I sit up, I rake my hand through my hair to try to calm my outlandish bedhead.

My movement alerts Charisma to the fact that I'm no longer asleep. "Greetings, Kricket," she says in a shy way as she uses the ribbon from the binding to mark the page before she sets the atlas aside on the table. "Are you well after your nap?"

"Where's Trey?" I ask, trying to stifle a yawn.

"He's down on the main level. He has been sequestered with the other Cavars and his brother and father for the past few parts."

"What are they talking about?"

"I don't know. They won't let me in the room with them."

"You didn't insist upon being in there too?"

"Well . . . no."

"Why not?"

"Trey asked me to sit with you."

"Would they have let you in there if you didn't have to sit with me?"

"No. Probably not."

"Why not?"

"They like to shelter me."

"Do you like them to shelter you?"

She's confused by the question. She shrugs. "I know no other way," she says simply.

"I don't believe that. You're strong and capable. You take care of spixes and know how to train them to move through courses where you shoot the crap outta stuff with your sonic sayzers. You should demand to discuss your future and any plans they make to protect it."

"How do I get them to listen to me?"

"*Make* them listen. Know your worth. Show them you're capable of whatever life throws at you. Don't expect them to understand you or like it."

A warm smile curls her lips. "Maybe you can show me how it's done."

"If you train me to use your sonic sayzers, I'll teach you how to earn their confidence."

"When do we start?" she asks in a conspiratorial way.

"After I shower?"

She rises from her chair and walks to the white-cushioned bench at the foot of the bed. Gathering a robe that was waiting there, she brings it to me. "It'll have to be after our repast. Mamon has been preparing food all day. She'll be disappointed if we don't partake of it."

As I don the robe, I try not to smirk at her formal way of speaking. I'm used to it, having been forced to speak it at the palace, but I much prefer the causal, humorous way the Cavars communicate. I nod. Charisma leads me to the lavare. It's a modern interpretation of a mountainous waterfall. The walls are gray stone, probably quarried from the hills in the distance. Enclosed glass hems in the cascade of water that spills out from a reservoir near the ceiling and down a round granite rock. When Charisma leaves, I stand beneath the rock, allowing the steaming water to pound away some of the tension that is my constant companion in this world.

The water shuts itself off the moment I step out of the glassed-in area. I head to the vanity and touch the stone wall, triggering warm air that blows down on me from the ceiling. I no longer marvel at all of the conveniences afforded us in this world. It's funny how fast I got used to them.

A long, lilac-colored gown is spread on the bed waiting for me when I return to the bedroom. I eye it skeptically.

"Vessey wants us to dress for dinner. It's in honor of your first meal as part of the family. I think secretly that she's also worried that it could be our last celebration together as a family."

I glance over at her. Her hair is stunning, pulled back on one side with a sparkling diamond comb. It allows for the beautiful soft waves to spill over her shoulders. Her dress is a ruby-colored silk and so thin that it looks liquid. It clings to her perfect silhouette.

"I'll wear it," I say softly, so that she doesn't feel the need to explain further. I understand the need for a last meal.

She offers to fix my hair and I agree, sitting with her as she pulls it into shapes that make me look older and more elegant. Braiding it off to the side, it falls over my left shoulder, leaving my back completely bare as the dress intended. She hands me the automatic makeup artist that she brought with her, and I quickly close my eyes after I bring it to my face to apply a thin, subtle layer of cosmetics.

"These shoes may be a little big," she says as she hands me a pair of silver sandals. They are too big, but since they're flats, and they wrap around the top of my ankle, they aren't too bad.

"I can manage with these. Thank you," I say.

We go down to dinner together. Charisma directs me through a maze of hallways and staircases to the main floor. The house is a large estate. It could have been used for hunting at one time, because it has that sort of manorlike feel to it that my other residence at the palace had. Linking arms with me, Charisma shows me to what must be the grand hall. The ceilings in the room have to be at least three stories high. Everything within the rectangular room is big. Big fireplace on the shorter wall, transparent walls that rise high above our heads. Four grand chandeliers spread soft light over all the occupants beneath them. Large, masculine chairs and divans anchor the room, presiding over sumptuously woven area rugs and a stone floor of the same gray that was in the mountain lavare.

Off to one side, beside the fireplace, Trey and his father sip amber liquor out of stout glasses. They both stop talking as Charisma and I join them. When we sit down to eat, I find myself between Trey and Charisma. Trey's dad raises a toast. We all settle in to eat.

I listen mutely to the banter as it flows around the table. Wayra tells stories about the first time he was at their estate in Thistle. Vanderline relates a story about how inseparable Trey, Victus, and Charisma were growing up. He calls them the tonic triad, because they managed to keep a constant tempo going without ever a lag in the action. I smile, because they were troublemakers.

"That was mostly Trey," Charisma says, smiling at Victus. "We were just trying to keep up."

Victus chimes in and relates some escapades from their youth. Throughout it all I listen, laughing with them, gleaning new information about these close-knit people.

From the other end of the table, Trey's mamon smiles at her husband, Vanderline. "All this talk of childhood and we haven't heard a thing from Kricket."

I smile and look down at my plate. "I'm enjoying hearing about life on Ethar. It's much more interesting."

She laughs. "Oh, we've heard all these stories before. Tell us something new. What was it like on Earth?"

"It was nice," I reply.

Wayra snorts and Jax winces a little.

"You must've played some games there, surely?" Trey's mom persists, trying really hard to draw me into the conversation.

I wrinkle my nose and shrug. "I played stickball a few times in my neighborhood—on the south side of Chicago—that's a game where you use a stick to hit a ball and then you run around three bases then try to run to the home plate before someone tags you with the ball."

"Were you good at it?" Vessey asks, happy that she's succeeding in having a conversation with me.

"No. Not really. I had to stop playing when I lost. As losers, my team had to give up our shoes. It took me a couple of weeks to earn enough money to get some new ones, so I didn't play it after that."

Vessey looks startled. "Surely there were games that you weren't expected to give up your shoes if you lost?" she asks in an unsure tone of voice.

"Where I'm from, most games are only played if there's a bet involved, or else why play them?"

"So no one plays games for fun?"

"No, they do. I just wasn't one of them." I can see that she's confused, so I sigh and explain, "One of my fathers was a hustler, so he taught me to play games that not many of the other kids' parents let them play like: find-the-patsy"—I tick that one off on my finger—"kick-the-bum's-can-and-steal-his-stash"—I add another finger—"pick-a-pocket-hide-and-seek"—a third finger joins them—"and convenience-store-boogeyman-candyland. That's when you shoplift as much candy as you can, and then sell it door-to-door pretending it's for charity. I got tired of playing boogeyman-candyland, so I just started stealing forties of malt liquor for Dan. It was more efficient and cut out a couple of steps."

I stop talking when Vessey abruptly rises from her chair. Picking up her own dinner plate and Victus's next to her, she doesn't seem to notice that he's not finished with his meal, or that his fork is halfway to his mouth. "That sounds very labor-saving, Kricket. Would anyone like anything else from the keuken?" she asks, but her voice is raspy like she has something stuck in her throat. Her eyes skim over the table and she patently ignores Wayra as he lifts his plate, about to ask for more of something. Before he can comment, however, Vessey clears out, practically running from the room to the kitchen.

I set my fork down, knowing I've said too much. I don't know what's wrong with me. I know that I should've softened that. I could've made something up or omitted parts and made it a nicer version of the truth, but I didn't want to; I want her to know me for who I am. I don't want her pity. I just want acceptance. This is my truth. I have entrusted her with it. Now I want to see what she does with it.

Trey reaches under the table and squeezes my knee. He pushes his chair back from the table. "Please excuse me, everyone, I believe my mamon needs help in the keuken." He nods and then follows his mom into the kitchen.

Wayra calls to me from across the table, "Kricket, I want you with us when we raid the enemy ammo sites. With your size and speed we can fit you between the beam spotters. You can blow the signal seekers and install the scanner jammers without them ever detecting you."

"That sounds like fun, Wayra. I'm in," I agree with a smile.

Drex, Hollis, and Gibon agree too, calling out several more things they think my skills as a thief and a grifter would translate into tactically.

Charisma covers my hand that is resting on top of my fork on the table. I glance over at her and see that her eyes are filled with tears, but she's fighting to keep them from spilling over. In a soft voice that doesn't carry too far, she says, "Trey gave us the talk while you were sleeping. He told us that you don't like sympathy, so if you say something that we find sad or troublesome, we should not show you that it bothers us."

"He told you I hate pity?"

"Yes, that's right," she says. "That's why Vessey left so quickly. She wanted to smother you with concern and love and kisses and cry her heart out for all that you've been through, but she didn't want to hurt you more or offend you, so she left so she could pull herself together."

"Thank you for telling me; it helps to have a translator."

"I'm more than that," she says with a sniffle. "I'm your friend, and hopefully, one day, your sister."

"I have something for you," I reply impulsively. Turning to Vanderline, I ask, "May we be excused?"

"Of course," he nods, as he stands up from the table. All of the other men stand as well. Charisma seems delighted that I've freed her from the table early.

I take her with me upstairs. Finding my bag near the bed, I pull out the black lacquer box. When I open it, I show her its contents. Charisma puts her hand to her mouth in shock. "My Crystal Clear Moments! You carried them with you all the way here from the Isle of Skye? And my sonic sayzers!" She picks one up and hugs it to her. "These are my favorite ones! I have another set, but they're not as pretty. I thought they were gone forever!" She peers into the box and picks up my starcross bracelet. "This is Trey's starcross."

I look at it in her hand. "Well," I say sheepishly, "it's sort of mine now. Trey gave it to me."

She looks startled. "Trey gave you this?"

I nod. "Yeah."

"It's been in his family forever."

"With luck it will remain in it forever."

"Here." She pushes the silver bracelet over my hand, and then gently pushes it over my wrist. The metal grows in size to accommodate the width of my arm as she slides it up onto my bicep. "There," she says, admiring the look of the silver starcross armband. "Some females wear them there. It's convenient if you use this hand to throw the starcross." She holds my opposite hand, crossing it over my chest.

My fingertips touch the etched silver crest on the armband. The panel opens up and a wickedly sharp star-shaped metal disk emerges to sit upon the cradle, waiting to be thrown. I press it back in, and it hides away once more beneath the crest.

Charisma holds up the sonic sayzers. "Did you use both of these?"

"No, just this one." I indicate the right one.

She hands it to me. "Here. You can practice with this one, then. I'll recalibrate the left one for me. Do you need to rest or can we try them out now?" she asks me.

I glance outside. It's really dark with no city lights, but the moons and stars are bright. I shrug. "I'm not tired. Let's try it."

She smiles broadly. "We'll take these and use them as targets." She picks up the lacquer box with the Crystal Clear Moments figurines inside. "All but this one." She reaches in and extracts the dancing couple that Trey said she received at her debut swank.

I laugh. "Trey said you hated that one!"

"I did hate it," she replies ruefully. "I thought it resembled Victus, and so it made me sad. But now, I love it. "

"Would it be all right if I kept one?"

"Of course," she says. "Pick whichever one you want."

"Thank you! Should I change?" I ask while gazing down at the lilac gown I'm wearing.

"We probably won't practice very long, and it's not too terribly exerting. I think we're fine in what we have on—maybe just bring that jacket there." She points to the black jacket of hers that I borrowed.

"You don't mind if I use it?"

"No! I have several that are very similar to that one. If you want another one, let me know."

She gathers the black box and waits for me to retrieve the jacket. When I pull it on, she walks with me to the terrace outside. Taking the staircase that leads to the grounds below, we descend the stone steps to a lovely courtyard. Charisma activates the lighting. Everywhere in the beautiful courtyard, hundreds of floating yellow, round lights the size of baseballs rise up from the ground to hover above us in the air. They hang at different levels in a staggered, firefly pattern; it's breathtaking and magical.

With the mountain range of the annexed area in the background, beneath the shine of the moons, Charisma sets up the zero-gravity apparatus and frees all the Crystal Clear Moments into the star chamber. Immediately, the figurines start to perform their tricks for us.

"Do you know which one you want to keep?" Charisma asks, watching the trift fly around performing daring maneuvers.

I reach into the pocket of the black jacket and show her the crystal spix that I had previously rescued from the star chamber. "I like the knight."

"It suits you," she says with a grin. Placing the box on the ground, she extracts the sonic sayzer cuffs from it. I lift my wrist for her to attach the right one to me. Immediately, the metal of the sonic sayzer grows and lengthens, covering my wrist to my elbow in a framework of Gothic-looking silver.

After the fingerless-glove part of it has grown over the back of my hand, Charisma advises, "Move your fingers to enter your security code." I do as she says, twitching my fingers so that it looks like I'm playing an invisible piano with my right hand. "You can extract the earpiece now," she advises as she dons the other weapon.

"Are you ready?" she asks me when I have the earpiece in place.

"Yes," I reply. We walk a short distance away from the targets.

She lifts her hand and concentrates on the shiny quarry ahead of her. When she fires, she hits the ballerina dead in its center, shattering the glass into showering bits. She squeals like a child! Turning to me, her face is a mask of elation and she smiles giddily. "That felt so good! I never would have dreamed that it would be so good!"

I laugh as she grasps my forearms while jumping up and down. She reaches around me and hugs me impulsively. "You have to kill one too! It's the best!"

When she releases me, I laugh some more and say, "I'll try, but I'm not sure what words to say to get it to work."

"I think you should try to shoot the mastoff first," she says, referring to the mastodon. "It's wide and it doesn't move very fast."

From somewhere behind us, a fast-moving, falcon-shaped ship sweeps through the dark sky, roaring over the stables and house. It's hard to see, but the sound of it is like a jet fighter breaking the sound barrier. Trailing it, in definite pursuit, is an Alameeda E-One. The waspish ship shoots blue-colored laser cannons at the falcon ship, trying to bring it down. The falcon ship banks to the left. It comes around to fly directly over the courtyard. As the E-One adjusts to follow it, it suddenly slows its progression when it comes upon us in the center of the courtyard. Allowing the falcon ship to escape, it instead hovers over Charisma and me in an eerie, menacing way.

Shouts from the Cavars come from every direction when a bright white beam of light hits us in a sickening spotlight. Beside me, Charisma glances my way and whimpers, "Kricket."

An instant later, her skin is melting from her bones from a flame-thrower directed at her. I scream her name, but it doesn't help; she's on fire. A tractor beam lifts me up into the air and I travel toward the belly of the ship.

"Are you ready?" Charisma asks me. I blink a couple of times. In front of me, the ballerina crystal figurine dances across the zero-gravity sky. I exhale a deep breath, seeing it curl with the icy smoke of a vision.

I shake my head no. When I find my voice, I shout at her, "Run, Charisma! Tell Trey that they're here—the Alameeda are here!"

Charisma hesitates, unable to process what I just said to her. I have to get her moving, so I push her hard in the direction of the house. "Run!" I shout again.

With terror in her eyes, she asks me, "What about you?"

"Just go!" I plead. This time she listens to me. She picks up the hem of her dress and she runs toward the house.

I pick up the hem of my dress too, as I run around the exterior of the house to the front of the estate. When I reach the orchard there, I try to catch my breath. I scan the hills by the pass where we entered the valley. Lifting my shaking right arm, I try to brace it with my left one. My breath comes out in raspy pants as I wait for what seems like an eternity.

I hear the rumble of the falconlike ship before I see it, but when I do, it flies so quickly over the ridgeline that it is almost impossible to track. Focusing on where that ship had crossed the ridge, I take aim with my sonic sayzer and then a deep breath. As I exhale, I see the Alameeda E-One coming over the crest of the ridge. Breathlessly I say, "The worst, Honey."

The recoil from the sonic sayzer lifts me off my feet; I find myself flat on my back looking up at the sky. The wind is knocked out of me, but I sit up anyway. Wheezing for breath, I cringe when I notice a hole in the ridgeline. *I missed!* Not only that: the E-One has halted its pursuit of the falcon-shaped ship and is now bearing down on me.

I rise quickly from the ground, lifting my aching arm again and pointing it at the enemy E-One, as it grows closer. "The worst, Honey," I say the words and I'm knocked over again.

Someone grasps me under my shoulders and lifts me up. Trey's sexy, masculine scent is as much around me as his arms as they go to my waist. He braces my back against his chest and his voice is calm as he says, "Try again."

He helps me lift my arm and aim at the Alameeda death ship bearing down on us. I whisper to Trey, "The worst, Honey."

Trey absorbs the recoil while the rotorless heli-vehicle in front of us explodes into a huge, flaming fireball. As pieces of the ship fall to the ground, shouts from the Cavars come from all angles. Trey turns so that his body is between the E-One and me as it crashes hard into the dirt, shaking the fruit from the orchard.

Trey straightens, before turning me around in his arms. He brushes the hair from my face, scanning it to assess my state of mind. I'm numb. I don't know how I feel right now, other than scared. A loud *boom* severs the sky again as the falconlike ship circles back around. Bracing myself, I lift my right arm, trying to track it, but Trey grabs my wrist. "It's a Comantre ship."

I lower my arm, relieved that I don't have to try to take it down. It flies overhead; its jets reverse, causing it to hover for a few moments before it descends from the sky and lands in the paddock by the stable. "Go back to the house," Trey says softly. "I'm going to see what they want. Make ready. Our position is compromised now. We'll have to leave within the part."

He lets go of me; I sag a little at the loss of him. He walks toward the Comantre ship, while the belly of it opens like a gaping maw. I lose my breath when Giffen emerges down the ramp with a score or more heavily armed Comantre Syndics in his wake.

I yell to Trey, "Not friendlies!" Lifting my arm, I aim the sonic sayzer at Giffen, whispering, "The worst, Honey."

Giffen raises his hand, redirecting the killer sound I throw at him. It ricochets off the grain silo, exploding it into a shower of confetti. Giffen retaliates, throwing energy at me so that I'm knocked down once more. I lie on the ground, dizzy and confused, trying to make my eyes focus on Inium, the moon above us, but the blue orb turns dark and fades away before my eyes.

CHAPTER 15
UNSPEAKABLE THINGS

I rouse to consciousness, feeling a tug on my hair. A large hand pulls the shorn strands of my tresses away from me. The blond mass in his palm curls and disappears. A knife passes in front of my eyes, and then disappears as the person behind me moves away. I try to lift my hands, but they're shackled around the stiff seat back behind me. Someone has removed the sonic sayzer from my wrist, I realize, as I clench and unclench my fingers.

"Kricket," Giffen says from his chair opposite me. We're both sitting at the table where I'd eaten with Trey and his family only a few hours ago. "Would you like some water?" He lays his hand on his rough, five o'clock shadow, rubbing it thoughtfully over the sharp angles of his jaw. I assess his beard; it's more in character for him now than the shaven version of him at our last meeting. His golden-brown dreadlocks are pulled back from his shoulders and secured in a ponytail. The Comantre uniform he's wearing is all wrong. He should have swim trunks on and a volleyball in his hand so all the girlies on the beach can line up to rub sunscreen on his back.

My mouth is dry. I nod my head. "Water sounds good." Giffen produces a canteen. Opening it, he takes a sip before setting it down on the table. He pushes it in front of me. I lean forward; my hands behind me rattle the metal shackles against the slats of the chair, causing them to clang. My eyes lift expectantly to Giffen's, but he doesn't move to put the canteen to my lips; he slouches back in his seat negligently.

I understand. I lean back in my seat too, squaring my shoulders against the hard wood. I glance at the man with the knife. He's moving away to stand by the hearth near the head of the table. I'm surprised that I recognize him. He's the Comantre conscript who was part of the team that came to remand me to Defense Minister Telek's office. *He called me something when I was with Trey in his apartment on the Ship of Skye. What was it—a baboon—boosha? What was his name—Randal? Rankin? Raspin!*

"I would like some water. Could you get some for me, Raspin?" I ask with a tilt of my head.

"She's a corker, that one! Remember me, do ya?" Raspin asks with an ear-splitting grin. It is quickly chased away by an anxious look. *He's worried about something.*

"I remember everyone who calls me a shefty boosha. How's your mouth?"

He rubs the auburn-colored stubble on his chin, probably remembering that I elbowed him in the face in the Premiere Palisade's rail station. "I did not have to cut my hair." He takes off his cap, and cornrows of wiry copper hair spill down his back.

He's one of us—a freak. I'd bet a venish on it. "You're a lost boy like Giffen, aren't you? You have the freak gene too, right?" I ask him.

Raspin moves forward to the long, rectangular table where Giffen and I are seated. With one hand he grips the wood, picking it up. Without much trouble, he pushes the table away from him, over my head. The wood splinters as it crashes into the transparent window wall behind me, spilling the water as well. My heart beats painfully in my chest at the sheer strength of him. "I'm not lost," he glowers. "But me truluv is. You have to get her fer me."

I blink at him as he scowls at me threateningly. "Your truluv?"

"His girl," Giffen translates.

"Who's your girl?"

"Astrid is me truluv," he breathes heavily, raw emotion in every word.

I blink again. *Astrid?*

Giffen clears his throat so that I'll look at him. "We need you so that we can get Astrid back."

I feel dizzy. "Who's Astrid?" I ask, really needing that water now.

Giffen's steady gaze never wavers from me. "Astrid is your sister."

"She's my what?" *I think I hit my head too hard.*

"She's your baby sister."

"I don't have a sister," I whisper lamely. *I have another sister.*

"You do. She has risked everything to extract you from the conflict in the Isle of Skye, but she miscalculated the Alameeda and was taken hostage by them."

He's not lying. "I don't remember her—she's nothing to me—"

Raspin's face turns red. He picks up a heavy wooden chair and throws it through the glass wall. So many cracks form in the surface of the glass that I can see what is left of the chair only by looking through the hole it made.

Giffen pulls his wooden chair close to mine; he turns it around so he can straddle it, resting his arms on the seat back. "You're something to her. You're her 'Kick-it.' That's what she calls you when she talks about you. If you'd gone with me when I came for you, you would've met her."

"So she wasn't in on your plan to kill me before?" I ask with a frown.

Giffen sighs heavily. "She knew it was a contingency plan so that you wouldn't be turned over to the enemy and used against us. She was not in agreement with it—she threatened to cut off my . . . she threatened to cut me if I killed you."

"Wow. This is quite a change for you, Giffen. Now you're okay with handing me over to the Alameeda because they have *her* and you want *her* back?"

His eyes narrow at the bad light I just put him in. "We didn't have any leverage with you before now!" he retorts as justification to his prior plan. "And we didn't know where your loyalties lie. We had no assurances that you'd work with us. I was not at liberty to tell you about your sister then. We had to protect her identity."

"You have no assurances now, either!"

"I beg to differ. I have all of your friends. All the ones you risked your life to save before," Giffen threatens.

"You're going to blackmail me?"

He scowls. "I shouldn't have to! You should want to help your sister who loves you!"

My mouth hangs open for a moment before I snap it shut. "Loves me?" I stick out my bottom lip and shake my head with a shrug. "I don't know her! Where has she been? I didn't even know who she was until a second ago. Where did she go?"

"She's been on Ethar—hidden with us since she arrived here."

"When was that?"

"When your mother died."

I try to process what Giffen is saying. "If she's younger than me, she couldn't have been more than three or four years old. She couldn't have gotten here by herself."

"Her father brought her."

I feel sick and hopeful at the same time, and the fact that I feel hopeful makes me feel sicker. "Her father brought her? You mean *our* father brought her?"

He nods, looking uncomfortable. "Pan brought her here when she was almost four floans old."

"Water," I manage to say, begging Giffen with my eyes.

It's Raspin who brings it to me; bending down, he tips a canteen to my lips. He's surprisingly gentle for such a strong, raging knob knocker. When I've had enough, I move my lips away. He manages not to spill any of it on me. I can't yet ask them the only question I want to ask them. I'm too afraid of the answer. Instead I ask, "When you said 'they've been with us,' where was that? Is there a Valley of Misfit Boys or something?"

A grudging smile appears on Giffen's lips. "Pan made a home for us in the Amster Rushes—in the annexed area. Then he set about finding all of us—all the Alameeda males with special talents who were being hunted down and slaughtered—bringing us there. He saved most of our lives."

"He must be a saint," I reply with sarcasm.

"He is," Raspin replies, believing every word of it.

I snort in disgust. "Did he happen to notice when he got to Amster that he was one daughter short?" The bitterness in my voice is extremely apparent.

"He rarely speaks of you, but when he does, it's always with the greatest respect and admiration for your sacrifices."

I laugh humorlessly. "My sacrifices? Oh, that's—" I shake my head and exhale a harsh breath. "Do you know why he abandoned me on Earth?"

"You're the prophecy. You're the one who sparks the war. He couldn't bring you back. He had to leave you there. It was your destiny."

I nod my head as if I'm okay with it. "Oh . . . it was my destiny! So it's all part of the plan?"

Giffen exhales in relief. "Yes."

Rage boils over as I yell at him, "Screw your plan! And screw him!"

"Not! Working!" Raspin yells at Giffen. He storms to the doors, ripping them off their tracks as he leaves the room.

"Now you've made him mad," Giffen sighs in frustration.

"Just let me see if I understand you. You want me to allow you to hand me over to the Alameeda in exchange for my sister, but you don't want me to retaliate against you by using my ability to see the future to harm you in any way."

"Yes, and—"

"Wait! There's an *and*? Why is there an *and*?"

"We need you to be our eyes on the inside. We want to communicate with you and—"

"You want me to spy for you."

"Yes."

"You guys have some big, fat, *huge*, bouncy—"

Raspin enters the room dragging Trey's unconscious body behind him. I don't know what they did to him, but he looks dead. With a hand around Trey's throat, Raspin lifts him up, ready to gut Trey with his knife if I blink at him the wrong way. "Ya shefty wee monster! I'll carve him to prove to ya that I am heartfelt," he seethes. He's being honest.

"Wait! Please!"

Raspin's hand stills just above Trey's chest.

"Okay, I'll do it! Just stop!"

"Ya swear upon it?" Raspin asks angrily.

"I swear on it," I reply in desperation, trying to reassure him. "Astrid gets saved and I get thrown away again. It's fine. We have a deal. Just don't hurt him, okay?"

Raspin looks like he doesn't believe me. "Should something happen to Astrid, it happens to him. I gut 'em all if she's harmed." He raises his knife, placing it to Trey's neck, drawing blood as he begins to cut.

"Nothing will happen to her!" I try to placate him in a stream of words. "I'll make sure of it!" He stops cutting. It's an eternity that I wait—those seconds I watch Raspin take as he decides whether or not

I'm telling the truth. A part of me isn't sure if he'll believe me. Even when Raspin lowers the knife in his fist, I have trouble breathing.

My legs are numb with fear. When he stops holding Trey by the throat, my chin drops to my chest for a second in relief and I let go of the breath. He places Trey on the ground against the wall. I stare at Trey for several seconds, trying to see if he's still breathing. There's a swollen knot by his left temple. It's hard not to lose my mind as I strain against the metal on my wrists, finding that I can't free myself. The cut on Trey's neck is slowly dampening his collar with his blood.

I turn my attention back to Giffen. He rises from his chair, pulling out his communicator from the pocket of his Comantre uniform. I can't believe that my father is associated with these two psychos—then I think about how he abandoned me—maybe it makes perfect sense. I clear my throat and ask, "Does Pan know about this plan?"

Giffen's eyes narrow in suspicion. "He knows."

In a shallow tone I ask, "Does he agree with it?"

He ignores my question. "I need to take your image." He holds up his communicator in front of me.

"What are you planning to do with my picture?"

Giffen snaps a couple of shots. "I have to send it to Kyon Ensin. We'll pretend to be Comantre Syndics. He doesn't know who we are or who your sister is. Hopefully, none of them have realized yet that she has Alameeda blood or that she's a priestess. When Kyon responds, I will demand a trade: you for her. I will tell him that she is Comantre and was working in the Isle of Skye when the unrest broke out. I will ask for her safe return in exchange for yours."

"How do you know she's not already dead?" I ask.

"She's too pretty for that. They'd keep her for entertainment."

Raspin smashes another chair, unable to contain his rage.

I blanch. "Why wouldn't they know that she's a priestess—or at least know that she has Alameeda blood? Isn't it obvious?" I ask in a near whisper, trying without success to keep my inquiries between the two of us.

"She wasn't born with pale hair like yours. She has Pan's coloring—black hair, but her eyes are blue. We altered them before she went in."

"How did you do that?"

"We injected pigment to make them green, but it only lasts a few rotations, then it reverts to her normal hue."

"Alameeda blue?" I ask.

"That's right, like her mother's."

His attention is back on his communicator again. "Wait," I say, seeing that he's about to send the pictures he took of me.

"What?" he asks.

"You want this to work?" I ask, meeting his eyes.

"Of course!"

"If you want this to work, you should hit me."

His eyes narrow. "What?"

"I look okay right now—I look like you're not serious about getting your supposed consort back. You have to make it urgent or Kyon will take a little time to find out exactly who Astrid is before he hands her over. You have to put it on a faster time line. You have to take the control away from him and keep it. If he thinks that you might kill me, he'll lose the advantage. He can't know how you got me or that you have Trey. When you meet him to exchange us, it can't be here and we have to go alone—just you and me, Giffen."

Raspin growls at me, "Going!"

"He can't go," I argue. "There's too much emotion there. He can't cope. A priestess could read him like a billboard. You can get out alive with Astrid because of your telekinetic gift. It's the only way I can think of where everyone has a shot at survival."

Giffen looks at Raspin. "It sounds like a good plan."

"That's because it *is* a good plan," I mutter.

Raspin nods his head. He starts to walk toward me. "Seriously?" My eyes shutter in scorn. "You're not hitting me, Incredible Sulk!" I glare at him like he's a lunatic, which he definitely is. He hesitates and looks at Giffen.

I shift my head and nod toward Giffen. "You," I assess him. "You do it."

Giffen glances at Raspin, who shrugs and gestures with his hand toward me. Giffen squares his broad shoulders and walks to me. As he stands above me, looking down into my defiant face, I can't tell if he wants to do it or if he's reluctant to do it. I just know that he *will* do it. I take a deep breath, trying to brace myself. "Ready?" he asks. I nod.

The open-palm slap to my cheek from his rough hand makes my face turn away from him. Blood sprays outward through my parted lips in an array of red. If I hadn't been in a fight before, the sting of it might've shocked me. I never know whether to clench my teeth or loosen my jaw when I see it coming. If I clench my teeth, I usually end up with a few loose ones. If I loosen my jaw, I run the risk of biting down on the soft, fleshy tissue inside and shredding a hole in it. The best thing to do would be to duck, but that would be counterintuitive, since I want him to hit me.

His green eyes lean near mine; his breath is warm on my rapidly swelling skin. "Does a priestess feel pain?" he asks.

Lowering my forehead, I drive it into his nose, hearing it crack as blood spurts out to spatter my cheeks and his. As I reel with dizziness and an aching skull, I try to smile when I murmur, "Yes. Do you?"

"Careful," he groans, his nose bleeding profusely as he smiles. "Don't make me fall in love with you, priestess."

"Shut up." I spit blood. "Uhh, that's so much worse the second time," I say to myself, trying not to groan as I gather my courage. "Okay, I'm ready. Hit me again, and then take my picture."

It's extremely scary how quickly Kyon responds to the images that Giffen sends to him. What's also frightening are the layers of signal blockers Kyon is able to hack through during each of the communications Giffen engages in with him. Giffen has to cut the connection off a few times so Kyon won't trace our location.

Seething over Kyon's lack of cooperation, Giffen glares at me. "Your Alameeda intended is a sneaky, blond wacker!" he says with disgust, but it sounds less dirty somehow because his speech is so refined.

"He's not my anything, lost boy," I state calmly, wishing I could brush my hair back from my throbbing face. They haven't uncuffed me from the chair, even though I agreed to all of their demands. I guess I'm just untrustworthy.

Giffen scowls at me. "Don't deceive yourself. The moment he returns you to his home you'll be made his consort."

"You say that like it bothers you."

"Why should it?"

I shrug, which seems to bother him more. He gets surlier. "He wanted to communicate with you last time to verify that you're alive. When I contact him now, be brief. I need to tell him the location of the exchange before he can track the signal."

I don't argue. *What's the point?* "Let's do this."

Giffen eyes me suspiciously, glancing uneasily at Raspin. Raspin is watching me as if he expects me to disappear at any moment and take with me his ability to get back his truluv, which I think might mean his "soulmate."

Giffen makes the connection. Kyon answers, "You keep ending our conversations just when they're getting interesting."

"Have you located my consort?" Giffen asks.

"I have. She's a bit untidy, but nothing you're not used to, I'm sure."

Charming, I think.

"Let me see her," Giffen demands.

His jaw eases somewhat when a feminine voice comes through the communicator saying, "Gif?"

"Are you well?" he asks Astrid, relief in his tone. I groan inwardly, *He's so bad at this!*

She's not allowed to answer him. Instead, Kyon asks, "What of *my* consort?"

Giffen glances at me. "According to her, she's not your consort," he states vehemently.

I glare at him with a what-the-hell-are-you-doing look on my face. He doesn't have to argue about something as stupid as my commitment status. *What happened to "be brief"?* I say with my eyes. Giffen glares back at me with an I-can-say-whatever-I-want-to look.

Kyon growls, "She belongs to me—make no mistake. If you do not show her to me in the next few breaths, I will kill your consort in the most painful way imaginable."

Giffen's jaw clenches. He taps a few buttons before sliding his communicator onto a small table he has placed in front of my chair. Kyon's head-and-shoulders image appears as a holograph, being projected from the communicator like a video speakerphone. He doesn't look happy about the state I'm in.

"Resist, did you?" he asks with a grim look. "How is that working out for you, Kricket?"

"I have it all under control." I try to smile but my fat lip and puffy, black eye hurt more when I do. I wince and sag a little in my chair, letting my actions belie my words. "You don't have to come get me. I can find another ride."

"It's not an inconvenience. It's probably on my way," he says quietly.

Giffen barks out, "Diadem Rock—in two parts."

"I will be there—and, oh, if you touch her again, I will cut off both your consort's hands."

"If you fail to deliver Astrid in one piece, Kricket dies."

Giffen ends the communication.

CHAPTER 16
DARKEN THE STARS

Raspin's knife is drawn as he walks toward me. I flinch for a second, worried about what he intends to do with it. When he moves behind me and gathers my hair in his fist, ready to slice it off to help me heal, I growl, "Stop! Don't cut my hair! It'll look suspicious if you do!"

He hesitates.

"You shouldn't know about what my hair does when you cut it. It's one of their secrets. He'll wonder how you know, and then he'll wonder why you would help me when you were the ones who beat me up."

Raspin drops my hair. Instead, he touches the tight cuffs that pin my hands behind me. He enters a code, and they spring open. I almost can't move my arms—their stiff ache is excruciating—but I slowly bring them in front of me, then bend over at the waist and hug myself. "You want to help me?" I ask Raspin when he hovers in front of me. He stares at me in an oafish sort of way. "When I save Astrid's life for you, you owe me. The only payment I'll accept from you is in the form of protection. You owe me Trey's life, Raspin. No matter what happens, you have to protect him."

I wait as he crouches down to my eye level. "It takes the best in us to tie ourselves up fer love."

"Did my father teach you that?" I ask with a bitter laugh. "Love is the worst, Raspin. It sets fire to us just to see who it can kill."

He looks at me almost helplessly. From behind him, Giffen nudges his shoulder with a canteen. Raspin takes it from him and holds it out to me. I drink, trying hard to ease my tight throat.

"We have to go," Giffen says in a quiet voice from behind Raspin. "Would you like to change before we leave?"

My torn and bloodstained lilac dress is a tale of sorrow. It's also grass-stained and split up the side, exposing my right leg and most of my thigh. I wouldn't actually care all that much, but thinking of facing Kyon in it makes me feel even more vulnerable. "Is Charisma still here?" I ask.

"Is she the older or the younger female?" Giffen counters.

"Younger."

Giffen goes to the doorway; one door still hangs askew from Raspin's rampage. He speaks to a couple of armed men in the corridor outside.

When Charisma enters the room, she gives a soft cry, seeing Trey bleeding and unconscious on the floor. Her face pales, but she fights it as her voice hardens. "Trey needs medical attention. Will you let us tend to him?"

Giffen seems to remember Trey. He appears about to argue with her, but Raspin pushes them both aside, clearing a path to Trey. He picks Trey up and hoists him over his shoulder before staring at Charisma expectantly. They start to leave the room together, but Giffen stops them. "You can get someone to treat him," he instructs, "but then you have to bring back something for Kricket to wear— something she can travel in."

Charisma's attention is drawn to me for the first time. She blinks back tears when she sees my swollen face. I lift my chin because I don't need pity. "Bring me what I wore here, Charisma," I murmur.

"All right," she replies in a weak voice.

She leaves the room, and with her departure I'm alone with Giffen.

Giffen paces for a bit, every once in a while looking in my direction. I confuse him, I can tell. I haven't tried to bargain with him, or attempt to get him to change his mind. I haven't asked him any questions about himself or the other lost boys, or Astrid, or Pan, or the prophecy. It's bothering him.

"Are you hungry?" he asks me in an irritated tone. "Do you want something to eat?"

"No. Kyon will feed me; it'll give him something to do. He'll want to show me how well he can take care of me." I don't really know if that's true. I just want Giffen to stop talking to me.

Giffen's frown darkens and he becomes surly again. "He won't be able to care for you long. He's going to die like the rest of them!"

I don't reply.

Giffen resumes pacing. In a few moments, he pauses to evaluate me. "You're nothing like her." I raise my eyebrow, wondering for a moment whom he means. "Astrid," he says, studying me. "You're nothing like her; she is all heart."

I don't react, except to say softly, "Well. I guess Pan picked the right one, then."

That response was not what he was hoping for from me, because he looks a little like I punched him in the stomach with my remark. "She's part of the prophecy too, did you know that? We have to protect her," he says cryptically.

"Then protect her."

"It's what I've sworn to do."

"Well, from where I'm sitting, you're not very good at it."

The silence stretches on for a bit. When he doesn't stop staring at me, I look at him with a level gaze and ask, "What? What do you want from me, lost boy? Do you want my understanding? Do you want me to say it's okay that you're kidnapping me and trading me to the enemy?" I keep my voice calm but full of scorn. "Do you want my forgiveness because you're just doing what you're sworn to do?" I shake my head before looking up at the ceiling. "If I had a nickel for every time I've found myself in this same situation, I could *buy* this *entire* planet!" I straighten and meet his eyes again. "So get away from me with your whining for absolution. You get *nothing* from me!"

In the very next moment, Charisma enters the room with clothes piled in her arms. Her eyes shift from me to Giffen. We both look primed to kill each other. She hurriedly comes to me, getting between us in an attempt to shield me from him. "I brought the clothes," she says in a voice that's an octave higher than normal due to fear. I rise from the chair, ready to get on with this. She turns toward Giffen, "Please excuse us while she changes."

His handsome jaw hardly unlocks as his mutters, "I'm not letting her out of my sight." He crosses his arms over his chest, leaning against the wall.

With reddening cheeks, Charisma faces me. "It's okay," I murmur to her. I shrug off the black jacket, exposing my silver crested starcross armband Trey gave me. Giffen is at my side immediately, lifting my arm and tugging it off me.

"What's this?" he asks.

"It's mine!" I try to grab it back from him. He moves it out of my reach above my head.

He backs away from me and studies the starcross in his hands. "I can't let you keep this," he replies.

"You can't keep it! It's mine!" I retort with a thread of desperation in my tone. "It doesn't belong to you." My stomach churns. *I'll never get it back now that I've shown that it means something to me. I know better.*

 it's from Kitten?"

Giffen surprises me. "I'll keep it for you." There's honesty in his high handedness. "You'll get it back. I promise. Now hurry. We're running out of time."

Taking the tight legginglike pants from Charisma, I slip them on underneath the lilac dress. I turn away from Giffen, ready to pull the dress over my head, when I feel his hand on my back. I shy away from his touch, looking over my shoulder. He's staring at my back. I try to see what has caught his attention. Long, deep scratches are almost entirely scabbed over and rapidly healing themselves. I must've gotten them when Giffen hit me with his telekinetic energy. It had lifted me off my feet and I'd landed on my back, skidding across the ground.

"I didn't mean to hurt you like that." He's not lying.

I turn away from him, lifting the ruined silky fabric over my head so that my entire back is exposed to his remorseful gaze. *Stew in it, lost boy*, I think, while putting the black blouse over my head. I grab the dirty, black jacket from the chair, easing it on gingerly. As I turn around, I gather up the front of my shirt, wiping it with the sweat, dirt, and blood from my face. It makes a disgusting pattern. "There," I say to myself, letting my shirt drop down again. "Now I look like I've been through something."

"We have to go," Giffen growls. He's angry with himself for showing me emotions he shouldn't have in the first place.

Hurriedly, I turn to Charisma. "Will you do something for me?"

Her violet eyes brim with tears. "Anything. I will do anything for you," she assures me, not even knowing what it is I'll ask her to do.

"Will you give Trey one of your Crystal Clear Moments? The saer?"

She nods her head in confusion. "Of course," she whispers.

"And will you tell him it's from Kitten?"

"Yes. Anything else?"

"Yes," I lean near her ear and whisper, "Please tell him that I'll take care of his soul until he finds us. I'll be expecting him soon."

282

Charisma starts to cry. She hugs me, forgetting about my hurt back. I endure it, returning her hug.

"Take care of Victus and the family," I whisper to her.

"I will," she whispers back.

When I straighten, I look at Giffen and nod. He takes me by my arms, pulling them behind my back once more and cuffing me. "Let's go."

He takes me outside toward the falconlike ship. Ground sconces illuminate the pathways leading to it. There are also floating orb lights hovering several feet above us, casting a soft phosphorus glow all around. It's nearly dawn; the spectral light is shining on the horizon by the ridge. As I pass through the courtyard, armed men in Comantre uniforms clutching machine-gun-like weapons crowd nearer, trying to get a look at me. One of them hurries over to Giffen, matching our steps. "You shouldn't do this," he says sternly, staring at Giffen's profile. "It's not right. He didn't authorize this."

"It's the only way to get Astrid back," Giffen says, looking straight ahead, never missing a step. "We need someone on the inside with eyes on the Brotherhood. She's perfect for the job."

"How are we going to face him and tell him that we handed over his daughter to the Alameeda?"

"*We're* not going to tell him. *I'm* going to tell him."

"But he won't—"

Giffen jerks hard on my elbow as he stops and faces the soldier at his side. This one has long, straight brown hair and soft brown eyes. "You want Astrid back alive or not?" he seethes.

"Of course I do!" The soldier is aghast at the question. He glances past Giffen and gives me an apologetic look.

Giffen starts striding toward the aircraft again, pulling me along with him. In frustration, he calls over his shoulder, "Don't worry, Fidar. This one will have the Alameeda begging us to take her back."

He guides me up the ramp and into a large bay. Fluorescent lights come on, turning our skin tone a pale whitish blue. This part of the ship is probably used for loading and unloading cargo and for transporting troops. High-backed seats attached to the walls run the length of the aircraft on both sides. Giffen turns me around and uncuffs one of my wrists. Guiding me to a jump seat, he puts his hand on my shoulder and presses me into it. The seat belts crisscross over me as he snaps the other cuff to the handrail by my head, locking it. "Don't go anywhere."

The comment was made to get a reaction from me. I just stare at him with loathing. With a frown, he straightens. He wants me to say something—he needs it. He's okay when he's fighting with me, but the quiet between us bothers him.

When I don't oblige him, he turns his back on me and closes the cargo bay door, then disappears farther into the ship. There is an emptiness in the dim, pale light of the cargo bay. Nothing is familiar. Lights flash, blue, red, yellow, and green on a control panel on the wall. Instruments buzz and beep at odd intervals. It's agony, this unfamiliarity. My hands begin to shake first, and then my legs—my knees bounce from it. I look down at my hands, seeing streaks of dried blood smear my skin. Rubbing them together, I can't get their marks to go away. My teeth chatter like I'm cold, but I don't know if I am or not, because I'm numb. I make hacking sounds with my breath, because I can't seem be able to get enough air past the lump in my throat.

The ship lifts off, moving straight up fast enough for me to lose my stomach. I clutch the belts surrounding me. Normally, this would've scared me and brought on a panic that we might crash. Now, it has the opposite effect: it calms me. *We might crash. If we do, this ends.* Another part of me whispers, *I need to know the future . . . I need to prepare . . .*

"I wish to see the exchange at Diadem Rock," I murmur. My icy breath curls out before me and I leave my body.

৵৵৵৶

Giffen's large hand is cupping my chin as he kneels in front of my jump seat. "Kricket," he says while shaking my head to try to get a response from me.

Groaning, I mutter, "Are you really shaking my head right now? It already hurts like a spix kicked it, so stop!"

"Getting in touch with your spirit animal, were you?" His question is flippant, but there's relief in his tone that he can't hide.

"Yeah, it said to give you this." I raise my middle finger at him. He stares at it, because the gesture means nothing to him.

"I should take your finger?" he asks.

"I hate you," I reply, burying my head in my hands. I know I must be ghost-pale, because I feel like all the blood has left my brain.

"Good"—his lips turn sullen—"because they should be here soon. I'll set up contact with you in a few rotations."

"I'd rather not see you ever again," I reply.

"Sorry to disappoint you. I'll be the one communicating with you while you're with the Alameeda."

I scoff at that. *The arrogance!* "Keep dreaming. I'm never speaking to you again, lost boy. This is it for us. You should say good-bye now."

He growls, "You should stop thinking of just yourself! There are people counting on us not to fail, you ignorant child!"

"You must be my father's favorite," I retort, like that's a bad thing.

"I am," he agrees with pride.

"Well, I'm the one he threw away, so I don't think I owe you, or him, or anyone else anything."

Soft beeping sounds overhead. "They're here." Giffen swears under his breath. Getting to his feet, he moves to the cargo bay doors. He opens them, and the ramp begins to descend. Sunlight streams in from the outside. As the ramp clunks down on gray stone, the panorama spreads out beyond. We've landed on a ridge atop a high peak. I know what it looks like outside; I was just here—the future me—or is it the past me now?

Smooth rocks circle the depression in the shape of a crown. If I had to guess, it appears as if a meteorite of some kind had struck the mountaintop here and to mark the event someone placed enormous, bone-white standing stones around it. The stones look ancient, the remnants of a long-dead civilization. Maybe it's fitting that we're meeting here, since this civilization might die soon and a new one rise to take its place. Beyond the stones, if you look through the gaps, you can see clear sky in every direction.

Cold wind, reminiscent of Chicago, drifts in. Giffen comes back to me and unlocks my cuff from the handrail before helping me to my feet with his hand upon my elbow. He releases me from the other cuff as well, tossing it aside. "You've been to the future?" Giffen whispers beside me on the crest of the ramp. We both watch as a beautiful chrome trift lands opposite us on the gray rock bed.

"Yes." The elegant door of the chrome trift appears in the almost liquid surface of the craft. A waterfall of chrome pours down from the doorway, forming floating stairs.

When I don't say more, Giffen exhales in frustration and asks, "How does it go?"

"It doesn't work out well. She hugs me and they shoot her in the back of the head. Focus on the one holding her. If he raises his gun, don't hesitate to stop him. I'm going to try to change the outcome my way. If I fail, you'll have to kill him and try to run."

Giffen doesn't seem thrilled with this information. "If we get out of this, is there anything that you want me to tell Astrid for you?" he asks. Both of us regard the broad-shouldered, Kevlar-like-coated Alameeda Strikers who debark from the aircraft with their weapons drawn in plain sight.

"Tell her never to save me again." The coldness of my reply hangs in the air.

His jaw clenches. "Do you have a message for Pan?" Giffen asks. "No."

From the corner of my eye, I see him grimace. "I promise to help you—after we get Astrid home safely."

I force myself to laugh, but it sounds desolate, even to me. "Ahh, don't change now, lost boy. You were doing so well as the bad guy."

Kyon descends the trift steps. He's attired in a long, black coat with a brown fur collar and brown fur cuffs. He looks regal and virile. Behind him, a young woman is half dragged, half thrown down the steps. She whips her dark hair back from her face and I'm struck again, as I was a short time ago in the future, by our lack of resemblance. She's much prettier than me with her black hair and big eyes. She's taller than me as well. She doesn't have my curves, either; her frame is more slender than mine. It's lucky we don't look alike. If we did, Kyon would notice.

I clench my hands to keep them from visibly shaking. Without looking at Giffen, I say, "We're done. I hope I never see you again."

I take a step toward Kyon, but Giffen holds my arm and won't let me go. He faces my profile. *This is different; I've already changed the future just by telling him what happens in it.* Leaning down, Giffen whispers in my ear. "We're not done!" His lips brush the shell of my ear, causing me to shiver. "I'll find you soon." I refuse to look at him. He lets go of my arm. Straightening my shoulders, I walk down the ramp toward Kyon, who tracks my every movement.

The harsh wind picks up my hair, stirring it around and into my swollen face. I ignore it. Astrid is released from the grasp of a brutish soldier, pushed forward so that she almost falls flat on her face. I try not to look at her because my eyes should never stray from Kyon too long.

As Astrid nears, her eyes rivet on me. I hear her voice inside my head, *Kick-it!* Her tone is desperate; it resonates in my brain like she's inside me.

Don't you dare hug me! I think in an angry tone. *Pretend like you don't know me, Astrid, or you're dead! They'll shoot you in the back of the head and leave you here. Just walk!*

Astrid stumbles a step. Her eyes widen and I know she hears me—it's her special gift: communicating nonverbally. I continue to walk by her, never once glancing at her. Out of the corner of my eye I watch the soldier who'd turned her loose. He doesn't move, but continues to stand idly by, allowing her to pass on to the ship behind me. When I near Kyon, he raises his fingers and snaps them. A soldier hands him a long, white coat with a white fur collar and white fur cuffs.

The wind stirs the fur as I pause in front of him. Kyon drapes the coat around my shoulders and takes me in his arms, hugging me to him. "I've missed you," he whispers in my ear.

I say nothing, already cowed by the events that are unfolding.

"Come." Kyon is gentle as he shifts his arm to my shoulder and guides me at an unhurried pace to the stairs of the sublime trift. As we board, the falconlike ship behind me fires up its engines. The sound is an anchor in my gut, weighing me down to the ocean floor as it sails away without me aboard.

Kyon leads me to an elegant, yet still extremely comfortable, white leather seat. It's part of a cluster of four seats: two on either side of a low, chrome table. He holds my elbow until I sink onto the seat, and then he sheds his coat before taking the seat next to mine. No one else enters this private compartment; we're alone for the first time since he killed Geteron.

The trift's engines hum to life, I feel the slight vibration of the ship beneath me. "Would you like me to take your coat?" he asks.

"No," I pull the edges closer to me. "I'm cold."

He doesn't argue. Instead he says, "On screen."

When a holographic screen pops up, Kyon orders from a menu.

As the screen fades away, an ice bucket containing a beautiful golden bottle emerges from the center of the table along with two long, fluted glasses. A platter of sumptuous sandwiches, fruits, and cheeses appears as well.

"Would you like a drink?" Kyon asks with a charming lift of his blond eyebrow. His blue eyes regard me with speculation.

I nod. "Please."

He opens the golden bottle with a *pop*, pouring the bubbling, golden concoction into the stemware. When he hands it to me, his fingers brush mine. They're warm, so much warmer than mine. I take the glass and drink. It's lovely and fruity and definitely intoxicating. I tip my head back and drink it all before holding my glass out for a refill.

Kyon frowns. "Do you intend to get drunk? It's not like you to willingly give up control." Without a word, I continue to hold my glass out to him, demanding more. He obliges me by refilling it. I tip the glass to my lips once more. Kyon asks, "Did they kill him? Your Cavar, Trey?"

I choke on my drink, swallowing hard. I cough and sputter as tears roll down my face. A large hand rubs my back. When I'm able to breathe normally again, he wipes the tears from my dirty face with his thumbs.

"It's okay. You're not alone anymore. I'm here to take care of you. I will teach you what you need to know. I will train you to obey us." Frowning, I look away from him, moving my face with a jerk so that his hands fall from my cheeks.

"I know you're not ready to hear that, Kricket." I feel a sharp pain in my neck. Kyon pulls a tranquilizer gun away from my throat.

My eyes half shutter while my hand goes to the injection site. "I will have to teach you what is expected of you. We'll start anew from this moment on. I'll be your master and you will be my priestess."

Losing focus, I sag against the seat back. The smooth glass stemware slips through my fingertips, spilling golden liquid onto the immaculate floor. "You belong to me now," I hear him say, as I slip away into darkness.

⚬➰⚬

I should be used to waking in strange places by now, but this one has me on edge immediately. I feel different, but I don't know why. Lying in the dim light of a cavernous bedroom, I know something's wrong. It takes me a few moments to remember what happened. The last thing I knew, I was on a trift with Kyon. I move my arms; they no longer ache. In fact, they feel lighter and softer as they travel over the silk sheet of the enormous bed I now occupy. The blankets are light and airy too. They're just the right density to keep me warm from the cool, salty breeze that's wafting in between the white, billowing curtains framing a patio outside.

Beyond the stone terrace, waves crash upon a beach in hypnotic ebbs and flows. I sit up in bed, and the blanket slips down to show a soft, white nightgown. I touch the material; it's so fine as to be just a hair short of transparent. Making my way to the side of the bed, I rise, cross the hardwood floors and the soft area rugs, and pause at the threshold of the patio. The sight that greets me is breathtaking. The blue sea beyond the stone balustrade glows with the fire of stars. It's as if the sky fell into the sea. As I walk forward, my hair is lifted away from my face by the sea breeze. I rest my elbow on the stone railing, marveling at the beauty before me.

"It's the Loch of Cerulean, but everyone refers to it as the Sea of Stars," Kyon says from behind me. I straighten my spine when I feel his hand on my hip. He draws me back against him. He's bare-chested and wearing just some loose-fitting linen slacks. A blush stains my cheeks. "I've dreamt of this moment for so long now. I've wondered what it would be like to hold you like this. Now I know. It's bliss. You are the brightest star among the Sea of Stars, Kricket."

Kyon leans down, kissing my throat. His light touch causes my stone heart to lie heavy in my chest. The deadening beat of it promises me that I will never love again. And with Kyon's lips on mine to seal the vow, I swear that I will darken the stars forever.

Glossary

Abersuctonal: an antidote for znou axicote poisoning.

AFA: Armored Fugitive Apprehender—a robot programmed to apprehend fugitives.

Alameeda: one of the five clan-houses of Ethar. An ally of Wurthem. Ruling body is the Alameeda Brotherhood. A member of the Alameeda House.

Alameeda Striker: a member of an elite body of troops trained to serve the Alameeda Brotherhood.

ALV: Air Lift Vehicle—troop transport.

Amster Rushes: an ancient city where skeletal remains of skyscrapers are located near the border of Comantre in the no-man's-land restricted/protected area of Ethar.

arrowing: a part on a troupedo hovercar that resembles a gill of a fish. Used to hold the snuffout. Located where an auxiliary mirror would be on a human car.

Ateur: a Rafian senator in the House of Lords.

basiness: an automated hand washer that uses steam to kill germs.

baw-da-baw: a war cry used by Cavars in the Rafian military—means "hoorah."

beam spotters: laser-beam security alarm lights.

Beezway: a hovercar track like an expressway for the bullet-shaped hover vehicles called skiffs on the Ship of Skye.

bender: a part on a troupedo hovercar that resembles the gill of a fish. Used to hold the snuffout. Located where an auxiliary mirror would be on an Earth car.

Biequine: a competition wherein a rider takes a spix through a course of obstacles and shoots targets for both points and the best time.

Black Math: a virus that decimated the population of Ethar approximately a thousand years ago.

blipisode: an episode of precognition that lasts only a few seconds and happens without the clairvoyant losing total consciousness. A glimpse of a future event.

blushers: young Etharian women.

Boosha: Etharian slang for slut.

Brigadet: a member of the Rafian military police on the Ship of Skye.

bubble-shields: round, bubblelike barriers that act as protection from weapons fire; force fields. Blue in color.

Cargo Goer: a monstrous, ellipse-shaped ship that resembles the Bean sculpture in Chicago's Millennium Park. Each Cargo Goer is a massive, chromelike ellipse weighing several tons. Its skin can be altered to blend in with the environment, but it is usually mirrored, reflecting everything around it.

Cavar: a member of an elite body of troops trained to serve on land and sea; a member of the Rafian military of Ethar, similar to Earth's Marine.

chester: a male sex offender.

chrome: a swordlike stick with a silver tip that shocks like a cattle prod.

circa: a unit of measure equivalent to a mil.

click: approximately one mile.

Comantre: one of the five clan-houses of Ethar. An ally of Rafe. A member of the Comantre House.

Comantre Crosses: a district within the Comantre territory where the Comantre Syndic military base of the same name is located.

com-link: a device used as an intercom system.

Commodus: a bathroom.

cookery: the place where food is prepared and then distributed by conveyor to commissary units.

copperclaw: the exotic flower symbolically used in the weddinglike commitment ceremony in which a Brother of the Brotherhood weds his consort priestess.

Coriness: an honorific of royalty used in Rafian society. Kricket is a coriness because she is the daughter of Pan Hollowell, a corinet.

Corinet: an honorific of royalty used in Rafian society. Pan Hollowell's royal title.

crike: fifty years.

Crue: the Etharian form of pneumonia.

crystal: awesome.

Crystal Clear Moments: small, crystal-like figurines that animate when put into a star chamber gravity field.

death drones: automated drones that terminate civilians with blue lasers and/or flamethrowers.

deet: a unit of time equivalent to about six months.

dicron: a unit of measure equivalent to one meter.

dishery: the place where dirty dishes are transported to be cleaned and stored by an automated process of conveyors and robots.

doorcam: a camera mounted outside a door.

drak: a unit of heat measure similar to a degree.

Dreykar: an honorific of minor royalty used in Rafian society. Trey Allairis's royal title.

Dreykaress: an honorific of minor royalty used in Rafian society. Kricket would assume this title if she becomes Trey's consort.

Dunder Sorrows: a type of virus.

Elle: an honorific denoting a priestess in Alameedan society.

Em: an honorific denoting an ambassador.

E-One: a rotorless, helicopterlike vehicle used by military personnel, usually the Alameeda, to attack enemies. A military aircraft that resembles a wasp.

Ethar: a planet in a dimension similar to Earth's.

Etharian: a native of Ethar.

fardroom: Etharian currency. One fardroom is approximate to one American dollar.

Fay: an honorific equivalent to *Lady* in Rafian society.

fazaria: an amber-colored liquor similar to champagne.

fritzer: a type of card game.

Fitzforest: Thursday.

Fitzlutzer: Monday.

Fitzmartin: Wednesday.

Fitzover: Sunday.

Fitzsetter: Tuesday.

Fitzsumptner: Saturday.

Fitzwinter: Friday.

fleat: one minute.

flesh-layering-bot: a medical robot that reapplies skin.

flester: one week.

flipcart: a hovercraft skateboard.

floan: a unit of time similar to one year.

Forest of Omnicron: also known as the Forest of O; a wilderness in the restricted/ annexed area of Ethar.

freston: the tricked-out, riflelike black gun.

gennet: Cavar military rank equivalent to general in Rafian society. Trey Allairis's military rank.

git: a grunt; a new soldier.

Grumrell tree: a kind of tree. Its bark contains enzymes that ward off parasites and insects, but it tastes like cat poop.

guide-bot: a holographic image of a person that is programmed as a guide assisting patrons to various places.

guideways: freeways that glow lavender and are edged in silver. The guideways are stacked as they flow around, over, and into tunnels through buildings. Shifting traffic moves from one glowing level to the next seemingly at a whim.

harassenger: a passenger who harasses; specifically, an Alameeda drone turned into a bomb.

harbinger: a matte-black, gunlike weapon.

Haut: an honorific that means *Sir*. Denotes a high royal rank.

Hautess: an honorific that means *Lady*. Denotes a high royal rank.

Hesterfastok: an antidote for znou axicote poisoning.

hordabus plant: an aloe-like plant that almost instantly heals skin tissue damaged by burns, rashes, open wounds, and the like.

hovercar: also known as a skiff; a car capable of flying. It is propelled by forced air and does not have wheels.

hover crim: a limousinelike hovercar that is both expensive and private.

hohoban: Etharian chocolate.

holovision: a holographic television.

hominie: Etharian honey.

inamorata: a female lover.

inamorato: a male lover.

Inium: the smallest of Ethar's moons. It is blue in color.

ipsacore: the name of a level in the detention area of the Ship of Skye.

Isle of Skye: the city where the Regent's palace and the corrective court are located. It's the legal center of the House of Rafe.

jackwagon: an Etharian curse word.

jade: one hundred years.

jamarch: one thousand years.

kafcan: a beverage that is similar in every way to dark-roast coffee.

kesek: Cavar military rank, equivalent to major.

keuken: the kitchen.

kiaser gat: a type of gun.

knob knocker: an Etharian curse word.

Lamb's Bottom: an antidote for znou axicote poisoning.

lavare: a shower room.

link: a measure of length equal to six feet.

Loch of Cerulean: the tropical island where Kyon's estate is located in Alameeda territory. A body of water on Ethar. The political seat of the Alameeda Brotherhood, reminiscent of a fiefdom.

lurker: a stalker, crazy ex-girlfriend type.

mamon: Rafian word for *mom*.

mastoff: Etharian word for *mastodon*; a large elephantine mammal.

Minness: an honorific title equivalent to *Miss* or *Ms.* in Rafian society.

nim: idiot.

ostioscope: a medical device, also known as *grandma goggles* or *visor*, that fits over the eyes like glasses and is used to perform a full-body scan. It checks vitals: synapse firing, dendrite chemical composition, reuptake rates.

overup: an elevator that moves up, down, sideways, and slantways.

part: an Etharian hour.

pasdon: Rafian word for *dad*.

Peney: one of the five clan-houses of Ethar. This House has always remained neutral in wartime. A member of the Peney House.

pinpointer: a homing beacon.

polar: sexy.

Rafe: one of the five clan-houses of Ethar. An ally of Comantre. A member of the Rafe House.

Rafian: a citizen of Rafe.

rapid ascenders: Rafian drone aircraft.

ratwacker: an Etharian curse word.

razorite: a black bulletlike hovercar—military model.

recurve: a crossbow.

regeneration: a medical procedure to regrow limbs and organs.

Regent: the acting king of Rafe. The current Regent is Manus Grayson.

Riker Pak: an Alameeda jet pack.

rotation: an Etharian day consisting of about sixteen hours.

sactum amps: percussion grenades.

saer: a saber-tooth tiger used as a symbol of the House of Rafe and the Regent.

scanner jammers: devices that jam scanners.

sensor jammers: technology that jams scanners capable of finding the heat signatures of living beings. It also jams sounds, light, etc.

Shefty: Etharian equivalent to English slang "shifty."

shickles: an Etharian curse word.

Ship of Skye: a floating military fortress owned and operated by the House of Rafe and their Skye Council.

signal seeker: an alarm.

skiff: also known as a hovercar; a hovering car capable of flying. It is propelled by forced air and does not have wheels.

skoolie: a lamb with googly eyes and a face that resembles a pug dog (plural is *skoolies*).

Skye Council: also known as Skye; the military branch of Rafian government, similar to the Pentagon, which is self-governing. Works in cooperation with the Regent.

skyscape: a skyscraper located on the Ship of Skye.

slipshield: a clear sticker resembling the symbol on a USB port that contains a code to unlock cell doors in the detention area.

sloat: an Etharian goat.

snuffout: a fire-extinguisher-like canister filled with flammable gas used as ammunition for flamethrowers.

someone-elsie: a virus uploaded into an Alameeda drone that allows it to be navigated and controlled by a hacker.

sonic sayzer: a weapon that shoots sounds at an amplified frequency. It is a metal sleeve worn on the wrist that shoots sound waves Spider-Man style when certain words are spoken into a mouthpiece connected to the earpiece. The sound waves it shoots are capable of rupturing cells.

soothsayer: a priestess who has the ability to know through intuition if someone is lying.

speck: an Etharian month.

spix: a horse with wicked-sharp horns behind its ears (plural is *spixes*).

squelch tracker: a heat-seeking automated bomb that can be programmed to assassinate a target.

star chamber: a gravity chamber that animates figurines know as Crystal Clear Moments.

starcross: a sharp, star-shaped weapon that resides in a bracelet housing. The star can be removed from the bracelet to throw at an enemy. It acts like a boomerang, returning to the bracelet after it's thrown.

Striker: a member of an elite body of troops trained to serve the Alameeda Brotherhood.

suckerfish-bot: an automated medical robot.

swank: an elegant party.

sweet furroo: an Etharian saying similar to "good Lord."

swimmi-bot: an automated medical robot.

Syndic: a member of the Comantre military.

Techtonic Peninsula: land owned by the House of Peney; it is land that both Alameeda and Rafe are interested in obtaining for its strategic location as a staging area in wartime.

toad thumper: idiot.

trift: a smaller jet that looks like a Stealth Fighter.

triple nitronium fritzwinter sonicdrites: Alameeda bombs.

troupedo: a type of military grade hovercar/vehicle.

truluv: Raspin's Comantre slang for *soulmate*.

turk: approximately one pound in weight.

underbits: lingerie.

Valley of Thistle: a district within the border of Rafe where spix races are held annually. Trey Allairis's family estate is there, and it borders Charisma Sandersault's estate.

venish: venisonlike meat pie.

venteur: Cavar military rank equivalent to captain.

Verdi Freckles: a type of virus.

Violet Hill: a district of Rafe.

visor: a medical device, also known as *grandma goggles* or *ostioscope*, that fits over the eyes like glasses and is used to perform a full-body scan. It checks vitals: synapse firing, dendrite chemical composition, reuptake rates.

vista: chloroform.

wacker: an Etharian curse word.

wester: a female sex offender.

Westway: a city in Comantre.

whahappened: a virus uploaded into Alameeda drones that causes them to explode when they dock onboard their mother ships.

wrap: a medical procedure that removes scars from skin.

Wurthem: one of the five clan-houses of Ethar. An ally of Alameeda. A member of the Wurthem House.

xerts: a measure of sound equal to a decibel.

znou: a dangerous flower known to be teeming with turbine worms. It grows in the restricted area of Ethar. The petals are poisonous if ingested, causing the erosion of organs. The plural is *znous*.

znou axicote: poison from the znou flower.

Acknowledgments

God, all things are possible through You. Thank you for Your infinite blessings and for allowing me to do what I love: write.

To my readers and bloggers: Thank you! The outpouring of love that I receive from all of you is mind-blowing. Your generosity toward me is humbling. You make me want to write a thousand books.

Tom Bartol, you're my best friend. I cannot imagine my world without you in it. I love you.

Max and Jack Bartol, I count myself as the most fortunate person in the world to have you both in my life. Thank you for knowing when to let me write and when to rescue me from my computer.

Jason Kirk, your thoughtful and intuitive questions and suggestions have made *Sea of Stars* a better story. Thank you for challenging me and inspiring me to grow as a writer. I'm grateful. I can't wait to dive into the next project with you!

To the team of experts at 47North, you guys are superstars! Thank you for your time and for your hard work on this project. It means the world to me.

Shelly Crane, thank you for beta reading *Sea of Stars* and for your insights on writing and on life. You are precious to me. I'm so fortunate to have you as my friend.

Gloria Lutz, your unwavering support and unconditional love are a guiding light in my life. Thank you for using your wicked editing skills to help me through the initial draft of *Sea of Stars*.

Tamar Rydzinski, one of the best days of my life was when you agreed to be my agent. Thank you for always having my back.

Regina Wamba, you're an artist. Thank you for sharing your marketing genius with me.

Trish Brinkley, I love The Occasionalist! Thank you for always including me in your circle!

Amber McLelland, you're insane and that's why we get along so well. Thank you for your friendship.

Janet Wallace, you're inspirational. I love seeing what you create. It's magical.

To my lovely Hellcats: Georgia Cates, Shelly Crane, Samantha Young, Rachel Higginson, Angeline Kace, Lila Felix, and Quinn Loftis. What can I say? You complete me. Thank you all for your unwavering support.

Michelle Leighton. I love you, man. I will cherish my pocket Jamie forever.

About the Author

Amy A. Bartol is the award-winning and bestselling author of the Kricket Series (*Under Different Stars*) and the Premonition Series: *Inescapable, Intuition, Indebted, Incendiary* and *Iniquity*. She lives in Michigan with her husband and their two sons. Visit her at her website: www.amyabartol.com